THE
BACILLUS OF BEAUTY

Legacy of the Corridor

Also from Hemelein Publications

THE
BACILLUS OF BEAUTY

Special Edition

HARRIET STARK

Edited by
JOE MONSON

HEMELEIN PUBLICATIONS

The Bacillus of Beauty: Special Edition

Legacy of the Corridor, volume 5. Special Edition.

A Hemelein Publications release. This edition Copyright © 2024 by Hemelein Publications. All rights reserved.

The original text by Harriet Stark was first published in 1900 by the Frederick A. Stokes Company in New York City. It is in the public domain due to being published prior to 1929. The story as published here is a faithful reproduction of the text, with only minor editing for modern audiences.

"No Truth in Beauty?: Harriet Stark and the Bacillus of Beauty" essay Copyright © 2024 by Lee Allred. Used by permission of the author.

"Legacy of the Corridor", "Patient Zero", "A Little Backstory on Harriet Stark", "About the Editor", and "About the Cover Artist" essays Copyright © 2022 by Joe Monson. Used by permission of the author.

The Bacillus of Beauty is a work of fiction. Any names, characters, people, places, entities, or events are products of the author's imagination, and any resemblance to actual names, characters, people, places, entities, or events is entirely coincidental. The opinions expressed in the essays represent those of the respective authors, and do not necessarily represent those of Hemelein Publications.

Cover art: *Choosing* (ca. 1864) by George Frederic Watts (1817-1904).
Interior illustrations Copyright © 2024 by Jess Smart Smiley. Used by permission.
Cover design and interior layout and design: Joe Monson.

Managing Editor: Joe Monson
Art Director: Joe Monson
Publisher: Heather B. Monson
Published by Hemelein Publications, LLC.
http://hemelein.com/

First Hemelein printing, July 2022
Special Edition printing, June 2024
10 9 8 7 6 5 4 3 2 1

ISBN:
978-1-64278-049-9 (hardcover)
978-1-64278-057-4 (case laminate)
978-1-64278-058-1 (trade paperback)
978-1-64278-064-2 (ebook)

Library of Congress Control Number: 2023945697

Contents

Book V: The End of the Beginning

Legacy of the Corridor

Way back in 1994, M. Shayne Bell put together *Washed by a Wave of Wind*, an anthology of short works by authors from "the Corridor", an area that covers Utah, most of Idaho, parts of Wyoming and Nevada, and stretches into Arizona and parts of northern Mexico. Sometimes, the area around Cardston, Alberta, Canada, is included, too. For those unfamiliar with this area, it was settled by Mormon pioneers, members of the Church of Jesus Christ of Latter-day Saints.

Shayne's anthology highlighted science fiction and fantasy works by authors from the area, as the Corridor contained an unusually high number of successful authors—for the population in the area—both genre and non-genre, both members and non-members of the predominant religion. That legacy continues today with an impressive list of authors such as:

Jennifer Adams · D. J. Butler
Orson Scott Card · Michael R. Collings
Michaelbrent Collings · Ally Condie
Larry Correia · Kristyn Crow
James Dashner · Brian Lee Durfee
Sarah M. Eden · Richard Paul Evans
David Farland · Diana Gabaldon
Jessica Day George · Shannon Hale

Mettie Ivie Harrison · Tracy Hickman
Laura Hickman · Charlie N. Holmberg
Christopher Husberg · Raymond F. Jones
Matthew J. Kirby · Gama Ray Martinez
Brian McClellan · Stephenie Meyer
L. E. Modesitt, Jr. · Brandon Mull
Jennifer A. Nielsen · Wendy Nikel
James A. Owen · Ken Rand
Brandon Sanderson · Caitlin Sangster
J. Scott Savage · D. William Shunn
Jess Smart Smiley · Eric James Stone
May Swenson · Howard Tayler
Brad R. Torgersen · Nym Wales
Dan Wells · Robison Wells
David J. West · Carol Lynch Williams
Dan Willis · Julie Wright

That's a big list of names, and it only barely scratches the surface. Hemelein Publications created this publication series to highlight authors from the Corridor, both well-known and lesser-known. We think Shayne did a wonderful job drawing attention to these amazing writers back then, and we want to continue what he started.

You can learn more about the series at:

http://hemelein.com/go/legacy-of-the-corridor/

Joe Monson
Managing Editor
Hemelein Publications

Patient Zero, SE

Joe Monson

One of the things I did when starting the Legacy of the Corridor series was to look up information on speculative fiction authors from the area. Sure, I knew a lot of them, but it's always good to see if there are people I might have overlooked. I found plenty of well-known authors from the area, and I found more and more lesser-known authors as I dug into things. That's when I found Harriet Stark.

I had never heard of her before. I had never heard of her story, *The Bacillus of Beauty*, either. As far as I have found, it's the only story she ever had published. Did you know that Stark claims to have formulated her idea for this story after visiting a professor at Wesleyan University who was using bacteria to create a richer, creamier butter? I found an article that discussed this in detail (though, as Lee points out in the essay following this foreword, the story may or may not actually be true).

She described how, after her meetings with the professor, she took a train where she noticed how several bright-eyed and happily chatting women made the entire car feel lighter and more cheerful. She spent the rest of the train ride thinking about how to write a story about the "bacillus of beauty".[1]

Several well-known magazines and periodicals of the time reviewed the book. Seymour Eaton, writing for *The Booklovers Library*, compared it favorably with *The Strange Case of Dr Jekyll and Mr Hyde*, saying it was "a story of modern, present-day society."[2] Harper's Bazar said "the story is clever, and will interest the reader".[3]

It was even reviewed in *Life* magazine! They hated it, saying "it passes the patience of the most consistent reader of trash".[4] But then I've never put a lot of stock in basing my opinion of works solely on reviews. In fact, after all the bad reviews I've seen of some of my favorite books, I figure they're just one person's opinion, and the reviewers may only like things wildly different from what I like (happens a lot when you like adventurous and fun science fiction and fantasy). I often like things critics dislike.

When I finally read *The Bacillus of Beauty*, I found the characters (especially the secondary characters) interesting and engaging, though it had a few notions about women and men that are, frankly, very outdated. There are a lot of characters expressing opinions on what women should or shouldn't do, what's proper, and so on. There are also opinions expressed about what men should or shouldn't do. There are phrases and attitudes about all kinds of people that you'd not find in works published now, for better or for worse. I'll let you decide on that one.

However, all of them line up pretty well with the overwhelming majority of opinions expressed in the various magazines, newspapers, and idle chit-chat of the day at the turn of the Twentieth Century. Those were different times, with different ideas, different ways of doing things, and definitely many different expectations of women and men. People had the same kinds of dreams, desires, and needs that we find now, but they had different acceptable ways (to society) to do and accomplish them. In fact, if you keep in mind the time period in which it was published, it was surprisingly forward-thinking.

It espoused women being as smart as men. It showed female characters who were clever and witty and not just ornaments to hang on their beaus' arms. It showed them studying, working, and excelling at science, music, and art. The main character (well, the *main* main character) is not stupid or even treated as stupid by most of the characters. She's not helpless or even dependent on the other main character—her erstwhile fiancé—to rescue her. She makes her own decisions, and has to deal with the consequences of those decisions—some good, and some less so.

Even the main character's parents and the family and folks from her hometown were shown to have a certain sound wisdom in much of what they expressed. They weren't treated as simple bumpkins in the story (though it's mentioned that many people consider such people to be bumpkinish). I think Stark was way ahead of her time with this story. *Harper's*

Bazar even pointed out that it was basically science fiction (though they didn't use those words).[5]

To think that a woman farmer from Payson could have such a progressive story published by a major publisher (at the time) in New York *in 1900* only goes to support the theory that there's something about The Corridor that inspires people to take up the writing of speculative fiction. The story has an obvious message, but it also tells a compelling story wrapped in the melodramatic tones common in contemporary stories of the time, and there are definite messages beyond the obvious, too. I'll leave those for you to find and consider.

This special edition also contains eleven illustrations by Jess Smart Smiley, done in the style of story illustrations in the early 1900s. The original didn't have any illustrations outside of the cover art, so having these is a special treat. Jess is an excellent artist, and I'm excited to be able to use his works to enhance this edition. I think they add just a little bit extra to this forgotten work.

Lee Allred has written an excellent essay, also included in this special edition, that delves into the time period in which *Bacillus* was originally released. It contains fascinating insight into Stark, her life, the likely influences that were used in creating this story, and how this story was received by the publishing and reading community. As far as I know, this is the first such essay written about Stark and *Bacillus*. (If you know of any others, I'd be delighted to read them.)

I hope you enjoy this tale, and can look at it without judging it under today's standards. When you seek to understand the context of the time in which it was written, you can truly come to understand how groundbreaking this story was in so many different ways.

And you'll get a fun story to enjoy, too.

Joe Monson
Managing Editor
Hemelein Publications

---

1. "General Gossip of Authors and Writers". *Current Literature: A Magazine of Contemporary Record*, Volume 30, Number 1 (January 1901). p.61.
2. Eaton, Seymour (ed). "Two Fine Books of Imaginative Humour". *The Booklovers Library* (1900), pp.126-127. Philadelphia, Pennsylvania.
3. "Books & Writers". *Harper's Bazar*, Volume 33, Number 45 (November 10, 1900), p.1787* (it's technically page 1797 due to a few pages being numbered incorrectly). New York, New York.

4. "Composite". *Life,* Volume 36, Number 936 (October 18, 1900), p.326. New York, New York.
5. See note 3.

No Truth in Beauty?: Harriet Stark and the Bacillus of Beauty

Lee Allred

1

October of 1900. The nineteenth-century is rapidly slipping into the past, and observers worry and wonder if perhaps all that that century treasured is also slipping into the past.

The eyes of the world's press are turned to the Boer War still raging in South Africa where rag-tag commandos of Dutch farmers on horseback are still humiliating and bedeviling the mighty British Lion. On the other side of the world, the so-called Boxer Rebellion—another rag-tag army of peasants, this one armed with but fists and bamboo spears—has risen up against European powers dismembering a prostrate China. For fifty-five tense days, the embattled Legation Compound in Peking holds out against the Boxer siege until relief columns from the combined armies of the world's industrial powers—Britain, Germany, Russia, America, and Japan—finally arrive. Photographs of the chaotic aftermath still fill American magazines.

That interest in far-off China lay in America's participation in the crisis. Much to its own surprise, the United Stated had only just recently emerged a World Power, having fought and won (with almost embarrassing ease) a foolishly unnecessary but splendid little war against the desiccated husk of the Spanish Empire. The ten-week-war had ended but its reverberations still echoed, particularly in the 1900 presidential election.

October marked the final turbulent throes of that election, a rematch between the staid incumbent William McKinley and the firebrand populist William Jennings Bryan. Bryan quixotically ran yet again on the issue of Free Silver. The issue may have resonated during the economic downturn back in 1896, but not 1900. Between a booming economy and his victory over Spain, McKinley's re-election was never really in doubt. McKinley won in a landslide: 292 electoral votes to 156.

Even so, the election was a bitter one. Disillusioned by what it saw as American Imperialism after American emerged from the war in possession of three overseas colonies—Puerto Rico, Guam, and the Philippines, America saw herself no better than the European colonial powers she had previously mocked and derided.

The press, who had so vociferously egged on the war, now derided its results with equal gusto, turning on McKinley. *Life Magazine* offered the following guide to voters: "For War, Teddy, Taxation and Trusts, vote for William McKinley. For the Constitution, Peace, Panic and Populism, vote for W.J. Bryan." *Life* accompanied this with a cartoon depicting Uncle Sam, draped in imperial robes, crown, and scepter, sitting dejectedly in on throne beside Lady Liberty bewailing that "darned if I can have any fun on Fourth of July with these things on."

Good Government types and reform-minded citizens had concerns closer to home. They bewailed that the GOP could raise $1 million of campaign contributions as easily as once it raised a mere $10,000 a few elections ago. Party machines and voting corruption were rampant.

Republicans might have had their squalid Pennsylvania and upper-New York State machines, but nothing on Earth could compare to the brazen, open, and total corruption of the Democrats' Tammany Hall machine of New York City. Votes were openly, publicly manufacture red as if on a factory assembly line. Just prior to the election, *Munsey's Magazine* could run an acidic sixteen-page expose complete with extensive photo spread of the inner sanctum on 14th Street and its fat cat denizens, and the Tammany crowd only laughed. Within the confines of New York City, Tammany was inviolate. For the moment.

The average citizen really didn't care much. In those halcyon days before personal income tax and three-letter agencies, government impinged very little on daily life. The business of America, one future president would say, is business. And business was good. Golden, even. Gilded.

The year 1900 marks the apex of the Gilded Age. Nothing better reflected the sheer vitality of the American economic miracle than the advertisements adorning the back pages of the magazines and newspapers of the day. The *Chicago Time-Herald* boasted that it had published over four-million lines of advertising copy. (New York ad agencies offered to effortlessly place your firm's latest ad on 14,000 street cars with a single stroke of your pen on their dotted line.)

Magazine advertisements hawked wares of all shapes, sizes, and budgets. From central heating furnaces to luxury yachts. Eight-dollar rollup desks, billiard tables, Pillsbury flour, Cream of Wheat, women's corsets, cures for baldness, wheelchairs for invalids, quack medicines, folding Kodak pocket cameras (prices ranged from $5 to $35, depending on model), and even mimeograph contraptions. Ads touted Sharp repeating shotguns, revolvers, and even Spanish Army rifles (Mauser 7 x 57s) captured as war booty and sold off as government surplus.

The Armour meat packing company (of later hot dog fame), who had furnished over half-a-million pounds of canned meat (much of it spoiled) for the Army during the Spanish war, admonished the general public that "You Don't Know Beans" and plastered this counter-intuitive slogan on a series of stylish proto-art deco ads designed to sell their new canned pork and beans product to every American man, woman, and child (presumably even those with chicken pox). Van de Camp's, who did know beans, countered with a stylish series of *art nouveau* pork and bean ads of their own.

And the gadgets! Magazine back pages were rife with ads for all the latest mechanical crazes. Typewrites ads for Underwood, Densmore, Remington, and Yost brands. Ads picturing horseless carriages of all seating configurations and models. Familiar, household brands like Riker, Columbia, and Locomobile automobiles (800 vehicles of the latter actually in use!).

One manufacturer, the Woods Motor company, offered a "Spider" model. With 42-inch rubber-shod wooden rear wheels, 36-inch front wheels, and a driver seat perched above and behind the passenger cab, it looked for all the world like a handsome cab minus horses. The Spider boasted speeds of 12 miles an hour and could go 30 miles on one charge, assuming a motorist could find 30 miles of uninterrupted macadamed roadway.

None of these contraptions would have been possible without the relentless march of science and progress. The 19th Century had been the story of the steam engine, the locomotive, and the telegraph. In the late 1860s, the pinnacle of sailing knowledge and design dating back to before written history—sailing like the fabled *Cutty Sark* had, John Henry-like, gone up against new-model steamships like the *SS Agamemnon* and lost out on transoceanic trade routes.

The newly-dawning Twentieth Century promised even more marvels. Rudyard Kipling would soon write "Transportation is Civilization"— transportation of not only people and finished goods and raw materials but the transportation of ideas and information. Telephones were already commonplace. Marconi had done Edison one better with his new wireless telegraphy. Already there was talk of the British Royal Navy fitting out its battleships with radios having an effective range of a staggering sixty miles. Perhaps even more amazing, some American newspapers were operating a machine that transmitted images over telegraph wires. Its inventor called the machine a "telediagraph." Other inventors had designed related machines like the telautograph (for sending signatures for legal verification), the Bildtelegraph, the tephane, and others. Perhaps one day Marconi would add images to his wireless communication as well.

Some observers worried this relentless march of progress came with a price. *The Outlook* magazine noted that after New York City replaced most of its horse drawn trolleys with new-fangled cable, electric, and steam-driven trolley cars, traffic fatalities in the past ten years rose from 155 to 235. "The new and quicker method is not safer," it bemoaned. Almost as an afterthought the article listed a single fatality caused by that new automobile contraption. This would change.

More pious publications worried less about mortality and more about immorality. They feared Darwinism, science, and atheism were de-churching people, turning them away from religion. Numerous religious censuses were taken, both in the US and Britain. A census conducted in Youngstown, Ohio by the Ministerial Association relieved some fears: in its population of 58,000, less than 6% claimed no religion affiliation. The Youngstown census wasn't all good news, however. Her largest denomination was revealed to be not right-minded Protestants, but Roman Catholicism (11.493). There were even 590 "Hebrews" lurking in town, and somewhat bizarrely, nine whole "Latter-Day Saints" who seemed to lack the migratory sense needed to decamp to far-off Utah where their sort belonged. "Otherwise," Pastor Sinks concluded in the pages of the September issue of *The Christian Work,* the survey was a "gratifying and fruitful accomplishment" Darwin hadn't quite won over God, not yet.

Nowhere was progress and new technologies more disruptive, however, than in the world of publishing. Doomsayers saw only the trees—that the camera had all but eliminated the illustrated travelogue book, that the typewriter meant no more languid Longfellows sending in handwritten manuscripts comprised of strips of differing scrap paper pasted together—and not the forest of real change.

Modern printing presses had brought an economy of scale to publishing and printing. Former telegraph operator Frank A. Munsey came to New York with $300 dollars in his pocket and an idea gleaned from staring all day at telegram form pads. Buying out a bankrupt publishing firm, Munsey set about implementing his idea. Instead of publishing on expensive "slick" paper and charging 25¢ a copy, publish magazines on cheap newsprint and only charge a dime.

His new "pulp magazines" revolutionized the magazine field and made Munsey a personal fortune (his worth at the time of his death was nearly half-a-billion dollars in today's money).

An explosion of pulp fiction magazines soon followed, establishing and codifying the fiction genres we know today: mystery, western, romance, science fiction. This same low-cost newsprint method would eventually give rise to the comic book in the 1930s, too.

Book publishers would be slower to adopt Munsey's cheaper methods (the paperback boom wouldn't occur until after World War II), but the pulp magazine boom meant more readers and more readers meant more book sales overall. Critics bewailed the increasing number of "blood-and-thunder" books catering to the pulp reader crowd.

The U.S. Copyright office announced that in the prior accounting year (July 1, 1899 to June 30, 1900) they'd issued copyrights for 6550 volumes of "books proper." This was nearly a 20% increase in copyrights issued the previous period, nearly 20%. *Publisher's Weekly* crowed that "there had been no growth approximating the phenomenal increase of demand for reading." Five out of six of those copyrights were new books—new books by American authors—a sea change in a book field traditionally dominated by reprinted classics.

Then as now, the center of book publishing was New York City. Instead of four or five (or is it down to only three now?) huge conglomerates, dozens upon dozens of independent publishing firms flourished. One major publisher of the day was the Frederick A. Stokes Company of

5 and 7, East Sixteenth Street, New York. At the close of 1900, Publishers Weekly listed the current Stokes catalog at 42 books (18 non-fiction, 25 novels, and 9 children's books).

Stokes' best-selling title in October, 1900 was *Robert Orange* by John Robert Hobbes (pen name of female author Pearl Mary Teresa Richards), the highly anticipated sequel to her *A School for Saints*, but the Stokes book generating the most critical buzz was future Boy Scouts founder Baden-Powell's topical account of the Boer War, *Sport in War*.

The Stokes firm was forward-thinking in promoting its products. They took out the usual ads in literary and book trade magazines and bombarded magazines from *Life* and *Munsey's* to *Christian Work* with review copies, but Stokes also employed innovative techniques.

Stokes ran up a second printing of Harold Frederic's 1898 novel, *The Market Place*, but called it a "special edition" instead. The only thing "special" about it was the addition of nine full-page house ads for the latest Stokes books. These ads feature advertising techniques still used today: excerpts from the novel touted, reviewer quotes from around the nation, blurb quotes from the authors themselves, plot summaries, readers' letters, and even hype about their decorative book covers.

Stokes could and did follow other publishers in capitalizing on current events like Baden-Powell's Boer War and cranking out didactic "moral" novels like *Orange*, but they could be forward-thinking in book acquisitions, too. Stokes aggressively sought what we'd call speculative fiction novels.

When *Ainslie's Magazine* paid a staggering $1750 sight unseen for the serialization right for H.G. Wells next novel, they'd hoped for another *War of the Worlds*. What they got was *Love and Mr. Lewisham*—a tepid, run-of-the-mill romance novel. A horrified *Ainslie's* declined to print it, preferring to eat the $1750 loss. The Stokes company stepped in and snapped up the rights, willing to take a financial hit in publishing *Lewisham* in exchange for cementing itself as Wells's American publisher for future (and hopefully more futuristic) titles.

Autumn of 1900 also saw Stokes publishing *Goops and How to Be Them* by Gelett Burgess. A sort of reverse-psychology moral primer for children, *Goops* featured Tim Burtonesque illustrations of naughty "children" with faces like moray eels. Never out of print (you can buy copies even today), *Goops* spawned several sequels and went on to scare the cheese-and-crackers out of generations of traumatized American kids.

October of 1900 also marked the Stokes release of another singular book. Trade ads listed it as "340 pages, 12 mo, cloth, ornate, $1.50."

(12mo is publisher shorthand for paper size: "duodecimo," a single printing press sheet divided into 12 pages approximately 4 3/4" by 7 1/2", the standard cut-size for fiction novels of that day.)

The book cover was indeed ornate. Dark olive textured cloth gilt in gold highlights. Two abstract golden shapes suggest twin bubbling, fizzing champagne glasses. Slender fluted letters of gold spell out, Roman-style, THE BACILLVS OF BEAVTY—*The Bacillus of Beauty*.

Reading the publisher's description of this strangely-titled novel, one wonders if in fact those aren't stemmed glasses of fizzing champagne but rather laboratory retorts containing teeming golden bacteria.

A novel with a fresh and unhackneyed plot and treatment. It is like nothing else ever printed.

It tells the story of a young girl from the West who is made the subject of an experiment by a Professor in Barnard College, which transforms her into the most beautiful woman in the world.

Beauty proves a key to the smart world, and for a time the houses of the rich are as familiar to her as the studios and "dens" of newspaper "girl bachelors" and art students had been. Both phases of life are treated with the sure touch that knowledge gives.

That last phrase intimates that author Harriet Star is equally at home with Manhattan's glittering high society, it's so-called "400," as well as the up-to-the-latest scientific laboratories. That she is intimately familiar with the scope of her novel—the pressrooms of Gotham's newspapers, the smoke-filled backrooms of Tammany Hall, and the ballrooms of high society. That she lives in a world of belted earls and European nobility, nights at the opera, and silver salvers bearing calling cards with corners turned back just so and scrawled with *Visete* or *Felicitations* or *Pour Prendre Congé*.

Nothing could be further from the truth. The author, Harriet Stark, was a church-going farmwife of Mormon pioneer stock and mother of six (later eleven) living in the town she was born in and would die in: the tiny rural hamlet of Payson, Utah.

3

Stark was Harriet "Hattie" Wride's maiden name. Her father, Daniel Stark, was a Mormon pioneer of note. A convert from Nova Scotia, Daniel Stark as one of the "California Saints" sailed around the Horn in the *SS Brooklyn* rather than trek across the plains. He participated in the disastrous "Muddy Mission," an ill-fated attempt to settle southwestern Utah. He surveyed the foundation for the St. George Temple. Eventually he settled in Payson, Utah where he was employed as a County Surveyor.

Daniel Stark married three plural wives. Harriet's mother was Priscilla Birkenhead Stark, a British convert, Daniel's third (and youngest) wife and an exceptional beauty. Priscilla bore Daniel six children (Harriet was the oldest). Daniel fathered fourteen other children from his other marriages.

Harriet's husband, Lewis William Barry Wride, was slight in height and build, almost impish. Of Welsh stock, he had a full head of reddish sandy hair and sported a lifelong mustache, grown to cover up a scar on his upper lip. By all accounts, he was as decent a man as ever lived. He ran a mixed-use family farm so typical of rural Utah: alfalfa, sugar beets, potatoes, onions, and other staples. The farm also had fruit orchards and a small dairy herd. Harriet loved him deeply.

Of Harriet herself, were it not for a one-page biographical sketch written by her youngest daughter Gwen and an unpublished, unfinished autobiography by Harriet herself, we would know little of Harriet Stark aside from vital statistics gleaned from stone headstones and yellowed newsprint obituaries: born September 23, 1866, Payson, Utah; married to Lewis Wrede, March 18, 1886, Logan, Utah; died, August 23, 1944 "from causes incident to old age," Payson, Utah.

Harriet's autobiography essentially covers only her childhood, breaking off at her marriage. Daughter Gwen Wride Fillmore—born eight years after publication of *Bacillus*—reminisces only about her own years growing up in the Wride household. Neither document mentions Wride's writing career.

They do, however, paint a hard life: raising eleven kids in a farmhouse without running water and constantly short on money (Lewis Wrede had many virtues, but ambition—a drive to improve his farm—didn't appear to be one of them). One November, the barn containing a whole year's harvest burned down (ironically, on Guy Fawkes Day). Harriet had to sew all her children's clothes, making her own patterns taken from photographs in magazines. She never owned a house with central heating, never owned an automobile, "Spyder" or any other model. Harriet spent her years caring for eleven children, then an invalid father-in-law, then an invalid husband, and finally cared for as an invalid herself, dying in the home of her youngest daughter.

In these family histories, we see a glimpse of Harriet as a cow-milking, apple-picking, hay-mowing, aproned farmwife. We get nothing at all of Harriet Stark the writer.

4

Current-day writers leave a bakery's worth of breadcrumbs behind during their careers. Social media, professional online forums, convention panels dutifully recorded by ubiquitous smart phones and posted online—scholars of current-day writers have a wealth of material to work with, not the least of which are a writer's papers and manuscripts now almost routinely donated to university libraries upon a writer's death.

Researchers of Harriet Stark have none of that. Harriet Stark left nothing behind except her one published novel. We have no original manuscript, no letters to her publisher, no unfinished drafts of other projects. Nothing. Not one word in her obituaries or her family histories even mention that she wrote at all, let alone that she was the first Utah author to be published by a New York publisher.

We don't know when *Bacillus* was written, how long it took to write, or how many publishers she sent it to before Stokes bought it.

What we have is one published promotional "letter" purporting to tell of how Stark came up with the central premise of *Bacillus*:

"Three years ago I spent a day with Prof. H. W. Conn of Wesleyan University, who was applying bacillus culture methods to butter. He was educating cream by indoctrinating it with microbes of ferment from older, better cream. I could see with my own eyes in his test tubes the little clusters of spores which not only hastened ripening. but made the new cream richer than it would have been if left to nature. Of course bacillus culture is a dairy commonplace now, and drummers hawk rival butter germs all over the country; but the idea was newer then, and it made upon me a deep impression. That night I took a way train from Middletown to Hartford. At one station. midway, a group of factory girls came aboard. Nearly all were very pretty; their bright eyes. their merry chatter, made everybody in the car more cheerful. The very lamps burned more smilingly. The strange alchemy I had seen, the beauty before me—was it any wonder that the idea flashed upon me: 'What if there were a Bacillus of Beauty! Would not all the world be at the feet of its discoverer? What would happen to his first client?' Forthwith I resolved that there should be in fiction at least, one perfectly beautiful woman..."

It is doubtful this promotional piece can be taken at face value. One the one hand, commercial dairy bacillus would be just the thing agricultural science-minded husband Lewis Wride would be interested in. On the other hand, the cash-strapped Wride family journeying back east to a prestigious university to hear a lecture is very out of character, especially within a time frame that includes the birth of three children (and the infant death of that third child). Easier to believe is that the letter was fabricated whole cloth by the promotionally-aggressive publisher were it not that the writing style of the letter is undeniably Harriet Stark's.

Harriet's only documented travel outside Utah was visiting grandchildren in Idaho. Lewis Wride did serve a Mormon mission to Great Britain 1891-1893, transiting through the East Coast both directions, but Harriet did not accompany him.

A number of theories have been floated trying to square the circle with perhaps the most credible positing that Harriet really *did* attend a bacillus lecture, but one closer to home at the University of Utah in Salt Lake City (thereby riding the 400 South street car down the hill back to the train station) and that publisher Stokes changed the venue from a rustic western school to the prestigious Wesleyan University for promotional reasons.

Regardless, the letter provides the one slim fact we have about Harriet's writing of *Bacillus*: she wrote it over a period of not longer than three years. We don't know when her promotional letter was written. After publication? As part of her manuscript submission? Depending on the time it took to sell the novel and how long between acceptance and publication, that three-year period might have been nearly anytime during the 1890s, a decade particularly trying for the Harriet Stark family.

Lewis Wride was abroad in Great Britain serving as a Mormon missionary from 1891-1893, leaving Harriet back home to look after two children (Ann and Beatrice Eloise) and presumably the farm as well. Harriet birthed three children during this decade—Mary (1896), Ronda (1897), Hattie (1899)—and lost one infant child, the one-year-old Ronda. Life as a rural farmwife with a wood burning stove and a kitchen cistern that had to be hand-filled by bucket would be challenging enough. Writing a novel (and selling) a novel in such conditions could only be described as superhuman.

We can infer where Harriet got some of the material she put into her novel, her New York setting, for example. Magazines were the one documented luxury afforded the Wride household. The most cursory perusal of the magazine publications of the day—*Munsey's*, *Frank Leslie's*, and *Century Illustrated Monthly*, for example—yield a plethora of densely informative articles and photographic essay about life in the metropolis, detailed enough to allow someone in Payson, Utah to describe the Gilded Age New York with confidence.

Articles like *Munsey's* "Journalism in New York" surely inspired Stark's female reporter Cadge character.

Inspiration for the novel's wonderfully quirky artist character, Kitty, for example, surely came from articles like the 11-page magazine photo-essay "The Art Student's League in New York" in *The Bookman*, detailing the rise of women's art schools in New York. Lingering over that essay's photographs, one can almost pick out Kitty amongst the unnamed photographed students replete with upswept Gibson Girl bouffants and paint-stained art smocks covering ankle-length dresses.

Even Kitty's fictional baroque insert illustrations of poor "beastesses" with clipped "noses and toeses" have their real-life magazine counterparts in the Art Nouveau feature headers scattered about the era's magazines, including ironically the very "Books Received" and "Books Reviewed" columns announcing the publication of *Bacillus* itself—one of which real-life header illustration actually shows a Cupid whose foot is clipped of all its "toeses," poor beastie

Even Stark's depiction in her novel of a prairie Bonanza grain farm came not from personal experience but surely from magazine articles depicting such farms down to accounts of mile-long processions of the huge for-hire convoys of mechanical combines necessary to harvest such large-scale operations.

The bonanza farms underscore a peculiar aspect of *Bacillus*. Critics like to say every novel is, at least in part, autobiographical. Harriet Stark turns this on its head, writing the opposite of what she knows. Large single-grain bonanza farms run by hired hands rather than the real-life Wride family mixed-use Utah family farm run by family members. Main character Helen Winship an only child rather than just one of twenty siblings and half-siblings Harriet grew up as. The Winships adhere to a generic Protestantism rather than Harriet's Mormon faith. She uses the glittering world of socialite Manhattan as fictional backdrop, not her rural (and economically depressed) Payson, Utah. Instead of married off to a farmer at twenty as Harriet was, her female characters have lives and careers of their own: Kitty a magazine illustrator, Cadge a newspaper reporter, and Helen Winship a graduate student. Male lead John Burke a New York lawyer imbued with a burning ambition to better himself rather than Payson farmer Lewis Wride's placid self-satisfaction with his station in life. And yet Harriet Stark manages these diametrical opposites with perfect confidence, causing readers to ascribe to her "that sure touch that knowledge gives" of subjects she herself had never experienced.

Is there anything of Harriet Stark herself in the novel. Again, there are those who say that all novels are—at least in part—autobiographical, yet trying to guess which portions is often a fool's game and reveals more about the critic than the writer. A writer often has no idea themselves why a particular plot element is used. For a critic trying to assign a reason from a remove of over a century? Near-certain folly.

For example, we have a group photograph of a bespectacled Harriet Stark standing somewhat awkwardly, somewhat ungainly next to her seated mother, Priscilla Stark, the noted beauty of the family. Stark's main character Helen Winship's obsession with beauty partially derived from comparisons between plain-faced Harriet and a beautiful aunt. Was Helen's insecurity reciprocated in real life with her creator's?

Did character Helen's frantic need for money later in the novel reflect the Wride family finances, perhaps after that barn burning down? Did Helen's lament about the difficulty of a woman in 1900 raising or earning money with no other path open save marriage or the arts mirror her creator being in a similar bind? Was *Bacillus* written to raise cold hard cash and was the reason the family never spoke of it was that it didn't?

We can suppose, we can theorize, but in all likelihood we will never know.

5

Publisher Frederick A. Stokes & Co. certainly pulled out all stops to try to make *Bacillus* a financial success. Stokes aggressively marketed the book, going all out. Beginning in September 1900, one month prior to the release of Bacillus, Stokes placed ads and sent out review copies to newspaper and magazine publications such as *The Literary Era*, *Book News Monthly*, *The Bookman*, *The Critic*, *The Literary World*, *The Book Buyer*, *Literary*

News, *Current Literature*, *Publishers Weekly*, *Munsey's*, *Life*, *The Outlook*, *The Nation*, *Century Illustrated*, even to specialty magazines such as *Christian Work*, *The Art Interchange*, and *Boston Home Journal*.

The New York magazine *Fame* (a monthly journal for advertisers examining advertising techniques and ad campaigns) reported that Stokes innovated a special marketing technique for *Bacillus*: sending out to newspapers excerpts of the novel on sheets pre-typeset into compositing "sticks" (or columns). (*Fame* neglects to mention if this tactic annoyed newspaper compositors more than it "aided" them.)

For five full months, from September 1900 to January 1901, magazines coast-to-coast were peppered by both ads and mentions of Harriet Stark's novel in "Books Received" and "Books Reviewed" features. Stokes even put an advertisement for *Bacillus* in the back pages of its own novels penned by other authors.

After January 1901, all mention of *Bacillus* ceases. The novel's publication life had run its course. Frederick A Stokes & Co. moved on to their next product. We can only surmise that despite the publisher's apparent faith in the novel, the book failed to sell. One final mention takes place in April 1901 in the back pages of the Salt Lake Tribune; undoubtedly Harriet Stark herself sending in promotional copy in a last-ditch effort to garner publicity in what was essentially her home town newspaper. After this, *Bacillus* and Harriet Stokes sank out of sight, out of memory so completely that she remained unknown up through the 1970s, even the 1990s, to scholars specializing in Mormon Literature studies.

The fault lay not with the publisher. Stokes did everything and then some to promote the book. The fault lay in the nature of the book itself. Harriet Stark was the victim of bad timing.

The American literary scene of the last part of the 19th Century was dominated by the iron-fisted aesthetics of one man: William Dean Howells, editor of *The Atlantic Monthly*, celebrated as "the dean of American letters." Up until then, American fiction had meant the likes of Washington Irving, James Fennimore Cooper, Edgar Allan Poe, Herman Melville, Mark Twain—raw, outsized stories for a raw, outsized nation spanning a virgin continent. Howells would have none of such fare, none of the "deadly engravings of 'Washington Irving and friends'" as he termed it.

In his seminal *Criticism and Fiction*, Howells explicitly called for literature where "nothing happens" (that is a direct quote!), literature where "nobody murders or debauches anybody else; there is no arson or pillage of any sort; there is not a ghost, or a ravening beast, or a hair-breadth escape, or a shipwreck, or a monster of self-sacrifice, or a lady five thousand years old in the whole course of the story."

Howells sought literature reflecting "the smiling aspects of life." Detractors would say, perhaps exaggeratedly, that the perfect Howell story was story about a clutch of ladies from the garden club sitting around for tea and discussing a chip in the china teapot. Regardless, Howell was willing to pay for what he wanted. His *Atlantic* paid astronomical rates and an entire generation of writers started writing to please Howells. Perhaps more importantly, an entire generation of literature critics and book reviewers became Howells-men as well. Stylistic writing and word choice were in. Plot was out. History, adventure, and anything smacking of the fantastic was derisively labelled "blood and thunder" literature.

Much to Howells's ire, in 1900 there was an entire cadre of prominent, well-respected blood and thunder writers: H. G. Wells, Robert Louis Stevenson, Jules Verne, Bram Stoker, Arthur Conan Doyle, H. Rider Haggard, among others. (Howells's derisive dig about a five-thousand-year-old woman quoted above specifically referenced Haggard's novel *She*, published just one year earlier than Howells' remark.)

Primarily British (and thus a good part of why Howells railed against European writers in *Criticism and Fiction*), these writers were joined by American authors such as Mark Twain, Ambrose Bierce, and Robert W. Chambers in writing everything Howells deplored: history, adventure, fantasy, and something new that would eventually be known as science fiction. Stories with plot. Stories where things happened.

Howellsian critics decried the then-deluge of "blood and thunder" novels (the very literary magazine issues reviewing *Bacillus* are replete with such complaints), but the dominant voice in literature, the colossus which bestrode the literary world at the turn of the century, was the foremost practitioner of blood-and-thunder: Rudyard Kipling.

It is almost impossible to convey to a 21st Century reader just how powerful a cultural influence Kipling once had on the English-speaking world. If you take the Beatles at their 1960s peak, add in the Michael Jackson of the 1980s, throw in *Star Wars* and the Marvel movies, you begin to approximate Kipling's ascendency. Blue collar workers quoted him to their shaving mirrors and literary critics used him as a yardstick to measure everything else published at the time. Harriet Stark referred to Kipling and his works no less than three times in the course of her *Bacillus* novel.

But colossi are fated for toppling, and the year 1900 marked the start of Kipling's fall. The reasons behind Kipling's slide are beyond the scope of this essay, but suffice it to say that in 1899 he was unassailable by the critics. Beginning in January of 1900, all that changed. "Just now I can discern a reaction from the Kipling craze," a writer in *The Book News Monthly* wrote. "A year ago one heard only praises of Kipling, but now…" it was open season on the "billiard ball in need of a shave."

January of 1900 saw the publication of Richard Le Gallienne's landmark *Rudyard Kipling: A Criticism*. An influential author himself, at the time, Le Gallienne was the "antithesis" of Kipling, in aesthetics and temperament. Said a reviewer of La Gallienne's diatribe: "He [Le Gallienne] is aghast at the prevalence and the popularity of blood-stained fiction. As Mr. Kipling is the Field-Marshall of this army he tilts his lance at him."

January also saw the publication of W. J. Peddicord's *Rudyard Reviewed* in which, as a reviewer writes, Peddicord "scarcely admits that Kipling has even a talent of mediocre kind…all that Kipling has written must pass in time into oblivion." (Rather like the oblivion Peddicord himself has passed into; of all his writings, ironically only his anti-Kipling book is readily remembered.)

Magazine literary critics soon jumped in as well, their article titles semaphoring their opinions: Frank Moore Colby's "The Writer Who Does Not Care: Kipling" in *The Bookman* and Robert Buchanan's "The Voice of 'The Hooligan'" in *Contemporary*, for example. Over the next five decades a veritable cottage industry of anti-Kipling books would see print, leading to the eventual complete unpersoning of Kipling in English Departments.

Kipling and blood-and-thunder literature still had supporters in the pages of book review columns in the autumn of 1900, but more and more the literary review columns were filled with editorials like those in the very influential *Munsey's Magazine* Literary Chat. The *Munsey's* January 1901 issue sarcastically proclaimed the book world was currently seized by blood and thunder mania in its "Literary Epidemics" item, subtitling it "Howells, Kipling, Du Maurier, the detective yarns, and the swashbuckler":

…[W]e were shaken, all of us, by the Kipling fever. Then we read "Sherlock Holmes" and had the detective delirium…Just now the swashbuckler has us in his grasp…

Fighting and bloodshed are the essentials we demand in our fiction today; with nothing else can our thirst be satisfied. That the life pictured is fantastic, absurd, or impossible, the no such persons lived or could live, and no such incidents could occur, is nothing...

[Stories]...filled with accounts of deeds no man ever did or could do. No matter; is there bloodshed? Do they fight? Is the villain slain? Is the hero a tremendous fellow ... rushing through the world making a loud noise? Then that is what we want, and plenty of it. Lay it on thick...

Mr. Howells once had some queer primitive notion that the object of fiction was to portray life as it is or might be. But Howells! Bless your soul, who is Howells?

The unnamed Harriet Stark novel found itself landing in this literary battlefield and the reviews weren't pretty.

The Critic, a review magazine dedicated to professional snark and cattiness, dismissed Stark's novel with as little space as possible, said review quoted here in its entirety: "*The Bacillus of Beauty*, by Harriet Stark, teems with the bacteriæ of bad novel writing."

Life's review was far more dismissive. It grudgingly admits that "[m]any an entertaining book has been written upon the basis of an absurd idea, well handled," but contends Stark's book "passes the patience of the most consistent reader of trash."

Stark's novel never had a chance of a favorable review from *Munsey's Magazine*. Firmly in the pro-Howells/anti-blood and thunder camp (their Kipling epidemic editorial quoted above appeared the month following their *Bacillus* review and a pro-Howells tongue bath, "Howells at His Best," reviewing his *Literary Friends and Acquaintance* ("Howells has written something that is not only worth reading, but worth keeping as well—which can be said of very few books") in February, but were also aesthetically opposed to any novel featuring a villain or anti-hero as protagonist, believing it to be a moral hazard for readers.

A month prior to reviewing *Bacillus*, the "Literary Chat" unnamed critiquer once again indulges in sarcastically "advocating" for what he obviously opposes in an item entitled "The Villain Hero." After trashing fictional spies and "morphine fiend" Sherlock Holmes and poor Rupert of the *Prisoner of Zenda* novels (all of which were to be considered "villains" for less than pure foibles and behavior), the Literary Chat caps off the article by saying what was really needed to shock the reading public out of the evils of anti-hero protagonists was facetiously suggesting substituting anti-hero novels with anti-*heroine* one instead:

It may be time for anxiety over modern degeneracy when the villainess begins to reign. Thus far she is rare. In books, as in existence, women's rights are by a myth, and equality in picturesque wrong doing is not permitted the downtrodden sex.

But the crux of the Literary Chat's complaint isn't merely that *Bacillus* has as its protagonist Helen a "villainess as heroine". The *Munsey's* literary chatterbox seethed at the very notion of women writers. A mere two items before his *Bacillus* review, he all but gave himself apoplexy over a news item that novelist Mary E. Wilkins, under contract to deliver her next novel to her publisher, had postponed her scheduled marriage a Dr. Freeman until after she'd finished the book.

For its December 1900 review of *Bacillus*, the Chat reprised a trick pulled the previous issue ("Hair Tonics and Piety"), disparaging a publication by associating it with a beauty aid, doubled and redoubled in Stark's case. Woman writer, woman protagonist, women's products, get it? *Har har har.*

The Chat subtitled its Harriet Stark review "A novel on looks which has not even the excuse of advertising a hair restorer or a nail polish" and proceeded to "quote" a string of purposely-histrionic fake paragraphs "from" the novel's main character Helen Winship's POV:

> "My incomparable beauty—my dazzling eyes, my glistening hair, my svelte figure, my pomegranate lips, my swan-like throat, my almost vulgar vigor, and, in brief, all the charms which I have inventoried on nearly everyone of the preceding [three hundred] pages—is all to be ascribed to the use of Mme. La Rose's Triune Tonic, which is equally good for skin, eyes, and general disposition. For sale at all druggists' and most department stores for sixty-three cents a quart bottle."

And on and on.

Pausing to take a swipe at the use of such an un-Howellsian story device as "the perennial story of the fountain of youth," the Chat pronounces the entire novel superfluous as "all of which [the novel deals with] has been more succinctly summed up in "Handsome is that handsome does," and other saws of similar import."

Other reviewers, thankfully, were more favorable.

The year 1900 edition of *The Booklovers Library* catalog, though lacking the term itself and quaintly listing it in its "imaginative humor" section, correctly describes *Bacillus* as a science fiction novel and approves of it as such:

> "Suffice it, therefore, to state that it is a 'twentieth century' sort of book, the main action of which would be scarcely possible with our range of faculties. But like a book with which it may, not inaptly, be compared—Robert Louis Stevenson's *Doctor Jekyl* [sic] *and Mr. Hide*—*The Bacillus of Beauty* is a book with a moral of tremendous importance…

Noting that it is a book that will interest women ("No woman will read it without strongly taking sides on the great question it brings up"), the catalog concludes that "[f]ew books will attract a larger constituency of readers."

But would women really be interested in reading what *Munsey's* Literary Chat would classify as a blood and thunder book? Certainly, *Harper's Bazar*, billed as "A Weekly Magazine for Women" (they spelled Bazaar with only one "A" at the time), was more positive in its female-targeted October review than *Munsey's* had been, despite using the same bromide to summarize Stark's book:

> "[It] illustrates those well-worn axioms, "Handsome is as handsome does" and "Beauty is only skin deep." The story is original in its plan…her beauty becomes dazzling, fairly scorching, indeed in its radiance. What she got out of this sudden acquisition it takes a good many pages and the introduction of a number of characters to portray. The story is clever and will interest the reader…"

6

The most useful review from the 21st century reader's perspective (certainly the most perceptive) comes from the November 1900 issue of *The Book Buyer*:

> There are as many possibilities in the creation of perfect physical or mental beauty as in the conception of Frankenstein's monster, or the dual personality of Dr. Jekyll; but Miss Harriet Stark, the author of *The Bacillus*

of Beauty, apparently has failed to see the potentialities of her plot. Tales of this kind are the natural property of romantic writers; only powerful imaginations can make them yield all they hold. But Miss Stark is not a romanticist, but a realist. The idea of the German professor who has discovered the bacillus of beauty, and with it inoculates a far from handsome girl, making her the most beautiful woman in the world, is full of promise. But what does the author make of it? She has dimly felt that the situation should yield some symbolic lesson of life, but has floundered into a chain of commonplace occurrences—making her beauty a nine-days' society wonder, a "special" for the yellow press, a social struggler laden with debts, wrecked in happiness…The clever invention is frittered away upon realistic things; the greater possibilities (if such there be, as we do not doubt) are neglected. The tale falls short through lack of imagination.

The reviewer puts a finger to a central debate that has flared up repeatedly throughout the history of science fiction, one often as fraught as Howellsians vs. blood-and-thunderers.

"Outsized" was the term this essay used earlier to describe the blood and thunderers—outsized characters grappling with outsized problems requiring outsized solutions against an outsized backdrop—science fiction most of all. In its purest form, science fiction's *raison d'être is* that scientific backdrop, *is* that scientific problem, a problem which—if not solved through swashbuckling and daring-do—must be resolved through scientific action (or, more rarely, scientific inaction).

Often those scientific backdrops, problems, and solutions are as much the main character of the story as the main characters themselves are. Sometimes excessively so. At its Gernsbackian worst, science fiction characters possess as much personality and free will as the wooden player tokens on a Cluedo game board and seemingly exist for no other purpose than to be advance the required number of spaces in order to declare that Space-Colonel Mustard did it in the airlock with the turbo encabulator, thus solving the story's super-science puzzle as with no more emotional stakes than a crossword puzzle.

The *Book Buyer* reviewer expected an outsized story such as a *Frankenstein* or a *Dr. Jekyll*. With an H. G. Wells novel about bacterium and bacillus and super-serums, you get toppling Martian invaders or invisible men. With a Harriet Stark novel, you get nights at the opera, visits to dressmakers, and high teas with belted earls. Instead of *War of the Worlds*, the reviewer—like Ainslie's poor acquisition editor—got something more akin to *Love and Mr. Lewisham*, It was almost as if *Bacillus of Beauty* was (whisper it!) a Howellsian novel.

Thus, the reviewer baffled and confused, accuses Stark of failing to see potentialities, of frittering away the book's promise, of floundering into the commonplace—similar to accusations made against the 17th Century poet George Herbert in his day.

In our day, Herbert is perhaps best known for his poem "Jordan (I)," a portion of which ("Is There in Truth No Beauty?") served as an episode title on the original *Star Trek* television series:

> *Who says that fictions only and false hair*
> *Become a verse? Is there in truth no beauty?*
> *Is all good structure in a winding stair?*
> *May no lines pass, except they do their duty*
> *Not to a true, but painted chair?*
>
> *Is it no verse, except enchanted groves*
> *And sudden arbours shadow coarse-spun lines?*
> *Must purling streams refresh a lover's loves?*
> *Must all be veil'd, while he that reads, divines,*
> *Catching the sense at two removes?*
>
> *Shepherds are honest people; let them sing;*
> *Riddle who list, for me, and pull for prime;*
> *I envy no man's nightingale or spring;*
> *Nor let them punish me with loss of rhyme,*
> *Who plainly say,* my God, my King.

Once again, it is outside the scope of this essay to delve into the literary feuds of the 17th Century or the history of what Samuel Johnson jeeringly coined the Metaphysical school of poetry. Suffice it to say that the complaint of Herbert's critics was essentially the same complaint voiced by Howells and Harriet Stark's *Book Buyer* reviewer: Herbert Wasn't Following The Rules.

Leaving aside the true nature of the multi-leveled "Jordan" poem— yes, a poem ostensibly about a poet advocating for plain language and against hidden meanings is in fact a multi-layered work; one of the main complaints against the Metaphysicals was their inordinate fondness of word play (modern critics have taken to calling their school the Baroque school instead)—the surface layer of the poem is an effective rebuttal to Herbert's critics. Herbert argues for writing what he wants in the language he wants, of seeking Truth in the beauties and Beauty in the truths he chooses.

More importantly, he essentially tells his critics "I don't begrudge you your kind of literature, don't begrudge me mine." That Herbert's fictive poet is arguing against some of Herbert's own aesthetics only lends it power.

The problem with William Dean Howells's dictums isn't that there's anything inherently wrong with the kind of stories Howells wanted by themselves. It's that Howells would brook no other kind. This *should* be the only kind of literature allowed quickly escalates into this *must* be the only kind. You must read only *this*, you must write only *this*. Likewise, the *Book Buyer* reviewer *this* is the only way to write science fiction.

But let us see what the reviewer's idea of what *Bacillus* should have been. We take as our text Stanley G. Weinbaum's 1935 short story, "The Adaptive Ultimate." This story is considered a classic in the field and has been dramatized multiple times on television as well as radio and film. It bares an uncanny resemblance to *Bacillus*. Indeed, in broad terms the main plot (up to a point) is almost identical:

> Kyra Zela, a miserable wretch even more drab and plain than Helen Winship, gets injected with a newly discovered super-serum that bestows perfect health and beauty. This perfection either changes her personality outright or brings to the fore latent negative traits. She begins to see herself superior to normal people and thus increasingly feels society's rules don't apply to her. She abandons all those close to her, betraying them even, in her rapid ascent up the ladder of society, embarking on a quest for position, power, and fortune. Ultimately, Kyra's estrangement from the rest of humanity comes in conflict with her desired ascent within its ranks, precipitating a final resolution.

Near-identical to *Bacillus*, and yet the exact opposite.

The bifurcation begins with the respective super-serums themselves. The perfection Harriet Stark's bacillus treatment imbues is static; the perfection Weinbaum's serum imbues is adaptive. Stark's perfection realizes the full potential of an individual's original genetics but no further. Weinbaum's perfection exceeds one's original genetics, adapting, mutating.

Helen Winship is human; perfect, but still human. Kyra Zela is a super-human who can adapt against any threat. She soon graduates from petty theft to callous murder, eventually poised to take over the world. The story becomes a race by the serum's creator to find a scientific way to kill the invulnerable Kyra before she can make good her conquest. Weinbaum writes exactly the outsized scope the *Book Buyer* reviewer call for, resolves it with just the sort of laws of science crossword puzzle that would please the reviewer.

Harriet Stark chose to write a different kind of story even though starting from an almost-identical setup. She chose to write a character study, an ordinary person set against an extraordinary backdrop, and work out the story's resolution based not on science but on the personality-driven actions and reactions of that character. As *Book Lovers* notes, *Bacillus* is "a problem story only as to its main theme."

Roughly eighty years later, another writer suffered similar grief from the science fiction community. Beginning in the 1980s and continuing on to the 2020s, Connie Willis has received an unparalleled string of Nebula and Hugo Awards (8 and 17 respectively) making her the most awarded writer in the history of science fiction, and yet in 1993 the late Gardner Dozois, editor of *Asimov's* magazine, felt the need to devote the bulk of his foreword to Willis's *Impossible Things* defending Willis and her fiction from both critics and certain portions of the reader base—"bored sophisticates" and "self-consciously Cool People" to use his phrasing.

On the surface, their complaint was that she was a housewife writing about housewives. True, Connie Willis was and is a housewife (one who by her own admission sings in church choirs and goes to Tupperware parties) and her stories do sometimes star housewives, but their real squawk was that Willis was "maudlin"—once again a writer dared juxtapose the commonplace, the domestic, against an sfnal background. In fictive Armageddons great ("A Letter from the Clearys") or small ("The Last of the Winnebagos"), Willis wrote of everyday concerns and honest emotions, just as Harriet Stark had a near-century earlier.

It wasn't that Willis couldn't write hard sf ("The Sidon in the Mirror") or New Wave ("Daisy, in the Sun"), but she chose to write what she wanted to write instead. And that seemed to irk her detractors all the more. (Even in 2021, even after all the awards, an otherwise-sympathetic 2021 *Clarksworld* interviewer cannot resist a little dig, titling the Willis piece "Science Fiction and Schmaltz.")

Unlike many writers who only specialize in one or the other, Willis has mastered both dark, traumatic tales and lighter fare. Her particular specialty, however, is her heartfelt homages to 1930s Hollywood screwball comedies full of, in Willis's own words, "all sorts of smart-aleck or daffy or obnoxious supporting characters."

To read *Bacillus* is to realize that Harriet Stark's supporting characters —witty quirky, off-kilter ones like Kitty and Cadge and the General and the surly theatre manager and even the seemingly-henpecked uncle, Judge Timothy Baker (who reveals himself later to be far more than he appears) —could very well walk onto a Connie Willis story or a 30s screwball comedy with nobody the wiser. Stark seems to be channeling the screwball comedies three decade before they were invented and eighty years before the Connie Willis stories.

This inevitable comparison by readers who have read both authors makes the fate of *Bacillus* and its author all the more poignant with what-could-have-beens.

A near-universal trait among authors is that they grow to hate or at least feel embarrassed by their first published work. Willis's "Santa Titicaca" appeared in late 1970. It is a serviceable enough story, a tale about intelligent frogs and Incan magic. Textual clues point to a 1969 *The Undersea World of Jacques Cousteau* TV special exploring the Peruvian lake, its frogs, and Incan treasure legends as the origin seed for the story. Gardner Dozois, who was responsible for the story's publication, admits that it "shows only a few flashes of her later wit and style."

It would be just short of a decade before Willis sold another science fiction story. A decade of honing her craft. The award nominations began rolling in a year after her return in print. But had she not sold a second work and then a third and a fourth and on and on, the author Connie Willis would have been remembered only for "Santa Titicaca."

Bacillus is Harriet Stark's "Santa Titicaca." Workmanlike enough to get published, showing flashes of what she might have been. What her future work may have been like we will never know, and we are poorer for it.

Portions of Stark's prose in *Bacillus* decidedly show their Mauve Decade origins. Overly long and at times overly melodramatic, almost Byronic—the *Munsey's* Literary Chat review is completely wrong about the book's faults. But other portions are surprisingly modern. Stark's style in those sections read like they came from the 1930s. It is easy to envision that by a second or third novel, Stark has sloughed off the Mauve Decade/Byronic prose altogether, writing solely in her modernistic voice.

Continuing to write of the ordinary juxtaposed against the fantastic, Harriet Stark may well have been to the 1910s and 1920s what the very successful Robert Nathan who also wrote of the ordinary and the inexplicable (*The Bishop's Wife*, *Portrait of Jenny*) was in the 1920s and 1930s, and not all the Howellsian critics in the world could stop her, anymore than they stopped George Herbert or Connie Willis.

Sadly, we will never get those second or third novels.

We don't know why *Bacillus* was Stark's only novel; neither Harriet or her family ever said. Perhaps family circumstances at home prevented her from following up on her success. Perhaps it may have been the publisher's decision; disappointing sales, perhaps, or disappointing reviews. Perhaps Harriet Stark only had the one novel in her, although this is extremely hard to believe of so inventive a mind as Starks. It remains an unsolvable mystery. We simply lack that sure touch that knowledge gives

7

To paraphrase L.P. Hartley, "the past is a foreign country; they write differently there." So how should we of the Twenty-First Century read *The Bacillus of Beauty*?

In a perfect world, writing is direct communication from the author to the reader. A writer's means of doing so is through the manuscript, an imperfect medium at best. Alfred Korzybski, the father of general semantics, readily reminds us that "the map is not the territory, the word is not the thing it describes." The manuscript is not the story the author meant to tell, it's the filter by which the writer tells it. Readers bring their own filters—personal experience. You are as much a product (and a prisoner) of your time—culturally, linguistically, artistically—as *The Bacillus of Beauty* is of its era.

Artforms change. You only have to sample popular music from different decades to discern that. Prose fiction evolves—slower than most other artforms, perhaps—but evolve it does. The science fiction novel has moved on in the almost one-and-a-quarter century since *Bacillus* was written.

The novel's language may seem stilted, even Byronic at times. The characters may not reflect current-day sensibilities or political positions.

And still, *The Beauty of Bacillus* is an enjoyable read.

Treat Harriet Stark's novel as a foreign film.

This essay has gone into considerable detail on the cultural, social, and political climate of 1900 American, Harriet Stark's life circumstances; and the literary scene that *Bacillus* landed in, all in an attempt to help bridge that foreign gap, help you look at the book from a 1900 perspective.

If the language seems stilted or Byronic, merely say to yourself that this film's subtitles were badly translated, garbling the meaning of its original language. Keep in mind that while *Munsey's* complaint about Stark's prose was not altogether unjustified, *Munsey's* reviewed the cream of the literature of its day and *Bacillus* is being held up to that. Stark's prose is scarcely purpler than the vast bulk of her contemporaries, like Gaston Leroux's later 1910 novel, *The Phantom of the Opera* for example. ("Santa Titicaca," after all, isn't a *bad* story; merely a weak one compared to the ghost of future Connie Willis stories to come.)

If the characters in the novel don't hew to certain current-year causes, remember they follow the foreign customs and mores of 1900. Remember that Harriet Stark wouldn't receive the right to vote for another twenty years after the novel's publication.

Characters like Kitty and Cadge are—by 1900 standards—almost scandalous in their independence. The fictional Helen Winship, by putting career over marriage, by delaying her engagement to John Burke until after her post-graduate degree, risked the same opprobrium in fiction as *Munsey's* heaped upon the real-life author Mary E. Wilkins. Helen Winship's almost manic hypergamic ascent up the ranks of society in pursuit of marriage is all but necessitated by the inability of women in 1900 to acquire money of their own. What Harriet Stark writes of was in her time truly stunning and brave when there was a real societal cost.

Because it was written before standard genre tropes became standard tropes, *Bacillus* doesn't always do what you expect. One of the great joys in reading *Bacillus* is that you're never sure what direction Harriet Stark will go.

Paradoxically, another joy in reading Stark's novel is noting how many themes and plot elements from later works she predicts years and decades in advance, whether it's watching an egotistical, irascible professor molding a woman to his whims in order to seamlessly fit into high society (Shaw's *Pygmalion*, 1913) or pondering on how perfection might alter the human condition—is imperfection necessary to truly be human? (Algis Budrys's "Silent Brother" [1953], The Falling Torch [1959], and "Be Merry" [1966]) or would perfection render human beings inhuman (the bulk of fellow Utahn and fellow Mormon Raymond F. Jones's mid-century output [*This Island Earth*, 1952] and others).

Harriet Stark only wanted to explore the truth of beauty, but an inventive, insightful mind such as hers couldn't help uncovering other truths— that is how truth works, that's the beauty of truth. But that a "mere" farmwife in Payson, Utah in 1900—working in isolation, snatching what writing time she can between raising children, doing daily domestic chores without running water, electricity, or labor-saving devices, pitching in with the farm work—could not only write a New York-publishable novel—the first person in her state to do so—but also presage so much of a yet-to-be-created literary genre is nothing short of miraculous.

And the sad part about miracles is that once granted one, you crave more.

Alas, *The Beauty of Bacillus* is all we have or will ever have of Harriet Stark. She appears in our midst, primly and properly presenting her Victoria-era calling card with inscribed with *Pour Prendre Congé* informing us that though she has just arrived, she must take her leave,

P.P.C.

THE
BACILLUS OF BEAUTY

Book I: The Broken Chrysalis

(From the shorthand notes of John Burke.)

1

The Metamorphosis

New York, Sunday, Dec. 16.

I am going to set down as calmly and fully as I can a plain statement of all that has happened since I came to New York.

I shall not trim details, nor soften the facts to humour my own amazement, nor try to explain the marvel that I do not pretend to understand.

I begin at the beginning—at the plunge into fairy tale and miracle that I made, after living twenty-five years of baldest prose, when I met Helen Winship here.

Why, I had dragged her to school on a sled when she was a child. I watched her grow up. For years I saw her nearly every day at the State University in the West that already seems so unreal, so far away, I loved her.

Man, I knew her face better than I knew my own! Yet when I met her here—when I saw my promised wife, who had kissed me goodbye only last June—I did not recognise her. I looked full into her great eyes and thought she was a stranger; hesitated even when she called my name. It's a miracle! Or a lie, or a wild dream; or I am going crazy. The thing will not be believed. And yet it's true.

This is my calmness! If I could but think it might be a tremendous

3

blunder out of which I would sometime wake into verity! But there has been no mistake; I have not been dreaming unless I am dreaming now.

As distinctly as I see the ugly street below, I remember everything that has befallen me since my train pulled into Jersey City last Thursday morning. I remember as one does who is served by sharpened senses. Only once in a fellow's lifetime can he look upon New York for the first time—and to me New York meant Helen. Everything was vividly impressed upon my mind.

When I saw my promised wife, I did not recognise her.

I crossed the Cortlandt Street ferry and walked up Broadway, wondering what Helen would say if I called before breakfast. I could scarcely wait. I stopped in front of St. Paul's Church, gaping up at a twenty-six story building opposite; a monstrous shaft with a gouge out of its south side as if lightning had rived off a sliver. I went over to it and saw that I had come to Ann Street, where Barnum's museum used to stand. The Post Office, the City Hall, the restaurant where I ate breakfast, studying upon the wall the bible texts and signs bidding me watch my hat and overcoat; the *Tribune* building, just as it looks on the almanac cover— all these made an instant, deep impression. Not in the least like a dream.

By the statue of Horace Greeley I stood a moment irresolute. I knew that, before I could reach her, Helen would have left her rooms for Barnard College; breakfast had been a mistake. Then I noticed that Nassau Street was just opposite; and, in spite of my impatience to be at her door, I constrained myself to look up Judge Baker.

Between its Babel towers, narrow Nassau Street was like a canyon. The pavements were wet, for folks had just finished washing windows, though it was eight o'clock in the forenoon. Bicycles zipped past, and from some- where north a freshet of people flooded the sidewalk and roadway.

Down a steep little hill and up another—both thronged past belief— and in a great marble maze of lawyers' offices I found the sign of Baker & Magoun.

The boy who alone represented the firm said that I might have to wait some minutes, and turned me loose to browse in the big, high-ceiled outer room or library of the place where I am to work. After the dim corridors, it was a blaze of light. On all sides were massive bookshelves; the doorways gave glimpses of other rooms, fine with rugs and pictures and heavy desks, different enough from the plain fittings of the country lawyers' workshops I had known. The carpet sank under my feet as I went to the window.

I stood looking at the Jersey hills, blue and fair in the distance, and dreaming of Helen, who was to bless and crown my good fortune, when I heard a step at the door and a young man came in—a tall, blonde, supple fellow not much older than I. Then the Judge appeared, ponderous, slow of tread, immaculate of dress; the same, unless his iron-gray locks have retreated yet farther from his wall of a brow, that I have remembered him from boyhood.

"Burke!" he said, "I am glad to see you. Welcome to New York and to this office, my boy!"

The grasp of his big warm hand was as good as the words and the eyes beneath his heavy gray brows were full of kindness as, holding both my hands in his, he drew me toward the young man who had preceded him. With a winning smile, the latter turned.

"Hynes," said the Judge, with a heartiness that made one forget his formal manner, "you have heard me speak of Burke's father, the boyhood companion with whom, when the finny tribes were eager, I sometimes strayed from the strait and narrow path that led to school. Burke, Hynes is the sportsman here—our tiger-slayer. He beards in their lairs those Tammany ornaments of the bench whom the flippant term 'necessity Judges,' because of their slender acquaintance with the law."

"Glad to see you, Burke," said Hynes, as dutifully we laughed together at the time-honoured jest.

I knew from the look of him that he was a good fellow, and he had an honest grip; though out where I come from we might call him a dude. All New Yorkers seem to dress pretty well.

Presently Managing Clerk Crosby came, and Mr. Magoun, as lean, brusque and mosquito-like as his partner is elephantine; and after a few words with them, I was called into the Judge's private room, where a great lump rose in my throat when I tried, and miserably failed, to thank him for all his great kindness.

"Consider, if it pleases you," he said, to put me quite at my ease, "that I have proposed our arrangement, not so much on your own account as because I loved your father and must rely upon his son. It brings back my youth to speak his name—your name, Johnny Burke!"

Yes, I remember the words, I remember the tremour in the kind voice and the mist of unshed tears through which he looked at me. I'm not dreaming; sometimes I wish I were, almost.

When I left the Judge, of course I pasted right up to Union Square, though I felt sure that Helen would be at college. No. 2 proved to be a dingy brick building with wigs and armour and old uniforms and grimy pictures in the windows, and above them the signs of a "dental parlour" and a school for theatrical dancing.

It seemed an odd place in which to look for Nelly, but I pounded up the worn stairs—dressmakers' advertisements on every riser—until I reached the top floor, where a meal-bag of a woman whose head was tied up in a coloured handkerchief confronted me with dustpan and broom.

"I'm the new leddy scrubwoman, and not afther knowin' th' names av th' tinants," she said, "but av ut's a gir-rul ye're seekin', sure they's two av thim in there, an' both out, I'm thinkin'."

I pushed a note for Nelly under the door she indicated—it bore the cards of "Miss Helen Winship" and "Miss Kathryn Reid"—and hurried away to look up this gem of a hall bedroom where I am writing; you could wear it on a watch chain, but I pay $3 a week for it. The landlady would board me for $8, but regular dinners at restaurants are only twenty-five cents; good, too. And anybody can breakfast for fifteen.

Then I went back to Union Square, where I hung about, looking at the statues. Once I walked as far as Tammany Hall and rushed back again to watch Helen's door. Finally I sat down on a bench from which I could see her windows; and there in the brief December sunlight, with the little oasis around me green even in winter, and the roar of Dead Man's

Curve just far enough away, I suppose I spent almost the happiest moments of my life.

I was looking at Nelly's picture, taken in cap and gown just before she graduated last June. My Nelly! Nelly as she used to be before this strange thing happened; eager-eyed, thin with over-study and rapid growth. Nelly, whose bright face, swept by so many lights and shadows of expression, sensitive to so many shifting moods, I loved and yearned for. Nearly six months we'd been apart, but at last I had followed to New York to claim her. As I sat smiling at the dream pictures the dear face evoked, my brain was busy with thoughts of the new home we would together build. I'd hoard every penny, I planned; I'd walk to save car-fare, practice all economie—

Wasn't that a face at her window?

I reached the top landing again, three steps at a time; but the voice that said "Come!" was not Helen's and the figure that turned from pulling at the shades was short and rolypoly and crowned by flaming red hair.

"Miss Winship?" said the voice, as its owner seated herself at a big table. "Can't imagine what's keeping her. Are you the John Burke I've heard so much about? And—perhaps Helen has written to you of Kitty Reid?"

Without waiting for a reply, she bent over the table, scratching with a knife at a sheet of bold drawings of bears.

"You won't mind my keeping right on?" she queried briskly, lifting a rosy, freckled face. "This is the animal page of the Sunday *Star* and Cadge is in a hurry for it, to do the obbligato."

I suppose I must have looked the puzzlement I felt, for she added hastily:—

"The text, you know; a little cool rill of it to trickle down through the page like a fine, thin strain of music that—that helps out the song—tee-e-e-um; tee-e-e-um—" She lifted her arm, sawing with a long ruler at a violin of air,—"but you don't have to listen unless you wish—to the obbligato, you know."

"Doesn't the writer think the pictures the unobtrusive embroidery of the violin, and the writing the magic melody one cannot choose but hear?"

I thought that rather neat for my first day in New York, but the shrewd blue eyes opened wide at the heresy.

"Why, no; of course Cadge knows it's the pictures that count; everybody knows that."

A writing table jutted into the room from a second window, backing against Miss Reid's. On its flap lay German volumes on biology and a little treatise in English about "Advanced Methods of Imbedding, Sectioning and Staining." The window ledge held a vase of willow and alder twigs, whose buds appeared to be swelling. Beside it was a glass of water in which seeds were sprouting on a floating island of cotton wool.

"Admiring Helen's forest?" came the voice from the desk. "I'm afraid there's only second growth timber left; she carried away the great redwoods and all the giants of the wilderness this morning. Are you interested in zoology? Sometimes, since I have been living with Helen, I have wished more than anything else to find out, What is protoplasm? Do you happen to know?"

"I'm afraid not."

"Neither does Helen—nor anyone else."

Miss Reid's merry ways are infectious. I'm glad Helen is rooming with a nice girl.

The place was shabby enough, with cracked and broken ceiling, marred woodwork and stained wall paper; but etchings, foreign photographs, sketches put up with thumb tacks and bright hangings made it odd and attractive. On a low couch piled with cushions lay Helen's mandolin and a banjo. A plaster cast of some queer animal roosted on the mantel, craning its neck down towards the fireplace.

"That's the Notre Dame devil," Miss Reid said, following my glance; "the other is the Lincoln Cathedral devil." She nodded at a wide-mouthed imp, clawing at a door-top. "Don't you just adore gargoyles?"

"Yes; that is—very much," I stammered, wandering back to Helen's desk. And then!

And then I heard quick steps outside. They reached the door and paused. I looked up eagerly. "There's Helen now," said Miss Reid; "or else Cadge."

A tall girl burst into the room, dropping an armful of books, and sprang to Miss Reid.

"Kitty! Kitty!" she cried, in a voice of wonderful music. "Two camera fiends! One in front of the college, the other by the elevated station;

waiting for me to pass, I do believe! And such crowds! They followed me! Look! Look! Down in the Square!"

2

The Most Beautiful Woman in the World

Both girls ran to the window. Miss Reid laughed teasingly. "I see nobody—or all the world; it's much the same," she said; "but you have a caller."

I rose from behind the desk with some confused, trivial thought that I ought to have spent part of the afternoon getting my hair cut.

I had had but a glimpse of the newcomer in her flight across the floor; I knew she had scarlet lips and shining eyes; that youth and joy and unimagined beauty had entered with her like a burst of sunlight and flooded the room. I felt, rather than saw, that she had turned from the window and was looking at me, curiously at first, then smiling. Her smile had bewildered me when she opened the door; it was a soft, flashing light that shone from her face and blessed the air. She seemed surrounded by an aureole.

But she—how could this wonderful girl know me?—she surely was smiling! She was coming towards me. She was putting out her hands. That glorious voice was speaking.

"John! Is it you? I'm so glad!" it said.

Had I read about her? Had I seen her picture? Had Helen described her in a letter? Was she Cadge? No; not altogether a stranger; somewhere before I had seen—or dreamed—

"John," she persisted. "Why didn't you write? I thought you were coming next week. Did you plan to surprise me?"

Miss Reid must have made a mistake, I felt; I must explain that I was waiting for Helen. But I could not speak; I could only gape, choking and giddy. I did not speak when the bright vision seemed to take the hands I had not offered. I could feel the blood beat in my neck. I could not think; and yet I knew that a real woman stood before me, albeit unlike all the other women that ever lived in the world; and that something surprised and perplexed her. The smile still curved her lips; I felt myself grin in idiotic imitation.

"What is the matter?" the radiant stranger persisted. "You act as if—"

The smile grew sunnier; it rippled to a laugh that was merriment set to music.

"John! John Burke!" she said, giving my hands a little, impatient shake, just as Nelly used to do. "It isn't possible! Don't you—why, you goose! Don't you know me?"

"Helen!"

Of course! I had known her from the beginning! A man couldn't be in the same room with Nelly Winship and feel just as if she were any other girl. But she was not Helen at all—that radiant impossibility! And yet she was. Or she said so, and my heart agreed. But when I would have drawn her to me, she stepped back in lovely confusion, with a fluttered question:
—

"How long have you been here, John?"

That voice! Sweet, fresh; full of exquisite cadences such as one might hear in dreams and ever after yearn for—from the first it had baffled me more than the beautiful face. It was not Helen's. What a blunder!

I gazed at her, still giddy. Who was she? I could not trust the astounding recognition. She returned the look, bending towards me, seeking as eagerly, I saw with confused wonderment, to read my thought as I to fathom hers. Then, as some half knowledge grew to certainty, the light of her beauty became a glory; she seemed transfigured by a mighty joy such as no other woman could ever have felt.

An instant she stood motionless, the sunshine of her eyes still on me. Then, drawing a long breath, she turned away, pulling the pins out of her feathered hat with hands that trembled.

I watched the process with the strained attention one gives at crucial moments to nothings. I laughed out of sheer inanity; every pulse in my body was throbbing. She lifted the hat from her shining head. She put it down. She unfastened her coat. In a minute she would turn again, and I should once more see that face imbued with light and fire. I waited for her voice.

"I'm sure of it!" she cried, wheeling about of a sudden, with a laugh like caressing music, and confronting me again. "You didn't know me, John; did you?"

"Why didn't I know you?" I gasped. "Why are you glad I don't know you? What does it all mean, Helen?"

Instead of answering she laughed again. It was the happiest joy-song in the world. A mirthful goddess might have trilled it—a laugh like sunshine and flowers and chasing cloud shadows on waving grass.

"Helen Winship, stop it! Stop this masquerade!" I shouted, not knowing what I did.

"But I—I'm afraid I can't, John."

The glorious face brimmed with mischief. In vain the Woman Perfect struggled to subdue her mirth to penitence.

"I—I'm so glad to see you, John. Won't you—won't you sit down and let Kitty give you some tea?"

Tea! At that moment!

Clattering little blue and white cups and saucers, Miss Reid recalled herself to my remembrance. I had forgotten that she was in the room. I suspect that she dared not lift her head for fear I might see the laughter in her eyes.

"I've made it extra strong, Mr. Burke," she managed to say, "because I'm starting for the *Star* office to find the photo-engravers routing the noses and toeses off all my best beastesses."

"Kitty thinks all photo-engravers the embodiment of original sin," said the Shining One. "They clip her bears' claws."

"Well," returned Miss Reid, making a flat parcel of her drawings, "this is the den of Beauty and the beasts, and the beasts must be worthy of Beauty. Mr. Burke, don't you know from what county of fairyland Helen hails? Is she the Maiden Snow White—but no; see her blush—or the Princess Marvel? And if she's Cinderella, can't we have a peep at the fairy godmother? Cadge will call her nothing but 'H. the M.'—short for 'Helen the Magnificent.' And—and—oh, isn't she!"

"Kathryn!"

Before that grieved organ-tone of reproach, Kitty's eyes filled. I could have wept at the greatness and the beauty of it, but the little artist laughed through her tears.

"Helen Eliza, I repent," she said. "Time to be good, Mr. Burke, when she says 'Kathryn.'"

Adjusting her hat before a glass, Kitty hummed with a voice that tried not quaver:—

> *"Mirror, mirror on the wall,*
> *Am I most beautiful of all?*
>
> *"Queen, thou art not the fairest now;*
> *Snow-white over the mountain's brow*
> *A thousand times fairer is than thou.*

"Poor Queen; poor all of us. I'm good, Helen," she repeated, whisking out of the room.

"Such a chatterbox!" the goddess said. "But, John, am I really so much altered? Is it true that—just at first, you know, of course—you didn't know me?"

She bent on me the breathless look I had seen before. In her eagerness, it was as if the halo of joy that surrounded her were quivering.

"I know you now; you are my Helen!"

Again I would have caught her in my arms; but she moved uneasily.

"Wait—I—you haven't told me," she stammered; "I—I want to talk to you, John."

She put out a hand as if to fend me off, then let it fall. A sudden heart sickness came upon me. It was not her words, not the movement that chilled me, but the paling of the wonderful light of her face, the look that crept over it, as if I had startled a nymph to flight. I was angry with my clumsy self that I should have caused that look, and yet—from my own Helen, not this lovely, poising creature that hardly seemed to touch the earth—I should have had a different greeting!

I gazed at her from where I stood, then I turned to the window. The rattle of street cars came up from below. A child was sitting on the bench where I had sat and feasted my eyes upon the flutter of Helen's curtains. My numb brain vaguely speculated whether that child could see me. The sun had gone, the square was wintry.

After a long minute Helen followed me.

"John," she said, "I am so glad to see you; but I—I want to tell you. Everything here is so new, I—I don't—"

It must all be true; I remember her exact words. They came slowly, hesitated, stopped.

"Are you—what do you mean, Helen?"

"Let me tell you; let me think. Don't—please don't be angry."

Through the fog that enveloped me I felt her distress and smarted from the wrong I did so beautiful a creature.

"I—I didn't expect you so soon," the music sighed pleadingly. "I—we mustn't hurry about—what we used to talk of. New York is so different!—Oh, but it isn't that! How shall I make you understand?"

"I understand enough," I said dully; "or rather—Great Heavens!—I understand nothing; nothing but that—you are taking back your promise, aren't you? Or Helen's promise; whose was it?"

I could not feel as if I were speaking to my sweetheart. The figure before me wore her pearl-set Kappa key—the badge of her college fraternity; it wore, too, a trim, dark blue dress—Helen's favourite colour and mine—but there resemblance seemed to stop.

Confused as I still was by the glory I gazed on, I began painfully comparing the Nelly I remembered and the Helen I had found. My Helen was not quite so tall, but at twenty girls grow. She did not sway with the yielding grace of a young white birch; but she was slim and straight, and girlish angles round easily to curves. Though I felt a subtle and wondrous change, I could not trace or track the miracle.

My Helen had blue-gray eyes; this Helen's eyes might, in some lights, be blue-gray; they seemed of as many tints as the sea. They were dark, luminous and velvet soft as they watched my struggle. A few minutes earlier they had been of extraordinary brilliancy.

My Helen had soft brown hair, like and how unlike these fragrant locks that lay in glinting waves with life and sparkle in every thread!

My Helen's face was expressive, piquantly irregular. The face into which I looked lured me at moments with a haunting resemblance; but the brow was lower and wider, the nose straighter, the mouth more subtly modelled. It was a face Greek in its perfection, brightened by western force and softened by some flitting touch of sensuousness and mysticism.

My Helen blushed easily, but otherwise had little colour. This Helen had a baby's delicate skin, with rose-flushed cheeks and red, red lips. When she spoke or smiled, she seemed to glow with an inner radiance that had nothing to do with colour. And, oh, how beautiful! How beautiful!

I don't know how long I gazed.

I was trying to study the girl before me as if she had been merely a fact —a statue, a picture. But here was none of the calm certainty of art; I was in the grip of a power, a living charm as mighty as elusive, no more to be fixed in words than are the splendours of sunset. Yet I saw the vital harmonies of her figure, the grace of every exquisite curve—the firm, strong line of her white throat, the gracious poise of her head, her sweeping lashes.

I looked down at her hands; they were of marvellous shape and tint, but I missed a little sickle-shaped scar from the joint of the left thumb. I knew the story of that scar. I had seen the child Nelly run to her mother when the knife slipped while she was paring a piece of cocoanut for the Saturday pie baking. That scar was part of Helen; I loved it. I felt a sudden revolt against this goddess who usurped little Nelly's place, and said that she had changed. Why was she looking at me? What did she want?

"You are the most beautiful woman in the world," said a choked voice that I hardly recognised as my own.

Instantly the joy light shone again from her face, bathing me in its sunshine, and the world was fair. She started forward impulsively, holding out her hands.

"Then it's true! Oh, it's true!" she cried. "How can I believe it? I— Nelly Winship—am I really—"

"Ah—you are Nelly! My Nelly!"

What happened is past telling!

With that jubilant outburst, as naive as a child's, she was my own love again, but dearer a thousand times. Would I have given her up if her hair were blanched by pain or sorrow, her cheeks furrowed, her face grown pale in illness? Need I look upon her coldly because she had become radiant, compellingly lovely? Why, she was enchanting!

And she was Helen. A miracle had been worked, but Helen's self was looking at me out of that goddess-like face as unmistakably as from an unfamiliar dress. It was seeing her in a marvellous new garb of flesh.

"Oh, I'm so happy! I'm the happiest girl on earth; I'm—am I really beautiful?"

The rich, low, brooding, wondering voice was not Helen's, but in every sentence some note or inflection was as familiar as were her tricks of manner, her impulsive gestures. Yes, she was Helen; warm breathing, flushed with joy of her own loveliness, her perfect womanhood—the girl I adored, the loveliest thing alive!

I seized the hands she gave me; I drew her nearer.

"Helen," I cried, "you are indeed the most beautiful being God ever created, and—last June you kissed me—"

"I didn't!"

"—Or I kissed you, which is the same thing—after the Commencement reception, by the maple trees, in front of the chapter house; and—"

"And thence in an east-southeasterly direction; with all the hereditaments and appurtenances—Oh, you funny Old Preciseness!"

"And now I'm going to—" The words were brave, but there was something in the pose and poise of her—the wonder of her beauty, the majesty —perhaps the slightest withdrawal, the start of surprise—that awed me. Lamely enough the sentence ended:

"Helen, kiss me!" I begged, hoarsely.

For just a fraction of a second she hesitated. Then the merriment of coquetry again sparkled in her smile.

"Ah, but I'm afraid—" she mocked.

Her eyes danced with mischief as she drew away from me.

"I'm afraid of a man who's going to be a great city lawyer. And then— oh, listen!"

Hurried, ostentatiously heavy footsteps sounded in the hall. They stopped at the door, and someone fumbled noisily at the knob. There was a stage cough, and Kitty plunged into the room, carefully unnoticing.

"Such an idea for—a hippopotamus comic," she panted; "a darling! Sent drawings down—messenger—rushed back to sketch—"

Here she paused to take breath.

"—lest I forget."

Snatching off her gloves she resumed her place at the big table, and began making wild strokes with a crayon on a great sheet of cardboard.

"I just *had* to do it," said she apologetically over her shoulder; "but— don't mind me."

The Hornets' Nest

I t was dusk when I left Helen. My head was buzzing.

Out of her presence, what I had seen was unthinkable, unbeliev-able. I could do nothing but walk, walk—a man in a dream.

I rushed ahead, jostling people in silly haste; I dawdled. I carefully set my feet across the joinings of paving blocks; I zigzagged; I turned corners aimlessly. Once a policeman touched me as I blinked into the roaring torches of a street repairing gang. Once I found myself on Brooklyn Bridge, looking down at big boats shaped like pumpkin seeds, with lights streaking from every window. Once I woke behind a noisy group under the coloured lights of a Bowery museum.

It rained, for horses were rubber-blanketed, and umbrellas dripped on me as I passed. I was hungry, for I smelled the coffee a sodden woman drank at the side of a night lunch wagon. But how could I believe myself awake or sane?

Again and again I found my way back to the bench on Union Square, from which I could gaze at Helen's window, now dark and forbidding. Across an open space was a garish saloon. When the door swung open, I saw the towels hanging from the bar. Two men reeled across the street and sat down by me.

"Oo-oo!" one gurgled.

"Dan's goin' t' kill 'imself 'cause 'is wife's gone," blubbered the other. "Tell 'm not ter, can't ye, matey? Tell 'im' t's 'nough fer one t' die!"

"Oo-oo!" bellowed Dan.

I walked away in the darkness, but I felt better. Drunkenness was no miracle: I was awake and sane, sane and awake in a homely world of sorrow and folly and love and mystery.

I went to bed thinking of Cleopatra, "brow-bound with burning gold"; of Fair Rosamond; Vivien, who won Merlin's secret; of Lilith and strange, shining women—not one of them like the goddess the glory of whose smile had dazzled me. At last I slept, late and heavily.

Next morning I was again first at the office; and by daylight in the bustling city, things took a different complexion. I had gone to my sweetheart tired by a long journey, and I felt sure, or tried to feel sure, that my impressions of change in her were fantastic and exaggerated.

Judge Baker, on his arrival, installed me in Hynes's room, behind the library, between the corridor and one of the courts that light the inner offices. In his own room, to the left, he detained me for some business talk, after which he said, carefully rubbing his glasses:

"I trust that you will not find yourself altogether a stranger in the city. My wife will wish to see you, and my sister, Miss Baker, cherishes pleasant recollections of your mother. I believe you are already acquainted with Mrs. Baker's young cousin, Miss Winship. You know that, since graduation, she has come to New York for the purpose of pursuing post-graduate studies in Barnard?"

"Yes."

I drew a breath of relief. There was nothing in the Judge's manner to give significance to his mention of Helen. I must have deceived myself.

"A most charming young lady."

He glanced at the letters on his desk and methodically cut open an envelope. Then he dropped the paper knife, raising his bushy brows, a gesture that indicates his most genial humour, as he continued with more than usual deliberateness:—

"You knew her, no doubt, as an intelligent student; you may be surprised to learn that she has developed extraordinary—the word is not too strong—extraordinary beauty."

"Always a lovely girl," I muttered.

"From her childhood Nelly has been a favourite with me;" the Judge leaned back in his big chair, seeming to commit himself to an utterance; "but her attractions were rather those of mind and heart, I should have said, than of personal appearance. The change to which I have alluded is more than the not uncommon budding of a plain girl into the evanescent beauty of early womanhood; it is the most remarkable thing that has ever come under my observation. I am getting to be an elderly man, Burke, and I have been a respectful admirer of many, many fair women, but I have never seen a girl like Miss Winship; she is phenomenal."

"You—you think so?"

It was true, then!

"I have ceased to think; I am nonplussed. Witchcraft, though not in the older sense of the word, is still no doubt exercised by young ladies, and there are certain improvement commissions that undertake, for a suitable consideration, the—ah—redecoration of feminine architecture, or even the partial restoration of human antiques. But this is a different matter."

"I saw Miss Winship yesterday."

"You will not then accuse me of overstatement?"

"She is indeed beautiful."

The restraint with which I spoke evidently puzzled him. He continued to look at me curiously, as he said slowly:—

"From a young man I should have expected more enthusiasm. At times I suspect that the youth of today are less susceptible than were those of twenty-five years ago. But this affair has perhaps occupied my thoughts more than otherwise it might, because Helen is in a measure my ward during her stay in the East, and because of my daughters' affection—"

"Judge, I had supposed you aware of an engagement between Helen and myself."

"Ah, that accounts for much. To you, no doubt, she is little altered. Your eyes have seen the budding of that beauty which but now becomes visible to those less partial. I believe Mrs. Baker did hint at something between you, but it had escaped my mind."

The Judge's bright eyes that contradict so pleasantly the heavy cast of his features began to twinkle. Little lines of geniality formed at their corners and rayed out over his cheeks. He beamed kindliness, as he continued:—

"Accept my congratulations. A most excellent family. Mrs. Winship is Mrs. Baker's cousin. Ah, time flies; time flies! It seems but yesterday that my little girls were running about with Nelly, pigtailed, during their visits in the West."

"Does Mrs. Baker also think Nelly—changed?"

"Only on Tuesday my wife returned from nursing an ailing relative. She has not seen Helen in some time. I believe we are to have her with us at Christmas. We must have you also. But I cannot altogether admit that the change is a matter of my opinion. It has been commented upon by my daughters in terms of utmost emphasis."

"She is the most beautiful woman in the world!"

"There we shall not disagree. To Nelly herself the riddle of nature that we seek to read is doubtless also a mystery, but one for whose unraveling she is happy to wait. My daughters have a picture of her, taken at the age, possibly, of six, which gives inartistic prominence to 'Grandpa Winship's ears'—the left larger than the right. You know the family peculiarity owned by the eldest child in each generation? The loss of this inheritance may not be, to a young lady, matter for regret; but as a mark of identification and descent, the Winship ears might have entitled her to rank among the Revolutionary Daughters. However, she is a poor woman who has not a club to spare."

"Judge, how long is it since this—transformation took place? You speak of it as recent."

"Nelly comes to me," said the Judge, "with—ah—natural punctuality for monthly remittances from her father. In November I was struck with the fact that New York agreed with her; yet even then I did not miss the family nose—a compromise of pug and Roman. But ten days ago, when I saw her last, I recognised her with difficulty. For more precise information you must ask my daughters."

"Then it was only ten days ago that you saw anything wrong—?"

"Wrong! My dear young friend, if Nelly's case obtained publicity, would not the world, which loves beauty, be divided between a howling New York and a wilderness?"

The Judge glanced up at me, slipping his paper knife end over end through his fingers.

"I have spoken of myself as nonplussed," he said more seriously, "and I am. I was never more so; but I see no occasion for anxiety. Since when has it been thought necessary to call priest or physician because of a young lady's growing charm? Confronted by an ugly duckling, we must congratulate the swan."

"Judge, how much money does one need to marry on in New York?"

"All that a man has; all that he can get; often more. But—ah—is the question imminent? Nelly is in school; you have come out of the West, as I understand it, to attack New York. Conquer it, Sir; conquer New York before you speak of marriage to a New York woman."

"Helen is not a New York woman."

"We naturalize them at the docks and stations."

"But you—" I repressed a movement of impatience. "Didn't you marry young?"

"Mrs. Baker and I began our married life in one room; cooked over the gas jet, in tin pails. And if little Nelly is the equal of other women of her family—but that is practice versus principle, my young friend; practice versus principle."

He turned again to his letters, and I understood that the interview was closed.

Right after lunch I started for Barnard. Helen has written so much about the college that as soon as I struck the Boulevard I knew the solid brick building with its trimmings of stone fasces. I turned into the cloistered court on One Hundred and Nineteenth Street and paused a minute, looking up at its Ionic porticoes and high window lettered "Millbank Hall."

Then I entered, and a page, small, meek and blue uniformed, trotted ahead of me through a beautiful hall, white with marble columns and mosaics, sumptuous with golden ceiling, dazzling with light and green with palms, to the curtained entrance of a dainty reception room.

"Stop a minute, Mercury," I said as he turned to leave; "where is Miss Winship?"

He reappeared from an office beyond, replying:—

"Biol'gy lab'r'tory. What name?"

Instead of waiting until Nelly could be summoned, I followed the mildly disapproving boy up a great, white stairway, past groups of girls, some in bright silk waists and some in college gowns. Even in the farthest corner remote from the hubbub, a musical echo blent of gay talk and laughter filled the air; a light body of sound that the walls held and gave out as a continuous murmur.

A second time piping, "What name, Sir?" Mercury opened the door of a large room with many windows. At the far corner my eyes sought out Helen in conversation with a keen-eyed, weazened little man, at sight of whom the boy took to his heels.

Three women besides Helen were in the room, bunched at a table that ran along two sides under the windows. They wore big checked aprons, and one of them squinted into her microscope under a fur cap. Wide-mouthed jars, empty or holding dirty water, stood on other tables ranged up and down the middle of the room, and there was a litter of porcelain-lined trays, test tubes, pipettes, glass stirring rods and racks for microscope slides.

Against the wall to the left were cabinets with sliding doors, showing retorts, apparatus, bottles of drugs, jars of specimens and large, coloured models of flowers and of the lower marine forms. Against the right hand wall were sinks, an incubator and, beyond, a door leading into a drug closet. There was the usual laboratory smell, in which the penetrating fume of alcohol, the smokiness of creosote and carbolic acid, the pungency of oil of clove and the aroma of Canada balsam struggled for the mastery.

In her college gown Helen looked more like herself than the day before and less so, the familiar dress accentuating every difference. Against the flowing black her loveliness shone fair and delicate as a cameo, I thought of the Princess Ida,

> *Liker to the inhabitant*
> *Of some far planet close upon the sun*
> *Than our man's earth; such eyes were in her head,*
> *And so much grace and power—*
> *Lived through her to the tips of her long hands*
> *And to her feet.*

She had not noticed my entrance, but as I stepped forward, she turned, and I was again lost in wonder at her marvellous grace. Her beauty seemed a harmony so vitally perfect that the sight of it was a joy approaching pain.

I had not been mistaken! She was the rarest thing in human form on this earth. I was awed and frightened anew at her perfection.

"Why, how did you find your way out here?" she asked with girlish directness. "I'm not quite ready to go; I must finish my sections for Prof. Darmstetter."

The Professor—I had guessed his identity—joined us, glancing at me inquisitively. His spare figure seemed restless as a squirrel's, but around the pupils of his eyes appeared the faint, white rim of age.

"You are friendt of Mees Veensheep?" he asked. "Looks she not vell? New York has agreed vit' her; not so?"

At my awkward, guarded assent, I thought that something of the same surprise Judge Baker had voiced at my moderation flitted over the old man's face.

"I find you kvite right; kvite right," he said, "New York has done Mees Veensheep goot; she looks fery vell."

He whisked into the drug closet, and Helen seated herself before a microscope next that of the fur-capped woman.

"Do you care for slides?" she said. "I'll get another microscope and while I draw you may look at any on my rack. But be careful; most of the things are only temporarily mounted—just in glycerine. Here is the sweetest longitudinal section of the tentacle of an *Actinia*, and here—look at these lovely transverse sections of the plumule of a pea; you can see the primary groups of spiral vessels. They've taken the carmine stain wonderfully! But my work is not advanced; I wish you could see that of the other girls."

"I mustn't interfere with your task; I'll look about until you are ready."

Her shining head was already bent over the microscope; her pencil was moving, glad to respond to the touch of that lovely hand.

I picked up a book, the same little volume I had noticed the day before, on "Imbedding, Sectioning and Staining." Near it lay a treatise on histology. I opened to the first chapter, on "Protoplasm and the Cell," but I couldn't fix my thoughts on *Bathybius* or the *Protomoeba*. I walked toward an aquarium, flanking which stood a jar half-filled with water in which floated what seemed a big cup-shaped flower of bright brown jelly with waving petals of white and rose colour.

While I looked, thinking only of the curve of Helen's lips and the dancing light in her eyes, and the glowing colour of her soft flesh, Prof. Darmstetter's thin, high-pitched voice grated almost at my ear.

"T'at is *Actinia*—sea anemone."

"I come from the West; I have never seen the sea forms living," I answered with an effort, fearing that he meant to show me about the laboratory.

"It is fery goot sea anemone; fery strong, fery perfect; a goot organism."

He bent over the jar, rubbing his hands. His parchment face crackled with an almost tender complacency. For a full minute he seemed to gloat over the flower-like animal.

"Very pretty," I said, carelessly.

"Fery pretty, you call it? T'e prettiness is t'e sign of t'e gootness, t'e strengt', t'e perfection. You know t'at?"

To his challenging question, in which I saw the manner of a teacher with his pupils, I replied:

"In your estimation goodness and beauty go together?"

A jar half-filled with water in which floated a cup-shaped flower with waving
petals of white and rose.

"T'ey are t'e same; how not? See t'is way."

He shook his lean, reproving forefinger at a shapeless, melting mass that lay at the bottom of a second jar, exuding an ooze of viscid strings.

"T'at,"—he spat the word out—"is also sea anemone. It is diseased; it is an ugly animal."

"The poor thing's dying," said Helen, coming to his side. "There ought to have been some of the green seaweed, Ulva, in the water. Wouldn't that have saved it?"

"Ugliness,"—Darmstetter disregarded the question—"is disease; it is bat organism; t'e von makes t'e ot'er. T'e ugly plant or animal is diseased, or else it is botched, inferior plant or animal. It is t'e same vit' man and voman; t'ey are animals. T'e ugly man or voman is veak, diseased or infe-rior. On t'e ot'er hand,"—I felt what was coming by the sudden oiling of his squeak—"t'e goot man or voman, t'e goot human organism, mus' haf beauty. Not so?" Again he rubbed his hands.

24

Helen glanced mischievously at me, as a half-repressed snort interrupted his dissertation.

The woman in the fur cap, who might have been a teacher improving odd hours, had knocked up the barrel of her microscope; she gazed through the window at the dazzling Hudson. Next to her, a thin, sallow girl, whose dark complexion contrasted almost weirdly with her yellow hair, slashed at a cake of paraffine, her deep-set eyes emitting a spark at every fall of the razor. The other student, a young woman with the heavy figure of middle age, went steadily on, dropping paraffine shavings into some fluid in a watch crystal. With a long-handled pin she fished out minute somethings left by the dissolving substance, dropping these upon other crystals—some holding coloured fluids—and finally upon glass slides. She worked as if for dear life, but every quiver of her back told that she was listening.

"You agree vit' me?"

"It seems reasonable; the subject is one that you have deeply studied."

"Ach so! T'e perfect organism must haf t'e perfect beauty. T'e vorld has nefer seen a perfectly beautiful man or voman. Vat vould it say to von, t'ink you? But perfection, you vill tell me, is far to seek," he went on, without waiting for a reply. "Yet people haf learned t'at many diseases are crimes. By-and-by, we may teach t'em t'at bat organism is t'e vorst of crimes; beautiful organism t'e first duty. V'at do you say?"

The fur-capped girl pushed back her chair.

"Prof. Darmstetter," she said, "will you be good enough to look at my sections?"

"He's stirred up the hornets' nest," whispered Helen. "But come; perhaps they will show us. Those girls are so clever; they're sure to have something interesting."

4

The Goddess and the Mob

As we descended the stairway and passed groups of students in front of the bulletin boards in the hall, Helen said:—

"I am afraid you shouldn't have called for me. It isn't usual here."

"We'll introduce the custom. How could I help coming—after yesterday? Helen—"

"Have you seen Grant's tomb?" she inquired hastily. "It's just beyond the college buildings, hidden by them. You mustn't miss it, after coming so far."

We had issued on the Boulevard, and a few steps brought us in view of the stately white shrine on Claremont Heights. But I looked instead at her brilliant face against the velvety background of black hat and feather boa.

The sun's rays, striking across the river, played hide-and-seek in her shimmering hair, warming it to gold and touching the rose of her cheeks to a clear radiance. Her eyes were scintillant with changing, flashing lights.

"Well?" she challenged at last, half daring, half afraid. "You know me today?"

"You are a sun goddess. Helen, what does it mean?"

"New York agrees vit' me," Her laugh was irresistible—low and sweet, a laugh that made the glad day brighter. "How not? It is vun fine large city."

We laughed together to the memory of *Actinia*.

"I am a goot organism. T'e bat organisms vish to scratch me; but t'ey are not so fery bat. In time ve may teach t'em gootness."

"If Darmstetter doesn't think you a perfect organism, he must be hard to satisfy. He's a peculiar organism himself. Has he true loves among sand stars or jelly fish, or does he confine his affections to sea anemones?"

"Prof. Darmstetter is a great biologist. It's a shame he has to teach. Don't you think such a man should be free to devote himself to original work? He might in England, you know, if he were a fellow of a University. But we're proud of him at Barnard; and the laboratory—oh, it's the most fascinating place!"

We came slowly down the Boulevard, looking out at the sweep of the Hudson, while she talked of her studies and her college mates, trying, I thought, to keep me from other topics.

I scarcely noticed her words; her voice was in my ears, fresh and musical. The new grace of her shining head and wondrous, swaying figure, the beauty and spirit of her carriage, filled my consciousness. A schooner with a deck load of wood drifted with the tide, her sails flapping; I saw her in a blur. When I turned from the sheen of the river, the bicyclists whizzing past left streaks of light. A man cutting brush in a vacant lot leaned on his axe to look after us. The sudden stopping of his "chop, chop"—he too was staring at the vision of beauty before his eyes—brought me out of my revery.

"Nelly," I said, "your father will expect a letter from me. What shall I say?"

"Tell him I am studying hard and like the city."

"But about us—about you and me?"

"Must we talk of that here—on the street?"

She spoke almost pleadingly, with the same soft clouding of her loveliness that I had seen the day before?

"But I must speak," I said. "You were right yesterday, I won't ask anything of you until I have made a start; but I must know that you still love me; that will be enough. I can wait. I won't hurry you. That is all, Helen. Everything shall be as you wish; but—you do love me?"

"Oh, you great tease! Why, I suppose I do; but—so much has happened, I don't know myself now; you didn't know me when you first saw me here. Why can't you wait and—don't you hope New York vill agree vit' you?"

She laughed with tantalizing roguery. "You *do* love me!" I cried. "And we shall be so happy with all our dreams come true—happy to be together and here! If you knew how I have looked forward to coming, and now—yesterday I thought myself insane, but I wasn't! You are the most marvellous—"

"Am I? Oh, I'm glad! So glad!"

I was confused, overjoyed at her sudden sparkle; the soft, flashing light of her was fire and dew. She made visible nature sympathize with her moods. The sky smiled and was pensive with her.

"But see," she cried with another of her bewildering changes; "we're at Columbia."

We had left the Boulevard, and were approaching the white-domed library.

"Look at the inscription," Helen said, as students carrying notebooks began to pass us. "'King's College Founded under George II.' Doesn't that seem old after the State University? Ours, I mean."

Our inspection was brief. Before the open admiration of the students Helen seemed, like a poising creature of air and sunshine, fairly to take wing for flight.

"Tell me about yourself," she commanded, when we were beyond the flights of terraced steps. "You are really in Judge Baker's office? You—you *won't* say anything more?"

"You—darling! You have almost said you love me; do you know that? Well, I'll be considerate. I will work and I will wait and I will believe—no, I'll be certain that some day a woman more beautiful than the Greeks imagined when they dreamed of goddesses who loved mortal men will come to me and, because it is true, will quite say 'I love you.' But I may not always be patient; for you do. After all, you are Nelly!"

I was almost faint with love of her and wonder; I adored her the more for the earnestness with which she lifted her flushed, smiling, innocent face to say:

"But tell me about the office, *please*. You wouldn't want me to say— would you, if I wasn't sure? Isn't the Judge the most delightful man? So— not pompous, you know; but so good. Don't you like Judge Baker?"

"I love you! Oh, yes, the Judge says, 'if we are confronted with an ugly duckling we must congratulate the swan.' Were you ever an ugly duckling? I'm sure you love me, Helen."

"Did he say that? Well, even when I last saw him why that was nearly two weeks ago—I—oh, I was an ugly duckling!"

We laughed like children. In the sunshine of her joy-lit eyes I forgot the miracle of it, forgot everything except that I had reached New York and Nelly, and that the world was beautiful when she looked upon it.

We came down from Cathedral Heights; and as we boarded a train on the elevated, eyes peered around newspapers. An old gentleman wiped his glasses and readjusted them, his lips forming the words, "most extraordinary," and again, "most extraordinary!" A thin, transparent-looking woman followed the direction of his glance and querulously touched his elbow. Two slender girls looked and whispered.

I thought at first that city folks had no manners, but presently began to wonder that Helen escaped so easily. She had drawn down a scrap of a veil that scarcely obscured her glow and colour and, as the train gathered headway, our neighbours settled in their places almost as unconcernedly as if no marvel of beauty and youth were present. Indeed, most of them had never looked up. The two young girls continued to eye Helen with envy; and I was conscious of an absurd feeling of resentment that they were the only ones. I wanted to get up and cry out: "Don't you people know that this car contains a miracle?"

Why, when Helen lifted to her knee a child that tugged at the skirts of the stout German hausfrau in the next seat, the mother vouchsafed hardly a glance.

"How old are you?" asked Helen.

"Sechs yahre," was the shy answer.

"Such a big girl for six!"

"So grosse! So grosse!"

The little thing measured her height by touching her forehead.

"Shump down," admonished the mother stolidly, while Helen bent over the child, wasting upon her the most wonderful smile of the ever-lasting years.

"It was long ago, wasn't it," Nelly asked, when the child had slid from her lap, "that Uncle promised to take you into his office?"

"Yes," I said. "When Father died, the Judge told me that when I had practised three years—long enough to admit me to the New York bar—he'd have a place for me. It was because the three years were nearly up, you know, that I dared last June to ask you—"

"You'd dare anything," she interrupted hastily. "Remember how, when I was a Freshman, you raced a theologue down the church aisle one Sunday night after service, and slammed the door from the outside? 'Miss

Winship,' you said—I had sat near the door and was already in the entry
—'may I see you home?'—"

"The theologue and the congregation didn't get out till you said yes, I
remember! They howled and hammered at the door in most unchristian
rage?"

"I *had* to say yes; why, I had to walk with you even when we quarrelled;
it would have made talk for either of us to be seen alone."

She breathed a sigh that ended in rippling laughter.

"You'll have to say yes again."

But at that she changed the subject, and we talked about her work at
Barnard until we left the train at Fourteenth Street, where we met the
flood tide of Christmas surging into the shops and piling up against gaily
decked show windows.

Street hawkers jingled toy harnesses, shouted the prices of bright truck
for tree ornaments, and pushed through the crowd, offering holly and
mistletoe. Circles formed around men exhibiting mechanical turtles or
boxing monkeys. From a furry sledge above a shop door, Santa Claus
bowed and gesticulated, shaking the lines above his prancing reindeer. I
had never seen such a spectacle.

"What a jam!" cried Helen, her cheeks flooded with colour. "Come,
let's hurry!"

Indeed, as we threaded our way in and out among the throng, her
beauty made an instant impression.

"There she goes!"

"Where? Where? I don't see her."

"There! The tall one, with the veil—walking with that jay!"

Not only did I hear such comments; I felt them. Yet even here there
were many who did not notice; and again I sensed that odd displeasure
that people could pass without seeing my darling.

It was a relief to leave the neighbourhood of Sixth Avenue and cross to
the open space of Union Square.

The east side of the little park was quiet.

"All right?" I asked.

"All right."

Her breath came quickly as if she had been frightened.

"But see," she said a moment later, "there comes Kitty trundling her
bicycle down Madison Avenue. You'd better come in, and be on your best
behaviour; yesterday Kitty thought we were quarrelling."

"Sorry I'm wanted only to vindicate—is it your character or mine that would stand clearing? And will you tell me—"

A little old Frenchman, with a wooden leg, who was singing the "Marseillaise" from door to door, approached, holding out his hat.

"Merci, M'sieu', Madame," he said, carelessly pocketing a nickel; then, as he fairly caught sight of the face that Helen of old might have envied, he started back in amazement, slowly whispering:—

"Pardon! Mon dieu! Une Ange!"

We left him muttering and staring after us.

"I'll really have to get a thicker veil," said Helen hastily; "stuffy thing! I like to breathe and see. At first it was—oh, delightful to be looked at like that—or almost delightful; for if no had one noticed, how was I to be sure that—that New York was agreeing vit' me? But now they begin to—"

"Then New York hasn't always agreed vit' you? Aren't you going to tell me—"

"Oh, I've been well," she interrupted, "ever since I came. But here's Kitty. Any adventures, Goldilocks?"

"A minute ago a tandem cuffed my back wheel," said Miss Reid, coming up. "My heart jumped into my mouth and—and I'm nibbling little scallops out of it right now."

And then we trooped upstairs together.

5

A High Class Concert

I stayed for supper, over which Kitty's big Angora cat presided; Kitty herself, her red curls in disorder, whimsical, shrewd, dipping from jest to earnest, teased Helen and waited on her, wholly affectionate and, I guessed, half afraid.

The little den was cosy by the light of an open fire—for it seemed to be one function of the tall, pink-petticoated lamp to make much darkness visible; and Nelly was almost like the Nelly I had known, with her eager talk of home folks and familiar scenes.

She asked about my mother's illness and death that had held me so long in the West, and her great eyes grew dim and soft with tears, and she looked at me like a Goddess grieving; until, sweet as was her sympathy, I forced myself to speak of other topics. And then we grew merry again, talking of college mates and the days when I first knew her, when I was a Sophomore teaching in Hannibal and she was my best scholar—only twelve years old, but she spelled down all the big, husky boys.

"I didn't know what I was doing, did I," I said, "when your father used to say: 'Bright gal, ain't she? I never see the beat of Helen Lizy;' and I would tell him you ought to go to the State University?"

"Think of it!" cried Helen. "If I hadn't gone to college, I shouldn't have come to New York, and, oh, if—but how you must have worked, teaching and doubling college and law school! Why, you were already through two years of law when I entered, only three years later."

"Well, it's been easy enough since, even with tutoring and shorthanding; six lawyers to every case—"

"Wasn't tutoring Helen your main occupation?" asked Kitty Reid audaciously. "I have somehow inferred that—"

But there was a sound of hurrying feet on the stairs, and she sprang to the door, crying:—

"Cadge and Pros.! They said they were coming."

On the threshold appeared a lank girl with shining black hair and quick, keen, good-humoured eyes.

"Howdy?" she asked with brisk cordiality; "angel children, hope I see you well."

In her wake was a tall, quiet looking young man with a reddish-brown beard.

"Salute; salaam," he said; "all serene, Kitty? And you, Miss Winship?"

Then as the two became accustomed to the light, I saw what I had nervously expected. There was a little start, an odd moment of embarrassment. They gazed at Helen with quick wonder at her loveliness, then turned away to hide their surprise.

It was as if in the few days since they had seen her—for the new comers were Kitty's brother and the Miss Bryant of whom everyone speaks as "Cadge"—Helen's beauty had so blossomed that at fresh sight of her they struggled with incredulous amazement almost as a stranger might have done.

Talking rapidly to mask embarrassment, they joined us round the fire, Reid dropped a slouch hat and an overcoat that seemed all pockets bulging with papers, while Miss Bryant and Kitty began a rapid fire of talk about "copy," "cuts," "the black," "the colour" and other mysteries.

"Wish you could have got me a proof of the animal page," said Kitty finally; "if they hurry the etching again, before my poor dear little bears have been half an hour on the presses, they'll fill with ink and print gray. I'll—I'll leave money in my will to prosecute photo-engravers."

"Oh, don't fret," said Miss Bryant. "Magazine'll look well this week. Big Tom's the greatest Sunday editor that ever happened; and I've got in some good stuff, too."

"Of course your obbligato'll be all right," Kitty sighed; "but—oh, those etchers and—Yes, Big Tom'll do; I never see him fretting the Art Department, like the editor before last, to sketch a one-column earthquake curdling a cup of cream."

"How *could* anybody do that?" cried Helen.

"Just what the artist said."

Miss Bryant looked slightly older than Helen; in spite of her brusque, careless sentences, I suspected that she was a girl of some knowledge, vast energy and strength of will. And suspicion grew to certainty that she and Reid were lovers.

I might have read it in his tone when in the course of the evening he asked her to sing.

"Then give me a baton," she responded, springing to her feet.

Rolling up a newspaper and seizing a bit of charcoal from the drawing table, she beat time with both hands, launching suddenly into an air which she rendered with dramatic expression as rare as her abandon.

"Applaud! Applaud!" she cried, clapping her own hands at the end of a brilliant passage, her colourless, irregular face alive with enthusiasm, her black eyes snapping. "If you don't applaud, how do you expect me to sing? *Vos plaudite!*"

"I'll applaud when you've surely stopped," said Kitty Reid demurely; "but before we begin an evening of grand opera, I want you to hear the Princess. Helen, you know you promised."

"Nonsense!" exclaimed Helen, colouring at the title, "I can't sing before Cadge; but if you like, I'll play for you. See if I'm not improving in my tremolo."

Helen did not sing in the old days, so that I was not surprised at her refusal. Taking her mandolin, she tinkled an air that I have often heard her play, but neither I nor anyone else had ears for it, so absorbed was the sense of sight.

Her long lashes swept her cheeks as she bent forward in the firelight, her vivid colouring subdued by the soft, playing glow to an elusive charm. At one moment, as the flames flickered into stronger life, her beauty seemed to grow fuller and to have an oriental softness and warmth; the next, the light would die away, and in the cooler, grayer, fainter radiance, her perfect grace of classic outline made her seem a statue—Galatea just coming to life, more beautiful than the daughters of men, her great loveliness delicately spiritualized.

If I were a beautiful woman, I'd learn to play a mandolin.

"Sing, Helen," begged Kitty in a whisper.

In a voice that began tremulously, low and faltering, and slowly gained courage, she sang the ballad she had been playing. It was easy to see that she was not a musician; but, as she forgot her listeners, we forgot everything but her.

Miss Bryant put down the compasses and scale rule she had been restlessly fingering, and her keen eyes softened and dilated. Kitty dropped on the floor at Helen's feet; the hush in the room was breathless. Reid sat in the dark, still as a statue; I clenched my hands and held silence.

The words were as simple as the air. But the voice, so clear, so sweet, so joyous, like Helen's own loveliness—to hear it was an ecstasy. We were listening to the rarest notes that ever had fallen on human ears—unless the tale of the sirens be history.

Her perfect grace of classic outline made her seem a statue—Galatea just coming to life.

As the last note died, the fire leaped, dropped and left us in dusk and silence. Kitty buried her face against Helen's dress. My heart was pounding until in my own ears it sounded like an anvil chorus. I don't know whether I was very happy or very miserable. I would have died to hear that voice again. It is the truth!

With a sudden sob and a sniffing that told of tears unashamed, Miss Bryant found frivolous words to veil our emotion.

"Ladies and gentlemen," she quavered, "this is a high class concert; three dollars each for tickets, please. Helen, you don't know how to sing, but—don't learn! Come Pros."—the big drops ran down her cheeks; "I've got to look up a story in the morning."

"Wait a minute," said Reid, his long, delicately shaped fingers trembling. "Let me recover on something."

Picking up Kitty's banjo, he smote the strings uncertainly and half sang, half declaimed:—

> "'With my Hya! Heeya! Heeya! Hullah! Haul!
> Oh, the green that thunders aft along the deck!
> Are you sick of towns and men? You must sign and sail again,
> For it's Johnny Bowlegs, pack your kit and trek!'

"By Jove! Kipling's right; nothing like a banjo, is there? Now then, Young Person, I'm with you. Good night; good night!"

While his voice was still echoing down the stairway, Miss Bryant came running up again.

"Say, got a photograph of yourself, Helen?" she asked.

She had apparently quite recovered from her emotion, and her tone expressed an odd mixture of business and affection.

"I believe if I showed Big Tom a picture of you," she explained, "he'd run a story—there's your science, you know, and your music—on the Society page, maybe."

"But I haven't any picture; at least, any that you'd want—only a few taken months ago, for my father."

"Show me those; why won't they do?"

"Oh, they aren't good; they—they don't look like me. Besides, I really couldn't let you print my picture, Cadge."

"All right. Good night, then; good night, Kitty."

"Perhaps I was just the least bit homesick; I'm glad you've come," Helen said to me at goodbye.

She did not withdraw the hand I pressed. She was still under the excitement of the music; the song had left on her face a dreamy tenderness.

"Don't you like Cadge?" she asked, checking with shy evasiveness the words I would have spoken. "She can do anything—sing, talk modern Greek and Chinese—Cadge is wonderful."

"I know someone more wonderful. Helen, when did you begin to sing?"

"I don't sing; tonight was the first time I ever tried before anyone but Kitty. Did I sing well?"

"I can't believe you're real! I can't—"

"Don't! Don't!" she laughed. "Remember your promise."

And with that she ran away from the door where I stood, and I came directly home. Home, to set down these notes; to wonder; to doubt; to pinch myself and try to believe that I am alive.

I am alive. This that I have written is the truth! This is what I have seen and heard since a common, puffing railroad train brought me from the West and set me down in the land of miracles.

It is the truth; but out of that magic presence I cannot—I am as powerless to believe as I am powerless to doubt.

God help me—it is the truth!

Book II:
The Birth of the Butterfly

(from the autobiography of Helen Winship)

The Psychological Moment

No. 2 Union Square, December 14.

I am the most beautiful woman in the world!

I feel like a daughter of the gods. Bewildered, amazed, at times incredulous of my good fortune—but happy, happy, happy!

There is no joy in heaven or earth like the joy of being beautiful—incomparably beautiful! It's such a neverending surprise and delight that I come out of my musings with a start, a dozen times a day, and shudder to think: "What if it were only a dream!"

Happy? I have no faith in the old wives' fables that we are most miserable when we get what we want. It isn't true that the weak and poor are to be envied beyond the powerful. Ask the fortunate if they would change! I wouldn't; not for the Klondike?

I'm so happy! I want to take into my confidence the whole world of women. I want them to know how the gift was gained that they are some day to share. I want them to know that there are still good fairies in the world; and how I was fated to meet one, how he waved his wand over me and how my imperfections fled. Every woman will read the story of my life with rapt attention because of the Secret. I shall tell that last of all. Now it's my own.

Is it true that I have longed for beauty more passionately than most women; or is it only that I know myself, not the others? I can remember the time, away back, when the longing began—when I was—

Incredible! Was I ever an ugly little girl, careless of my appearance, happiest in a torn and dirty dress; and homely, homely, homely? Oh, miracle! The miracle!

They say all girls begin life thus heedless of beauty; but none get far along the road before they meet the need of it. So it was with me; and now I love to recall every pitiful detail of the beginning of the Quest of Beauty, the funny little tragedy of childhood that changed the current of my life— and of your lives, all you women who read.

It was one day after school, in the old life that has closed forever—after the prairie school, dull, sordid, uninspiring, away in the West—that a playmate, Billy Reynolds, was testing upon me his powers of teasing. I remember the grin of pleasure in his cruelty that wrinkled his round, red face when at last he found the dart that stung. His words—ah, they are no dream! They were the awakening, the prelude of today.

"Janey's prettier'n what you be," he said; and of a sudden I knew that it was true, and felt that the knowledge nearly broke my heart.

But could there be any doubt of the proper reply?

"Huh!" I said, shrugging my lean shoulders. "I don't care!"

The day before it would have been true, but that day it was a lie. I did care; the brave words blistered my throat, sudden tears burned my eyeballs, and to hide them I turned my back upon my tormentor.

It was not that I was jealous. I cared no more for Billy than for a dozen other playmates. It was just the fact that hurt. I was homely! Not that the idea was new to me, either. Dear me, no! Why, from my earliest years I had been accustomed to think of myself as plain, and had not cared. My earliest recollection, almost, is of two women who one day talked about me in my presence, not thinking that I would understand.

"Ain't she humbly?" said one.

"Dretful! It's a pity. Looks means so much more to a gal."

"But she's smart."

By these words—you can see that I was young—I was exalted, not cast down. And for five years, remembering them, I had been proud of being "smart." But now, in the moment of revelation, the law of sex was laid upon me, and the thought failed to bring its accustomed comfort. Smart? Perhaps. But—homely!

With feet as light as my heart was heavy because of Billy's taunt, I flew home and ran up to my room. I had there a tiny mirror, about two-thirds of which had fallen from its frame. I may before that day have taken in it brief, uncritical glimpses at my face, but they had not led to self analysis. Now, with beating heart and solemn earnestness, I balanced a chair against the door—there was no lock—and looked long and unlovingly at my reflected image.

The broken mirror gave no hint of my figure.

I saw many freckles, a nose too small, ears too big, honest eyes, hair which was an undecided brown; in short, an ordinary wind-blown little prairie girl. Perhaps I was not so ill-looking, nor Janey so pretty, as Billy affected to think, but no such comforting conclusion then came to me. Sorrow fronted me in the glass.

The broken mirror gave no hint of my figure, but I know that I was lean and angular, with long legs forever thrusting themselves below the hem of my dress; the kind of girl for whose growth careful mothers provide skirts with tucks that can be let out to keep pace with their increasing stature.

Yes, I was homely! I could not dispute the evidence of the bit of shivered glass.

My heart was swelling with grief as I slowly went down stairs, where my mother was getting supper for the hired men. I think it must have been early spring, for prairie schools need not expect boy pupils in seeding time; I know that the door was open and the weather warm.

"Ma," I said as I entered the dining room, "will I ever be pretty?"

"Sakes alive! What *will* the child think of next?"

"But will I, Ma?"

"'Han'some is as han'some does,' you know, Nelly," my mother responded, as she set on the table two big plates piled high with slices of bread. Then she went into the buttery and brought out a loaf of temperance cake, a plate of doughnuts and a great dish of butter.

"Oh, come now, Ma; please tell me," I wheedled, not content with a proverb.

"Why, Nelly, I don't know; the' ain't nobody does know. I was well-favoured at your age, but your pa wan't much on looks. But Pa had a sister who was reel good-lookin', an' some says you've got her eyes. Maybe you'll take after her. But land! You can't never tell. I've seen some of the prettiest babies grow up peaked and pindlin' an' plain as a potato; whilst, on the other hand, reel homely children sometimes come up an' fill out rosy-cheeked an' bright-eyed as you please. There was my half-sister Rachel, now, eight years younger'n me. I remember well how folks said she was the homeliest baby they ever see; an' she grew up homely, too, just a lean critter with big eyes an' tousled hair; but she got to be reel pretty 'fore she died. Then there's my own Cousin Francie, she that married Tim'thy Baker an' went to New York to live. She's a bright, nice lookin' woman, almost han'some; an' her little girls are, too; about your age they be. An'—"

I suppose the lonely prairie life had made Ma fond of talking, without much regard for her audience. Often have I heard her for an hour at a time steadily whispering away to herself. Now she had forgotten her only auditor, a wide-eyed little girl, and was fairly launched upon monologue, the subject answering as well as another her imperious need.

"Which of Pa's sisters, Ma?" I asked, interrupting.

"W'ich of his sisters—w'at? Wat you talkin' 'bout now?"

"Which is the good-looking one?"

"Oh, your Aunt Em'ly, o' course. Nobody ain't ever accused S'renie or Keren-Happuch o' bein' sinfully beautiful, fur's I know."

My Aunt Em'ly was invested for me with a new interest. Perhaps some day I might take after her and grow equally well favoured. I did not remember having noticed that she was beautiful, and resolved to study her at the first opportunity.

2

A Sunday School Lesson

oing to church was a good old New England custom that in our family had borne transplanting to the West. Sunday was almost the pleasantest day in the week to me—not elbowing school-less Saturday from its throne; not of course even comparing with the bliss of Friday just after school, but easily surpassing the procession of four dull, dreaded, droning days the ogre Monday led.

The beauty and fragrance of the summer Sabbath began in the early morning, when I went out into the garden, before putting on my Sunday frock, and picked a quantity of the old fashioned flowers that grew there. I arranged them in two flat bouquets, with tall gladiolus stalks behind and smaller growths ranging down in front so that they might see and be seen, peeping over each other's heads, when placed against the wall in church.

Then after the great toilet-making of the week, we were off. The drive over the prairie in the democrat wagon behind our smartest pair of plough horses was a pleasure that never grew tame from repetition. Arriving at the church, I would give my bouquets to the old stoop-shouldered sexton and watch him anxiously as he ambled down the aisle with them. Perhaps my flowers—yes, the very flowers that I had dashed the dew from that morning—would be placed on the pulpit itself, not on the table below, nor yet about the gallery where sat the choir. Then indeed I felt honoured. But wherever they might be, I could watch them all through the services,

46

perhaps catch their fragrance from some favouring breeze, and feel that they were own folks from home.

Even sermon time did not seem long. After I had noted the text to prepare for catechism at home, I was free to dream as I chose until the rustle of relief at the close of the speaking. And the droning of bees and buzzing of flies, or the sudden clamour of a hen somewhere near would come floating in through the open window, and the odour of the flowers and the twigs of the "ellum" tree tapping at the pane helped to make the little church a haven of restfulness.

But on the Sunday following my awakening I had no care for sounds outside, no eyes for my bouquets, though they stood at either hand of the pulpit; I got permission to sit in Aunt Keren's pew, where I could see Aunt Em'ly's face; and all through the sermon I studied it with big, round eyes.

Yes, and with sorrow growing leaden in my heart.

For I was not old enough to see in her face what it had been, nor to appreciate the fine profile that remained. Hers was not the pink-and-white of rosy girlhood, the only beauty I could understand; and wherein her toil-set features differed from those of the other drudging farmers' wives or the shut-in women of the little village, I could not see.

A lump rose in my throat; this wrinkled and aging person was the beautiful woman I might take after!

I'm afraid I returned from church that day without the consolations of religion.

There followed an anxious time of experimenting. Someone had told me that lemon juice would exorcise freckles, and surreptitiously I tried it. How my face smarted after the heroic treatment, and how red and inflamed it looked! But then in a little while back came the freckles again and they stayed, too, until—but how they went, I am to tell you.

I wheedled from mother the privilege of daily wearing my coral beads —the ones my cousins Milly and Ethel Baker had sent me from New York —and had an angry fit of crying when one day, while we children were racing for the schoolhouse door at the end of recess, the string broke and they were nearly all trampled upon before I could pick them up.

Youth is buoyant. Next I begged the sheet lead linings of tea chests from the man who kept the general store, and cut them into little strips that I folded into hair curlers, covering them with paper so that the edges should not cut. I would go to sleep at night with my short, dampened hair twisted around these contrivances, and in the morning comb it out and admire it as it stood about my head in a bushy mass, like the Circassian girl's at the circus.

Thus beautified, I happened one day to meet our white-headed old pastor! How he stared!

"Stand still a minute, Nelly, child, and let's look at you," he commanded. "Why, what have you been doing to yourself?"

The good man's accent wasn't admiring; sadly I realised the failure of my attempt to compel beauty. When I reached home I sternly soaked the curl out of my hair, brushed it flat and braided it into two exceedingly tight pigtails. Ah, me! It's easy—afterwards—to laugh at the silent sorrows of childhood, bravely endured alone. At least, it's easy for me, now!

I began to worry Ma about my clothes. I grew ashamed of red-and-black, pin-checked woollen frocks, and sighed for prettier things. One of the girls wore at a Sunday school concert a gray and blue dress with many small ruffles, that seemed to me as elegant as a duchess could want. The children whispered that it had cost $20, and I wondered if I should ever again see raiment so wonderful. I knew that it was useless to ask for such a dress for myself; I should be told that I was not old enough for fine feathers.

It was our Sabbath day custom to pass directly from the church services to those of Sunday school, and drive home after these. One stormy day I was the only scholar in my class, and when we had finished the Bible Lesson Leaflets and I was watching the long rows of bobbing heads, flaxen and dark, in the pews full of restless, wriggling children, I turned to the teacher with a question that I had long been meditating.

"Miss Coleman," I began desperately, "ain't there any way to get pretty?"

"I wish there were a way and I knew it," she responded with a smile. "But you should say 'isn't,' you know."

"Oh, but you are pretty," I cried, not with the intent of compliment, but as merely stating a fact.

I do not now think that it was a fact. Miss Coleman's features were irregular, her nose prominent, her forehead too high; but she had a fair, pure complexion and fine eyes, and somehow reminded me of the calla lilly that Ma was always fussing about in our sitting room.

And she was good and wise. I have often thought how different my life might have been if her orbit had not briefly threaded mine. If I had asked that question of some simpering girl a few years older than I—the average Sunday school teacher—she would have replied, from under the flower-burdened hat that had cost her so much thought, that all flesh was grass and beauty vain; and I should have known that she didn't believe it.

"For that matter," said Miss Coleman, after a little pause in which she seemed considering her words with more than usual care, "there are ways of growing beautiful; and, so far as she can, it is a woman's duty to seek them; would you like to know how?"

A duty to be beautiful! Here was novel doctrine.

I gazed with eyes and mouth wide open as she continued: "For one with good lungs and a sound body, the first law of beauty is to be healthy; and health is not just luck. To get it and keep it seek constant exercise in the open air. Middle-aged women lose their looks because they stay in too constantly; when they were girls and played out-of-doors, they had roses in their cheeks. Most handsome women of sixty are those who go among people and keep their interest in what is going on.

"And the second law is intelligence. For thinking gives the eyes expression. A foolish girl may be fair and rosy, yet far from beautiful. Many of the world's famous beauties have suffered serious blemishes; but they have all had wit or spirit to give their faces charm. You have planted flowers?"

"I guess so; yes'm." I didn't see the connection.

"You know then that if you kept digging them to see if they had sprouted, they never would sprout. So it is not well to think too much about growth in beauty. Don't be impatient. It is a work of years. But the method is certain, within limits. I should think that by exercise for the body and study for the mind you might easily become a beautiful woman. Another thing; don't slouch."

I sat up straight as a grenadier, my shoulders absurdly stiff.

"No, nevermind your shoulders," said Miss Coleman, smiling; "they'll take care of themselves if you keep your head right. Practise sitting and standing erect. And never wear a corset. If the Almighty had meant woman to be corset shaped, He'd have made her so."

The superintendent's bell, tinkling for the closing hymn, and the rustle of the leaves of singing books broke in upon our talk; for the first time I failed to welcome the interruption.

"Why, I've delivered quite a lecture upon beauty," Miss Coleman said. "Now just a word more. Try to remember that by making yourself a good and wise woman you will also make yourself more beautiful."

"Oh, I'll remember; I will!" I cried.

And I have done so! Every word! And if Miss Coleman could only see me now! How could I forget?

I was silent all the way home. At the dinner table, as my father was tucking his napkin under his chin, he said: "Well, Nelly, w'at was Mr. Stoddard's text?"

"I—I guess it was something about the children of Israel."

"Yes, prob'ly it was something about 'em," Pa assented with a chuckle.

But Ma spoke more sharply: "I guess you won't get let to set in Aunt Keren-Happuch's pew again right away, Helen 'Lizy." For before my lesson I had once more been studying Aunt Em'ly's face.

I didn't mind the prohibition the least bit. I had a new idea and a new hope. The idea was exaggerated, the hope vain.—Was vain? Ah, it has been more than realised, as you shall hear; realised in a way that amazes me the more, the more I think upon it. Realised as yours shall be, some day, through me!

Realised! Great Heavens! It is a miracle!

3

The Quest of Knowledge

Our district schoolhouse was a shadeless, unpainted box. Within, whittled desks, staring windows and broken plastering made it a fit prison for the boys, whose rough ways were proof of the refining influence of their daily intercourse with the hired men. I wonder such places are tolerated. What a contrast to Barnard's white and gold!

John Burke was our teacher the following winter. He was only seventeen then, but already tall and well grown, in appearance quite a man. He was a student working his way to an education, and his example was a help to me. For I no longer hated lessons. Miss Coleman's talk had filled me with such zeal for knowledge that I became, before the term was over, the phenomenon of the school. Mr. Burke boarded at our house and he would bring home shining tales of my prowess, and often I would listen open-mouthed as we sat about the table at night and he told stories of the State University and the students and the merry life they led.

Everyone was amazed at my industry. I played as heartily as I worked, but I studied with a will, too, and passed a score of mates. That was easy enough, for home study was never dreamed of by most of them, and leisure hours in school were passed in marking "tit-tat-to" upon slates or eating apples under the friendly shelter of the desks.

At the end of the term I received a prize—a highly coloured print of "Washington Crossing the Delaware," which Pa and Ma used long after to bring out and exhibit with pride. It is still somewhere in the old house—

hung up in Ma's bedroom, I think, along with the blue-and-tinseled crown, marked "Charity" in gilt letters across the front, which I wore in the exciting dialogue of "Faith, Hope and Charity" at a Sunday school exhibition.

But more than any prize, I valued the help and friendship of John Burke and the consciousness that he considered me his most promising pupil. Upborne by new ideals, I resolved to study through the vacation that followed, and to my surprise this was not an infliction but a pleasure, now that I was my own task mistress.

Next term the "girl teacher"—for economy's sake we had them in summer when there were no big boys to thrash—was astonished at my industry and wisdom, and as I could see, a little afraid of them. At the end of the first week I went home bursting with an idea that in secret I had long cherished. Aunt Keren was at tea, I remember, and the talk fell upon my work in school, giving me my opportunity.

"Who'd a thought a mischeevious little tyke like her would ha' turned out a first-rate learner, after all?" queried Auntie, beaming upon me good naturedly from behind her gold-bowed spectacles. "I al'ays tol' ye, Ezry, ye'd be proud o' her some day."

"I guess Sue Arkwright's a famous good teacher; that's one thing," said Ma, amiably. "Sis never done near so well before; at least, not till last term."

"I never thought Sue was anythin' remarkable," Pa broke in. "How is that, Sis? Is she a good teacher?"

"No, she ain't," I responded, with quickened beating of the heart. Criticism of teachers was admissible in my code of ethics, but justification must follow; there must be proof—or reproof.

"What's that?" said Pa, looking at me curiously. "Ever ketch her in a mistake?"

"Yes, Sir."

"Bring the book."

I ran and fetched a well-thumbed book from the sewing machine and turned to the definitions of familiar foreign words.

"There," said I, spreading the speller flat on the table and pointing with my finger. "French word for 'Mister.' Teacher called it 'Monshure,' just as they all do. But that's wrong. Today I showed her how it is. See, the book says it's pronounced 'm-o-s-s-e-e-r' and that little mark means an accent on the last syllable and it's 'long e.' 'Mosseer' is right. But when I showed it to teacher, she looked at it awhile, and then she wrinkled up her eyebrows, and whispered it once or twice and said: 'Oh, yes; "mosser."' And she made us call it 'mosser' all the rest of the day, too," I ended triumphantly.

"Why, o' course that ain't right; 'mosser' ain't it!" volunteered one of the hired men, who had lingered to hear the discussion. "I've heerd that word a thousan' times; right way seems like 'M'shoo.' Shucks! Can't get my tongue 'round it, nohow."

"Yes, I know", said Pa "you go call Frenchy."

Joe Lavigne, summoned from the barn, came, followed by all the rest, curious to see what was wanted—a rough, kindly gang of men in blue overalls and big, clumping boots.

"Joe," said Pa; "you say 'Mister' in French."

"Ya-a-as, M'sieu' Weensheep, so I call heem: M'sieu'; M'sieu'; M'sieu'."

Very carefully Frenchy pronounced the clipped word.

"That's all, Joe; I s'pose book French is a good deal diff'rent from ord'-nary Kanuck. 'Mosseer' is right anyhow, for the book says so. Teacher had ought to know enough to go by the book, I sh' think."

"Tain't her fault, Pa," I said, relenting. "She never went to any good school. I want to go somewhere where the teachers know a real lot; not just a little bit more than me. I want to go"—I paused to gain courage—"I want to go to the University, like—like Mr. Burke."

"The State University!" Pa repeated, in a tone of awe; "Thunder! Don't believe we could manage that, Sis."

"W'y, yes, y'can, too, Ezry," Aunt Keren argued, "seems to me you're forehanded enough, to do for an only child. 'Tain't 's if you was like me 'n' Ab., with our four chunies."

"She'd have to go to an academy first to get fitten for it," said Ma. "She couldn't go to the Univers'ty for three or four years yet."

"Of course not," I answered; "but you might write to Mr. Burke to send me a catalogue to find out how much I'd have to know to get taken in. Then I could study at home till I got pretty near ready, and then take a year at the Academy."

The words flowed easily, eagerly; I had so often gone over the plan.

"Good idee," said Pa, nodding his head, relieved to find that I wasn't seeking to leave home at once; and so it was arranged.

Isn't it wonderful? Plain and bald and homely the house, unpretending the surroundings, simple and primitive the life, that sent forth the world's first beautiful woman, the Woman of the Secret! I have tried to set it all down exactly as it happened—the quaint, old fashioned dialect, the homely ways, the bearded, booted men. For this place, just as it was, was the birthplace of the new glory; out of this homely simplicity dawned the new era of beauty that is to make the whole world glad.

A catalogue was sent for, books were bought and I set to work unaided, though Mr. Stoddard took an interest in my studies and often helped me out of difficulties. I chose the classical course, undeterred by parental demonstrations of the "plum uselessness" of Latin and Greek; I had for the choice no better reason than that it was more difficult. I no longer went to the little red schoolhouse.

All this time I had almost forgotten Billy, to whom I owed such a debt of gratitude for sending me upon the Quest. Once I met him on the road.

"Ain't ye never comin' to school no more?" he queried.

"No, I am never going again; I am preparing for the State University; I shall take a classical course," I answered with hauteur, looking down upon him as I spoke. Only that morning Ma had let out another tuck in my gown.

"I'm aw'fly sorry," Billy murmured with a foolish, embarrassed grin. "Guess I'll walk along of ye, if ye don't care."

My triumph found me cold. The sting of Billy's words yet rankled, and perhaps I was not so grateful to the little wretch as he deserved. It was about a quarter of a mile to our house; we walked the distance in unbroken silence. Once there, Billy rallied.

"Goodbye, Miss Winship," he said, holding open the gate for me. It was the first time that anyone had addressed me by that grown-up title.

"Goodbye, Billy."

And that was the end of the beginning of the Quest.

In blizzard time and through the fierce heat of summer I toiled at self-set tasks in our ugly, comfortable home. During the blessed intervals when we could induce "girl help" to stay with us I had scarcely any housework to do. Fairly regular exercise came to be a habit and I worried admiring relatives into thinking me a candidate for an early grave by taking a cold bath every morning. In the end I managed, with a single year in a cheerless boarding house near a village academy, where I studied greedily, devouring my books, to enter the State University with a scholarship to my credit.

I took half the examination in Spring and read extra Virgil and Ovid all summer. Then in August, when the long vacation was nearly over, came the village dressmaker. Ma had promised me two new dresses, and I would sit hemming towels or poring over Greek and Roman history while they turned the leaves of fashion magazines and discussed materials and trimmings.

I secretly hoped for a silk, but Mother, to whom I suppose I am even now—now!—a little girl, vetoed that as too showy, and the dressmaker added her plea for good, durable things. The choice fell upon a golf suiting for school and a black cashmere for church.

I begged hard to have the cashmere touch the ground, but both women smiled at the folly of the child who forgot the many rebindings a long skirt would call for. There was a comic side to my disappointment, for I guessed that the widow Trask could not make the designs I coveted, nor anything of which she could not buy a paper pattern.

But when I went up to the University and became entitled to join in the cry:—

S!—U!
We're—a—few!
S!—T!—A—T—E!
U!—ni—ver—si—tee!
Wow!—Wow!—Wow!

—I found that I compared favourably enough with my mates. Dress played little part in every day college life, and for such occasions as socials or Friday night debating society I soon learned from upper class girls to mitigate ugly gowns with pretty ribbons. And I congratulated myself upon the fact that I was not by any means the plainest girl in my class. My face was hopeless, but my hard-won fight for an erect posture had given me a bearing that seemed almost distinguished. And—well, even my face wasn't so bad, I thought then!

We were a jolly set; most of us poor as church mice, and caring little. Making rather a boast of it, indeed. John Burke's roommate, Jim Reeder, cooked his own meals—mostly oatmeal—in his room and lived on less than a dollar a week until fairly starved. I suppose they'll call him "old Hoss" to his dying day. Until his mother moved to town, John was almost as ill fed. He was just completing his law course when I was a Freshman, and used to make brave jests at poverty, even after his admission to the bar.

Of course I was glad to meet him again, and, though I was puzzled just at first, to see how little older than I my former teacher was, yet afterwards—why, I haven't answered his last—I don't know how many letters; I simply must remember to write to him!

I think the best part of the teaching wasn't in the books. Some of the students were queer and uncouth when they came, the boys eating with their knives in the fashion of the farm; some of the brightest girls in ill-fitting clothes—perfect guys they'd be thought in the city. But there were others of quite different manner, and from them and from professors who had seen the world, we learned a little—a very little—of its ways. And perhaps we were not unfavourable specimens of young republicanism, with our merry, hopeful outlook upon life, and our future governors and senators all in the raw—yes, and our countesses and vice-reines!

4

Girl, Bachelor, and Biologist

Merrily flew the years and almost before I realised it came graduation. In the leafy dark of the village street, in the calm of a perfect June night, John Burke told me that he loved me, and I plighted my troth to him.

We laid plans as we bade each other goodbye, to meet again—perhaps —in New York in the fall; and even that little separation seemed so long. We did not guess that the weeks would grow to months, and—oh, dear, what will he think of me when he gets here? And what—now—shall I say to him?

Father for the first time visited college to see me graduate. Between his pride in my standing at the head of my class and his discomfort in a starched collar, he was a prey to conflicting emotions all Commencement week, and heaved a great sigh of relief when at last the train that bore us home pulled out of the station. But as we approached our own he again grew uneasy, and kept peering out at the car window as if on the watch for something.

At length we descended in front of the long yellow box we called the "deepo." And there was Joe Lavigne to meet us, not with the democrat wagon, but with a very new and shiny top buggy.

When we reached the farmhouse, I saw proofs of a loving conspiracy. The addition of a broad veranda and a big bay window, with the softening effect of the young trees that had grown up all around the place, made it look much more homelike than the bare box that had sheltered my childhood. A new hammock swung between two of the trees.

Mother met me at the door with more emotion than I had ever before detected upon her thin face. Then I saw that the dear people had been at work within the house as well. Cosey corners and modern wall paper and fittings such as I had seen at the professors' houses and had described at home to auditors apparently slightly interested, had been remembered and treasured up and here attempted, to make my homecoming a festivity. The house had been transformed, and if not always in the best of taste, love shone through the blunders.

"Oh, Father," I cried, "now I am surprised! How much wheat it must have cost!"

"Well, I guess we can stand it," he said, grimly pleased and proud and anxious all at once. "We wanted to make it kind o' pleasant for ye, Sis; an'—an' homelike."

There was something so soft and tremulous in his voice that it struck me with a great pang of contrition that I had left him for so many years, that already I was eager to go away again—to the great city where John was soon to be.

I turned quickly away and went from room to room admiring the changes, but after supper, when we were all gathered about the sitting room table, Father returned to the subject most upon his mind. He had seen me with John during Commencement week, and must have understood matters.

"Ready t' stay hum now, I s'pose, ain't ye?" he asked with a note in his voice of cheery assurance that perhaps he did not feel, tilting back and forth in his old fashioned rocking chair, as I had so often seen him do, with closed eyes and open mouth, his face steeled against expression. And the slow jog, jog, jog of the chair reminded me how his silent evening vigils had worn away the rockers until they stood flat upon the floor, making every movement a clacking complaint.

Tonight—tonight, he is rocking just the same, in silence, in loneliness. Poor, dear Pa!

"I'm glad to get home, of course," I said; "but—I wanted to speak with you. But not tonight."

"Why, ye're through school."

"Yes, but I—I wish I could go on studying; if I may."

The words tripped over each other in my embarrassment.

The jog, jog of the chair paused suddenly, leaving for a moment only the ticking of the clock to break the silence.

"Not goin' to put up 'ith us an' stay right alon', eh?" he asked; and rocked twice, then stopped again, in suspense for the answer.

"Why, Father," I stammered, "of course I don't want to do anything unless you're willing, but I had thought I'd like—I did want to go and study in the city—I think—or somewhere."

"Dear me! Dear me!" he mused, his voice very low and even; "an' you just through the University; 'way up to the top, too. Can't ye—seems as if ye better stop alon' of us an' study home, same's you used to? Mebbe—mebbe 'twon't be good for ye, studyin' so much."

"Of course I can, you dear old Dad," I cried; and horribly guilty I felt as I looked at the kindly, weather-beaten face. "I shall do just whatever you say. But oh, I wish I *could go to the city*! Don't you suppose I could?"

"Chicago, mebbe?"

"I had thought of a post-graduate course in Barnard College—that's in New York, you know."

Father knew John's plans. I blushed hotly. In the pause that followed I knew that he was thinking of a well-thumbed map in my old school geography; of the long, long journey to Chicago, and the thousand weary miles that stretched beyond. Hastily I went on:—

"But I know how you have saved for me and worked for me and pinched; and I'd be ashamed to be a burden upon you any longer; I can teach to get money to go on with."

"No;" said Pa, sitting up straight and striking the arm of the chair with his clenched fist a blow that gave some hint of the excitement that moved him. "Guess a child o' mine don't need to teach an' get all dragged out, alon' of a passel o' wild children! No, no, Helen 'Lizy;" he added more softly, sinking back into the old attitude and once more closing his eyes; "if the's so much more to learn, an' you want to go ahead an' learn it, just you go an' get it done with. I'm right sorry to have ye go so fur away; I did think—but it's nat'ral, child; it's nat'ral. I s'pose John Burke's goin' to the city, too, and you kinder—I s'pose young folks likes to be together."

"I—I—we have talked of it."

Talked about it! John and I had talked of nothing else for a week. I sat very still, my eyes on the carpet.

"Guess John Burke'll have all he cares to do for one while, gittin' started in the law office, 'thout runnin' round with Nelly," said Ma. "Ye seem bent on spoilin' the child, Ezry. Al'ays the same way, ever sin' she's a little girl."

Her lips were compressed, the outward symbol of a life of silent hours and self restraint.

"There, there, Ma," said Father, jogging his chair again. "Don't ye worry no more 'bout that. What's ourn is hern in the long run, an' she may as well have some of it now when she wants it, an' it'll do her some good. I s'pose Frank Baker—she that's your mother's cousin an' married Tim'thy Baker an's gone to New York to live—I s'pose she might look after you; but it's a long way off, New York—seems like a dretful long way off. What ye goin' to learn, Sis, if ye should go t' the city?"

"Well, I was good in chemistry; Prof. Meade advised me—I might study medicine; I don't know. And I want to know more about books and pictures and the things that people talk about, out in the world, though I can hardly call that a study, I suppose."

The words somehow disappointed me when uttered. They didn't sound convincing. Such pursuits seemed less serious, there in the old farmhouse that spoke of so much painful toil, than when John and I had discussed them on the sunny campus.

"I—I don't know yet, just what to do; there's all summer to plan; but I want—somehow—to make the very most and the best of myself," I added earnestly.

It was true, and the nearest I could come to the exact truth; that love urged me yet more eagerly upon the Quest, and that with all my heart I longed to become a wise and brilliant woman, for John's sake, and as a step towards beauty, according to Miss Coleman's words.

"I don't hold with women bein' doctors," said Ma, as she energetically knitted into the middle of her needle before looking up. "I don't know what we're comin' to, these days."

"There, there, Ma, I don't know why women shouldn't be doctors, if they want to. They make better nusses'n men. Mebbe—mebbe Sis'll be gettin' married some day, an' I tell ye a little doctorin' know-how is mighty handy in a house. A doctor an' a lawyer, now, would be a gret team, right in the fambly, like. Well, Sis, we'll see; we'll see."

I knew that the matter was practically settled; and there was little sleep for me, or for anyone, that night in the old farmhouse.

I stayed at home until September, and then one morning Father drove me again to the little yellow station whose door opens wide upon all the world.

"Well, goodbye, Helen 'Lizy," he said.

"Goodbye, Father."

For weeks I had been eager to be off, but as the train began to move and I looked back at his patient figure—he made no more show of his deep emotion than if the parting were for a day—a big lump rose in my throat at leaving him and Ma—old before their time with toil and privation and planning and striving for me.

I knew how lonely it would be in the sitting room that night without me. Father with closed eyes jogging away in his chair, Mother bolt upright and thin and prim, forever at her knitting or sewing; no sound but the chair and the ticking clock upon the shelf—that night and every night. And the early bedtime and the early morning and the long, long day— what a contrast to this!

I pressed my face against the window, but a rush of tears blurred all the dear, familiar landmarks—Barzillai Foote's red barn, the grain elevator at the siding, the Hartsville road trailing off over the prairie; I would have given worlds to be in the top buggy again, moving homeward, instead of going swiftly out, out, alone, into the world. Three months ago! I did not dream what miracles were in store!

And so one day I reached the New York I had dreamed about. It wasn't as a shrine of learning that it appealed to me, altogether; but as a wonderful place, beautiful, glittering, feverish with motion, abounding with gayety, thronged with people, bubbling with life.

How it fascinated me!

Just at first of course I was lonely because John had not yet come, and Mrs. Baker, mother's cousin, was away from home. But I soon made friends with my cousins, Ethel and Milly; shy, nice girls, twins and precisely alike, except, that Ethel is slightly lame. And at my boarding place I made the acquaintance of an art student from Cincinnati three or four years older than I, who proposed that we should become girl bachelors and live in a studio.

"But I didn't know people ever lived in studios," I objected.

"Oh, you dear goose!" said Kathryn Reid—it's really her name, though of course I call her Kitty—"Live in studios? Bless you, child, everybody does it. And I know a beyewtiful studio that we can have cheap, because we're such superior young persons; also because it's ever so many stories up and no elevator. Can you cook a little? Can you wash dishes, or not mind if they're not washed? You got the blessed bump of disorder? You good at don't care? Then live with me and be my love. You've no idea the money you'll save."

That's just the way Kitty talks. You can't induce her to be serious for three minutes at a time—I suppose it's the artistic temperament. But she's shrewd; studio life *is* better than the kind of boarding house we escaped from. And so jolly! Kitty has more chums than I, of course. Her brother, Prosper K., and Caroline Bryant—"Cadge," for short—a queer girl who does newspaper work and sings like an angel, are the ones I see most. Though for that matter the city's full of girls from the country, earning or partly earning their living. One will be studying music, another art; one "boning" at medicine, another selling stories to the newspapers and living in hope of one day writing a great American play or novel. Such nice girls —so brave and jolly.

My new home is in a building on Union Square. And I like it—the place, the people, the glimpse of the wintry Square, the roaring city life under my window. I'm sure I don't want a quiet room. It's such fun, just like playing house, to be by ourselves and independent of all the world. I think it's an intoxicating thing, just at first, for a girl to be really independent. Boys think nothing of it; it's what they've been brought up to expect.

Well, I tore myself away from the dear place to get at my work. I really mean to work hard and justify Father's sacrifices. I tried to take singing lessons, because John is so fond of music, but there I made a dismal failure; I had, three months ago, neither ear nor voice. The day before the fall semester opened, I climbed the long hill to Barnard College, fell in love with its gleaming white and gold, so different from the State University, and arranged for a course in biology. Then I began physical culture in a gymnasium.

I couldn't have made a queerer or a better combination. For it was in the Barnard laboratory that I met Prof. Darmstetter; and it was my bearing, my unending practice of the West Point setting-up drill, my Delsarte, my "harmonic poise" and evident health that drew his attention to me.

How well I remember the day I made his acquaintance! I had entered the laboratory without knowing what manner of man he was, for all my arrangements about my course had been made with clerks. So it was with genuine surprise that I turned from an inspection of the apparatus to answer when a squeaking voice at my elbow suddenly saluted me:—

"Mees Veenship, not so?"

The owner of the voice was a little old fellow, whose dry, weazened face gave no hint of his years. I guessed that he was probably seventy, though he might as easily be much younger. His skin was parchment-coloured and cross-hatched by a thousand wrinkles and the hair under his skullcap was as white as snow, but he was as bright of eye and brisk of manner as a youth of twenty.

"Yes, sir," I replied rather awkwardly; "I am Miss Winship."

"V'at for you study biology?" was his surprising query, uttered in a tone between a squeak, a snarl, and a grunt.

"Because I wish to learn," I replied, after a moment's hesitation.

"No, mine vriendt," he snapped, "you do not vish to learn. You care not'ing for science. You are romantic, you grope, you change, you are unformed. In a vord, you are a voman. You haf industry—mine Gott, yes! —and you vill learn of me because I am a man and because you haf not'ing better to do. And by-and-by behold Prince Charming—and you vill meet and marry and forget science. V'at for I vaste my time vit' you? Eh? I do not know any voman who becomes a great scientist. Not so? T'ose young vomen, t'ey vaste t'eir time and t'ey vaste mine."

I followed his gesture and saw two or three nice looking girls in big checked aprons amiably grinning at me. One of them by a solemn wink conveyed the hint that such hazing of new arrivals was not unusual.

"You're paid to waste your time on me," I answered hotly. "I'm here to work and to listen to you; my plans are my own affair, and if I never become a great scientist, I don't see what difference that makes to you."

The meekest looking girl gasped, wide eyed at my temerity. But Prof. Darmstetter's shrewd little eyes twinkled with reassuring good nature.

"Vell, vell, ve shall see," said he, wagging his head; "maybe I find some use for you. I vatch you. Maybe I find for you some use t'at you don't expect, eh? Ve shall see."

So he walked away, shrugging his shoulders and snapping his fingers and muttering to himself: "Ve shall see; we shall see." And at times throughout the session he chuckled as if he had heard of an excellent joke.

"Good gracious!" I whispered to one of the aproned girls that had watched the encounter—students like myself—"that's an encouraging reception, isn't it?"

"It is," she gravely replied. "We're all jealous of you. You are evidently destined to become Prof. Darmstetter's favourite pupil. I know I cried half the night at the way he greeted me. We were all watching you and you got off easy. Brought an apron? I can lend you one, if you didn't. It's pretty mussy here."

"Thank you," I said, "but really I can't get my mind off Prof. Darm-stetter, all in a minute so. What sort of a man is he?"

"Oh, irritating sometimes, but a genius; I suppose his treatment of the girls is a sample of his Early Teutonic ideas of civility. He likes better to teach the Columbia boys—says their work in future years'll do him more credit. But we get used to him and don't mind it, we who were here last year. And he's a great scientist; has a worldwide reputation. He almost lives in the laboratory, here and at Columbia; has no home life or friends or relatives. And oh, it's such a privilege," she said with a sudden change of tone, a school-mistressly manner, looking upon me more austerely, "to study under such a man. He is a Master."

The Master! She little knew how true was the word! Tomorrow, if his secret and mine were known, the world would hail him as its lord. He would be a greater man than has yet lived on the earth. Armies would fight for his favour at the bidding of queens—to get what I have! And to think that chance led me from two thousand miles away, straight to him.

From the first, he seemed to take an interest in my doings. He never troubled himself to be polite, but he watched me; always he watched me. I often saw him chuckling and rubbing his hands as if in approbation. But of what? Not of my work, for of that he never took the slightest notice, except when I compelled him to do so by some question.

Then, in quick-flung sentences, he would condense the results of a life-time of study into phrases filled with meaning, that seemed to cast light upon principles, not facts, and make wonderfully clear the very purpose of Nature. Then indeed, he almost forgot that we were women, and talked with kindling enthusiasm of his pet subject. I ceased to wonder that he held such high rank in college.

Under such conditions I made rapid progress. I thoroughly enjoyed the work, though I was not absorbed in it, like most of my companions; but I was quick enough to keep pace with them and to make occasional shrewd suggestions that pleased Prof. Darmstetter not half so much as some sudden display of spirit. He did not seem to care whether I became a student. And always he watched me, for what purpose I could not determine.

My home life—if existence in a studio can be so called—was merry. I was learning the ways of the world. I liked the life. I wrote to John almost every day. The freedom of the den, the change from rote lessons to post-graduate work was pleasant. I was happy.

Happy? I must have dreamed it.

What I thought happiness was nothing to what I now know happiness can be.

The Finding of the Bacillus

I f I have dwelt so long upon the laboratory and its master, it is because there the great blessing came that has glorified my whole existence. This was the way of it.

One day I asked Prof. Darmstetter some question about the preparation of a microscopic slide from a bit of a frog's lung.

"Vait!" he snapped, "I vill speak vit' you aftervards."

The girls prophesied the terrible things that were to happen, as they lingered in the cloak room, waiting their turn on the threadbare spot in the rug which a rich girl had bought to cover the threadbare spot in the carpet in front of the mirror. "Now you'll catch it!" the last one said, as she carefully put her hat straight with both hands and ran out of the room.

When I returned to the laboratory Prof. Darmstetter motioned me to a chair and took one opposite, from which he fixed his keen eyes upon my face. Again he seemed weighing, judging, considering me with uncanny, impersonal scrutiny.

"How I despise t'ose vomen!" he said at last, throwing up his hands with an impatient gesture.

Used to his ways, I waited in silence.

"I teach t'ose vomen, yes; but I despise t'em," he added.

"If you do, you ought to be ashamed of it," I retorted hotly. "But I don't believe you really despise them. Such a bright lot of girls—why, some of them are bound to be heard from in science some day!"

"In science? Bah!"

"Why not? There was Mary Somerville and—and—and Caroline Herschel and—well, I can't think of their names all in a minute, but I'm proud to be one of the girls here anyway."

"You are not one of t'em," he cried angrily. "T'ey are life failures. You fancy t'ey are selected examples, but t'ey are not; t'ey are t'e rejected. T'ey stood in t'e market place and no man vanted t'em; or else t'ey are fools as vell as failures and sent t'e men avay. You know me. I am biologist, not true? I hate t'e vord. I am physiologist, student of t'e nature of life—all kinds of life, t'e ocean of life of v'ich man is but a petty incident."

"You were speaking about—"

"Ach, so! Almost t'ou has t'e scientific mind t'at reasons and remembers. I said, I am physiologist. I study v'at Nature is, v'at she means to do. V'en Nature—Gott, if you vant a shorter name—makes a mistake, Gott says: 'Poor material; spoiled in shaping, wrong in t'e vorks; all failures; t'row t'em avay. Ve haf plenty more to go on vit'. You know. You study Nature, also, a little. You know she is law, she is power. To t'e indifidual pitiless, she mofes vit' blind, discompassionate majesty ofer millions of mangled organisms to t'e greater glory of Pan, of Kosmos, of t'e Universe. She vastes life. And how not? Her best vork lives a little v'ile and produces its kind, and t'e vorst does not, and t'ey go down t'e dark vay toget'er and Nature neit'er veeps nor relents Kosmos is greater t'an t'e indifidual and a million years are short.

"T'ose young vomen—Nature meant t'em to desire beauty and dream of lofe. Vat is lofe? It is Nature's machinery. T'ose vomen are old enough for lofe, but t'ey haf it not. So t'ey die. T'ey do not reproduce t'eir kind, not'ing lifing comes from t'em, to go on lifing, on and on, better and better —or vorse, as Nature planned—vit' efery generation. If a voman haf t'e desire of lofe and of beauty, and lofe and beauty come not to her, t'en I pity her, because I am less vise and resolute to vit'hold pity t'an Nature is. Efen if she haf not lofe, but only t'e ambition of power or learning or vealt', I might pity her vit' equal injustice, but I cannot. She vill not let me. She does not know t'at she is a failure. She prides herself upon being so mismade. She cannot help t'at; neit'er can I help despising her. Such vomen are abnormal, monstrous, in a vord, failures. Let t'em die! You, I t'ink, are not so. You study to bide t'e time. You haf a fine carriage. You comb t'e hair, you haf pretty ribbons, you make t'e body strong and supple, you look in t'e glass and vish for more beauty. Not so?"

66

"Of course I do," I cried angrily, wondering for the moment if he had lost his senses. It seemed as if he knew little about women for a man who professed to make all life his study. If there were one of his despised girls who lacked the desire of beauty and the dream of love, I am much mistaken. But I came to see afterward that he understood them as well as myself.

"I t'ought so," he mused, his eyes still upon my face. "And you are not too beautiful now; t'ey could not doubt. Yes; I vatch you, I study you. Seldom I make t'e mistake; but it is fery important. So I vatch you a little v'ile longer yet. T'en I say to myself: 'Here is t'e voman; yes, she is found.'"

And he chuckled and rubbed his lean hands together as I had so often seen him do.

The thought flashed across my mind that this extraordinary man meditated a proposal of marriage, but I dismissed the notion as ridiculous.

The Professor leaned forward and, fixing me with his eye, spoke in a hoarse whisper, tense with excitement:—

"Mees Veenship, I am a biologist; you are a voman, creature of Nature, yearning for perfection after your kind. I—I can gife it you. You can trust me; I am ready. I can gif you your vish, t'e vish of efery normal voman. Science—t'at is I—can make you t'e most beautiful being in t'e vorld!"

Another Sunday school lesson! Miss Coleman and her unforgotten lecture upon beauty flashed upon my mind. But this man was promising me more than she had done, and his every word was measured. What was the mystery? What had he to say to me?

"T'e most beautiful—voman—in t'e vorld," he went on in a slow, cadenced whisper. "Do you vish it?"

His glittering eyes held mine again. No, he was not jesting at my expense; rather he seemed waiting with anxiety for me to make some decision upon which much depended. He was in very serious earnest.

But was ever a question more absurd? Who of women would not wish it? But to get the wish—ah, there's a different matter! I thought he must be crazed by over-study, and I could only sit and stare at him, open-mouthed.

"Listen!" he went on more rapidly, as if to forestall objection. "You are scholar, too, a little. You know how Nature vorks, how men aid her in her business. Man puts t'e mot'er of vinegar into sweet cider and it is vinegar. T'e fermenting germs of t'e brewery chemist go in vit' vater and hops and malt, and t'ere is beer. T'e bacilli of bread, t'e yeast, swarming vit millions of millions of little spores, go into t'e housevife's dough, and it is bad bread; but t'at is not t'e fault of t'e bacilli—mein Gott, no!—for vit' t'e bacilli t'e baker makes goot bread. T'e bacilli of butter, of cheese—you haf studied t'em. T'e experimenter puts t'e germs of good butter into bad cream and it becomes goot. It ripens. It is educated, led in t'e right vay. Tradition vaits for years to ripen vine and make it perfect. Science finds t'e bacillus of t'e perfect vine and puts it in t'e cask of fresh grape juice, and soon t'e vine drinkers of t'e vorld svear it is t'e rare old vintage. T'e bacillus, inconceivably tiny, svarming vit' life, reproducing itself a billion from one, t'at is Nature's tool. And t'e physiologist helps Nature.

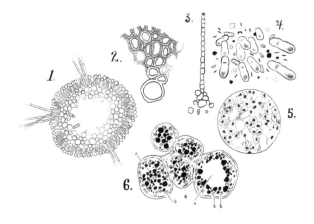

"I haf discofered t'e Bacillus of Beauty."

"See now," continued Prof. Darmstetter. "I haf a vonderful discofery made. I must experiment vit' it—*experimentum in corpore vili!* Impossible, for the subject is mankind. I must haf a voman—a voman like you, healt'y, strong, young—all t'e conditions most favourable. She must haf intelligence—t'at is you. She should know somet'ing of biology, and be fery brave, so t'at she may not be frightened, but may understand how t'e vonderful gift is to come to her; and t'at is you. She should not be already beautiful, lest t'e change be less convincing. Yes, you are t'e voman for t'e test. You may become more famous in history fan Cleopatra or Ninon, and outshine t'em and all t'e ot'er beauties t'at efer lifed. Do you vant triumphs? Here t'ey are. Riches? You shall command t'em. Fame? Power? I haf t'em for you. You shall be t'e first. Aftervard, v'en beauty is common as ugliness is now—ah, I do not know. Efen t'en it vill be a blessing. But to be t'e first is fame and all t'e ot'er t'ings I promise you. Now do you trust me?

Now do you beliefe me? Vill you make t'e experiment? I haf—let me tell you!—I haf discofered—"

Cautiously Prof. Darmstetter looked about the room. Then he leaned toward me again and added in a hoarse whisper:—

"I haf discofered t'e Bacillus of Beauty."

6

The Great Change

The Bacillus of Beauty! Was the poor man insane? Had much study made of him a monomaniac babbling in a dream of absurdities? Do you wonder that I doubted?

And yet—the thought flashed through my mind that things almost as strange have become the commonplace. I had seen the bones of my own hand through the veiling flesh. I had listened to a voice a thousand miles away. I had seen insects cut in two, grafted together, head of one and tail of another, and living. I had seen many, many marvels which science has wrought along the lines of evolution. And yet—

My dream; my desire always! If it could be!

As I stared open-mouthed at the Professor, he began once more:—

"T'e danger, t'e risk—t'ere is none. You shall see. It is as harmless as—"

"Never mind about that!" I interrupted. "How would I look? Would it change me totally? Would I really be the most beautiful?—"

I stopped, blushing at my own eagerness.

"Absolutely; I svear it. T'e most perfectly beautiful voman in t'e vorld. Mein Gott, yes. How not? Never vas t'ere yet a perfectly beautiful voman. Not von. All have defects; none fulfills t'e ideal. You? You vill look like yourself. I do not miracles. T'e same soul vill look out of your eyes. You vill be perfect, but of your type. T'e same eyes, more bright; t'e same hair, more lustrous and abundant; t'e same complexion clear and pure; t'e same voman as she might have been if t'e race had gone on defeloping a

70

hundred t'ousand years. Look you. Some admire blondes; some brunettes. You are not a Svede to be white, an Italian to be black. You are a brown American. You shall be t'e most beautiful brown American t'at efer lifed. And you shall be first. Vit' you as an example we shall convince t'e vorld. Ve shall accomplish in t'ree generations t'e vork of a hundred t'ousand years of defelopment. How vill humanity bless us if we can raise, out of t'e slums and squalor, out of t'e crooked and blind and degraded, out of t'e hospitals and prisons, t'e spawning dregs of humanity and make t'em perfect! T'ey shall valk t'e eart' like gods, rejoicing in t'eir strengt'. No more failures, no more abnormalities. Nature's vork hastened by science, aeons of veary vaiting and slow efolution forestalled by—by me!"

The little Professor stood erect, his eye fixed on mine, his mien commanding. I had never looked on man so transfigured.

The thought was intoxicating me, driving me wild. I tried to think, to struggle against the tide that was sweeping me away. He seemed to be hypnotizing me with his grave, uncanny eye. I could not move, I could not speak.

"You may ask," Darmstetter went on—though I had not thought of asking—"if t'e beauty vould be hereditable; if as an acquired characteristic, it vould pass to descendants, or, if each child vill not haf to be treated anew. I believe no. It is true t'at acquired traits are not hereditable. T'ere Weissmann is right, v'atefer doubters may say. You know t'e t'eory. T'e blacksmit's muscles are not transmitted to his son t'e clerk; but t'e black hair t'at he got from his fat'er. Only after fery many generations of blacksmit's could a boy be born who vould grow up as a clerk vit' blacksmit' muscles. Efolution shapes t'e vorld, yes; but t'e process is so slow, so slow! So education, modification, must begin afresh vit' each generation and continue forefer. But t'is bacillus does not add ornament to t'e outside. It is not like t'e masseuse, vit' her unguents and kneading. It changes all t'e nature. It is like compressing a million years of education by natural selection into von lifetime. T'at is my t'eory. I do not know—it is not yet tried—but how ot'ervise? Ve but hasten t'e process, as t'e chemist hastens fermentation; Nature constructs, she does not adapt or alter or modify. Ve produce beauty by Nature's own met'od. V'y not hereditary?"

I had made up my mind.

"I'll do it," I cried, no longer able to resist, for the fever of it was in my blood. "You shall make your attempt on me! It can do no harm. I do not see how it can accomplish all you claim, but if you think—it's an experiment full of possibilities—in the interests of science—"

"Interest of humbug!" snapped Prof. Darmstetter, his own sarcastic self again. "You consent because you vant to be beautiful. You care not'ing for science. I can trust you vit' my secret. You need svear no oat's not to reveal it. You vant to be t'e only perfect voman in t'e vorld, and so you shall be, for some time. T'at is right. T'at is your revard."

My cheeks flushed at his injustice. I do care for others. I am not selfish —not more than everybody. And yet—at that moment I feared him and his knowledge; I shuddered at nameless terrors.

Really, I often wonder that I ever had the courage to try. And oh, I am so glad!

Now there is no more fear. Darmstetter is my servant, if I will it. As for his marvellous power, I shall bless it and reverence it all my life. I thank God for letting me know this man. It is too wonderful—too wonderful for words!

The transformation was slow at first. The beginning—such an anxious time. Every day I studied myself and watched and waited for the first sign of growing grace, for the dawning glory. Sometimes I thought I could see the change already under way, and then again the same plain Nelly Winship looked at me from the uncomplimentary glass, and away flew all my hopes.

It was the fading of a little scar on my thumb that first let me know the blessed truth. Now I can scarcely see the place where it was, and I'm sure no one else would notice it. It will never go away entirely. Prof. Darmstetter says I am not proof against wounds and old age, because these are a part of Nature's great plan. But it faded, faded!

And my ears! How I used to hate their prominence! But soon they snuggled closer to my beautiful, beautiful face—and I'm in sure I don't blame them. Every morning when I woke, my shining eyes and the bloom of my cheeks told me I was growing perfect, just as he said I must do. Though I'm not yet quite perfect.

I could sit at my glass and look for hours at my reflected image—if it weren't for Kitty—and—

Why, it seems like another girl, and such a girl as never the world saw before—not me, but Her. Sometimes times I fear Her; but oftener and oftener, as I get used to the lovely vision, I want to hug Her right out of the cold mirror and kiss Her and pat Her smooth cheek like a child's, and put pretty clothes upon Her, as if she were a doll.

And then I try to realise that Her is Me, my own self, and I just cannot believe it! I look from the reflected image to a little photograph of the

Helen Winship I once knew, and back again to the glass, and wonder, and thank God, and shudder with awe of my own loveliness. I luxuriate in it, I joy in it, I feel it in every fibre of my being. I am as happy as a queen. I am a queen—or She is.

I am but slightly taller. My form is more rounded and of better mould, but I am still slender. My face is the same face but—how can I express it? A Venus with the—the expression of a Western schoolgirl pursuing special studies in New York, looks at me with Her eyes. They are the eyes of Helen Winship, but larger and fuller orbed and more lustrous, with an appeal that makes me fall in love with myself, as I look. The nose is longer and straighter, the cheeks fuller and fairer, the chin daintier, the neck—ah, well, why shouldn't I be frank? I am beautiful!

And the complexion—still so strange I do not say "my complexion"— clear, fair, rosy all in one, with the fineness and purity of a baby's; it is the most indescribable of all the marvels that glow in my glass. Before, I had the rather sallow, powder-excusing skin of so many Western girls. Now it is perfect. I love to gaze by the hour at my own beauty. I should be renamed Narcissa.

My voice, too, is glorious. I have to school myself not to start at the sound of it when I speak. And most of all, what most impresses me when I try to consider myself fairly—candidly—critically—is the appearance of strength, of health, of unbounded power and deathless youth—as if the blood of generations of athletic girls and free, Viking men ran in my veins. I am, I believe, the only perfectly healthy woman on earth.

Will the gods smite me for my happiness? Are they jealous? Ah, well, I have never lived until now, and if I can stay a little while like this, I shall be satisfied; I shall be ready to die. If only beauty does not vanish as suddenly as it came! If it did, I should kill myself.

There are disadvantages. Such a time as I'm having with my clothes! Money to buy new is not so plenty as I could wish, though the $75 a month that Father sends was more than enough until the change. I'm saving to buy a microscope—a better one than those loaned to students at the laboratory; so I have to let out and contrive—I who so hate a needle!

And the staring admiration that is lavished on me everywhere! I suppose I'll get used to it; but it's a new experience. I like to be looked at, too, much as it embarrasses me. My loveliness is like a beautiful new dress; one is delighted to have it, but terribly shy about wearing it, at first.

Admiration! Why, the mystified music master is ready to go down on his knees to me, the janitor and the page boys are puzzled. I wonder—I wonder what John will say, I almost dread to think of his seeing me so; yet it will be the greatest test. Test! I need none!

The girls in the laboratory are divided between awe and envy, and Kitty Reid—poor Kitty! She began by being puzzled, then grew panic stricken.

The first time she noticed—I shall always remember it—was when I came in from the college one day, still skeptical of change, yet hoping it might be so.

"Why, you've a new way of doing your hair—no; same old pug—but somehow—you're looking uncommon fit today," she said glancing up from her drawings.

My heart leaped for joy. It was true then! It was true! But remembering Miss Coleman, I forced myself to reply as quietly as I could:—

"My genius must be beginning to sprout."

A little later Kitty was in constant mystification.

"How do you do it?" she would demand. "What have you got? Can't you let me into the secret? I just think you might introduce me to the fairy godmother."

If I were to tell anyone, it would be Kitty, of course. Such a dear little red-headed angel she would make! But it would not be fair to Prof. Darmstetter. He is not ready yet. So I can only sham ignorance and joke with her about milk baths and cold cream and rain water. Now that she has reached the stage of fright, I have great fun with her.

"The age of miracles has come again," she says a hundred times a day. "I can't believe my eyes! How is it that you are growing so beautiful? Is it witchcraft?"

"Am I better looking?" I inquire languidly. "Well, I'm glad of it. I had an aunt who was well-favoured when she was young; it's high time I took after her, if I'm ever going to."

"No living aunt ever looked as you do now," Kitty will mutter, shaking her head. "I don't know what to think. I'm half afraid of you."

To tell the truth, she's more than half afraid of me, and I delight in mystifying her all I can.

But the strangest thing of all, the most ridiculous thing, considering his age, the oddest thing when one remembers that he himself is its creator—Professor Darmstetter is half in love with the beauty he has made; he would be, if he might, the gray and withered Pygmalion of my Galatea!

7

The Coming of the Lover

December 15.

R eally, I don't know which is the more aggravating, John Burke or Kitty. Such a battle as I've had with them today!

I had quite stopped fretting over John's absence. Indeed, though of course I wished to see him, I dreaded it; I was so happy, just as I was, and I had so many things to think about, so many dreams to dream and plans to make.

I liked John when he taught the little prairie school and praised me to my wondering relatives. All through my college course I was proud of his regard, because everyone respected him; and last June I promised to marry him.

We said then that our love wasn't just a "coed. flirtation," because he was a grown man and not a student any more. But—but—but last June I wasn't—

Why, I've but just come to possess the gift that I wouldn't exchange for the proudest throne on earth, and I mean to make it my throne in the great world. I haven't yet had time to think things out or realise my fairy fortune; but John and I mustn't do anything foolish. Wise love can wait.

He came while I was at school.

When I found him here, he actually didn't know me.

He stared as if I were a stranger whose face drew, yet puzzled him. Then he was attracted by my beauty, then for a moment dismayed, and then—why, he was really so much in love that I—I—he gazed at me as if I were not quite real; with reverence. His eyes mirrored my power; the wonder of the new Me, the glory and the radiance of me shone in them. He worships me and—well, of course nobody could help liking that.

He was just as he has always been, but somehow, here in the city, I couldn't help finding him bigger, stronger, more bucolic. His clothes looked coarse. His collar was low for the mode, his gloveless hands were red. There was something almost clerical in his schoolmasterly garb, but his bold dark eyes and short hair aggressively brushed to a standstill, as he used to say, looked anything but ministerial. It was plain that he was a man of sense and spirit, one to be proud of; plain that he was a countryman, too.

I couldn't help seeing his thick shoes any more than I could his hurt face when I was distant and his ardour the moment I grew kind; and I was so ashamed—thinking of his looks and picking flaws, when three months ago I was a country girl myself—that I know—I don't know what I should have done, if Kitty hadn't returned.

I was so relieved to see her, for John has been writing of marriage soon and of a home, in one room if need be; and we have too much to accomplish, with beauty and woman's wit and brain and strength, for that. It is my duty to think for both, if he's too much in love—the dear, absurd fellow! And yet—

As soon as he was gone, Kitty jumped up from the drawing table. She was on pins and needles for anxiety, her eyes dancing.

"Well, when's the wedding?" she cried.

"What wedding?"

I was vexed and puzzled, and distressed, too, after sending John away as I had done. I wanted to be alone and have a chance to think quietly.

"Oh, any old wedding; will it be here, in the den? You going to invite us all?" asked Kitty.

"Isn't going to be any wedding."

"I'm sorry; I always did lot on weddings."

"You'll have to be the bride, then. Honest, Kitty, I don't like jokes on such subjects. Mr. Burke and I haven't an idea of being married, not for centuries."

Kitty went white all in a minute. She is so quick tempered.

"Oh," said she, "you're going to throw him over. I thought as much! You were always writing to him when you first came to the city, and talking about him, at night when we brushed our hair; but lately you haven't spoken of him at all. You used to look happier when the postman brought you something from him. And you had his picture—"

"The postman's?" I interrupted, but Kitty kept on as if she were wound up:—

"—on the mantelpiece, in a white-and-gold frame with your own. You hid 'em both when you began to grow beautiful. I suppose you think you're too good for him. But don't go and break his heart; please don't, Princess; there's a dear."

"Goose! I haven't the least notion of breaking his heart. I—why can't you let me alone? I'm—I'm very fond of him—if you will insist on talking about it."

"Oh, I can see! If you'd noticed the poor fellow's face—"

"'Poor fellow!' If you'd seen him before you came! He doesn't need your pity. Why, it seems to have been with you a case of love at first sight," I said mockingly. "He was rude to you, too; he never even noticed that you were in the room, after I came."

"I don't care. I don't expect a man to notice me when he meets his sweetheart for the first time in ever so long; and such a sweetheart! But you—you—oh, I'm afraid of you! I'm afraid of you! What is this mystery? What is it? Why have you grown so grand and terrible? What has become of my chum?"

She sat down flat on the floor and burst into passionate weeping.

"Get up!" I cried.

"I won't!"

A sense of great loneliness came over me and I threw myself down beside her.

"Oh, Kitty," I said, "why aren't you old and wise and sensible instead of being just a silly girl like myself? Then you wouldn't sit here howling, but you'd kiss me and cuddle me and comfort me and tell me what to do."

"I'm afraid of you! I'm afraid of you! It's—it's no' canny."

"Kitty, Kitty! Why aren't you my fairy godmother, so that you could show me in a magic glass what to do, instead of scolding me, when I'm wretched enough already?"

"Wretched! You!" Her eyes fairly blazed. "I wouldn't ever—*ever* be wretched if I looked like you—not ever in this world!"

"Yes, you would. You'd be so puzzled about things; and bad girls would scold you, and there wouldn't be a single soul within two thousand miles to rely upon. And you'd be awkward and shy when folks looked at you. And then you'd—you'd—you'd cry."

Afterwards we both wiped our eyes and made it all up; and I told her again that I really was fond of John.

Well, folks must eat. I went out to get some chops, a half dozen oranges and the other things for supper—we have lunch and supper, no dinner—and though I started so blue and wretched, I simply couldn't stay melancholy long, people stared at me and admired me so much. They crowded after me into the little corner grocery, and the room was so full that someone upset a tub of pickles and there they stood around in the vinegar to look at me.

It was frightful! But it was nice too; though I was so embarrassed that I wanted to run away. I'll get used to it; but—why, my own mother wouldn't know me! It's no wonder Kitty is frightened.

I wish I could see Ma. But she couldn't advise me. I ought to have a home, though, and someone older than Kitty to look after me. I must leave the den; but where to go? Suppose I burned myself broiling chops or beef-steak, or blistered my face with steam from the kettle! That would be frightful, now. It's the least I can do for Prof. Darmstetter to keep free from harm the beauty he gives me. And besides,—I never before was afraid, but now I go scurrying through the halls and up and down the stairs like a wild thing; the place is so public, so many people notice me.

I wonder if I couldn't talk to Mrs. Baker. She's at home now. Or there's the Judge's sister, Miss Marcia, the dearest old maid. I've only seen her once or twice, but I believe she'd be good to know.

I have too many problems to stay here. I must make some settled plan, now that my life means so much to all the women in the world. And—how to deal with a headstrong young man who won't take "no" for an answer or "wait" for wisdom I simply don't know. If he would only give me time to make my own acquaintance! There are so many things to think of. A great world is open to me. I have the key and I am going to live the most beautiful life.

I must think and plan and learn how not to be frightened at my own face in the mirror; I must—I simply *must* have time.

Dec. 17.

I HAVE JUST SEEN John again; he came up to Barnard, which won't do at all. And he came home with me, and—how he loves me!

But I can manage him. Indeed, he was more reasonable today.

Book III:
The Joy of the Sunshine

1

Christmas

No. — East 72d Street, Dec. 28.

M illy and I have just come from a run in the Park, and here I am this shining white morning scribbling away in my own cosey room.

My very own room—for the most delightful thing has happened; I'm visiting Mrs. Baker—Aunt Frank I am to call her, though she is really Ma's cousin—and she has asked me to spend the rest of the winter here.

So I've really left the den. And I didn't deserve it. Why, when Mrs. Baker invited me to dinner on Christmas day, I dreaded the visit. I hadn't seen her since I came from the West, and I wondered what she'd think of me, and what she'd write to Mother. If Pa and Ma could see me now, would they say their little Nelly'd "filled out well-favoured?"

What *would* they say to me?

Why, Christmas morning, when I read the home letters, I felt as if I had betrayed my parents' confidence, as if I'd robbed them of their child by changing into such a lovely creature. Then I laughed; they won't mind my getting rid of freckles and a pug nose. And then I cried, almost, and felt so lonely, for even Kitty had gone off with Pros.; and so far away and so happy, and a good deal troubled with it all; for John had sent me some roses and a ring, and I knew I should find him at my Aunt's, eager to see whether I wore them.

John's such a problem. All that day I sat alone in the den, trying to think, and trying to let down the hem of my waterproof, for it was snowing and I have only one good dress; and every few minutes I would slip on the ring and pull it off, watching the rainbow lights that flashed and paled in the heart of the stone, and smiling because John had chosen an opal; I wonder if he knows it's the gem of the beautiful woman.

In the end I let it stay on my hand, of course, for, after all, I suppose I am betrothed to him.

So it happened that I was almost late for dinner at the Bakers', and quite late when I really got inside the house; for I walked past the door two or three times before I could muster up courage to ring the bell. When I finally ran up the steps, my umbrella was powdered white, and snow and water were dripping off my skirts. My heart was beating fast with dread and expectation; I was sure no one would know me.

"I—I'm too wet for the parlour," I said to the maid who came to let me in; and after a single startled, puzzled look, she went to tell someone of my arrival. There I stood in my shabby mackintosh, looking at a huge, gilt-framed picture of the Judge, until a plump little robin of a woman, in a black dress with a dash of red at the throat, came trotting out to meet me.

That was Aunt; in spite of my fright and self-consciousness I wanted to laugh to see her bright eyes look at me in amazement that grew almost to panic. She didn't know me; the servant could not have caught my name.

"Did you—wish to see me?" she finally managed to say.

"I'm Helen Winship—" I faltered. I felt as if I had done something very wrong.

"Nelly!" she cried, clutching my hands and almost lifting herself on tiptoe, as she blinked into my eyes in the uncertain light of the outer hall. "This isn't—can't be—not *our* Helen Winship—oh, it's some message from her—some—"

Her voice died away in incoherent mutterings. She drew me into a big hall like a sitting room behind the small parlour.

"Come into the light, child, whoever you are. I want to look at you," she said.

An open fire was burning in the grate, and in the room were Milly and Ethel and white-haired Miss Marcia and a tall, blonde young man.

All rose to their feet, then stopped. There was an awkward pause, the answering thrill of tense amazement shot from mind to mind like light-ning. They stood as if frozen, gazing. The room was for a moment so still that I could hear my own quick breathing and the hammering of my heart. I was grateful for some far shout upon the street that drowned the noise.

"But—you—but—I thought—" Milly began in a half-hushed, awestruck whisper; she never finished the sentence, but continued to gaze at me with big, round eyes, her lips parted, her breath quick and tremulous.

I was transported with joy and fright; I almost wished I might sink into the floor, but just then down the stair came the Judge with John behind him, and little Joy perched on his shoulder. I think the others were as grateful as I for the interruption.

"Put me down! Put me down!" screamed Joy as she saw me sprinkled with sleet. "Mamma, ith that Mithith Thanta Clauth?"

At the welcome laugh that helped to break the ice she ran with a flirt of her short skirts to hide her head against her father's knee.

"Helen!" repeated Mrs. Baker, only half recovering from her stupefaction, "this isn't—why, it can't be you!"

"I—oh, I'm afraid I'm late," I stammered.

Miss Marcia began to unbutton my raincoat, and her kindness somewhat relieved my embarrassment, though I don't know how I managed to respond to the hubbub of greetings, especially when Mr. Hynes, the stranger, was presented.

He had been looking at me more intently than he knew, with dark blue brilliant eyes, and he flushed as he touched my hand, until I was glad to take refuge with Joy, who hovered about, eying me as if she still suspected some ruse on the part of Santa Claus.

"Joy, you know Cousin Nelly?" I said; and at sound of my voice, they all looked again at each other and then at me.

"Why, I can't believe my eyes, though Bake here said you'd altered. Altered!" twittered Aunt Frank. She turned indignantly upon the Judge, who wisely attempted no defense. "I didn't dream—Bake, here, never can tell a story straight. Have you—what is it? Nelly, dear, it's two years since I've seen you; of course you've—grown!"

But no amazement could long curb her hospitable instincts. Her incoherence vanished as she grasped at a practical consideration.

"But let Milly take you up stairs and get your things off," she said with an air as of one who solves problems.

"Are you truly Cothin Nelly?" Joy lisped. "All wight; come thee my twee."

Though she couldn't recognise me as the cousin of a few weeks earlier, the child was eager to claim me as a new friend. So I escaped with her and Milly to the nursery, where I stayed as long as I dared, letting my cheeks cool.

"The twee ith mine and Mamma'th," said Joy; "we're the only oneth young enough to have Christhmath twees, Papa thayth."

"Hoh, guess I'm younger'n Mamma, ain't I?" scoffed my other little cousin who had been sent to inquire into our delay. He is perhaps a dozen years old, is called "Boy" officially, and Timothy, Jr., in the family records, and—like Joy—wasn't in the least afraid of me, after five minutes' acquaintance.

Boy led me down to the others, but dinner was nearly over before I felt at ease. I'm not used to having at my back a statuesque servant—though this one was not too statuesque to be surprised by my appearance almost out of decorum. And I couldn't help knowing that everyone wanted to look at me all the time, which was delicious, but embarrassing. I blushed and gave stupid answers when addressed, and even feared that I might show myself at fault in the etiquette of a city table. It was strange to have forks in so many cases where I've always used spoons. And, though of course I knew what the finger bowls were, I wasn't quite sure how to use them.

No one was more puzzled by my appearance than Uncle Timothy himself. As he looked at me—and this he did through most of the meal—certain long gray hairs in his eyebrows seemed to wave up and down, as I had often noticed with the frightened curiosity of a child, like the questioning antennae of an insect.

"And what is the school work now?" he asked when the dessert came. "The last time I had the very real pleasure of seeing you, it was—perhaps animalculae?"

"The cell," I replied, relieved at the introduction of a topic that I could talk about, "and the cell wall. Protoplasmic movements, you know, and unicellular plants and animals. I'd been making sketches that day of the common amoeba of standing water."

"I am not familiar with the—ah—with the amoeba; but doubtless its habits are interesting. And when do the school days end? A young lady looks forward with pleasure, I fancy, to release from—"

"Is the amoeba a—some horrid bug, I suppose?" interrupted Aunt Frank; "and you—er—do things to it in that laboratory? How can you? The very thought of such a place! It makes me shiver!"

"Oh, but you should see it, so clean and bright; the laboratory's simply beautiful!"

"But this is your first winter in the city, and you ought to be enjoying concerts and theatres, meeting people, seeing things."

"Oh, I only keep such hours as I elect, being a post graduate; and I've been to several theatres," I said; "Kitty and I get seats in the top gallery."

"The—the top gallery?"

"At matinees," I hastily explained, "and not—not lately."

And then I felt more confused than ever, for Mr. Hynes was watching me. John was looking at me, too, with that great light in his face that had been there ever since my arrival, when he first saw the opal gleaming on my finger; and I—oh, how could I have hinted that I don't dare go where so many people might look at me? But it's the truth. And though the truth may be inconvenient, it's wonderfully sweet!

After dinner we passed into the big drawing room behind the hall. Joy did some clumsy little dances in her short white frock—she is really too chubby to caper nimbly—and Ethel and Milly played and sang neither well nor ill.

I think they were more afraid of me than I had been of the servants at dinner. They are not very pretty, with their light, wavy hair and pale flower faces, though I'm afraid I set my standard too high now—now that I know what is possible.

I went to the piano myself afterwards and played. Played! It was terrible! Never would I have believed that I could make such a mess of it. I didn't sing until they began trying carols. I didn't mean to do so then, but I chimed in before I thought, when they sang:—

> *He set a star up in the sky*
> *Full broad and bright and fair.*

"That song was taken from the Ormulum," said the Judge; "a poem of the thirteenth century—"

"Nelly! Was that you?" cried Aunt Frank, interrupting.

The music of the new, fresh, vibrant voice had thrilled them all—all except the unconscious Judge—and there they sat, spellbound. But as they shook off the witchery, there was all at once a babble of voices, and before I quite knew what had happened, I was at the piano again, singing "The King in Thule:"

There was a king in Thule
True even to the grave
To whom his mistress, dying,
A golden goblet gave.

Perhaps it wasn't very appropriate to Christmas, but Cadge had drilled me upon it. In the middle of the first stanza I happened to glance up, and noticed that Mr. Hynes was again looking at me with an absorbed, indrawing gaze, colouring with amazed pleasure. It woke in me a flutter of consternation and delight, for he has the sensitive face of a musician; but my presence of mind was gone, and for one horrible instant I thought I was going to break down, and just sat there, gasping and blushing. My heart sank and my voice dwindled to a quavering, unfamiliar whisper. I couldn't remember the words; but then I seized hold of my courage and sang and sang and sang, better than I had ever done before.

I didn't look up again until I had finished; then somehow I got away from the piano, and shyly slipped into a chair near Miss Baker. Of course there was a clamour that I should sing again, but I couldn't. The flaming of my cheeks made me ashamed.

Perhaps some time I shall learn the city way of not seeming to care very much about anything.

Aunt must have had it at her tongue's end all the evening to invite me to come to her; and when she was bidding me goodnight she could wait no longer.

"You're living right on Union Square?" she said; "in the same building with—with—"

"A milliner, a dentist, a school for theatrical dancing," I enumerated, laughing happily. I knew that it was I myself, and not my mode of life, that bewildered her.

"But—is it—*nice?*"

"Better than a boarding house. Two or three other girls lodge there, the housekeeper is obliging, and the experience—well, at least it's enlightening."

"I wish you'd come here. Why don't you?"

"Oh, could I?" I cried with sudden frankness. "You can't think how glad I'd be! The studio was awfully nice at first, and I've made the best of it, but I know Ma—Mother and Father would be pleased. If it wouldn't be too much trouble—"

And so easily it was all arranged. Of course after she had seen me, heard me, felt the charm of me—of Her—Aunt Frank couldn't leave Her in the studio!

I'd have been glad to avoid the journey back to Union Square with John; for the evening, with all its perplexities, had been paradise, and I dreaded to have him bring me back to earth with words of love. I ought to be more than usually tender towards John now, when he has just lost his mother; but when the Bakers' door had closed behind us, and we stood together under the crispy starlight—for it had cleared and turned cold during the evening—I talked feverishly of things that neither of us cared about, and kept it up all the way home.

John scarcely seemed to listen to my chatter. He was as if under a spell, and his dark, strong face glowed with the magic of it. As we approached the Square, he looked down at me, and slipped my hand from his arm into the clasp of his warm fingers. Through my glove he felt the ring, and gave the hand a little, almost timid pressure.

"Am I doing right? Ought I to wear it?" I cried. "Won't you help me think, just as if you didn't—didn't care? This isn't like last summer. We are different; I am very different. You must have seen tonight, that I am not at all the same girl. I've told you that I can't be certain; I am dazed."

"I shall remember everything—all you told me when I came, and now," he said. "But you are doing right—darling!"

He held my hands when we parted and looked into my eyes, and I saw that his own were shining. His love seemed too deep for any outburst of passion, or else he feared to alarm me; and yet he seemed so sure.

I wish—I wish—oh, I don't know what I wish; I ought not to be bound to anyone; but I suppose I love John.

2

A Looking Over by the Pack

Jan. 2.

If women are not meant to study, Prof. Darmstetter should be pleased with me. Instead of working up my laboratory notebooks, I have sat until midnight, dreaming.

"Go to bed early and get your beauty sleep," says Aunt, but I push open the window and lean upon the sash and let the cold air blow over me. I'd like to dance a thousand miles in the moonlight; I'm so young, and so strong, and such glorious things are coming!

Tomorrow I shall have a foretaste of the future; I shall know what other people—not John and my relatives—think of me. Ah, there's only one thing they can think! Tomorrow'll be the beginning of the world to me.

Tomorrow! Tomorrow! Aunt Frank has sent out cards for an "At Home." And it's tomorrow!

Oh, I'm glad I came here! I revel in the new home.

I like the house; it looks so big and solid. I like my cousins—quiet little creatures. They wait upon me, anticipate my smallest wish, and defer to my opinions as if I were a white star queen dropped from the ether; all but Boy, and even he respects me because I can construe Caesar.

I like my Aunt—devoted to clubs and committees, though she's forgotten them now in her eagerness to introduce me. Ah, tomorrow!

Blessed tomorrow! And I like Aunt Marcia Baker. I wonder if, when I am older, I too shall be serene and stately, with a face that seems to have outlived sorrow; I can hardly believe now that I shall care to live at all when people's eyes have ceased to follow my beauty. When for me there are no more tomorrows.

I think I shall like Mr. Hynes; he's almost one of the family, for he is betrothed to Milly, and I'm glad—ah, so glad I'm not she! What a life she looks forward to—each day exactly like its fellows; a droning, monotonous existence, keeping house, overseeing the cooking—perhaps doing it herself; for he's only a young lawyer, just starting in life!

But I like his face, so full of impulse and imagination. I believe he's a man who might go far and achieve much. Why should he handicap himself with an early marriage?

It's well enough for Milly; she doesn't understand her limitations. Why, she's almost as eager over tomorrow as if it could mean to her what it does to me; and that is an outlook into a life so glad, so wonderful!

Dear, good Aunt Frank proposed the tea before my trunks were fairly unpacked.

"Won't your Professor give you a holiday from—is it microbes you study?" she inquired. "Sure they're not dangerous?"

"The afternoon tea bacillus is not wholly innocuous," suggested Uncle, pinching her cheek.

It was good to see the loving look that reproved and repaid him.

"Why, Bake," she protested, "tea never hurt anybody."

"Oh, I've time enough," I said; "I have no regular days for going to Prof. Darmstetter, and the other studies—"

It was on my tongue to add: "and the other studies don't matter," but I checked the words.

"Well, you'll find it takes time," Aunt reminded me. "How about clothes, now? Suppose you show me what you brought."

And in a few minutes we were all chattering at once in discussion of my modest little wardrobe. I could feel, as each new dress was shaken from its folds, that Aunt was more dissatisfied than she would confess.

"Everything's pretty and tasteful," she conceded at last; "but—for a tea —if you could—"

If she had dared, she'd have offered to get me a dress herself.

"Oh, of course I'll need something new," I said hurriedly; "I meant to ask your advice. Nothing very costly," I was reluctantly adding. But at that moment an inspiration came to lighten the gloom.

The very thing! I'd use the money I'd saved for the microscope! I don't need one the least bit.

So I was able to add with some philosophy:—

"I never did have a nice dress, and I'd like something pretty good this time. Why, I haven't nearly spent all my allowance," I cried with kindling enthusiasm, jumping up to pace the floor. "Tell me what I ought to have— just exactly what is most suitable. I don't know much about teas, but I'd like something—fine!"

Aunt's face glowed with excitement. I think she saw in imagination fifty Helens dancing before he eyes in a kaleidoscopic assortment of dresses.

"You're right. We'll get—oh, what shall we—what shall we get that'll be good enough for you?" she cried in a flutter. "Something simple of course, you're so young; but—I'll tell you: We'll go right to Mrs. Edgar!"

Perhaps my own face burned, too.

"Who's she? Someone on the Avenue?"

"No; no one knows her, but—she's a marvel! It'd mean the world and all to her to please someone sure to be noticed, like you. She's a widow; has two children."

So to Mrs. Edgar we went. Her eyes devoured me. She is a mite of a woman, young, white-faced, vivacious.

"For a tea?" she asked. "A—a large one?"

She spoke with forced calmness, but her hands had the artist's flutter, the enthusiast's eagerness to be doing.

"I'll get samples," she went on; "there's not a minute to be lost; not— one—moment! I'll work all night rather than fail her. You will not wish"— she dismissed us abruptly—"to go with me to the shops?"

"No; Miss Winship attracts too much attention."

Alas, it's true! It has become an ordeal for me to venture into a shop. But what a blessed thing if my beauty should bring success and ease to this poor, struggling little widow—just by my wearing a dress she has made! Oh, she'll not be the only one! What if Kitty sometime wins fame by painting my picture, or Cadge by writing of me in her "Recollections?" Why shouldn't I inspire great poems and noble deeds and fine songs, like the famous beauties Miss Coleman told about? Yes, even more than they; there was not one of them all like me!

Next evening when Aunt brought the samples upstairs, I was reading to the Judge in the library, and the others were listening as if stocks and bonds were more fascinating than romances.

"Shall we pray for a second Joshua, arresting the sun, pending deliberation?" asked Uncle, displeased at the interruption.

"Why, Bake, there's scarcely ten days, and how we'd feel if Nelly didn't look well!" cried Aunt Frank; and we all broke out laughing at the bare idea of my looking ill!

"I never saw anyone to whom dress mattered so little," Aunt Marcia said, as she folded up her silk knitting. "But Mrs. Edgar insists upon her four fittings like any Shylock haggling for his pound of flesh; it is written in the bond."

When she had trotted away home with her prim elderly maid, like a pair out of "Cranford," Ethel made an impressive announcement:—

"The General will pour."

"Returned hero from the Philippines?"

"Oh, dear, no. Meg Van Dam could face Mausers, but a Red Cross bazaar was as near as she got to the war. We call her the General because —oh, you'll find out. Meg is Mrs. Robert Van Dam."

"Oh, I think I've seen that name in the papers. Aren't they grand people?"

"Why, yes; rather; we don't know the Van Dams; Meg's only just married. You might have read about her mother-in-law, Mrs. Marmaduke Van Dam, or her aunt-in-law, Mrs. Henry Van Dam, or Mrs. Henry's daughters; the family's a tribe. But Meg, why, we went to school with Meg; she's just the General."

My dress came home tonight—white and dainty. Ah, at last I've something to wear that's not "good" and "plain" and "durable"! But there was an outcry, as there has been at every fitting, because I won't wear stays. Eccentric, they call me; as if Nature and beauty were abnormal!

When I was arrayed in it, Aunt and Ethel led me to the library for Uncle's inspection.

"Is tomorrow the day set to exhibit to Helen other aspects of New York than the scholastic?" he asked, looking up from his paper. "The first appearances of a young girl in modern society are said to be comparable with a 'Looking Over by the Pack,' as described by Mr. Kipling. May Mrs. Baloo and Mrs. Bagheera and Mrs. Shere Khan have good hunting tonight, and be kind tomorrow to our womanling."

"Why, Bake, you know just as well as I do there aren't any such people coming. I believe it's just one of your jokes," sputtered Aunt. "Nelly, dear, turn slowly round."

She had dropped on her knees beside me, busy with pins and folds, and Joy was lisping the caution, born perhaps of experience, "Don't you thoil it, Cothin Nelly, or Nurthey'll vip you," when Milly came into the library; and with her was Mr. Hynes.

"Lovely! Isn't it, Ned?" cried Milly. "It's for tomorrow."

Mr. Hynes scarcely glanced at the dress, then looked away again, with indifference that somehow hurt me.

"Very pretty," he said languidly. "Classic, isn't it? By the way, Judge, I think you'd be interested—"

And then he began to tell Judge Baker about some horrid auction sale of old books!

I was surprised. I couldn't account for it. To hide my disappointment—for I do want to look my best tomorrow, and then everybody has taken so much pains—I bent over Joy, tying and untying the ribbons that held the rings of soft hair in front of her ears.

"Thop, Cothin Nelly; you hurt!" she screamed.

As soon as I could, I ran to take off the dress. How could Aunt so parade me? Of course the women Mr. Hynes knows must have all their dresses from city dressmakers.

But I believe, after all, he did notice, for I saw him colour before he turned sharply away. To please Milly, he might at least—

He called the dress classic; it's just long, soft folds without messy trimmings; and, oh, it's not vanity to peep at myself again and again and to dream of tomorrow. I'm gloriously, gloriously beautiful! If John comes tomorrow, I do hope he'll wear gloves. He has good hands, too; well-shaped—

Why, of course; Mr. Hynes must admire me.

Snarling at the Council Rock

Jan. 10.

T oday has been heaven!

There was a famous lawyer among Aunt's guests and a United States Senator and a real author, a woman who has written books; but people brushed past them all for a word with me!

And I'm going to the Opera! I shall sit in a box. Mrs. Van Dam says I'll make the sensation of the season! I'm going to the Opera!

When men came this morning with palms and flowers to decorate the house, I ran off to the Park. I did almost run, really. There was a song at my lips: "Gladdest, oh, gladdest, most beautiful in the world; blessed, most blessed, most beautiful in the world!" and the "tap-tap" of horses' feet on the asphalt, the "b-r-r-rp" of the cable cars and the rattle of elevated trains kept time, until all the city seemed ringing with my joy.

I know it's foolish; if I had been beautiful from my childhood; if I could have grown up to think of it as a matter of course; if I had been used to the awe of men and women's envy, I might think less about it, might even fancy that I would have preferred learning or wealth—for we all love what we have not. But now—it is so new, so marvellous!

I had plenty of things to think about when I could calm myself. Only yesterday I'd had a long talk with Prof. Darmstetter.

"The experiment is not yet complete," he declared. He had asked me to stay for—but that is a part of the secret which is to pass with this record from me to all women.

"You are beautiful," he said; "mein Gott, yes! More beautiful t'an any ot'er voman since t'e appearance of man on eart'. But perfectly beautiful? I do not know; I t'ink not yet. Who can tell for v'at ultimate perfection Nature destined t'e human body? But we shall see. T'at perfection you shall reach. In a veek, a mont', t'ree mont's—I cannot tell. Ve must vait and experiment and still vait, but success is assured—absolute success. I shall gif it. I do not know if t'e human type is t'e highest t'at eart' is capable of supporting, but it is t'e highest present type, and it shall be my vork to gif it t'at for v'ich it has hungered and t'irsted, and towards v'ich slowly it has groped its vay; it shall be my vork to gif humanity beauty and perfection."

The light that illumined his yellow, wrinkled face made me cry out, "All the world will bless you! All women will be grateful as I am grateful!"

"Ach!" he snapped with a sudden change of countenance. "I shall be von more name and date to make harter t'e student's lessons and longer t'e tables—t'at is gratitude! Vit' t'e vorld we haf at present no concern. For t'is, indeed, you bless me—t'at I am not a quack to make public an incomplete discofery, for ot'er quacks to do mischief. You are glad t'at it is vit' you alone I concern myself. But you are not grateful; you are happy because I say t'at you shall be yet more beautiful; t'at is not gratitude. You might—"

At the eager shrillness of his voice I drew a step away.

"Indeed I'm grateful, whether you believe it or not!" I cried. "You think all women so selfish! Of course I'm glad that I alone am in the secret, but you proposed it yourself, and I rejoice as much as you do that some day— by and by—other women will be happy as I am happy—"

"Yes—by and by! You emphasize t'at," he snapped mockingly, but then he recovered himself and his queer new deference. "And you haf t'e right; I vish you to rechoice in your own lofeliness. Ve haf engaged toget'er in t'is great vork, and it is vell t'at we bot' haf our revards—I t'at I aggomblish somet'ing for t'e benefit of my kind, and you—since vomen cannot lofe t'eir kind, but only intifiduals—you haf t'e happy lofe t'at is necessary to a voman."

His eyes rested on my ring.

I couldn't tell him—proud as I am of it—that John had loved me before I ever heard of the Bacillus. But I could punish his gibes.

"Oh, by the way—I'm not coming tomorrow," I said. "My Aunt is to give a tea."

Strange to see him struggle with his disappointment like a grieving child! But he bravely rallied.

"T'at is goot," he said, "you shall tell me v'at people t'ink of you. You vish to go about—to be admired; you vish to gif up science; not so?"

"Oh, no! I couldn't be a doll, for men to look at and then tire of me. I must study the harder—to be worthy—"

The look of his face, of the thin, straight-lipped mouth, the keen old eyes, stopped me.

"You vill not gif up study now, at least," he sneered; "not until you haf t'e perfect beauty. You haf need of me."

Prof. Darmstetter is so irritating! Why, he has just as much need of me! He himself said I was the best subject he could find for the experiment. But even if he had finished his work with the Bacillus, he'd rather teach me, a despised woman, all the science I could master than develop the budding talent of the brightest Columbia boy. The sight of my beauty is a joy to him. Really, I pity the poor man. He makes the great discovery when he's himself too old to profit by it; the Bacillus will not work against Nature. It has brought him only a hopeless longing—

But I shall study. He shall see! Not in the laboratory, of course; that is hardly fitting now. I wouldn't go there again except for the lure of promised beauty—can more loveliness be possible? But I do feel the responsibility of beauty. The wisest and best will crowd about me, and they must find my words worthy the lips that shape them and the voice that utters. And I shall learn from their wisdom.

"There was Hypatia; she was both beautiful and learned," I found myself confiding to a gray squirrel in the Park, and then I laughed and ran home to make my last preparations.

Ethel arranged my hair today, though I could hardly yield her the delight of its shining, long undulations. Then she did Milly's as nearly like mine as possible, and Milly did hers. The girls wore white like me, and my aunt was in black. The house was full of flowers; as if it had plunged into seas of them, it dripped with an odourous rosy foam. John sent a box—the extravagant boy!—and there were big American Beauty roses, with stems as long as walking sticks from Pros. and Cadge. Milly had flowers, too, from Mr. Hynes.

At first I wasn't a bit afraid, while acquaintances were dropping in one by one—Mrs. Magoun, Mrs. Crosby, the wife of the managing clerk in Uncle's office, Aunt Marcia—all allies.

Then there came a stir at the door, the magnetic thrill that foreruns a

Somebody. And there upon the threshold stood a tall, dashing girl, superbly turned out; not handsome, but fine-looking, dark, decisive, vital—a creature born to command.

I knew her at the first glance. She was the General!

I was for a moment surprised to see her so young and girlish, though I might have known; for she was Milly's school-mate. I doubt if she's two years my senior, but in social arts and finesse—ah, the difference!

The house seemed to belong to her from the moment she entered. She moved like a whirlwind—a well-mannered and exquisitely dressed whirl-wind, of course—with an air of abounding vigour and vitality, up to where we stood, and there stopped short.

"How d'y'do?" she said, in the clipped New York fashion, looking at me with the confidence of one who is never at a loss—and then—

Oh, the joy! For all her *savoir faire*, it was her turn to be confused. For a moment she peered at me with a short-sighted squint; then after a little hesitation, she put up her lorgnette, making an impatient gesture, as if to say: "I can't help it; I *must*"—and stared.

Her eyes grew big as she gazed; but at last she drew a long breath, and put down the quizzing glass with an effect of self-denial. When she spoke there was little to remind me of her momentary loss of self-command.

"Are you enjoying New York?" she demanded.

"Milly tells me you've never been in the city before; that you are studying at Barnard."

"Yes."

I knew that I had impressed this strong, splendid woman, but I was a little afraid of her.

Quite herself again, she began asking questions about myself, my home, my studies; quick, probing, confusing questions, while in my cheeks the awkward colour came and went. But it would never have occurred to me to parry her queries. I could not help liking her, though when at last she left me and began a progress through the rooms, I drew a breath of relief, like one who has passed with credit a stiff exam-ination.

At the door of the dining room she paused again, judging through her glass the table and its dainty decorations.

"Those flowers are rather high," she declared, and calling upon Milly for help, she began rearranging the roses, and laying the twigs of holly upon the cloth in bolder patterns. She seemed to take charge, to adopt me with the house, to accept and audit and vouch for us.

Then people began coming all at once, all together, and I had to take my place beside Mrs. Baker and Aunt Marcia in the reception room.

I can't tell anything about the next hour; it's a blur. But I wouldn't have missed a minute. I had never before seen a reception, except at the University where sometimes I used to serve as an usher, pouncing upon people as they entered and leading them up to the row of Professors and Professors' wives backed against the wall. But now I had to stand up myself and meet people. And oh, that was different!

At first two or three women would approach, putting out their hands at an absurd height, and start to say: "How d' you—" or "I'm so—"

And Aunt would make some excited, half-coherent remark and look at me, anxiously but proudly, and say my name.

But they never heard her! As they really saw me, each in turn would start, and, wide-eyed, look again. And as the awe and wonder grew in their faces—as there came the little stop, the gasp, that told how their reserve was for once overthrown, then, to the utmost, I tasted the sweet of power and felt the thrill of ecstasy.

Red spots burned in Aunt's cheeks; she talked fast in her company voice, and somehow the lace at her throat got awry. Aunt Marcia was as calm and stately in her soft black velvet as if nothing were happening. And really there was little to disturb one's composure. New Yorkers aren't like our whole-souled, emotional Western folks. Not one of these women but would have suffered torture rather than betray her surprise beyond that first irrepressible gasp of amazement. After that one victory of human nature, they would make talk about the weather, or the newest book, and then get away to discuss me in undertones in the hall or drawing room.

Quickly the sixth sense of a strange agitation went through the house. I knew what they were all talking about, thinking about. Subtle waves of thought seemed to catch up each new comer so that she felt, without being told, that something extraordinary was happening. Women now approached not unprepared; but for all their bracing against the shock, not one could be quite nonchalant at the first sight of my superb, compelling beauty.

My eyes flashed, my pulse rioted as I felt the vibrant excitement of the gathering, the tiptoe eagerness to reach our neighbourhood, the hush that fell upon the circle immediately around me, the reaction of overgay laugh and chatter in the far corners.

Oh, it was lovely, lovely! No girl could have been quite unmoved to feel that all those soft lights were glowing in her honour, those masses of flowers blooming, all that warmth and perfume of elegance and luxury wafted as incense to her nostrils. And the undercurrent of suppressed excitement, the sensation of Her!

At times I grew impatient of conventionality. How was it possible for these people to look so quietly, eye to eye, upon the most vitally perfect of living beings? How could they turn from me to orange frappé or salted almonds?

Once or twice I caught some faint echo of the talk about us.

"Where is she?" asked one voice, made by curiosity more penetrating than its owner realised.

"Julia's seen her; she's talked and talked till I had to come."

"And she's still studying?"—Another voice—"How can she? Great beauty and great scientist—bizarre combination!"

How that would amuse Prof. Darmstetter!

By and by I saw John towering above the others while he bobbed about helplessly in the sea of women's heads that filled the rooms and even rose upon the "bleachers," as he calls the stairs. There were not really so very many people, but he didn't know how to reach us, he is so awkward. When he had steered his course among the women and had spoken to my Aunt, his face was radiant as he turned to me.

"I knew *you* wouldn't fail us, Mr. Burke," Aunt said hurriedly. "Mrs. Marshall—so glad—this is—Nelly, dear—"

Behind John was a lady waiting to meet me.

"—So glad you've come," I said to him; and the words sounded curiously to me because in my excitement I also had spoken in my "company voice."

But I had no time to say another word to him, as I turned to greet Mrs. Marshall.

He mumbled something, flushing, while his eyes devoured my beauty in one dumb, worshipping look. Then he dropped quickly out of our group. I was sorry, but he'll understand that I was flurried. He ought to learn self control, though; he shouldn't look at me before so many people with all his heart in his eyes.

And I was so vexed about his clothes, too! His old, long, black coat, such as lawyers wear in the West, would have been pretty nearly right—something like what the other men wore—but he seemed to think it was not good enough, and had put on a brand new business suit. Of course there wasn't another man there so clad, but he never seemed to notice how absurd he was.

The Viewing of the Pack didn't last long. Before my cheeks had ceased flaming, before I had grown used to standing there to be looked at, people seemed to go, all at once, as suddenly as they had arrived.

Just as the last ones were leaving, some instinct told me that Mr. Hynes had come. Before I saw him, I felt his gaze upon me, a wondering, glad look, as if I were Eve, the first and only woman.

Milly brought him to me and left us together, but at first he was almost curt in his effort to hide his sensibility to my beauty—as if that were a weakness!—and I was furiously shy, and felt somehow that I must hold him at still greater distance.

"Am I never again to hear you sing?" he asked. "Sweet sounds that have given a new definition to music are still vibrating in my memory."

I knew he was thinking of Christmas!

"I don't often sing, except for Joy," I mumbled; "I've had so few lessons."

"Joy doesn't know her joys; but—wouldn't she share them?"

"Sometime—perhaps—"

I couldn't answer him, for hot and cold waves of shyness and pleasure were running over me. Oh, I hope, for Milly's sake, he doesn't dislike me. He seems to feel so intensely, to be so alive!

When he had gone, I went to the dining room with Aunt Marcia, and found there Ethel and the General and Peggy Van Dam, the General's cousin, a pale girl, all eyes and teeth. Kitty was with them, and she darted towards me, but Mrs. Van Dam was before her.

"Sit down, both of you," she commanded.

She fairly put us into chairs, and brought us cups of something—I don't know what.

Aunt Marcia breathed a little sigh of relief.

"Helen," she said, "you haven't been standing too long?"

"It wasn't an instant! I could stand all day!"

Mrs. Van Dam smiled, and I felt *gauche*, like a schoolgirl. I am so impulsive!

"It was all delightful!" cried Kitty; "and yet—while you were my chum, Helen, I *did* think you rather good looking!"

"You find yourself mistaken?" the General inquired.

"Oh, no-o-o; not exactly; a beautiful girl, certainly; but—oh, I could have made pincushions of some of those pudgy women, nibbling wafers, and delivering themselves of lukewarm appreciations! 'Too tall'—'too short'—'too dark'—'too light'; 'I like your height bettah, my deah.' Helen, you dairymaid, powder! Plaster over that 'essentially improbable' colour."

Mrs. Van Dam broke out laughing at Kitty's mimicry. I wish the child wouldn't let her hair straggle in front of her ears and look so harum-scarum.

"I doubt if we have had many harsh critics," said Miss Baker.

"Not a thing to criticise," cried Aunt Frank, entering just then and catching the last word. "Everybody so interested in Nelly! Bake, if you'd only come earlier, I'd have been perfectly satisfied."

They say that Uncle Timothy can never be coaxed home to one of his wife's receptions, but he answered with great solemnity, as he loomed up behind the little woman:—

"I am privileged to be here, even at the eleventh hour. I could not wholly deny myself the sight of so much youth and bloom."

"Don't be hypocritical, Judge," said the General reprovingly. "You're too big and honest to achieve graceful deceit. But before I go—I've seats for the Opera Monday night in Mother's box. Miss Winship must come, and—" her glance deliberated briefly—"and Milly."

Milly cried, "How delightful, Meg!" But my tongue tripped and my cheeks flamed as I tried to say that I had never seen an opera and to thank my new friend.

Little she heeded my lack of words. Gazing at me once again as she had upon first seeing me, she exclaimed:—

"You great, glorious creature! They sha'n't hive you in a schoolroom; you must come out and show yourself; why, you'll set New York in a furore!"

I think she's splendid.

No sooner was she gone than I was summoned to the reception room, and Cadge rushed to meet me. She looked much smarter than Kitty, with her black hair curled and her keen eyes shining with excitement.

"All over but the shouting?" she asked. "Meant to get here in season to see you knock 'em in the Old Kent Road, but woman proposes, Big Tom disposes. Shall I turn in a paragraph? Just—did you have music? What's your dress—in the Sunday society slush, of course, not the daily; 'fraid the *Star* won't take over a stick—. Greek a little bit? M-m-m—not modistic exactly, but—but—."

Her abrupt sentences grew slower, paused, dropped to an awestruck whisper, as she looked upon me. She added in her gravest manner: "Say, you're the loveliest ever happened! The—very—limit!"

But awe and Cadge could not long live together. In a moment her mouth took a comically benevolent quirk.

"And 'among those present'—" she asked; "who was that leaving just as I got here?"

"Mrs. Robert Van Dam, schoolmate of my cousins. But you're not writing me up, Cadge?"

Cadge whistled.

"Van Dam! How calmly the giddy child says it! Does your youngest cousin make mud pies with duchesses? Say, she comes pretty near being one of the '400.' But I'm off; a grist of copy to grind—talk of raving beauties, you'll be the only one that won't rave!"

Of course Cadge wouldn't have talked just like that before the others, if she had come earlier.

At bedtime Milly and Ethel ran to my room to talk things over, and my Aunt came to shoo them off to bed, but she stayed and talked, too; and I've no business to be writing at this shocking time of night, except, of course I couldn't sleep and so I might as well.

"Everybody thinks you resemble your cousins," Aunt said; "and really there *is* a family likeness."

Poor Aunt! Ethel and Milly are washed out copies of me, in dress and hair, if that constitutes resemblance; and they imitate even my mannerisms.

I should think Mr. Hynes would be too critical to admire Milly.

I had a partial engagement for Monday with John; but he'll let me off, to go to the Opera.

4

In the Interests of Music

Tuesday morning, Jan. 14.

I am writing before breakfast. They told me to lie quietly in bed this morning, but I'm not tired, not excited. Nothing more happened than I might have expected. I couldn't have supposed that in my presence people would be stocks and stones!

But oh, it was beautiful, terrible! How can I write it? If I could only flash last night—every glorious minute of it—upon paper!

And I might have lost it—they didn't want to let me go! There was a full family council beforehand. John had taken quietly enough the cancelling of our half engagement for the evening, but he had strong objections to my going to the Opera.

"If you prefer that," he said, "but do you think it wise to appear in such a public place with strangers?"

"But why not?"

I was impatient at so much discussion and discretion. My mind was made up.

"There's no reason why you shouldn't, I suppose." John drew a great sigh. "But I shall feel easier if—I think I'll go too."

"We'll all go," cried Aunt Frank—it was so funny to have them sit there debating in that way the problem of Her—"we'll enjoy it of all things—the Judge and I, and especially Ethel."

And so, when the great night came, Milly and I left the others in the midst of their preparations, and went off to dine with Mrs. Van Dam; we were to go with her afterwards to see Mascagni's *Christofero Colombo*.

It seems impossible now, but I was excited even about the dinner. I thought it the beginning of recognition—and it was!—to be seized upon by this splendid, masterful young General.

She lives not far from us—on Sixty-seventh Street near Fifth Avenue, while we are on Seventy-second Street near Madison. The wall of her house near the ground looks like that of a fortress; there are no high steps in front, but Milly and I were shown into a hall, oak finished and English, right on the street level; and then into a room off the hall that was English, too—oak and red leather, with branching horns above the mantel and on the floor a big fur rug; and, presently, into a little brocade-lined elevator that took us to Mrs. Van Dam's sitting room on the third floor.

"You ought to see the whole house," Milly whispered, as we were slowly ascending.

I had eyes just then for nothing but the General herself, who met us, a figure that abashed me, swishing a gleaming evening dress, her neck and hair a-glitter with jewels, more dominant and possessive and—yes, even more interested in me than when I had first seen her.

When we went down to dinner, I did see the house; for at a word from Milly, partly in good nature and partly in pride, Mrs. Van Dam led the way through stately rooms that kept me alternating between confusion and delight, until she paused in a gilded salon, with stuccoed ceiling and softest of soft rose hangings, where I scarcely dared set foot upon the shining floor.

Less in jest than wonder, I asked if Marie Antoinette didn't walk there o' nights.

"It's *Diane*, isn't it, who walks here this night?" she said, linking her arm in mine and leading me to a tall mirror. Then she changed colour a little, took her arm away hastily and walked from the great glass. Kind and friendly as she was, she couldn't quite like to see her own image reflected there—beside mine!

"*Diane* and the Queen of Sheba!" exclaimed Milly, for beside our simple frocks the General was indeed magnificent.

Her brow cleared at this, and she laughed with satisfaction. When I blurted out something about having once run off to a shop parlour, before I came to Aunt, for a peep at a full-length glass, she laughed again at the confession and called me "a buttercup, a perfect *Diane*."

At dinner we met Mr. Van Dam—a small man who doesn't talk much; and it seemed so exciting to have wine at table, though of course I did not taste it, or coffee.

And it was delightful to lean back in the carriage, as we drove to the Opera House, and remember how Kitty and I used to pin up our skirts under our ulsters and jog about in street cars. Mrs. Van Dam wore a wonderful hooded cloak of lace and fur, and her gloves fastened all the way to her elbows with silk loops that passed over silver balls.

I had been so impatient during dinner, because they didn't sit down until eight o'clock, and then dawdled as if there were no Opera to follow; but I needn't have worried, for although the performance had begun when we arrived, there were still many vacant places in the great house. I drew closer about my face the scarf that Ethel had lent me until we had passed through the dazzling lobby, up the stairway and through the corridors, and until the red curtains of the box had parted, and I had slipped into the least conspicuous chair. Muffled as I was, I trembled at the first glance at the great, brilliantly lighted house, from which rose the stir of a gathering audience and a rustle of low voices.

"Why, you're not nervous, are you?" the General asked. "I've brought you here early on purpose; you'll be comfortably settled before anybody notices."

And she good-naturedly pushed me into a front place. The music was all the while going on, but no one seemed to pay much attention.

"Who'll notice me in this big building?" I asked with a shaky little laugh.

But just at first, as I looked out over the house, I clutched the lace that was still around my throat. It was warm after the chill air without, and my head swam. There was mystery in the swarming figures and the murmur. The breath of the roses that lay over the box rails, the gleaming of bared shoulders, the flash of jewels seemed to belong to some other world—a world where I was native, and from which I had too long been exiled. Surely in some other life I must have had my place among gaily-dressed ladies who smiled and nodded, bending tiara-crowned heads above gently waving fans. I felt kinship with them; I passionately longed to be noticed by them, and feared it even more intensely.

Almost immediately after our arrival the curtain fell upon the first scene. We had missed every word of it! Mrs. Van Dam left me for a few minutes to myself, and as I became more composed, I put back my scarf and looked about a little more boldly. The house was yet far from full, but every moment people were coming in.

The boxes at each side of us were untenanted, but at no great distance I saw Peggy Van Dam, seated beside a large woman—her mother, Mrs. Henry—and chatting busily with a stout, good-natured-looking young man. Even Peggy had not noticed our entrance and, quite reassured, I lifted my opera glass and began studying the audience.

We were near the front of the house in the first tier on the left, and I had in view almost the whole sweep of the great gold and crimson horse-shoe. Down in the orchestra some of the women were as gorgeous in satins and brocades as those in the boxes, while others wore street attire. Nearly all the men had donned evening dress, and I thought at first—but soon saw how absurd that was—that I could pick out John by his office suit. I could not repress a little glow of pride, as I looked down upon those rows and rows of heads, to think that somewhere among them, or above them, John was watching, rejoicing with me, fearing for me where for himself he would never fear. He'd lift, if he could, every stone from my path. Mr. Hynes, now, would carry you forward so fast that you'd never see the stones.

I had no thought that Mr. Hynes was in the house, but, amusing myself with the idea, I lifted my glass—dear little pearl trinket with which the General had provided me—and looked for him, wondering how often a poor young lawyer attends the Opera. Of course I couldn't see anybody I knew, nor could I read my libretto, for the words danced before my eyes; and Mrs. Van Dam, smiling at my interest, began chattering about the people around us, speaking as if I would soon be as familiar with the brilliant world of fashion and society as herself.

"I wonder," she said in her energetic way, "what it feels like to be at one's first opera."

Excitement was flashing from my eyes and burning on my cheeks as I answered, "It's—it's—oh, I can't tell you! But in the West," I added hastily, "we had oratorio."

"What a buttercup you are!" she said again.

Soon the curtain rose upon the second act—or scene. Whichever it was, that was all that I was fated to see or hear of the Opera. And for the little while I could consider it, I must say I was disappointed. The scenery was superb, but the voices—

"You've spoiled us, Nelly," Milly whispered.

"Colombo's not bad."

I squeezed her hand ecstatically.

I find that I don't criticise men so shrewdly; but oh, the thin, shrill pipe of Isabella, compared with what a woman's voice may be! Yet I admired her skill, and did not wonder that the house applauded.

The second scene was just closing, and I was lost in dreams of the fine things that I shall do for art and music when I'm a great society leader, when the box door opened, and there entered an elderly couple, much alike—tall, thin, rather stately and withered. I knew that they must be Mrs. Marmaduke Van Dam, the General's mother-in-law, and her husband. Impulsively I sprang up to allow them to come to the front places.

And then—the catastrophe!

I was conscious at first only of an instant's confusion, of a hurried introduction in undertones. Then I found myself again sitting, my arm tingling to the clutch of Milly's fingers. In her pale, pretty face her light eyes glowed with a fright that was not all painful.

The blood seemed to flow back to my heart as I realised what I had done. The sudden stir in our box had called attention, and I had been standing in the glare of electric lights overhead and at my feet, my white dress outlined against the blood-red curtains.

"Take this fan," Milly whispered from behind me. "Will you have my seat?"

Shame dyed my face. After such a heedless act I couldn't look at the General. I knew that, in his surprise at my appearance, Mr. Marmaduke Van Dam had fumbled noisily with his chair, and that Mrs. Marmaduke had dropped her shoulder wrap—she was in evening dress; how can elderly women do it?—I knew that in spite of their rigid politeness they found it hard to keep their eyes from me. I hoped the General had been too busy to appreciate my folly, and I drew a quivering breath of relief that it had had no more serious consequences.

Yet I was queerly dissatisfied. The Metropolitan Opera House is a big building, and the part of the audience to which I could have been conspicuous was small. Yet some people must have seen; had they taken no notice?

For some space—minutes or seconds—it seemed so.

Then a confused murmur, a shifting, restless movement, began near us in the orchestra. A good many people down there, as well as in the boxes at each side, had noticed me earlier. Now they began whispering to their neighbours. Heads were turned our way; people were asking, answering, almost pointing. I could see the knowledge of me spread from seat to seat, from row to row, as ripples spread from a stone thrown into still water. Opera glasses were levelled. Comment grew, swelled to a stir of surprise. The curtain had dropped for the interval between scenes; our box became for the moment the centre of interest, and the lights were high. Even the orchestra was resting.

Then it was given me to see how in a great audience Panic may leap without cause from Opportunity.

The stir grew, spread. Fascinated, I gazed down at the disturbance. I knew that a frightened smile still curved my lips. I felt my eyes glow, luminous and dilated. My heart almost stopped beating, gripped by triumph and horror. Afterwards I realised that I had not availed myself of the screen Milly offered; I hadn't lifted the fan to shield my face; I had not stirred to hide myself.

"Bob!" whispered the General. "Quick! Don't you see?"

Robert Van Dam sprang to his feet, offering, as I thought, to exchange places with me. Once more I started up, and chairs were moved to give me passage.

While again I stood under the glare of the lights, and while for the second time the movement in the box drew attention thither, somebody below half rose to look at me. Two or three—a dozen—followed. As I dropped into my seat at the back of the box, and cast the scarf again about my head, twenty, thirty people were struggling out of their chairs.

From my shelter I watched as, farther and farther away, the heads began to turn. From places where I had not been visible I heard the murmur swelling, the scuffle of people rising. I had disappeared from sight, the first to rise had dropped back into their seats as if ashamed, but others increased the uneasy tumult of low, tense sounds.

My brain worked quickly. I understood the shuddering thrill that passed over the audience. It was as if all my life I had seen such vast assemblies, and knew the laws that rule their souls. Even before it came I guessed it was coming; a voice—it was a man's—crying out:—

"What is it? Is it—fire?"

And from away across the house came the answering call—not a question this time, not hesitant, but quick and sharp:—"Fire!"

What should I do? Why was not John or Mr. Hynes there to tell me? Wild thoughts darted through my mind. Should I stand once more? Show myself? Should I cry: "It was I, only I! They were looking at me. There is no fire!"

Crazy, crazy thought! For the thing was over as soon as it began.

Those who had started the confusion and who understood its cause, began shouting:—

"Sit down! Sit down!"

From the topmost gallery a tremendous great voice came bellowing down:—

"What—*fool*—said—that?"

There was a little laugh, a hiss or two rebuked the disorder; then the baton signalled the orchestra, and the music recommenced, smoothly and in perfect time; the conductor had never turned his head. The curtain went up; the incident was closed.

I drew a long, sighing breath of relief as one, then another, then all together, as if by a single impulse, the people sat down in their places. It had been but an instant. The painted stage, the glittering court ladies, Isabella on her throne, the suppliant Colombo, were as if nothing had happened.

"First-rate orchestra," muttered Robert Van Dam.

The General turned in her chair and looked at me. She did not speak, but I could see that she was excited; it seems to me now that her eyes were very bright, and that her strong, square-chinned face looked curiously satisfied.

"Let's go," I gasped; "I want to go home."

Choking with sobs, though not unhappy, I felt as if I wished to run, to fly; but, as I tottered out of the box, I could scarcely stand. Mr. Van Dam helped me, the General and Milly following. In the corridor we were joined by Peggy and the florid young man whom I had seen with her.

"Why—why, you're not going? You are not going?" Peggy cried. She breathed quickly, and her teeth and eyes alike seemed to twinkle. "Can—can't Mr. Bellmer or I—do something?"

"Nothing at all," said the General in brisk staccato, fastening my wraps with an air of proprietorship; "nobody's in voice tonight, do you think? Miss Winship doesn't care to stay."

Before we reached the lobby, John came from somewhere, hurrying towards us. I was walking between Mr. Bellmer and Robert Van Dam, but with scarcely a look at them he tucked my hand under his arm, just as he would have done in the old days at the State University. At the door Mr. Van Dam looked for a cab.

"I'll take her home," said John grimly.

"I'll go with you; I must see her safe with Mrs. Baker," the General replied, understanding at once. "Mr. Bellmer, tell Mother, please, that Bob and I have gone with Miss Winship. Or—Bob, you won't be needed; you explain to Mother."

The two men hurried away upon their errand, though I fancied they went reluctantly. Peggy had not come down.

All the way home John's brows were black, and he looked straight ahead of him. As we passed under the glow of electric lamps, Milly smiled bravely at me across the carriage, respect and awe mingling with her sympathy. The General sat at my side erect; her eyes glittered, and she looked oddly pleased—not like a woman who had been at the focus of a scene, and had been dragged away from the Opera before it was over, but like a General indeed, planning great campaigns.

As for me, I felt that I must laugh—cry. Did ever such a ridiculous thing, such a wonderful, glorious thing, such a perfectly awful thing, happen to any other girl that ever lived?

I was living the scene again—seeing the mass of heads, the sea of upturned faces. Again I was gazing into the one face that had been distinct, the eyes that had drawn mine in all that blur and confusion, that had looked back at me, as if in answer to my voiceless call for help, with strength and good cheer. Even in the moment of my utmost terror, I had been sustained by that message from Ned Hynes. How did I chance to see him just at that crisis, when I didn't know of his presence? And why didn't he come to us afterwards, as John did?

Mrs. Baker and Ethel saw us leave the box, and were at home with Uncle almost as soon as we.

"Are you safe, Nelly?" Aunt cried, rushing at me; then, with the sharpness of tense nerves, she rebuked the Judge: "Ba-ake, you hissed her!"

"Nay, my dear; in the interests of music, I frowned upon disorder." He added, with waving of his antennae eyebrows: "It was Helen's first opera."

We all laughed hysterically, and then Mrs. Van Dam and John went away.

Could—*could* Mr. Hynes have gone to the Opera just because he had heard that I would be there?

5

A Plague of Reporters

Saturday evening, Jan. 18.

Since Monday I have left the house but once. The Judge has given me a microscope so that I may study at home instead of going to Barnard; and to please him I make a pretence of cutting sections from the plants in Aunt's conservatory; but oh, it's so dull, so dull! Or would be but for my happy thoughts. It isn't interest in apical cell or primary meristem that makes me fret to return to Prof. Darmstetter!

It's all on account of reporters that I am shut up like a state secret or a crown jewel. From daylight until dark, men with pencils and notebooks, cardboard-bearing artists and people with hand cameras have watched the house; and it's so tiresome.

The siege had already begun when Mrs. Baker came to my room the morning after the Opera, but I knew nothing about it. I couldn't understand why she scolded with such vehemence upon finding me writing in this little book instead of lying in bed; why she exclaimed so nervously over my escape and the horrors of jumping from windows, or sliding down ropes, or of being hurried along in fire panics until I was crushed to death.

"Why, you talk as if there had *been* a fire," I cried, kissing her.

Millions of fires have flamed and roared and sunk and died again; but never before has there been a Me!

The dear fussy little woman said that John had been telephoning inquiries. I could see that she wished to keep me in my room, and finally, at some laboured excuse for withholding the morning papers, I understood that she and John were hiding something; she is so transparent!

"You must be calm, Nelly, dear; you mustn't excite yourself," she chirped anxiously.

"Unless I see the papers, I shall have a fever, a high fever," I threatened; "I must—oh, I must see every word about last evening!"

At last the *Record* and the *Messenger* came upstairs already opened to the critiques of the new opera. Mrs. Baker wished to read aloud, but I almost snatched the papers from her; my eyes couldn't go fast enough down the columns. But in neither sheet did I find more than a reference to a "senseless alarm" that marred the rendition of "Christofero."

My cheeks flamed with annoyance. It was the reporters who were senseless; they had seen men adoring the wonder of this century, and had not flashed news of it—of me—to all the world!

Aunt couldn't understand. She thought to comfort me by saying that my share in the disturbance would never be suspected; she unblushingly averred that no one had seen me; she begged me to rest, to forget my fright, not to be distressed by the newspapers.

Distressed? Not I! Events had been too startling for me to heed the stupidity that whined over missing a few bars of a silly overture when *I* was in sight. Indeed I had been frightened; yet why should not the world demand to look upon me? I thought only of hurrying to Prof. Darmstetter that he might share my triumph. But Aunt wouldn't hear of my leaving the house; scarcely of my coming down stairs. Fluttering into my room she would bring me some fruit, a novel; then she would trot away again with an air of preoccupation.

I was getting out of patience at all this mystery, when, during one of her brief absences, Ethel tapped at my door, and a minute later Kitty Reid dashed at me, while in the doorway appeared Cadge, scratching with one hand in a black bag.

"Oh, Helen, Helen," cried Kitty, laughing and half crying, "*have* you seen Cadge's exclusive?"

"Cadge! You were there? Cadge!"

"Sure," said that strange creature, her keen eyes glancing about my room; "you don't deserve half I've done for you—not letting me know beforehand—."

"Or me!" Kitty broke in. "Oh, I've have given a—a tube of chrome yellow to see you!"

"—but we've made the Row look like nineteen cents in a country where they don't use money. See you've got the fossils." Cadge nodded towards the papers I had been reading. "But the *Star's* worth the whole— now where the mischief—"

"Cadge! Show me!"

From the black bag she drew several sheets of paper, upon each of which was pasted a cutting from a newspaper, with pencilled notes in the margin; a handkerchief, a bunch of keys, six pointed pencils, a pen-knife, a purse, rather lean, a photograph of two kittens.

"There," she said, relieved at sight of these, "knew I couldn't have lost 'em. Brooklyn woman left 'em $5,000 in her will. They'll stand me in a good little old half column. Now—where—ah, here you are!"

She unfolded a *Star* clipping and proudly spread it upon my knee.

"There, Princess! That's the real thing!"

I caught my breath at the staring headlines.

BEAUTY OF A WOMAN THREATENS A PANIC AT THE OPERA HOUSE

—

PRESENCE OF MISS HELEN WINSHIP CREATES SENSATION THAT MIGHT HAVE RESULTED IN A PERILOUS STAMPEDE

—

Alarm of Fire During the
Third Scene of "Christofero Colombo"

—

GREAT AUDIENCE AT THE METROPOLITAN ENDANGERED BY FRENZY OVER REMARKABLY LOVELY GIRL

"Hot stuff, ain't it?" said Cadge, beaming with satisfaction. "I never like that Opera assignment—dresses and society, second fiddle to the music man—but I wouldn't have missed last night! Minute I saw you in the Van Dam box I knew there'd be the biggest circus I ever—why—why, Helen—"

The horror of it—the pitiful vulgarity! My father, the University folks

—all the world would know that I had been made notorious by a—that I —oh, the tingling joy, the rapture—that I was the loveliest of women!

"Cadge! Oh, Cadge!"

I threw myself into her arms.

"Why, Helen, what's this? Can't stand for the headlines? Built in the office and I know they're rather—"

"They're *quite*" interrupted Kitty. "Of course the Princess wouldn't expect a first page scare. But cheer up, child; there's worse to come."

The girls were soothing me and fussing over me when Aunt Frank opened the door. At her surprised look I brushed away my tears of joy. I understood everything now—her uneasiness, the long telephonic conferences, my confinement to the house.

"Aunt," I managed to say, "here is Kitty come to condole with me and congratulate me; and this is my friend, Miss Bryant of the *Star*. You remember? She was here at the tea."

"A reporter!"

"Oh, I had to know! Don't worry. Cadge, dear, did nobody but you see me?"

"The fossils never have anything they can't clip," said Cadge in the tone of absorption that her work always commands. "I'm surprised myself at the *Echo*, though it did notice that a 'Miss Winslow' fainted in the Van Dam box. But haven't you had reporters here—regiments? Expected to find you ordering Gatlings for the siege."

"We're bombarded!" said Aunt. "With—er—"

"Rapid fire questions," suggested Ethel.

"—but the servants have their orders. Of course," Aunt added uneasily, "we're glad to see any friend of Nelly's."

"Oh, by the way, I'm interviewing you," Cadge announced; *Star* wants to follow up its beat. You haven't talked?"

"Why, no; but—do I have to be interviewed?"

Just at first the idea was a shock, I must confess.

"Do you *have* to be interviewed? Wish all interviewees were as meek. Why, of course, Helen, you'll want to make a statement. I 'phoned the *Star* photographer to meet me here, but he's failed to connect. However, Kitty can sketch—"

"Oh, Miss Bryant!" wailed Aunt. "An interview! How frightful! Can't you let her off?"

"Why, I don't exactly see how—though I might—" Cadge deliberated, studying Aunt's face rather than mine, "—might wait and see the red extras. I know how she feels, Mrs. Baker—they're always that way, at first —and I'm anxious to spare her, but—I can't let the *Star* be beaten. If I were you—"

She turned to me, hesitated a moment, then burst out impulsively, "If I were you, I wouldn't say a word! Not—one—blessed—word! I'd pique curiosity. There! That *is* treason! Why, I'd give my eye teeth, 'most, for a nice signed statement. But I'll wait—that is, if you really, honest-Injun, prefer."

"You're very kind," said Aunt Frank, with a sigh of bewildered relief. "We'd give anything, of course—*anything!*—to avoid—"

"Mind," Cadge admonished me as she rose to go. "I'm running big risks, letting you off; the office relied on me. If you do talk to anybody else, or even see anybody, you'll let me know, quick? And if you don't want to give up, look out for a little fat girl with blue eyes and a baby stare; she'll be here sure, crying for pictures; generally gets 'em, first time, too. Snuffles and dabs her eyes and says: 'If I go back without any photograph, I'll lose my j-o-o-o-b! Wa-a-a-h! Wa-a-a-h! until you do anything to get rid of her. Ought to be on the stage; tears in her voice. I wouldn't do stunts like that, if I never—you will look out, won't you?"

Aunt is so funny, not to have guessed who wrote the *Star* article. But she never saw it. Her precautions had all been taken at John's officious suggestion over the telephone. Busybody! An interview is nothing so terrible. The world has a right to know about me; and I don't suppose Aunt had an idea how grievously Cadge was disappointed.

No sooner had Cadge left us than Mr. Bellmer, pink and stammering in my presence, and after him the General, called to inquire for me.

It was wonderful to see the change in the strong, self-confident girl's manner. She beamed at my appearance, and her every word was caressing and deferential. The night before had had a magical effect. I was no longer "Diane," the ingenue whom she patronized as well as admired. I was a powerful woman, a great lady.

"Did our Princess enjoy waking this morning to find herself famous?" she asked, echoing Milly's word for me; and then, to Mrs. Baker's horror, she, too, had a tale to tell about reporters; they had been besetting her for information about her companion of the Opera.

"But I never see people of that sort, you know," she said, with an accent that piqued me, though I couldn't help feeling glad that Cadge had gone.

She showered me with messages from Mrs. Marmaduke Van Dam and from Peggy and Mrs. Henry. She had a dozen plans for my entertainment, but Mrs. Baker opposed a flurried negative:—

"We'll run no more risks like last night's; Nelly must stay at home—till folks get used to her."

"Then I can never go anywhere; never!" I cried in despair, yet laughing. It's impossible sometimes not to laugh at Aunt. But Mrs. Van Dam gave me a look that promised many things.

"You won't be left in hiding after such a début; you'll electrify society!" she said; and when she had gone, I wore away the day wondering what she meant, until I could send for the afternoon papers.

I laughed until I cried when they came, and cried until I laughed. The red extras reviewed the occurrence at the Opera from Alpha to Omega, publishing "statements" from ushers who had shown us to our box; from people in the audience and from the cab man who drove us home. And they supplemented their accounts with pen and ink sketches of "Miss Helen Winship at the Opera," evolved from the fallible inner consciousness of "hurry-up artists."

When Uncle came home, he found me reading an interview with him which contained the momentous information that he would say nothing.

"We shall not again forget," he said with a deep sigh of relief, "that

—the face that launched a thousand ships
And burned the topless towers of Ilion

—was Helen's. But the Metropolitan still stands. An argument not used on heart-hardened Pharaoh was a plague of press representatives."

I'm afraid he'd had a trying day.

The worst of my day was still to come.

After dinner, when I happened to be alone a minute in the library, Mr. Hynes came in. Oddly enough I'd been thinking about him. I had determined that the next time he called I would for once be self-possessed; I would act as if I had not seen how oddly he conducts himself—now gazing at me as if he would travel round the earth to feast his eyes upon my beauty and now actually shunning Milly's cousin. I was quite resolved to begin afresh and treat him just as cordially as I would any other man:

But the moment he appeared away flew all my wits.

"I think Milly'll be here in a minute," I stammered, and then I stopped, tongue-tied and blushing.

He came towards me, saying abruptly: "May I tell you what I thought when I saw you above us—" I didn't need to ask when or where. "—I thought: The Queen has come to her coronation."

One's own stupid self is so perverse! Of course I meant to thank him for his silent help the night before, but I asked with a rush of nervous confusion:—

"You—were you there?"

I could have suffered torture sooner than own that I had seen him.

"Were you there, Ned?" repeated Milly, blundering into the room. "Why, we didn't see you."

Of all vexatious interruptions! Behind her came John and most of the family.

"The servant of The Presence would fain know if The Presence is well," John said, coming quickly to my side and peering down at me with a dark, worn look upon his face, as if he hadn't slept, and a catch in his voice that irritated me, in spite of his playful words. I knew well enough that his anxiety had been on my account, but it was so unnecessary!

"The child bears up wonderfully," cried my Aunt, before I could answer; "but tomorrow'll tell the story; tomorrow she'll feel the strain."

Then they all broke out talking at once. John drew a big chair for me to the fire, and there was such an ado, adjusting lights and fending me with screens.

"You *are* well?" John asked, obstinately planting himself between me and the others.

"Perfectly. How absurd you are!"

It was so ridiculous that I should be coddled after the triumph of my life, as if something awful had happened to me.

I had felt annoyed all day, so far as anything can now annoy me, by John's too solicitous guardianship, and it vexed me anew when he began to pile up cautions against this and against that—to warn me against going out alone upon the street, and to urge care even in my intercourse with Cadge. He is quicker than my Aunt; he divined the source of the *Star* article, and he almost forbade me to cleave to such an indiscreet friend.

"Oh, last night won't happen again," I said carelessly; "and you don't know Cadge; she's as good as the wheat."

I wasn't listening to him. I was twisting his ring impatiently on my finger and watching in the play of the fire a vision of the great Opera House, the lights, the jewels, the perfumes, the white, wondering faces.

"Can't you see, Nelly," replied John, with irritation, "that this Bryant woman's article practically accuses you of risking lives to gratify a whim of vanity?"

"Why, John Burke, how can you say such a thing?" exclaimed Aunt Frank, overhearing his words and as usual answering only the last half dozen. "Risking lives! Poor Nelly!"

"I didn't say it," John patiently explained; "but other people—"

"Nobody else will talk about Nelly's vanity. Why, she hasn't a particle. As for the papers, I won't have one in the house—"

"Except the *Evening Post*?" suggested Aunt Marcia.

"Which Cadge says isn't a newspaper," I contributed.

"—so we needn't care what they say."

I was ready to laugh at John's discomfiture, but the possible truth of his words struck me, and I cried out:

"People won't really believe I did it on purpose, whatever the papers say—that I went there just to be looked at! Oh, that would be horrible! Horrible!"

"Of course not," John said with curt inconsistency to bring me comfort; but I had a reply more sincere—a fleeting glance only, but it said: "The Queen can do no wrong."

"Oh, I hope you are right; I hope no one thought that," I said confusedly in answer to the glance. And then I bent over the Caesar that Boy laid upon my lap, while Uncle asked:—

"Well, my son, is there mutiny again in the camp of our Great and Good Friend, Divitiacus the Aeduan?"

A few minutes later John said goodnight with a ludicrous expression of pained, absentminded patience. I didn't go to the door with him; I scarcely looked up from Boy's ablative absolutes.

Oh I treated him shabbily. And yet—why did he use every effort that day to keep me ignorant of my own rightful affairs, only to come at me himself with a club, gibbering of newspapers?

Why, John's absurd! He would have liked to find me—not ill, of course, but overcome by the Opera experience, dependent on him, ready to be shielded, hidden, petted, comforted. He can not see me as I am—a strong, splendid woman, ready to accept the responsibilities of my beauty.

6

Love Is Nothing!

Monday, Jan. 20.

Dear me! Beauty is a responsibility! Such troubles, such trials about nothing! It's photographs this time!

Last Wednesday—the day after the papers published so much about me—a strange man called in Mrs. Baker's absence and begged me to let him take my photograph—as a service to Art. If Aunt had been at home I wouldn't have been permitted to see him. But the man was pleasant and gentlemanly, and so sincere in his admiration that he won the way to my heart. I'm afraid devotion is still so new to me that it's the surest road to my good graces. He hesitated and stammered, blinking before my shining loveliness as if blinded, as he offered to take the pictures for nothing, if he might exhibit them afterwards; and at last I went to his studio, though I said that his work must be for me only, and that I must pay for it.

I wonder at myself for yielding, for I didn't mean to have any photographs until the experiment was quite finished—to mortify me in future with their record of imperfection; but I'm so nearly perfect now that, really, it's time I had something to tell me how I do look. Of course, as fast as I can lay hands on them, I'm destroying every likeness of the old Nelly. At the studio it was such a revelation—the care and intelligence the man displayed, the skill of the posing—that when I got home full of the subject and found Cadge waiting, I had to tell her all about it.

"H'm!" she said after I had finished; "what sort of looking chap?"

When I had described him, she sat silent at least a third of a minute, establishing for herself a new record. Then she said:—

"Princess, I'll have to take back every word I said yesterday about letting you off from being interviewed. I agreed to wait, but it's up to you. Every rag in town'll have some kind of feature about you next Sunday, and you wouldn't ask me to see the *Star* beaten? You'd better come right now to the *Star* photographer, or—see last night's papers?—you'll wish you'd never been born. I tell you the situation's out of my control."

"Well, come on then, before Aunt Frank gets back."

So we started out again. The sun and air made me so drunken with pure joy of living that I didn't mind the scolding sure to follow—though it certainly has proved an annoyance ever since to have Aunt's fidgetty over-sight of me redoubled, and to be shut up, as I have been, closer than ever, like a Princess in a fairy book, just as my splendid triumphs were beginning.

Worst of all, almost, Mrs. Baker told the tale of my misdeeds to John.

"Why, Helen," he said at once, "no photographer of standing goes about soliciting patronage; the man who came here wants pictures of you to sell."

"Like the great ladies' photographs in England?" I asked flippantly, though I was really a little disturbed.

"Just what I told her!" groaned Aunt Frank. "Bake must see the man; or —Mr. Burke, why can't you find out about him? Perhaps it's all right," she added weakly; "from her accounts he didn't flatter Nelly one bit; simply raved over her."

"Yes, I'll run in and converse with the art lover," John grimly agreed; but just then in came Milly with the General, and the subject was changed.

Indeed, though I don't know just how she managed it, from the moment the brilliant woman of the world entered the room, poor clumsy John was made to seem clumsier than ever, and before long, without quite knowing why, he went away. I'm pretty sure that Mrs. Van Dam dislikes to see us together.

John was wrong and yet not wrong about the photographer; his threat-ened interposition came to nothing, for the very next morning—only yesterday, long ago as it seems—I was enlightened as to the cheap and silly trick that had been played upon me.

"Thee, Cothin Nelly; pwetty, pwetty!" cried Joy, running towards me and holding up a huge poster picture from the Sunday *Echo*.

"Isn't it—why—give it to me!" I almost snatched the sheet from her baby hands.

My portrait! I knew it in spite of crude colour and cheap paper. It was my portrait, and it was labelled:

"HELEN WINSHIP, MOST BEAUTIFUL WOMAN IN THE WORLD. POSED BY MISS WINSHIP ESPECIALLY FOR—"

And then—the insolence of the man!—there followed the name of the bashful stranger whose devotion to Art had drawn him to my door! The fellow had practised upon my credulity to obtain my likeness for publication.

Never before had I realised what a great thing a newspaper is!

I threw down the sheet, quivering with anger. I felt that I should never again dare look at a paper; but half an hour later I sent Boy out to buy them all, and, locked into my room, I shook all about me a snowstorm of bulky supplements and magazines.

Having posed for Cadge, I knew, of course, that the *Star* would print my picture, perhaps several of them. But at any other time I should have been overcome to find a "special section" of four pages filled with halftone likenesses of me, cemented together by an essay on "Beauty," signed by a novelist of repute, and by articles from painters, sculptors, dressmakers and gymnasts, all from their respective standpoints extolling my perfections. Cadge had written an interview headed "How It Feels to be Beautiful."

But the *Echo!* Besides the poster which Joy had shown me, it published two pages of portraits framed in medallion miniatures of celebrated beauties with whom it compared me, making me surpass the loveliest women of history and legend, from Helen of Troy to the reigning music hall performer. And, with a shock of surprise, I not only saw in the pictures the dress I had worn and the theatrical things the deferential artist had loaned me to pose in, but in the article appeared every word I had said to him; and the skill with which fact, fiction, clever conjecture and picturesque description had been stirred into the sweetened batter that Cadge calls a "first-rate delirious yellow style" was maddening.

This is the beginning of the stuff:—

Chapter 1
A Prairie Bud

So fair that, had you Beauty's picture took,
It must like her or not like Beauty look.

—ALEYN'S HENRY VII

A Western Wild Rose!

As sweet! As perfect!

By all who have seen her, Helen Winship is pronounced the most beautiful of women.

Last Monday night, at the Opera House, a great audience paid her such spontaneous tribute as never before was offered human being.

At the sight of a young girl, trembling and blushing, staid citizens were lifted to their feet by an irresistible wave of enthusiasm.

Not for anything this girl has done, though Science will hear from her; not for her voice, though no nightingale sings so melodiously; but for a face more glorious than that other Helen's, "Whose beauty summoned Greece to arms and drew a thousand ships to Tenedos."

This modern Helen is a niece of Judge Timothy Baker, at whose residence, No. — East Seventy-second Street, she is staying.

The Judge and his family are reticent concerning their lovely guest, of whom the *Echo* presents the first authentic picture.

Miss Winship cannot be described.

Artists say that by their stern canons she is a perfect woman. Her beauty is that of flawless health and a hitherto unknown physical perfection.

She is cast in Goddess mould. The loose, flowing robe of her daily wear is of classic grace and dignity.

Tall as the Venus of Milo, she incarnates that noble figure with a lightness and a purity virginal and modern.

She is neither blonde nor brunette; of a type essentially American, she has glorious eyes and for her smile a man would lose his head.

It is a fact for students of heredity and environment to consider that Miss Winship is not a product of the cities. Jasper M. Winship, her father, is a bonanza farmer. Mrs. Winship was in her youth the belle of prairie dances, and still has remarkable beauty.

Born of pioneer stock, baby Helen was reared to a life of freedom; learning what she knew of grandeur from the sky and of luxury from the lap of Mother Earth. Child of the sunshine and sweet air, she danced with the butterflies, as innocent as they of cramping clothing that would distort her body, or of city conventionalities that might warp her mind.

Year by year she grew, a brown-faced cherub, strong-limbed and supple. Springtime after springtime her marvellous beauty budded, unnoted save by the passing traveller, who put aside the bright, wind-blown hair to gaze long into her fathomless eyes.

Roystering farmhands checked their drunken songs at the little maid's approach, but no wild thing feared her. Birds and squirrels came at her call and fed from her hand.

And so it went. Chapters **II** and **III** described with brilliant inaccuracy my University life and made me a piquant mixture of devotee of science and favourite of fashion. Ah, well, it was all as accurate as Pa's name or Mother's beauty or her love of dancing—she thinks it's as wicked as playing cards.

Before I had read half the papers, between dread of Father and John and the absurdity of it all, I was in a gale of tears and laughter. More than once Milly crept to the door, or I heard in the hall the uneven step of lame little Ethel. But I wouldn't open. I was swept by a passion of—

Not grief, not anger, not concern, not fear of anything on earth; but—Joy!

Joy in my beauty, about which a million men and women had that morning read for the first time! Joy in the fame of my beauty which should last forever! Joy in my full and rapturous life!

What did I care for the spelling of a name or the bald prose about my college course? What concern was it of mine how my photographs had been obtained? Trifles; trifles all! Here were the essential facts set broadly forth, speeding to every part of the country—why, to every part of the world! Cadge or Pros. Reid now—anyone who knows how such things are done—might note the hours as they passed, and say: "Now two millions have seen her beauty, have read of her; now three; now five; now ten millions."

And the story would spread! In ever widening circles, men warned by telegraph of the new wonder would tear open the damp sheets; and pen and pencil and printing press would hurry to reproduce those marvellous lines—tomorrow in Philadelphia, Boston, Baltimore, Montreal; next day in Chicago, St. Louis, Atlanta; and so on to Denver, Galveston and the Golden Gate.

The picture—*mine;—my picture!*—would be spread on tables in the low cabins of pilot boats and fishing smacks; it would be nailed to the log walls of Klondike mining huts; soldiers in the steaming trenches around Manila would pass the torn sheets from hand to hand, and for a moment forget their sweethearts while they read of me.

And the ships! The swiftest of them all would carry these pages to London, Paris, Vienna, there to be multiplied a thousand fold and sent out again in many tongues. Blue-eyed Gretchen, Giuseppina, with her bare locks and rainbow-barred apron, slant-eyed O Mimosa San, all in good time would dream over the fair face on the heralding page; women shut in the zenanas of the unchanging East would gossip from housetop to housetop of the wonderful Feringhe beauty; whipped slaves in midmost Africa would carry my picture in their packs into regions where white men have never trod, and dying whalers in the far North would look at my face and forget for a little while their dooming ice floes.

The wealth of all the earth was at my command. Railroad train and ocean grayhound, stage and pony cart, spurring horseman and naked brown runner sweating through jungle paths under his mail bags, would bear the news of me East and West, until they met in the antipodes and put a girdle of my loveliness right round the world!

Never before had I realised what a great thing a newspaper is!

My heart was beating with a terrible joy. And so—prosaic detail—I threw the papers down in a heap on the floor, combed my hair in a great loose knot, put a rose at my belt, and went down to smile at my Aunt's anxieties. I even went with my cousins to supper with Aunt Marcia. And in the early evening Mr. Hynes came to walk with us home. I knew his step, and my heart jumped with fright. What would he, so fastidious as he was, think of that poster?

But his look leaped to mine as he entered, and I—oh, it seemed as if there had never been such a night; never the snow, the delight of the cold and dark and the far, wise stars! I couldn't tell what joy elf possessed me as we walked homeward. I wanted to run like a child. Yet I couldn't bear to reach the house.

"Why, Helen," said Ethel; "you're not wearing your veil."

"Will the reporters git me ef I don't—watch—out?" I laughed. How could I muffle myself like a grandmother?

"We'll keep away the goblins," he said; and—it's a little thing to write down—he walked beside me instead of Milly. We would pass through the shadows of the trees, and then under the glare of an electric lamp, and then again into blackness; and I felt in his quickened breath an instant response to my mood; as if newspapers had never existed, and we were playing at goblins.

I hope he didn't think me childish.

Of course John had come before we reached home, and of course he had been all day fuming over the papers, as if that would do any good; but I had drunk too deep of the intoxicating air to be disturbed by his surprised look when Mr. Hynes and I entered the library; can't I go without his guarding even to Aunt Marcia's?

I like the library—bookshelves, not too high, all about it, and the glow of the open fire and the smiling faces. Sometimes I grow impatient of Aunt's fussy kindness, and of the slavish worship of limp and characterless Milly and Ethel; but last night I was glad to be walled about with cousins, barricaded from the big, curious world. I could have hugged Boy, who lay curled on the hearth, deep in the adventures of Mowgli and the Wolf Brethren. I did hug little Joy, who climbed into my lap, lisping, as she does every night: "Thing, Cothin Nelly."

I looked shyly at Mr. Hynes, who had stooped to pat the cat that purred against his leg, muttering something about a "fine animal." I knew

—I begin to understand him so well—just how he felt the charm of everything.

"Thing," Joy insisted, putting up a baby hand until it touched my cheek and twined itself in my hair, "Thing, Cothin Nelly." And I crooned while breathlessly all in the room listened:—

> *"Sweet and low, sweet and low,*
> *Wind of the Western sea—*

"He'll be a bad man, won't he, Joy," I broke off, as John came to my corner, "if he scolds a poor girl who has had to stand on the floor all day for the scholars to look at, and get no good mark on her deportment card?"

"I am no longer a schoolmaster, Nelly," said John so icily that Aunt looked up at him, surprised. "Come, Joy," she said, "Cousin Nelly can't be troubled with a great big girl. Why, Mr. Burke, she's cried herself ill, fairly, over those dreadful newspapers. I do so hope they'll leave her in peace now. But of course we tell her it's all meant as a tribute."

> *"Over the rolling waters go,*
> *Come from the dying moon and blow—*
> *Blow him again to me,*
> *While my little Joy, while my pretty Joy sleeps."*

"Thing more about your little Joy! More about me."

The sleepy child cuddled closer and, as I continued to sing, I knew that at least one person in the room understood that a creature so blessed as I could never cry herself ill.

> *"Father will come to his babe in the nest,*
> *Silver sails all out of the West—"*

"Milly and I have tributes, too," laughed Ethel. "The *Trumpet* says we're just as charming girls as our wonderful cousin. And the *Record* prints snapshots at Joy and her nursemaid. Aren't newspapers funny?"

"Someone of us should be running for office," said Uncle Timothy. "It seems gratuitous to subject an unambitious private family to the treatment expected by a candidate or a multimillionaire. Yet I have seldom had occasion to complain of the press. In its own perhaps headlong manner, it pursues such matters as are of greatest public importance. A household, to avoid its attentions, should be provided with good, plain, durable countenances. The difficulty with this family is its excess of attraction."

He patted Aunt's hand affectionately, while I sang:—

> "—*Under the silver moon*
> *Sleep, my little Joy, sleep, my pretty Joy, sleep*—"

"—but, Uncle, what shall I do?"

"Nothing. In a shorter time than now seems possible, another topic will supersede you. Then, as one of our Presidents has aptly said, you will sink into 'innocuous desuetude.'"

But of course I sha'n't!

As I rose to carry Joy to her bed, I felt from all in the room a look that said I was like a great, glorious Madonna, and I bent lower over the sleeping child's still face; it is good to have everybody admire me.

Oh, I do wish John were more reasonable. Not satisfied with seeing me Saturday and yesterday, he came again today and asked me to marry him at once. He's so ridiculous!

"Perhaps I'm selfish to wish to mould your brilliant life to my plodding one," he said wistfully, as if he were reading my thoughts. "But I don't mean to be selfish. I love you—and—you're drifting away from me."

"What a goose you are, John!" I said, laughing impatiently. "I'm just the same that I always was; the trouble is, I'm not a bit sentimental."

John *is* selfish. He'd hide me somewhere outside the city, he'd bury alive the most lovely of women. He prosed to me about a "home"; as if I could now endure a Darby and Joan existence!

Tonight his ring distracts—torments me. I pull it off and put it back and it galls my finger, as if it rubbed a wound. I used to go to sleep with it against my lips—I love the opal, gem of the beautiful women. I wonder if it's really unlucky.

I suppose John's talk today annoyed me because I'm in such a restless mood—waiting for the barriers to fall, for the glorious life ahead of me to open. How could he expect me to feel as in the days when we were boy and girl, when we dreamed foolish dreams about each other, and were romantic, and young? I have changed since then, I have a thousand things to think about in which he doesn't sympathize; if I answered his words at random it was because I couldn't fix my mind upon them. I drew a long breath when he left me—when I escaped the tender, perplexed question of his eyes.

It's true; I'm not a bit sentimental. I used to think I was, but now I feel sure that I could never love anyone as John loves me.

But I mustn't drift away from him. I remember so many things that tie us together, here in this strange, stormy city. What happy times we used to have! He'll understand better by and by, and be less exacting.

But I can't marry; I must be free to enjoy the victories of my beauty; I told him at Christmas that I can't marry for a long, long time.

7

Love Is All!

Thursday, Jan. 30.

I 've been trying to read, but I can't. Pale heroines in books are so dull! Last night came the Van Dams' dance and my triumph—and a greater triumph still; for today I have a wonderful, beautiful chapter to add to my own book, to the story of the only woman whose life is worth while.

I see the vista of my future, and—ah, little book, my eyes are dazzled! A rich woman would be a beggar, a clever woman a fool, an empress would leave her throne to exchange with me. Nothing, nothing is impossible to the most beautiful woman that ever lived, whose life is crowned by love. Love is all; all! In a palace without Ned I'd weep myself blind; with him a desert would be Eden. Love is all!

That blessed dance!

The General invited me ten days ago, the afternoon when—when John Burke— poor John!—scolded me about the photographs.

"Just a 'small and early,'" she said, broaching her errand as soon as she had fairly driven John off the field—there was just the faintest suggestion of relief in her tone—"Peggy's mother's giving it—Mrs. Henry Van Dam."

She looked at Aunt with an assurance as calm as if there were no interdict upon social experiments.

"Impossible!" gasped Aunt, glancing despairingly in the direction in which her ally had disappeared. "Why, Nelly doesn't leave the house; I've stopped her attendance even at Barnard."

"And quite right; but a private house isn't a big school, nor yet the Opera. Of course you say yes, don't you, Helen?"

"Yes, yes! A dance! Oh, I'm going to a dance! Play for me, Milly; play for me!"

Humming a bar of a waltz, I caught Aunt Frank in my arms, and whirled her about the room until she begged for mercy.

"Oh, you dear people, I'm so happy!" I cried as I stopped, my cheeks glowing, and, falling all about me, a flood of glistening hair; while the General, whose creed is to wonder at nothing, gazed at me in delighted amazement.

"You splen—did creature!" she cried.

"I—I would like to go; Aunt Frank, you will let me?" I said meekly, as too late I realised how differently a New York girl *bien élevée* would have received the invitation. But, indeed, my heart jumped with rapture.

Without John, Mrs. Baker really didn't know how to refuse me.

"But—but—but—" she stammered.

"Surround her with a bodyguard, if you like," said the General. "You'll have Judge Baker and Hynes, of course; and that—what's the name of that shy young man who's just gone? He looks presentable."

"But—but—" protested Aunt; "Bake'd never go; and—Nelly—has—do you suppose Mr. Burke has evening clothes?"

"Naturally," I said with nonchalance, though my quick temper was fired. I was as sure he hadn't as I was that Mrs. Van Dam knew his name, and that he would oppose the dance even more strongly than did Aunt; and I wished that I could go without him. But it was useless to think of this, with even the General suggesting a bodyguard. I resolved that he should at least consult a decent tailor.

"Why not have detectives as guards—as if I wore a fortune in diamonds?" I grumbled.

"Let us at least have Mr. Burke. Now, Helen, what do *you* propose to wear?" concluded the General.

Mrs. Van Dam took an extraordinary interest in my toilette. She even came to see my new evening dress fitted, and put little Mrs. Edgar into such a flutter that she prodded me with pins. I'll simply have to ask Father to increase my allowance; cheap white silk, clouded with tulle, was the best I could manage.

"H'm—Empire; simple and graceful," pronounced Oracle. "Square neck, Helen, or round?"

"Why—I've never worn a low dress—not really low," I said, longing but dubious. "Pa says—"

"Nonsense!"

"A shame!" chimed Mrs. Edgar.

And it would have been a shame to hide my neck and arms. I laughed when they cut away their interfering linings from the white column of my throat, and left across my shoulders only wisps of tulle. And last night, when I came to dress, I laughed again, and kissed the entrancing flesh, so firm and soft and gleaming faintly pink, and then I blushed because Aunt Marcia saw me do it. I worship the miracle of my own fairness. I could scarcely bear to put gloves on, even.

Miss Baker gathered all my shining hair into the loose knot that suits me, and put roses at my girdle and into the misty tulle about my shoulders. Ethel fitted on my slippers, and brought her fan and her lace handkerchief, and when I had smiled for one last time at the parted scarlet lips and the brilliant eyes that smiled back at me from the mirror, and had turned reluctantly from my dressing table, I was still joyous at remembrance of the light, the grace, the marvel of the vision I had seen reflected, that had seemed fairly to float in the dancing rose light of its own happiness.

Down in the hall the family were waiting, with John and Mr. Hynes; and, as I glided into sight on the stairway, Milly behind me, the Judge looked up at us, quoting with heavy playfulness:—

> *"She seizes hearts, not waiting for consent,*
> *Like sudden death that snatches unprepared.*

"How many conquests will satisfy you tonight, fair Princesses? Milly, will two young men answer instead of one old one?" He had been exempted from serving on my bodyguard.

"Bake! Death! How can you," sputtered Aunt. "Come, girls, the carriage is waiting."

"Wish I could dance," whispered Ethel, reaching up to touch my flowers—a pathetic little figure poised on her best foot.

"Oh, I wish you could! I wish you were going," I replied hastily, bending to kiss the little creature, the better to hide my sudden consciousness of my bared shoulders.

All in the room were looking at me as if never before had they beheld my beauty. John's strained eyes seemed to plead with me for an answering glance of affection, and I knew that Ned—though I wasn't conscious of looking at him at all—was alternately white and red as I was myself. I felt his glance so confused and passionate and withal so impetuous that, as Aunt Marcia lifted my wrap and I went down to the carriage, my heart beat violently, and I sank back into my corner in a frightful, blissful maze of fear and ecstasy.

But even then I didn't know what had happened to me.

We had but a few blocks to go, and before I had recovered, a man in livery was opening the carriage door at the mouth of a canvas tunnel which seemed to dive under a great house that towered so far above the street as to look almost narrow. We passed through the tunnel, another man opened a door almost at the street level, and we advanced into a hall extending the entire width of the house, so brilliantly lighted and so spacious that I caught my breath at thought of our errand, seeing that the size of the place and its splendour so far exceeded what I had supposed.

I clutched at Aunt's hand as if to stop her in front of the huge fire-place, where logs, crackling on tall "firedogs" of twisted iron, gave out a yellow blaze; but then quickly such a different terror and wonder and joy came again upon me that I lost consciousness of everything but Ned; and the masses of ferns and palms through which we were moving—the doll-like servants in silk stockings and knee breeches, their scarlet coats emblazoned with the monogram of the Van Dams—faded out of sight. Yet I never once glanced in his direction.

We had to go to the third floor for the dressing rooms; but in spite of those minutes of grace, when a maid had removed my wraps—she started with amazement as she did so—my cheeks were still aflame.

Mrs. Baker and Milly fussed with my dress, and Aunt became incoherent in her efforts to soothe and encourage me; for she feared the ordeal before us, and thought that I feared it also. And I was afraid, but not of meeting any person in that house, save one. I quivered at the thought that outside the door Ned was waiting, that we must go out to him, that I might even be obliged to speak to him. And yet I longed to see him again, to be with him—somewhere, away from them all.

Perhaps at last I was beginning to understand.

The General had been sent for, and I kept close to her and to Peggy, when they went down with our party to the parlours on the second floor. There, at our entrance, groups of people seemed to divide with an eager buzz that at any other time would have been ravishing music. Last night I

didn't know that I heard it, though now I remember how splendidly appar-
elled women and sombre-coated men turned their heads as we passed. Of
course word had spread that the beautiful Miss Winship was expected.

It was almost in a dream that I stood before Mrs. Henry Van Dam—a
short, heavy woman, in purple velvet, flashing with diamonds. Without a
vestige of awkwardness or timidity I answered her effusive welcome, and
the greetings of her grayish wisp of a husband, and of Mr. and Mrs.
Marmaduke Van Dam—both thin and grave; her neck cords standing out
under her diamond collar. And of little Mr. Robert Van Dam. And of Mr.
Bellmer—a pink, young, plump thing, all white waistcoat and bald head,
just as I remembered him at the Opera.

I held a reception of my own. I did it easily. After the first moments
Ned's presence excited me. I was always conscious of his nearness; I felt
that whether I talked or was silent—though I was never allowed to be that
—to whatever part of the room he went, his glowing eyes never left me.
And there came to me a thrilling confidence that he understood. He knew
that to me all these people were so much lace, so many blotches of white
complexion, so many pincushions of silk or lustrous satin stuck through
with jewels. He knew that I cared for no one of them; for nothing; not
even for my beauty, except that—thank God!—it pleasured him.

I knew that perfect beauty had come to me last night—had come
because I loved and was loved; and because Love was not the pale shadow
I had called by its name, but a rapture that was in my heart and in my face
and in the faces 'round me and in the music that swelled from the great
ballroom!

I had no idea of time, but perhaps it wasn't long before the General
manoeuvred me from the sitting-out rooms and across the hall to join the
dancers. Mrs. Baker and John were with us; Ned was not, but I knew that
he would follow.

It was a big apartment that we entered, occupying the entire end of
the second floor towards the street, perhaps thirty feet by forty and twenty
high; for an instant I was dazzled by the gleam of white and gold, the rise
of pilasters at door and window, the shimmer of soft, bright hangings and
everywhere the cheat of mirrors. I breathed delight at sight of the lovely
ceiling all luminous—no lights showed anywhere, yet the air was trans-
fused by a rosy glow. The next minute I had forgotten this in the pulse of
the music and the blur of moving figures; my favourite waltz was sounding,
and the scene was one of fairyland.

"Shall we dance?" asked John, and I came to myself in a panic. Dance with John—there? I hadn't thought of that. Of course I must, but—why, his step is abominable! It always was!

"As you please," I said with the best grace I could muster, glancing nervously up at him. He looked well in his new evening clothes, but his face was set in grim lines of endurance, and I went on with guilty haste to forestall question or reproach:—

"I hope you waltz better than you used."

"I'm afraid I don't," said he dryly.

And he didn't. I simply couldn't dance with him. He never thought about what he was doing or where he was going. I looked back despairingly at the General, grimacing involuntarily as I gathered my skirts from under his feet; and I had an odd notion that she smiled with malicious satisfaction. Could she have reckoned upon weaning me from him by a display of his awkwardness? I felt nettled at both of them.

"Helen," he said abruptly, as we laboured along the crowded floor, "do you remember our last dance—at the Commencement ball?"

The night of our betrothal! What a time to remind me of it! I had just seen Ned and Milly join the group we had left; and as they, too, began to dance, I felt a stab of pain that made me answer angrily—we were barely escaping collision with another couple:—

"If it's only at Commencement that you care to dance—"

He tightened his grip upon me almost roughly, then took me back to my Aunt without a word.

I tried to reason myself out of my pettishness, to atone to John, poor fellow! But my eyes followed Ned and Milly among the graceful, flying figures, and my feet tapped the floor impatiently until, presently, the music stopped and they came to us. Then Ned's parted lips said something, and then—as the music recommenced, I was in his arms and, almost without my own knowledge or volition, was moving around the room.

Moving, not dancing—floating in a rosy light, away and away from them all, into endless space, my hand in his, his breath on my cheek; always to go on, I felt; on and on, to the dim borderland between this earth and Heaven.

Presently his eyes told me that something was happening. The dancers had been too busily engaged to pay much heed to my first brief adventure, but in the intermission of the music I had been noticed, and now I saw that there was an open space about us. Here and there a couple stood as they had risen from their seats, while others, who had begun to dance, had come to a pause. Slender girls in clouds of gauze and fat matrons panting in satins were gazing in our direction. In the doorway were gathered people from the parlours.

"Are they looking at us? We must stop," I whispered.

"Looking at you, not us. But don't stop; not yet—Helen!"

"Helen!" He had called my name! My eyes must have shown with bliss and terror. I had an almost overmastering desire to whisper his name also, to answer the entreaty of his voice, the clasp of his fingers. But I forced myself to remember how many eyes were watching.

"I—we must stop," I said.

"Not yet; unless—we shall dance together again?"

I scarcely heard the "yes" I breathed. I shouldn't have known what I had said but for the sudden light in his eyes, the firmer pressure of his arm.

My feet didn't seem to touch the floor, as he gently constrained me when I would have ceased to dance, and kept me circling round with him until we came opposite my seat; then he put me into it as naturally as if I had been tired.

Tired! Our faces told—they must have told our story. But the others were blind—blind! John had risen as if to meet us, but if he took note at all of my flushed face, he doubtless thought me frightened.

It was exultation, not fright. I did not heed the following eyes, when, as gliding figures began to cover the floor again, John took me back to the parlours. I went with him submissively; I thought of nothing but the joy of my life, the love of my lover. I shall think of nothing else to the end of my days.

Ned went with me, confused and impulsive and ardent as John was attentive and curiously formal. But I wasn't allowed to remain with either of them. I didn't wish to do so. I was glad that people crowded about me —men in black coats all alike, whose talk was as monotonous as their broad expanses of shirt front or their cat's eye finger rings. But I tried to listen and answer that I might hide from John my tumult.

Before long I danced again—this time with some black coat; then with another and another and another; and, at last, once more with Ned.

We scarcely spoke, but he did not hide from me the fervour of his look, nor I from him the wild joy of mine. There was no need of words when all was understood, but as he put his arm around me, the tinkling music receded until I could hardly hear it, the figures about us grew indistinct— and in all the world there were left only he and I.

"Once there was another Helen," he said. His voice caressed my name.

"There have been many; which Helen?"

I so loved the word as he had spoken it that I must repeat it after him.

"*The* Helen; there was never another—until you. She was terrible as an army with banners; fair as the sea or the sunset. Men fought for her; died for her. She had hair that meshed hearts and eyes that smote. Sometimes I think—do you believe in soul transmigration?"

My heart beat until it choked me. Some voice far in the depths of my soul warned me that I must check him—we must wait until I—he—Milly—

"Sometimes; who does not? But Prof. Darmstetter would say that it was nonsense," I whispered, and waited without power to say another word.

"It is true; Helen is alive again, and all men worship her."

His eyes were so tenderly regardful that—I could not help it. Once more I raised mine and we read each other's souls. And the music seized us and swept us away with its rapture and its mystery.

The rest of the evening comes to me like a dream, through which I floated in the breath of flowers and the far murmur of unheeded talk. I saw little, heard little, yet was faintly conscious that I was the lodestar of all glances and exulting in my triumph. It was marvellous!

I didn't dance much. People don't at New York balls. But whether I danced or talked with tiresome men, my heart beat violently because he would see the admiration I won—he would know that I, who was Helen, a Queen to these others, lived only for him, was his slave.

There was supper, served at an endless number of little tables; there was a cotillon which I danced with Mr. Bellmer. John stayed in the parlours with Aunt, and Ned danced with Milly, but I was not jealous.

Jealous of Milly, with her thin shoulders rising out of her white dress, her colourless eyes and her dull hair dressed like mine with roses? Jealous, when his glance ever sought me; when, as often as we approached in a figure, if I spoke, his eyes answered; if I turned away my face, his grew heavy with pain?

Once in the dance I gave a hand to each of them. His burned like my own; hers was cold.

"Tired, Milly?" I asked, and indeed I meant kindly.

"No," she said sulkily, turning to the next dancer.

I couldn't even pity her, I was so happy.

I couldn't bear to have the beautiful evening end, and yet I was glad to go home—to be alone.

When John lifted me from the carriage, his clasp almost crushed my hand; poor John, how he will feel the blow! I didn't wait to say goodnight to Aunt; I didn't look at Milly, but ran away to my room.

Oh, indeed, the child doesn't love him! Milly knows no more about Love than I did two months ago. She's bloodless, cold; I do not wrong her. Some day she will learn what Love is, as I have learned, and will thank me for saving her from a great mistake. I hope she will!

I have saved myself from the error of my life. I'm not the same woman I was yesterday. It makes me blush to think how I looked forward to the adulation of the nobodies at that dance. I care for no praise but his. Why, I'll go in rags, I'll work, slave—I'll hide myself from every eye but his, if that will make him love me better. Or I will be Empress of beautiful women, if that is his pleasure, and give him all an Empress's love.

I couldn't sleep last night. I know that he could not. I know that he has been watching, waiting, as I have, for today, when he must come to me.

8

A Little Belted Earl

F ive wasted days; and nothing more to tell, though some women mightn't think so; nothing but—another triumph!

I've been to the Charity Ball. I've danced with a Lord—such a little fellow to be a belted Earl! I have scored over brilliant women of Society.

It isn't the simple country girl of a few weeks ago whom Ned loves, but a wonderful woman—a Personage; and I am glad, glad, glad! Though no woman could be good enough for him. I'm not; I am only beautiful enough. And oh, so feverishly happy, except that waiting is hard, so hard. I'm so restless that I scarcely know myself.

If I might tell him that I love him—as other Queens do! I am afraid of his glance when he is here, because he knows. But when he's not here, I imagine that he does not know, that he will never come again unless he learns the truth, and I say it over and over: "I love him! I love him!" and am glad and panic-stricken as if he had heard.

I have never had any other secret, but the Bacillus, I would sooner die than tell that, to Ned. My love I would cry aloud, but I cannot until he speaks, and he cannot speak until—has Milly no pride?

I thought—I thought that the very day after the dance—why, I could have rubbed my eyes, when I went down to a late breakfast, to find Mrs.

Baker chirping with sleepy amiability, and Milly doling out complacent gossip to Ethel. The very sky had fallen for me to gather rainbow gold—and here we were living prose again, just as before.

I had struggled with my joy through all the short night, for I had imagined them suffering and angry; but I do believe that on the whole Milly had enjoyed the dance, and liked to shine even by her reflected importance as the beautiful Miss Winship's cousin. She had been vexed by Ned's admiration for me; and yet—and yet she didn't understand. The stupid! Didn't see that his love is mine.

There may have been a pause as I came, dazzling them like a great rosy light; but then my aunt stifled a yawn as she said, "Here's Nelly," and the chatter went on as before.

But I didn't hear it. Gliding confusedly into a seat, I had opened a note from John. "—Called West on business; start today," it said; and then indeed I began to feel the tangle, the terrible tangle—my cousins blind, John gone, when I was counting the minutes until I could see him. Oh, I must be free! It is his right to know the truth, and—what can Ned say while I'm affianced? I am Milly's cousin, and he John's friend.

I hurried to escape. I longed to be by myself that I might recall Ned's every look and word. Without reason—against reason—I felt that at any minute Ned might come, and waves of happiness and dread and impatience swept over me, and kept me smiling and singing and running anxiously to my glass.

Ned loves my beauty; I pulled down my hair and reknotted it and pulled it down again, fearful—so foolish have I grown—lest I might fail to please him; and frowned over my dresses and rummaged bureau drawers for ribbons, until Milly, who had tapped at my door and entered almost without my notice, asked abruptly:—

"Who's coming?"

"No one; John—no, he's out of town."

I flushed to see her regard the litter about me with calm deliberateness.

"Oh, you don't have to take pains for John," she said with a short laugh. "But come; Meg's down stairs."

The General had followed Milly up; she whisked into the room, showering me with congratulations on my success at the dance, she claimed me for a dinner, a concert—half a dozen engagements.

"Oh, by the way," she said, checking her flood of gossip. "Who d'you suppose is to be at the Charity Ball? Lord Strathay. You'll talk with a real Earl, Nelly—for of course he'll ask to be introduced."

"Another dance!" groaned my aunt, who had trotted panting in the General's wake; "I'm sure I wish I'd never said she might go; I'm as nervous as a witch after last evening."

Poor Aunt; she looked tired. She's really becoming the great objector.

Such a day as it was! I started at every footstep; my heart gave an absurd jump at every movement of the door hangings. Of course I knew that Ned couldn't—that we mustn't see each other until—but Ned is mine; it's so wonderful that he loves me. If I were Milly, I wouldn't remain an hour—not a minute!—in such a false position.

Yet the next day passed just like that day, and the next and the next and the next; every morning a note from John, scrawled on a railway train, and begging for a line from me. I wrote, poor fellow; so that's settled, and I'm very sorry for him.

I got rid of one morning by calling on Prof. Darmstetter. It was three weeks since I had seen him, and he was testy.

"I see much in t'e newspapers about t'e beautiful Mees Veensheep, but v'y does she neglect our experiment?" he demanded, following me across the laboratory to my old table. "V'ere are my records, my opportunities for observation? Has t'e beautiful Mees Veensheep no regard for science?"

"You've always said she hadn't, and pretended to be glad of it; I won't contradict," I returned. "But hurry up with your records; it doesn't need science or the newspapers, does it, to tell you that the beautiful Miss Winship cannot go about very freely?"

"Ach, no," said he humbly; for he could not look upon my face and hold his anger. "If I haf not alreaty gifen to Mees Veensheep t'e perfect beauty t'at I promised, I cannot conceive greater perfection. You are satisfied vit' our vork—vit' me?"

"Yes, I'm satisfied," I said coolly.

Just as soon as I could, I left him. Oh, I ought to be grateful, more than ever grateful now that the Bacillus has won for me the most blessed of earth's gifts—the gift of love. But I'm not; I wish I might never again see Prof. Darmstetter; he reminds me—he makes me feel unreal. As for his records, the experiment is finished. We have succeeded, and I want to enjoy our success and forget its processes. And why not? He knows in his heart that we have no further need of each other.

My real records now are public; the Charity Ball last night added a brilliant chapter.

The Charity Ball! How calmly I write that! I hope it may be the last triumph I need to win in public without Ned; but I enjoyed it. There was no awkward John to spoil my dancing, no jealous Milly, no over-anxious Aunt. I had Mrs. Marmaduke Van Dam for my chaperon—more the great lady, with all her thin rigidity, than Mrs. Henry; and for companion the General, almost as young and lighthearted as I.

And I was mistress of myself, strong and self-contained. Instead of being confused when all eyes were bent upon me, I had a new feeling of glad self-command. I felt the rhythm of my flawless beauty, my pure harmonies of face and form, and found it natural that fine toilets should be foils to my cheap white dress, and that I should be the centre around which the great assembly revolved. I'm really getting used to myself.

I danced constantly, danced myself tired, holding warm at my heart this one thought: that in the morning Ned would read of my triumphs and be proud of them, and rejoice because she about whom the whole city is talking thinks only of him.

My partner in the march was "Hughy" Bellmer, as the General calls him; I begin to know him well. He's harmless, with his drawl and his round pink face that shines with admiration. Deliciously he patronized the ball.

"Aw, Miss Winship," he said, "too large, too public. People prefer to dawnce in their own houses."—The ball was at the Waldorf-Astoria. —"The smaller a dawnce is, the greater it is, don't ye see."

"But aren't any great people here?" I asked demurely. "I am just a country mouse, and I've really counted on seeing one or two great people, Mr. Bellmer—besides you, of course."

"The Charity Ball is—aw, y'know, Miss Winship, an institution," he explained, fairly strutting in his complacency at my deference; "and as an institution, not as a Society event, ye understand, it is patronized by the most prominent ladies in the city."

"How good of them!" I cried, laughing.

He was so funny! But he was useful, too; he knew about everybody.

Some of the women I shall remember—Mrs. Sloane Schuyler, leader of the smallest and most exclusive of Society's many sets—a handsome woman with well-arched eyebrows; and Mrs. Fredericks, of the same group; sallow, with great black eyes, talking with tremendous animation; and Mrs. Terry—of the newly rich; Mr. Bellmer's aunt; dumpy, diamonded and disagreeable-looking.

"But where are the famous beauties?" I asked eagerly. "Won't they dance, even for charity, except in their own houses?"

Some of them were there; tall, pale, stylish girls, or women whose darkened eyes and faces mealy with powder told of a bitter fight with time.

Why, I haven't seen a woman whom I thought beautiful since—since I became so.

"Aw, Miss Winship, really, y'know, you have no rivals," said my partner.

I hadn't supposed him clever enough to guess what I was thinking.

"Oh, yes I have—one," I said; "isn't there somewhere here a real live Lord?"

But just then we joined Meg, and it was she who pointed out to me "The Earl of Strathay—the Twelfth Earl of Strathay," in a whisper of comical respect and deference.

He wasn't very impressive—just a thin, pale young fellow with a bulbous head, big above and small below; but I was glad to do Meg a service; for of course she wished to meet him, and of course Lord Strathay was presented to the beautiful Miss Winship and her chaperons.

Then I danced with him. I felt as if I were amusing a nice boy; he hardly came to my shoulder. I asked him if he liked America.

He wasn't too much of a boy to reply:—

"Like is a feeble word to voice one's impressions of the land of lovely women."

And then he looked at me. Oh, he did admire me immensely, and I took quite a fancy to him in turn, though it seemed pathetic that such a poor little fellow—I don't believe he's twenty-one—should carry the weight of his title. I danced with his cousin, too, a Mr. Poultney; and wherever I went Strathay's eyes followed me wistfully.

Meg danced with Strathay and amused me by her elation. She hadn't really recovered from it today.

Today! Blessed today! Lord Strathay's only an Earl; today there came to me—Ned! Oh, this has been the gladdest, most provoking day of my life, for I had only a moment with him.

It was Mrs. Baker's "afternoon," and we had a good many callers; the fame of my beauty has spread. They gazed furtively at me as they talked and sipped their tea, and it was all very stupid until—oh, I didn't know how perturbed, how unhappy I'd been, until—I glanced up for a word with the General, who came late, and behind her I saw—Him. He came to me as if there were no one else in the room.

Ah, I have been unhappy! I have known that he would try to keep away from me. Useless! Useless to fight with love! It's too strong for us. At sight of him joy like a fire flashed through my veins.

But there were my cousins; there was Meg—she looked at him impatiently, I fancied, as she has sometimes looked at John. Poor John, it didn't need her surveillance to break his feeble hold upon my heart. And there they stayed. They wouldn't go. They stayed, and talked, while I shivered and grew hot with fear and gladness and the excitement of his presence; they talked—of all senseless topics—about the ball.

"Why, Mr. Hynes, we've missed you," said Ethel carelessly, at sight of him. "Oh, Meg, tell us about last night, won't you? Helen's said nothing; almost nothing at all."

"Oh, what is there to tell?"

It made me impatient. How could I chatter nothings when Ned was by my side, smiling down at me so confusedly?

"Most girls would find enough! You should have heard the dowagers cluck, Ethel!" exclaimed the General, her face losing its vexed look at the thought. "It was bad weather for their broods. You never saw such a scurrying, pin feathers sticking every which way. The proudest hour of Hughy Bellmer's life was when the march started, and he walked beside Helen—same parade as always—through that wide hall between the Astor gallery and the big ball room; committeemen and patronesses at the head and the line tailing. You may believe the plumes drooped and the war paint trickled. Nelly was the only girl looked at. Milly, you should have been there? Headache? You look pale beside Helen."

"Oh, I don't hope to rival Nelly's colour; she looks like—like somebody's '*Femme Peinte par Elle-même.*'" said Milly with a laugh that might have been innocent. Since Ned's entrance she had grown white and my cheeks had burned, until there was reason for her jest.

"Is Mr. Bellmer handsome—handsome enough to be Nelly's partner?" persisted Ethel, impatient for her gossip—to her it's all there is of gayety. "And is Lord Strathay—nice?"

"Mr. Bellmer's an overgrown cherub with a monocle," I laughed. Ned shall not think me one of those odious, fortune-hunting girls.

"Hughy's pretty good looking, Ethie," said Meg, amiably; "and the best fellow in the world; but probably not of a calibre to interest a college girl. And Lord Strathay"—the name rolled slowly from her tongue, as if she were loth to let it go—"is a charming fellow. Just succeeded to the title. He's travelling with his cousin, the Hon. Stephen Allardyce Poultney. Nelly danced with him. And did she tell you that Mrs. Sloane Schuyler begged to have her presented? Sister to a Duchess, you know. We'll have Helen in London next. Nobody there to compare with her. Just what Strathay said, I do assure you."

London! Men of title, and great ladies and the glitter of a court! Once

I may have dreamed of power and place and the rustle of trailing robes, and being admired of all men and hated of all women, but now in my annoyance I longed to cry out: "Why can't you talk sense? Why babble of such silly things?"

To make matters worse, Uncle came just in time to hear the General's last remark.

"I do not think our Princess would leave us," he said, "even if—

> *'at her feet were laid*
> *The sceptres of the earth exposed on heaps*
> *To choose where she would reign.'"*

It was scarcely to be borne. I knew he was thinking of John, and I caught myself looking down at my hand, praying that Ned might see that I no longer wore the opal ring.

Then came Aunt Frank with a headache, looking ill enough, indeed; and I was glad to jump up and serve her some tea.

"Milly has a headache, too," I said; and she looked from Milly's vexed, cold face to mine, almost peevishly replying:—

"Nothing ever seems to ail you, child."

After all the weary waiting, Ned and I exchanged only a word. But the word was a delight and a comfort.

More than once the Judge has suggested for me a short absence from the city to win a respite from the newspapers; and this morning, when he saw that the *Echo* had smuggled an East Side girl into the ballroom last night to tell the Bowery, in Boweryese, how the other half lives, her descriptions of me so incensed him that he almost insisted upon Aunt's packing for Bermuda at once. Ned must have heard of that.

"You will not go away?" he said when he took leave of me.

"You know that Uncle—"

"You will not?"

"No."

I couldn't speak steadily. The low, passionate entreaty told me that he had come to receive that pledge, and I gave it.

Oh, now, now, I cannot be unhappy! I know that he has tried to stay away from me, and why he has not succeeded. Love has been too mighty for us both. Love has conquered us, and I—I shall never again be unhappy!

Book IV:
The Bruising of the Wings

1

The Kiss That Lied

H e said he did not love me.

It is not true. I saw love when he spoke, when he kissed my hands. He does love me, but he guards a man's honour.

I have broken John's heart, given up my home, estranged my friends; I have given up even Ned for love of him. But I'd have gone to the ends of the earth in gladness, I'd have given up for him all else in life—even my beauty; which is dearer than life.

He'll come to me yet. Milly won't forgive, won't trust. She will not try to understand. Her only thought will be to hurt, to punish. She'll drive him to me again; but oh, the shame of taking him so, given to me by her severity!

I won't believe he doesn't love me.

What have I done to be so tortured? I didn't know it was cruelty not to break the bond with John earlier; I didn't know I gave him only a girl's passing fancy.

It was when I met Ned that my heart awoke.

I knew that he was Milly's betrothed and I had not thought of thus repaying Aunt's kindness. Her kindness! Kind as a stone.

But it wasn't Ned's fault. He couldn't help himself. If he could have left me alone! If he could only have gone away!

I suppose he tried to control himself, but his eyes glowed when he looked on me; and I, thinking I knew what love was, because I was affianced, did not see—did not know what the wild joy meant that his look woke in my heart.

To keep faith with John and Milly, should I have shunned him? But there was nothing to warn me; he never spoke of love; I never thought of it. If he had spoken earlier, I might have known what to do. It might have been the danger signal. Why could he not have kept away? Why did he not speak a word of love until it was too late—until—ah, I was so happy!

But he does love me. There's truer speech than that of words, and his lips—that kissed me, but said he did not love—have told two stories. I know which to believe!

And Milly knows. She is too wise to contend with Me.

I shall never know what brought Ned to the house—three weeks ago, but I haven't dared to write of it—I shall never know what happened before I saw him.

I ran into the library with a song bubbling to my lips—for I was thinking of him—and the gladness of it was in my eyes when I found him there. He started and turned to me a face of confusion—yes, and of worship. He fumbled with a book on the table, and glanced toward the door as if he would have left me. I saw that, but I didn't think—there was no time to think, but I must have felt that a crisis had come that would decide our lives. All the fear, all the sweet shame that I had felt before him vanished. My heart beat wildly for happiness, but I was calm.

At last we were alone together!

I waited for him to speak. Slowly he turned as my questioning eyes had willed. His were black with passion and grief. A look of pain contracted his face, and he said, jerking the words out hoarsely:—

"I'm going away."

The suddenness of it almost took my breath. I had expected different words. Indeed his eyes had shot another message; *they* said that he would never leave me!

Confused by lips that lied and eyes that confessed, I stammered:—

"Going—not going away? Why? Why should you go?"

I couldn't keep appeal out of my tone, and I could see him brace himself to resist. I think I knew that, if he could, he meant to sacrifice our love to John and Milly. I think I had seen this earlier; but I had thought the struggle past when he came to me and begged me not to leave the city. But perhaps, this time, I didn't understand him; perhaps I was simply confused by his distress.

I thought he tried in vain to look away from me. Then he moved a step nearer, slowly, as if reluctant. His face was haggard.

"Tell me why you are going."

I scarcely knew I spoke. It was as if some will independent of my own had dictated the words. Yet I did not try to hide my heart's wish; it was too late. He was my life, and in all but words—yes, and in words even—I told him so. We had confessed our love. It was his right.

"Listen," I said. "If anything is—is wrong, I must know it. I—I *must* know it. Tell me. I must know everything. Ned, you must tell me."

A vein stood out upon his forehead, but still he gazed silently at me. After a time he said hoarsely:—

"I'm going because for your beauty I have thrown away the love of the woman I was to marry. For you I have lost her, and yet—I loved Milly. My God, I love her!"

Once he had begun, the words came with fierce swiftness. He seemed to mean them to sting, to cut, to stab. It was hard not to cry out with the pain of hearing them. All that I understood was that he meant to wrench himself from me with a force that should make the breach impassable. This I felt, though still his eyes gave the lie to his words; his eyes that said I was dear as life to him.

"Don't think I blame you for the inevitable," he went on. "You do not know, and I pray God you may never understand, how contemptible I have been. And don't think me a fool; I'm not crying for the moon, nor dreaming that a glorious creature like you—ah, you're as far above me as the stars above the sea—to you I have been only—"

"Don't speak like that!" I cried. White-faced, I stared at him, tremblingly, pleadingly. There was a cloud in my brain that seemed to be coming down; it threatened to smother me—but I held fast to my courage. It was life itself for which I was fighting.

"You have—you are—"

The truth was at my lips, but he interrupted:—

"I know you have reason to hate me, for I have done you wrong. Because of my folly, your place here is not what it was; and you love Burke, whom I have wronged, as I love Milly, whom I have estranged. I must keep away from you. You can see that. For the sake of all, I must keep away from you."

The cloud was choking me, but I put forth my strength.

"You have done nothing wrong; I do not—"

Words failed me. I hadn't the temerity to speak John's name. And Ned —could he not see?—only stood there saying:—

"Why I've wrecked Milly's life and mine and turned your friends against you, only God knows, who made men what they are; only God knows—I don't. Can you forgive me?"

Didn't he love me? His despair was beating conviction into me. He was pale, his lip quivered. Why was he humbled and ashamed? I was palsied with doubt, and the golden moments were fleeting, were fleeting. I must act! But I felt as if I were dead and could not, though that strangling cloud still hurt me.

"There is nothing to forgive," I faltered at last. "Or—you must forgive me. Perhaps I should understand, but—oh, I'm not wise. Indeed I have not meant to—to—Shall I speak to Milly for you? But that would only make matters worse. They may take me—to Bermuda—anywhere; or—I will leave this house; she'll forget if I go away."

At the last words my tremulous voice broke almost into a scream. Must I go away—go away that he may make Milly happy?

"You will stay here," he said, his lips quivering more and more. "Why should I drive you from home? I have lost Milly. She understands no more than you, and I hope she never may! You need not fear that I shall trouble you. I shall not see you again. You are maddening—no, not that—but I am mad. Mad!"

He turned abruptly to go, came back as hastily, caught my hand and pressed hot kisses on it. His burning eyes looked passionately into mine. He was indeed like one insane.

Then with a great groan of contrition he put his hands before his face and rushed blindly from the room.

"Ned! Ned!" I cried out, but it was too late; he didn't hear me.

I don't know how I reached my chamber. I fell in a heap on the floor, shivering, laughing, sobbing, moaning for death.

Going away! I was going away from Ned! My beauty had meshed him; I almost hated it. I saw his haggard face, I heard again his voice, solicitous for Milly's grief. I know now that pain cannot kill, or I should have died.

Going away! He did not love me. He cared nothing for my hurt, only for Milly's. He loved that little white piece of putty that hadn't life enough to love any man!

I heard rain against the windows and felt a sudden fierce longing to go out and fight the storm. Could not a strong woman compel love? No other woman since the world began had been so fit for love, had yearned for it so hungrily.

Going away! Yet I felt his kisses upon my hand. Are men so different? What is a man, that he should love and not love?

How cold the old Nelly was! Since coming to the city, I had never let John kiss me; yet I thought I loved him. I thought love was a brook to make little tinkling music, and it had become a mighty ocean sweeping over me, sweeping over me!

But I must act at once, I thought; I must go away. I must find my aunt, must tell her—what? Where could I go? Not back to Kitty; she had left the den. Not to Miss Baker, who would share Aunt's wrath. Where could one such as I find refuge? A woman whom all women must hate for her loveliness?

"Ned! Ned! I am alone!" I cried in my agony of soul. "You must—you will!—come back to me, come back to me."

I bathed my eyes and hurried from the house to forget the thought, but it followed everywhere. The rain had not stopped, but it suited me to be drenched, to hold my face to the whiplash of the water snapped by the wind. I went to Meg Van Dam, who had long urged me to pay her a visit. This time I was ready to consent, for she at least was glad to have me; and before I left her I had agreed to go to her.

It was dinner time when I reached home, glad that it was to be home to me no longer; the house made me shudder as a dungeon might. It was so changed since morning, seen now with different eyes. The dining room was so heavily respectable, with its fussily formal arrangements—like Uncle, for it's big; like Aunt, for it's crotchety.

I suppose there must have been a scene with Ned. Aunt Frank was depressed, fitfully talkative. Milly scarcely spoke, but in the curtness with which she turned her sullen head when poor Ethel asked some question, I wasn't slow in finding a meaning.

Joy begged in vain for her nightly lullaby. I couldn't respond to her "Thing, Cothin Nelly!" I'd never before noticed how like she is to her sisters. With her snubby nose and her yellow braids, she'll grow into just another white-faced doll as Milly.

Miss Baker talked persistently about Bermuda; as if my exile had ever been a possibility! In all my blind whirlwind of pain, I was glad that this was the last night I should have to writhe under the click of her knitting needles, and sit opposite her large, solemn features.

"A change will do you good, Frances," she purred. "By either the *Orinoco* or the *Trinidad* you'll have only a two days' voyage. Helen will be in her element among the coral, and Milly must come home with a coat of tan."

Milly bent lower over her magazine; in an hour she hadn't turned a page. Her thin hands, like claws, that held the book, disgusted me, fascinated me! They were the hands that Ned had kissed, as he had mine; clasped and pressed, as he had—how could he!

I called Aunt to me at bedtime, and told her I'd trespassed upon her kindness too long, and that Mrs. Van Dam was pressing.

"But we can't let you go," she said, even while the wonder whether she might not shone through her face. "You and Meg have become friends, I know, but Bake and I feel responsible to your mother."

Of course we understood each other, but neither cared to speak the truth. She had no pity, in her feeling for her own child, for the hurt I might conceal. And I don't want her pity!

At least I shall no longer have to tear my heart out, meeting Ned in her house.

The parting was easier than might have been expected, for we all rose to the occasion. Uncle had been drilled over night, and his perplexity and Aunt's preparations for leaving home amused me. The trip to Bermuda had been proposed for my sake, Aunt had only half desired it; but now she forgot her fears of winter storms, seasickness and shipwreck, and clutched at the excuse to whisk Milly out of reach of Ned Hynes and out of sight of me.

Her tone was dulcet sweet.

"We can't blame you for preferring New York, when the Van Dams are so lovely to you," she said complacently. "But Ethel is delicate. Bermuda'll do her a world of good; though of course it's not fashionable.'"

"I'm sure you'll have a lovely trip," I said. "You must let me help you pack."

She was turning the house topsy-turvy in her zeal to sail by the next boat, the very next day. She succeeded; and when she left the house I left it, too; to come here; to the General; to a house that would two months ago have seemed a palace such as I could never dream of living in. It would suit me better to be independent, to be sometimes alone, to feel that

I shouldn't have a shrewd woman's eyes so much upon me. But for the present—it is my refuge!

At Christmas I should have broken down and sobbed when I saw the last of the Bakers, instead of dropping honeyed sentences and undulating out of the room—like—like—. He called me once the Goddess glowing in her walk. I have changed this winter, mentally as well as physically.

2

The Irony of Life

I've been feverishly gay since I came to Meg. I have walked between stormwinds—grief behind and grief that I must enter. I've dined and danced, and I've clenched my hands lest I might shriek, and I've longed to hide away and die.

But I won't die. I'm not like other women—a silly, whining pack, their hearts the same fluttering page blotted with the same tears wept in Hell or Heaven. Love is a draught for two—or one; wretched one!—to drink. My life is for the world.

Oh, I've been a child, caring only for the lights and the pretty things and the music; but I'm not blind now. I understand many things that were hidden from the plain girl from the West. I have lived a year in every day. I see as they are these people I have thought so kind. So rich I call them now; so smug, so socially jealous.

There's Meg Van Dam, now; surely she knows why I have come to her, and she was Milly's friend; yet she fawns upon me. I thought her a great person, but now I know she's eager to rise by hanging at my skirts, and I amuse myself with her joy that I've rejected Ned, as she thinks; with her talk of Strathay, her dismay at John Burke's wooing.

John's so persistent. He called to see me the very day—almost in the hour I came here; the hour I was pacing the dainty little room Meg assigns me, picturing the scene on board the Bermuda boat, wondering if Ned had gone to the dock on the chance of a parting word with Milly, torturing myself with the vision of a lovers' reconciliation.

When John's card was brought, I was tempted to refuse to see him. But at the thought that he would know too well how to interpret reserves, I went down, nerved to meet him with a smile.

"Why, John," I said with my most pleased expression, "back from the West so soon? You've heard the news, I suppose—my cousins sailed this morning."

He had turned from the window at the rustle of my dress, and the grimness of his square-set jaws, warning me of a coming struggle, relaxed into a look of perplexity. Men have so little insight; he could not see that, as I sank, still smiling, into a chair, my breath came in gasps that almost choked me. After a moment's silence he said sharply:—

"Helen, we must be married."

"Married! Didn't you get my letter? John—"

"Listen!" he interrupted. "I must have the right to take care of you. You need me."

"Indeed?"

My tone was purposed insolence; I met his look with bravado. I hated him because he—because I—because he dared to know—because he offered to come to my relief when my aunt—Ned—perhaps he thought me deserted—lovelorn. His awkward figure woke in me a sudden physical repulsion.

"*I* need *you*?" I repeated with a cool laugh. "And except the good deed of providing me with a husband, what services do you propose to—"

"Nelly," he said, disregarding my taunts, "I have just come from the *Orinoco*. When I reached the office this morning and heard that the party was starting, I assumed that you would be with it and hurried to the pier. If I'd missed the boat, I might not have learned the truth until—when? Why have they gone without you? What does it all mean?"

I pulled a flower nonchalantly from a vase beside me, but I felt my cheeks burn and grow white with deadly cold and fever.

"Didn't Mrs. Baker tell you," I said, "that 'Nelly dear' thought Bermuda unfashionable? You got my letter?"

"No; you did write, then? You so far recognised the claim of your promised husband—"

"Not now; not one minute—"

In a blind frenzy of rage I held out his ring; but he knew the master word to my heart. I stopped short as, ignoring what I said, he hurried on.

"Why wasn't Hynes at the boat?" he demanded. "Did he know what I didn't—that it was not the place to seek you?"

He grasped my wrists, he looked into my bloodless face—caught the defiant, exultant look that flashed upon it at the news he gave; then he dropped my hands but immediately seized them again.

"If he dares come near you, he shall answer! Speak!" he said. "Is it for his sake that you've stayed here?"

"If you will let me go—"

He loosed his grasp and I ostentatiously chafed my wrists. I was in a fury. I was driven to madness by the thought that John might force a quarrel upon Ned—the man I had rejected and the man that had rejected me!

"I'll never marry you nor any poor man!" I cried out. "What have you to offer me? What can you do? Oh, yes, you can come and insult me, and talk to me of love—Love! The love that would make me a poor man's drudge!"

Again I thrust his ring at him, the opal spitting angry blue and orange fires. I thought he would have struck at it. Heaven knows what mad instinct was at the back of his brain. I believe every man's a brute when the woman he loves defies him. I think his fingers tingled for the Cave man's club. At any rate, I shrank in terror from his eyes.

But quickly the red light sank in them, and a puzzled look grew there instead, turning them very soft and pitiful.

"Nelly, I cannot think you serious," he said. "We have always talked of marriage, and—is it an insult to press you for the day? Heart of me, I've been so much worried about you! Are you very sure that you have chosen the wisest part? If you are, I can only leave you to think it over, perhaps to—"

"Don't preach!"

I flung out at him a torrent of abusive words, resolved that he should think about me what he chose, so long as it was not the truth.

He had no plea for himself; he saw that it would be useless. I stabbed him the more viciously as the anger died out of his face and left it only grave and pained. He looked older than I had ever seen him before; and on his temple, where he turned toward the window, gleamed a little streak of gray.

"But, Nelly, what will you do?" he said at last.

His tone was as level as if he were discussing some trivial matter. He had given up the fight, and, paying no heed to my unkindness, had fallen back upon the old habit, the instinct of looking out for me, smoothing my way after his own fashion that is so irritating.

"You can't stay among these—these strangers, can you?" he continued. "Are you going home?"

"To the farm? Never, I hope. Mrs. Van Dam, my chaperon, has many plans for me—better form than talking things over with a man. In the spring we may go abroad."

He tried—poor, foolish fellow—to read from my face the riddle of a woman's heart before he answered:—

"I'm afraid I don't altogether understand you, Nelly."

Presently he left me, wondering, even as I wonder now: Why don't I care for John? He's a strong man and he loves me. Just another of Nature's sorry jests, isn't it?

It was all so hopeless, so tangled. I leaned against the mantel, relieved by his going, but unutterably lonely. Just for a moment I feared the brilliant future that stretched in vista—without love, it looked an endless level of tedium and weariness. My bitterness towards John melted and the years we had known each other unrolled themselves before me—happy, innocent years. I felt his strength and gentleness, and of a sudden something clutched at my throat. Sob followed sob; I shook in a tearless convulsion.

Only for an instant. Then I, too, turned to leave the room, but fate or instinct had brought John back and I was startled by his voice:—

"Nelly, tell me!"

He did not come near me. There was no gust of passion in his tone, yet I felt as never before the depth of his tenderness. He had not come back to woo, but as the old friend, ambitious of helpfulness.

"Helen," he said, "how can I leave you, who need protection more than any other woman, so terribly alone?"

I didn't fear I might be tempted, but I quavered out:—

"John, go away. I've wronged you enough. I never loved you; I've no faith in love. I never loved you at all, and—you must have seen, lately, that I have changed—that I've become a very—a very mercenary woman. I can't afford to marry a poor man."

My lips quivered, for this was the cruelest lie of all; I have changed, but I'm not money loving. And I couldn't deceive him. He smiled queerly, but he must have thought time his ally, for he only said:—

"Money can buy you nothing; you might leave gewgaws to other women. But you are less mercenary than you think yourself; and you will always know that I love you; let it rest with that, for now."

So he went away the second time, leaving me with my hands clenched and my teeth set—so fierce had been my fight to seem composed. As I sank breathless into a chair, and my tense fingers relaxed, out from my right hand rolled the little opal ring. I hadn't returned it, after all; had been gripping it all the time, unknowing. At sight of it, I burst into hysterical laughter.

And that madly merry laughter is the end. I should go crazy if I yielded to love that I can't return, and I should despise him if he accepted. A husband not too impassioned, a fair bargain—beauty bartered for position, power, for a name in history—that is all there is left to me, now that love has vanished.

The farm! I couldn't go back, to isolation and dull routine! I told John I might go abroad. Why not? I might see the great capitals, and in the splendour of palaces find a fitting frame for my beauty. There may be salve for heartache in the smile of princes. At any rate, the seas would flow between me and Ned Hynes.

I had forgotten my ambitions. I'd have said to Ned: "Whither thou goest I will go;" but if what he feels for me is not love—if in his heart he hates me for the witchery I've put upon him—

I could go abroad with a title, if I chose. If love lies not my way, there is Strathay.

How listless I am, turning from my sorrow to write of what to most girls would be a delight—of that pathetic little figure, toadied and flattered, but keeping a good heart through it all; of his marked attentions, which I permit because they keep other men away; of his efforts to see me —for the Van Dams' position isn't what I imagined it, and we are not invited to many houses where I could meet him; of Meg's rejoicings over a few of the cards we do receive.

Oh, I win her triumphs, triumphs in plenty! Because the Earl admires me, hasn't she once sat at the same table with Mrs. Sloane Schuyler, who refuses to meet intimately more than a hundred New York women; and hasn't she twice or thrice talked "autos" with Mrs. Fredericks; and isn't she envied by all the women of her own set because the Earl and his cousin shine refulgent from her box at the Opera?

Triumphs, certainly; doesn't Mrs. Henry wrangle with Meg over my poor body, demanding that I sit in her box, and that I join Peggy's Badminton club, and bring the Earl, who would bring the youths and maidens who would bring the prestige that would, some day, make a Newport cottage socially feasible?

That's her dream, Meg's is Mayfair; she thinks of nothing but how to invest me in London and claim her profit when I am Strathay's Countess, or mistress of some other little great man's hall. Oh, I understand them; Mrs. Henry's the worst; oily!

I wonder if London is less petty than New York; if I should be out of the tug and scramble there. But I mustn't judge New York, viewing it through the Van Dams' eyes. If I did, I should see a curious pyramid.

At the top, a sole and unapproachable figure, the twelfth Earl of Strathay, just out of school;

Next a society, two-thirds of whose daughters will marry abroad, and to all of whose members an Earl's lack of a wife is a burning issue;

Hanging by their skirts a thousand others, like the General and Mrs. Henry, available for big functions, pushing to get into the little ones;

Hanging by these in turn, ten thousand others outside the pale, but flinging money right and left in charity or prodigality to catch the eyes of those who catch the eyes of those who nod to Earls;

And after them nobody!

And the problem: "How high can we climb?"

Why, there are twenty thousand families in New York rich enough to be Elect, if wealth were all. I could almost marry Strathay to save him from the ugly millioned girls! How they hate me!

I know what love is like, now; Strathay means to speak. If Ned would only—but three weeks—three long, long weeks, and he doesn't—oh, I won't believe that, deep in his heart he does not love me. It's not time—not time, yet, to think about the little Earl!

At any rate I won't be flung at his head; last night I taught Meg a lesson she'll remember. She meant to bring him home to supper after the Opera, where, in spite of my first experience, we're constant now in attendance; but, to her surprise, then dismay, then almost abject remonstrance, I prepared to go out before dinner to inspect the new studio Kitty and Cadge have taken.

"Be back in good season?" she pleaded. "How *could* you make an engagement for the night when Strathay.—Not wait for you! Why Helen, you can't—what would Strathay think if I allowed you to arrive alone at the Opera?"

"Then can't you and Peggy entertain him?"

"Peggy?" She looked at me with blank incredulity. "You wouldn't stay away when Strathay—why, Helen, you didn't mean that. Drive straight to the Metropolitan when you leave your—those people, if you don't wish to come back for me. Where do they live?" she groaned despairingly.

"Top of a business block in West Fourteenth Street."

I thought she would have refused me the carriage for such a trip, but she didn't venture quite so far as that; and the hour I spent with the girls was a blessed breathing spell.

"What a barn!" I cried, when I had climbed more stairs than I could count to the big loft where I found them. "Girls, how came you here?"

"Behold the prodigal daughter! Shall we kill the fatted rarebit?" And Kitty threw herself upon me; while Cadge, waving her arms proudly at the Navajo rugs, stuffed heads of animals and vast canvasses of Indian braves and ponies that made the weird place more weird, replied to my query:—

"Borrowed it of an artist who's wintering in Mexico; cheap; just as it stands."

Then they installed me under a queer tepee, and we had one of the old time picked-up suppers, and for an hour my troubles were pushed into the background. The girls are in such frightful taste that I really should drop them, but they're loyal and so proud of me!

"Princess," said Cadge, "time you were letting contracts for the building of fresh worlds to shine in. You're the most famous person in this, with all the women thirsting for your gore; and you've a real live Lord for a 'follower.'"

"That's nothing."

Cadge thinks me still betrothed to John, so she affected to misunderstand.

"Nearly nothing, for a fact," she said; "it isn't ornamental, but we seldom see specimens and mustn't judge hastily. And it is a Lord.—See the handout he gave me for last Sunday—full-page interview: 'Earl of Strathay Discusses American Society?'

"Some English won't stand for anything but a regular pie-faced story, but Strathay's a real good little man."

"You said he had sixty-nine pairs of shoes," said Kitty reminiscently.

"No; twenty-nine."

"What's His Lordlets doing in New York?" inquired Pros., who was there as usual, a queer and quiet wooer.

"Tinting the town a chaste and delicate pink, assisted and chaperoned by his cousin, the Hon. Stephen Allardyce Poultney. Ugh! Glad the *Star* doesn't want an interview with *His* Geniality; don't like S.A.P. Esq.," said Cadge energetically. "But, Helen, now you've got people where you want 'em, you play your own hand. You don't want any Van Dam for a bear leader. That crowd's been working every fetch there is to get in with the top notchers, and they just couldn't. Knowing you is worth more to them than endowing a hospital. You're a social bonanza."

Perhaps I shouldn't have let her talk so about Meg, but, after all, she told me nothing new.

"Did I send you a marked paper with the paragraph I wrote about the important 'ological experiments you couldn't leave, even for the 'land of the lily and the rose?'" she proceeded. "Don't wonder you didn't want to go to Bermuda, everything coming so fast your way. I crammed your science into the story because it's good advertising. Don't really study at Barnard now, do you? I wouldn't; would you, Kitty?"

Her white, mobile face gleaming with animation, Cadge declaimed upon one of her thousand hobbies:—

"What's women's science good for but dribbling essays to women's clubs? If some 'Chairwoman of Progress' were to grab off the Princess, does it take science to give 'em 'Fresh Evidence that Woman was Evolved from a Higher Order of Quadrumanous Ape than Man?' We all know what the clubs want, and if they get it, they'd vote anyone of us as bright a light as Haeckel.—Pros., you saved any clippings for the Princess?"

Pros. gave me a quantity of articles about my beauty cut from out-of-town and foreign papers. I believe I'll subscribe to a clippings bureau. I hadn't thought of that.

I stayed and stayed; it was so pleasant in the eyrie; but when at last I rose to go, Kitty sighed:—

"Why, you've only been here a minute, and in that gorgeous dress, you're like a real Princess, not my chum. I shall suggest a court circular —'The Princess Helen drove out yesterday attended by Gen. Van Dam.'—'Her Serene Highness, Princess Helen, honoured the Misses Reid and Bryant last evening at a soiree.'—leaded brevier every morning on the editorial page. Oh, Nelly, can't I have your left-off looks? A homely girl starves on bread and water, while a pretty one wallows in jam."

"Princess must be wallowing in wealth," said Cadge, inspecting my evening dress; "suspect she didn't dress for us; it's Opera night. Stockholders share receipts with you? Beauty show in that first tier box must sell tickets."

"Wish they would divide; I'm as poor as a church mouse," I said, laughing.

I didn't go to the Opera, though the girls had cheered me up until I hurried home prepared to do Meg's bidding; but she had gone—angry, I suppose—and I didn't follow.

I gained nothing; the Opera gives me my best chance to see and be seen. I might as well have had my hour of triumph, the men in the box, the jealous glances of the women. I might as well have scanned with feverish expectation the big audience that turns to me more eagerly than to the singers, searching—oh, I'm mad to think that Ned might come there again to look upon me.

I didn't even escape the Earl. Meg and her husband came home early, bringing him and Poultney; we had the supper, and, for my sins, I made myself so agreeable that Meg forgave me, almost.

It was easy; I just let the poor boy talk to me about his mother and sisters, and watched his face light up as he spoke of them in a simple, hearty way that American boys don't often command. He is really very nice. One of his sisters is a beauty.

"But not like you," he said.

He's as boyishly honest as if he were sixteen; and as modest. To be Countess of Strathay would be a—

Of course Mrs. Henry and Peggy were here, smiling on Mr. Poultney, Strathay's cousin. Oh, I'm useful! I believe Mrs. Marmaduke is the only Van Dam who's kind to me without a motive; they're not Knickerbockers at all, as I supposed.

Cadge is right; I gain nothing socially by remaining with Meg; and her guesses come too close to my heart's sorrow. She watches and worries, forever concerned lest some "folly" on my part interfere with her ambitions. Why, I'm frantic at times with imagining that even the maid she lends me—an English "person"—reports upon my every change of mood.

Oh, I ought to be independent, independent in all ways. With a little money I could manage it.

There's a Mrs. Whitney, a widowed aunt of Meg's husband, who lives alone in an apartment where a paying guest, if that guest were I, might be received. Meg would raise an outcry, of course, but I can't keep on visiting her indefinitely; and I should still be partly in her hands.

But I have no money. My allowance is the merest nothing, spent before it comes. Why, I owe Meg's dressmaker, for the dress Cadge admired and for others—Mrs. Edgar was cheaper; I must go back to her. And in the Nicaragua, where Mrs. Whitney lives, the cost of—but it wouldn't be for long.

If Ned doesn't—

I won't think about Strathay. I must wait. It's my fault that I haven't plenty of money. I've been so unhappy that I haven't explained to Father how my needs have increased, how my way of life has changed. But I'll write tonight; he refuses me nothing. He must send me a good sum at once; as much as he can raise.

Mrs. Whitney's a harmless tabby—a thin, ex-handsome creature struggling to maintain appearances; but I can put up with her. I will go to the Nicaragua. I'll go at once.

3

The Suddenness of Death

The Nicaragua, March 29.

How could I have known that he would die?

I had never seen anyone die. It was as if life were a precious wine rushing from an overturned glass that I could not put right again. I did not dream a man could be so fragile.

For weeks I have not added a word to this record. But now I have looked upon death, and I must write. There is no one to confide in but this little book, stained by so many tears, confident of so many sorrows, so many disappointments.

Prof. Darmstetter is dead.

Dead, but not by my fault. I was not the thousandth part to blame. Yet I tremble like a leaf to think of it. I shall get no sleep tonight and to-morrow look like a fright to pay for it—no! I can never do that now, thank God! Thank God for that!

Yes, I'm glad; when I try to be calm, I am glad he's dead—no, not that—sorry he's dead, of course, but glad that my rights are safe—when I am calm.

But I can't be calm; it was too horrible!

It happened yesterday in the laboratory; we were alone together. I have seldom been to the laboratory of late, but I had begun to suspect that the Professor was planning treachery, preparing to try the Bacillus upon other women. He had been so impatient because I had not gone often enough, that he might make his records, his comparisons, his tests—I don't know what flummery. All at once he ceased his importunities; some instinct taught me that he was about to seek a more tractable subject. I was resolved that if he did contemplate such injustice, I should put a stop to it. And I went to watch him.

Was that wrong? Why, he had promised me that I should have pioneer's rights in the realm of beauty. Sole possession was to be my reward? I had the right to hold him to his promise. But I didn't think—

Yesterday I spoke to Prof. Darmstetter. That was how it came about. He had looked disconcerted at my appearance in the laboratory, and my suspicions had suddenly grown to certainty. I said to him:—

"I wish to see you alone."

A guilty look came to his face. I was watching him as he had watched me before the great change, and when he started at my words I knew he was thinking of playing me false; his conscience must have warned him that I had read his thoughts. But he knew that my strength was greater than his and he bowed assent.

When the other girls had gone—some of them with frightened looks at me, as if mine were the devil's beauty they tell about—and when Prof. Darmstetter was ready to begin his own work, I faced him with a challenge:—

"Prof. Darmstetter, you are about to break your word."

"You are mistaken," he said; but he could not face my look.

"I am not mistaken; you are planning to try the Bacillus upon other women, and you promised that I should be first."

"And so you are! I dit not promise t'at you should be t'e only beautiful voman all your life, or ten years, or von year. You haf t'e honour of being first. It is all, and it is enough. You shall be famous by t'at. I am an old man and must sometime brint my discofery for t'e goot of t'e vorld; but first I must make experiments; I must try the Bacillus vit' a blonde voman, vit' a brunette voman, vit' a negro voman—it vill be fine to share t'e secrets of Gott and see v'at He meant to make of t'e negro."

If his enthusiasm had not run counter to my rights, I might have admired it.

"I must try it vit' a cripple," he went on, "vit' an idiot, vit' a deaf and dumb voman. I must set it difficult tasks, learn its limitations. T'en I must publish."

"You shall do nothing of the kind. You are not a very old man and I am young. I have your secret safe, and it shall not be lost to the world even if you die. I shall see that your name is coupled with the Bacillus as that of its discoverer. Do you think I care to rob you of your honours? I value them little, compared with the beauty you have given me. Think what you promised me! That I should be first! And I have had the perfect beauty only a few days and already you are planning to make it cheap and common. This injustice I will oppose with all my might, but I will be fair with you."

"Fair vit' me!" he shouted. "Vat do you mean? T'at I shall die unknown, vit' t'e greatest discofery of all time in my hands? You call t'at fair? It is not fair to me, because I haf hungered for fame as you for beauty. But t'at is not'ing; t'at is for me only, and I am not'ing. It is not fair to t'e vorld to vit'hold t'is precious gift one hour longer t'an is necessary to exper-iment, to try, to make sure. To keep t'is possession all to yourself vould you deny it to millions of your sisters?"

"Yes, I would; and so would they, in my place," I cried. "I care as much for my beauty as you for your fame. And I hold you to your promise. I was to be first, and I shall be first. I haven't yet begun to live. You have barely finished your experiments, and now you're planning my ruin. I will not be balked."

"I vill not be balked by such selfishness," screamed Prof. Darmstetter, his parchment face livid with rage; "*I* vill be master of my own vork."

My beauty! My hold on life and power and success and love! My only hope of Ned, if he loves me—and God knows whether he does or no! See such beauty multiplied by the thousand, the million? Never!

I forced myself to be calm. My anger left me in a moment. I knew how useless it was, and I remembered that he himself had armed me for my protection. I smiled and held out both my hands to him, and I could see him falter as he looked.

"Look at me!" I said. My voice was a marvel even to myself, so rich and full and musical! "Look at me! Of what use was it to make me beautiful if you are now to make me unhappy? Ah, I beg of you, I implore you, don't be just, but be kind! Let me have my own way and see—oh, see how I shall thank you!"

His face changed as I moved toward him with a coaxing smile, and dropped my hands on his shoulders. The tempest of his wrath subsided as suddenly as it had risen, and he stood short-sightedly, his head thrust forward, peering into my eyes, helpless, panting, disarmed.

"You will not—ah, you will not!" I whispered.

"Ach, Du!" he murmured. "Du bist mein Frankenstein! Ich kann nicht —ich—ich habe alles verloren, verloren! Ehre, Ruhm, Pflicht, Redlichkeit, den guten Namen! Verloren! Verloren!"

A touch of colour that I had never seen there before grew slowly in his cheeks. It was the danger signal; but I did not know; indeed I did not know!

"Come," I said, shaking him lightly, playfully; "promise me that you will not do it for a year."

He lay limp, unbreathing, sprawled upon the bare boards.

"Delilah!" he whispered from behind set lips, his breath coming quicker, a hoarse rattling in his throat.

Then he snatched my hand and began pressing kisses upon it—greedily, like a man abandoning himself to a sudden impulse.

But the next moment, before I could move, he threw back his head and tottered to a chair, where he sat for an instant, breathing heavily. Just as I sprang toward him his frame stiffened and straightened and he slipped from the chair and fell heavily to the floor, where he lay limp, unbreathing, sprawled upon the bare boards in all the pitiful ugliness of death.

I was terribly frightened.

For a moment wild thoughts raced through my brain—foolish impulses of flight lest I be found with the body and somehow be held responsible. Then, with scorn for my folly, I ran out into the hall, crying for help.

The janitor rushed in, and seeing what had happened, went for the nearest physician, who came at once and knelt by the fallen man's side. But before he closed the staring eyes, rose from his examination of the prostrate figure and slowly shook his head, we both knew that Prof. Darmstetter was dead.

"His heart—." he began, turning for the first time toward me, whom as yet he had not noticed; and then he started back and stood open-mouthed, transfixed, staring at me—at my beauty.

In that sweet instant, call it wicked or not, I was glad that Darmstetter was dead! I could not help it. So long as he lived, I was not safe.

I did not blame him for planning to experiment with others, any more than I would have blamed a cat that scratches or a snake that stings. I will be just. His love of learning overbore his honour. He could not have kept faith. I should never have been safe with him in the same world. Yet am I sorry for him. I owe him much.

In the Doctor's wondering gaze at me over the body of my beauty's creator I felt anew the sense of power that has inspired me by night and day since my great awakening.

I have had bitter experiences of late; this has been the worst, yet in a way the most fortunate. By no fault of mine I am relieved of the danger of seeing beauty like—like this too common.

And I will be fair to the dead man, though he was not fair to me: if there is a God above, by Him I swear that I will write out the secret of the Bacillus this day, so that it shall not be lost if I too die suddenly, as he—

I will devise it to humanity, and John Burke shall execute the will. Poor fellow! Poor John!

I can't see that I was wrong. I did not know, Prof. Darmstetter himself probably did not know, that he was liable to such an attack. Even if I had known—I had the right to defend myself, hadn't I? It was not like the Nelly Winship I once knew to use such weapons against him; but that Nelly is as dead as he, and this glorious vision of white and rosy tint and undulant form shall be rival-less for years; marvel of every land, the theme of every tongue.

I sit alone in this huge palace in which I have come to live—feeling that at last I have a home of my own, where no one can overlook my thoughts—I sit alone and think of the future; and it is rosy bright, if only I could forget—if only I could forget!

In all the world I am the sole guardian of the Secret. I shall be the most beautiful woman for years and years and years; blessed with such beauty that men shall know the tale of it is a lie, until they, too, come from far countries to look upon it; and they shall go home and be known as liars in their turn, and always dream of me. When I am old and gray, I will tell the world how Darmstetter died, on the eve of publishing his discovery. Perhaps I shall cling to it until I, too—

Ah, I can see that ghastly Thing, the dead, hideous eyes staring up at me! Shall I be like that some day? As ugly as that!

It was not my fault, dead, staring eyes; not my fault!

Some Remarks about Cats

The Nicaragua, April 27.

I've been sitting for my portrait to Van Nostrand. It is an offering to the shades of Prof. Darmstetter. I must preserve some attempted record of my beauty for his sake; though the Bacillus couldn't have made, if he had lived, another woman as beautiful as I. It isn't conceivable.

I believe I'm a little tired with that, and with rearranging Mrs. Whitney's flat, and a little worried, too, about bills, the money from Father comes so slowly. Not that I need mind owing a trifle at the shops; half the women run accounts; but it's embarrassing not to have ready money. Why, I have to buy things to ward off gifts; Meg simply won't see me go without.

Perhaps I'm depressed too, because today has been a succession of petty squabbles, and I hate squabbling.

This morning came Aunt Frank. I knew she had returned from Bermuda, so I wasn't surprised to see her dumpy figure appear in Mrs. Whitney's parlour, followed by Uncle Timothy's broad back and towering head. I did with zest the honours of the apartment. It was sweet revenge to see Mrs. Baker's nervous discomfort at meeting me, and to watch her stealing furtive glances at my beautiful home.

"Well, Nelly, dear," she said, "you look very cosey, but we expected that, after your visit to Mrs. Van Dam, you would go to Marcia until our return."

"Oh, I couldn't think of troubling either of you," I said sweetly; "I have friends to whom it is a real pleasure to advise me."

That shot told.

"You don't know what anxiety you've caused, leaving us for—for strangers, that way," she retorted, bridling; "but since you *would* go, I'm glad everything's turned out so—been having your portrait painted? Why, it's a—it *is* a Van Nostrand!"—She had spied the painting.—"It's like you, rather; but—doesn't he charge a fortune?"

Then she rattled on, about the rooms, about Bermuda lilies and donkey carts, trying now and again to pry into my plans and urging me, not too warmly, to return to her, until she had reached the limits of a call of courtesy. I think it was with real relief that she rose as she received my final refusal. Uncle, who had sat silent in kind, or blind, perplexity, was unfeignedly glad to go.

"Run in often, won't you?" she said, at parting. "I hear—but perhaps I shouldn't speak of that. Is—is Lord Strathay like his pictures?"

Fussy! She'd gladly wash her hands of me, yet thinks she has a duty. But I was glad, for once, to see her. It's not for nothing that I have run society's gauntlet; I can aim confetti with the best of them; innocent looking but they hurt.

Scarcely had they gone when in rushed the General and my prim duenna, Mrs. Whitney; they'd been waiting until the coast was clear. It was with something like a scream that the two flew at me, crying in one voice:—

"Have you *really* refused to be one of Peggy's bridesmaids? Why didn't you consult *me*?"

Peggy despairs of Mr. Poultney; she's going to marry some person in Standard Oil, and her wedding will be a function.

"Yes," I said, ignoring the latter question.

"But why—*why*—" Mrs. Whitney squeaked and panted, and her breath failed.

"Because—was it because Ann Fredericks was asked too?" Meg demanded.

"Yes, if you must know."

"But what has Ann done?" said Meg. She planted herself in front of me, her hard, handsome eyes blazing with impatience. "She's as homely as the Sunset Cox statue and as uncivil to you as she dares; but she's only a cousin of *the* Frederickses, you mustn't mind her. What has Ann done, Helen?"

"She weighs two hundred and they call her 'Baby'! She's a fat slug on a currant bush! I won't talk about her."

I dashed into my room but Meg's staccato reached me even there.

"Just like Helen! Imagine Mrs. Henry's state of mind."

"And Ann's," said Mrs. Whitney.

"Oh, Ann's in mortal terror. But how can Helen expect pasty girls like Ann Fredericks—out last fall and already touching up—to forgive her beauty? Trouble is, every girl who comes near Helen knows she makes her look like a caricature."

Meg paced the floor a minute, then slapped herself into a chair.

"Oh, I've seen the women scowl at her," said Mrs. Whitney.

"Scowl?" said Meg. "Why, I've seen a woman actually put out her foot for Helen to trip over. Old women are the worst, I do believe; some of the young ones admire her. What do you think old Mrs. Terry said—Hughy Bellmer's aunt—at the last of her frightful luncheon concerts, where you eat two hours in a jungle of palms and orchids, and groan to music two hours more in indigestion. 'A lovely girl, my dear Mrs. Van Dam,' she said; 'a privilege to know her. Pity that so many of our best people fight shy of a protégée of the newspapers.' *That* from Mrs. Terry, with her hair and her hats—"

"And her divorce record," added Mrs. Whitney.

"She fears for her nephew; as if Helen would look at him! But the newspapers *have* hurt Helen. I wish she'd announce her engagement; she has the cards in her hands, but she's got to play 'em; and poor Strathay's so devoted!—Why didn't you shade the lights Tuesday at your dinner? In that glare we were all worse frights beside her than usual."

"I hate murky rooms!" I cried, breaking out upon them, for I couldn't stand it any longer. "It's your 'rose of yesterday' who insists on twilight and shaded candles. I enjoy electricity!"

Meg gazed at me in despair.

"Helen, are you really bent on making enemies?" she asked. "What *did* Ann Fredericks do?"

I couldn't have answered; it would have been no answer to say that she angers me with a supercilious stare; but the trouble of replying was spared me, for Mrs. Henry appeared that minute in the doorway, greeting me in her nervous puffy voice, "How *well* you look!" she said. "*Such* a treat to get a peep at you! Peggy really must try your dressmaker—but she's *so* disappointed! You *must* let me beg of you—*just* like an own daughter and Peggy couldn't think more of a sister! You *will* reconsider—"

Something in the way she thrust forward her head reminded me of how her tiara slipped and hitched about, on the night of her dance, and how Ned and I giggled when it had to be repinned.

"I'm afraid Peggy should have consulted me earlier," I said with a spite born of the recollection.

It would have been more than mortal not to take offense at that. Mrs. Henry's face grew red, and after a few perfunctory words she and Meg left, and Mrs. Whitney went out with them.

As Mrs. Henry backed into the hall, she almost collided with Kitty, who had just come up.

"Talking wedding?" that tease asked, following me back into the parlour and pirouetting before a mirror. "Chastening experience for once in a way to see mysel' as ithers see me. Big wedding, won't it be? Florist told Cadge he was forcing a churchful of peach and apple blossoms. You're a bridesmaid, ain't you? That *was* Mrs. Henry? Know I've seen her here. Looks apoplectic; and there's too much musk in her violet."

"That was Mrs. Henry, but I'm not on Peggy's list. How are the beast-esses' noses and toeses?"

"Ambulance rung for." Kitty darted to another looking glass. "Regular hall of mirrors, ain't it? Helen, why are photo-engravers—but say, I've seen a list of bridesmaids; Ann Fredericks was one, cousin of *the* Frederickses; great for Helen, we all said—Pros. and Cadge and—"

"Has the list been printed?"

Kitty looked puzzled.

"What are you cross about?" she said finally. "I don't wonder you get tired of such doings, tugging a ton of bouquet down a church aisle, organ grinding Lohengrin. If ever I marry, I sha'n't ask you to stand up with me; I propose to be the central figure at my own wedding; Cadge can do as she chooses."

"Why, Kitty! Cadge and—why, Pros., of course."

"In June. Came to tell you."

For a moment Kitty's eyes danced, then the mist followed the sunlight, and the poor little creature buried her head in my lap, sobbing.

"Oh, what'll I do," she cried, "when Cadge takes away my brother and my brother takes away Cadge, and you—they say you're going off with that Englisher to be a Countess—not that I ever see anything of you now."

"Oh, hush, child; don't you know you're talking nonsense?"

Kitty took me at my word.

"Earl's lady is a Countess, ain't she?" she asked, her voice still shaky.

Then she sat suddenly upright and put back her red curls from her brow, winking vigourously. "Oh, if you do live in a castle, put in bathtubs and gas; and if you go to court, please, Princess, hide a kodak under your bouquet for me and—"

Crying and laughing by turns and tossing back her flaming locks, she started for the door.

"Helen," she said, turning as she reached it, "I have such bad symptoms! Am I really the only girl that's jealous of you?"

"The only one that isn't jealous, you—you dear!" I exclaimed; and I believe it's almost true!

Kitty paused in the hall, playing with the roses in a bowl upon the table.

"We hear something of how the dowagers adore you. But let 'em wag their double chins; you'll scat the old cats from their cushions!" she said.

At the impetuous outflinging of her hands, the floor was strewn with pink petals.

"Cats?" repeated Mrs. Whitney, who just then made her appearance, "are they a hobby with Miss Reid?"

"I'd drown 'em," cried Kitty, vanishing, "nine times!"

Oh, I'm weary of these bickerings; so womanish! Every creature whose rival I could possibly become is my enemy. I don't blame them. What chance have they while I am present? Women who agree about nothing else make common cause against one who surpasses them. They are like prairie wolves that run in packs to pull down the buffalo, and I shall pity them as I would pity wolves. They shall find that I have a long memory.

I have decided. I shall marry Strathay.

February—March—April—three long, long months, and still Ned doesn't come, does not write. Yes, it's time to act; thank God, I've still some pride!

While Darmstetter lived, I couldn't have left New York; but now, now that I am safe, why should I stay here, flatting with a shrew, provoking the Van Dams, to whom I owe some gratitude, wasting my life for a man who —who said he didn't love me?

Milly's at home again; let Ned return to her, if he chooses. I shall marry Strathay. Meg shall be friend to a Countess. Then I shall be quits with her and with Mrs. Henry and with Peggy. And the "best people" will no more fight shy of me—though they don't now; they don't need to. Except Mrs. Schuyler, who has snubbed me just enough to leave herself right, whatever happens, few of them have ever met me.

I owe no thanks to Mrs. Whitney, with her prunes and her prisms and her penny-pinchings. I must secure my future.

And there's only one way—Strathay. I've been foolish to hesitate. He tried to speak yesterday, after the flower tea—for that's the extent of my social shining now; I am good to draw a crowd at a bazaar!—and I should have let him; I meant to do so.

But I can't blame myself for being sentimental, weak, and for putting him off; I was tired out. What an ordeal I'd undergone! What black looks from the women! They'd rather have starved their summer church in the Adirondacks than nursed it with my help!

But he must have understood; I think he saw everything that happened. The girls at my stall were sulky because no one bought of them, while I was surrounded; and one, in lifting a handful of roses, drew them towards her with a spiteful jerk that left a long thorn-scratch across my hand.

I pretended not to notice. Then in a minute I cried, "Why, see; how could that have happened?"

And I laid my perfect hand beside hers, ugly with outstanding veins, that she might note the accident—and the difference. People giggled, and she snatched her hand away, blushing furiously.

I was in high spirits, with a crowd about me. I knew how tall and graceful I looked behind my flowers; and to tease Mrs. Terry, I pinned Bellmer's boutonniere with unnecessary graciousness, and smiled at her while he sniffed it with beatitude beaming from his moony face.

"Awf'ly slow things, teas," he said regretfully, as she bore him off; "awf'ly slow, don't you think?" Really the man's little better than a down-right fool; if he were poor, no one would waste a better word upon him.

As he went, I caught sight of a slight figure, a pair of jealous, worship-ping eyes. Poor Strathay had seen the incident; had perhaps thought—

I took pains to be cordial to him, when he had made his way with Poultney to my side; and to Mr. Poultney, too; though I don't like him much better than Cadge does, with his cold eyes and his thin smile, that seems to say: "Hope you find my schoolboy entertaining."

An Earl is always entertaining!

Yet I ran away from him. I left the tea early. I wanted to think. All the way home in the carriage I marshalled arguments in his favour. I saw myself at court, throned in my brilliant circle, flattered by princes, consulted by statesmen, the ornament of a society I am fitted to adorn. I saw a world of jealous women at my feet and Ned convinced that I had been playing with him. I even rehearsed the scene we should enact when Strathay should speak; I foresaw the flush upon his face, the sparkle of his eyes when I should tell him that I would try to love him.

He must have slipped his cousin's leash, for he was at the Nicaragua almost as soon as I was. But there at home, with the boy's eyes fixed on mine, with the tremour of his voice telling me how much he cared, I couldn't listen.

I made talk with him, for him. I gave him no chance to speak, determined as I was that he should speak. I was conscious of but one desire—to put off the avowal.

At last he said: "Sometimes I fancy you're not happy."

His voice was tense. He was leaning forward in his eagerness; he looked so zealous to be my champion—so honest!

I tried to smile. I really liked him.

Happy! Out of memory there came to me a picture: I was creeping to Ethel's bed at night, whispering to her that I was the happiest girl in the world; she kissed me sleepily, and said she was happy too, and then I groped my way back to bed, and lay there in the dark, smiling. That was years ago. Three months? Years, long, long years ago!

Now it flashed across me that Lord Strathay loved me as I had loved Ned. That gave me a measure of the gift he was to offer. I felt Ned's kisses on my hands, bidding me be honest.—I felt other kisses, too; I saw—good God, how long must I see?—a gray old face—the face of Darmstetter! Happy! I closed my eyes to shut out the vision. I shuddered.

"You—really, I'm afraid you're very tired," he said, after waiting a little.

"Yes; tired," I gasped; "that's all."

But I knew I must marry him. I controlled myself. I smiled; I waited. I wished him to go on, but he was peering into my straining eyes with anxious sympathy.

"I'm afraid you're too tired to talk with me today," he said; "but—you will let me come again?"

"Yes."

Such a relief! Though what was to be gained by waiting? What must be must be.

Indeed an older man might have seen the wisdom of speaking at once. But Strathay looked wistfully at me for a moment, then turned away with a big, honest schoolboy sigh; and something like a sob broke his voice as he whispered:—

"I—I would do anything to serve you."

Then he went away.

Perverse! I *will* marry him. Other women take husbands so. I like him; I should like him even if he were not an Earl—and his name a career.

I shall make Strathay as fine a Countess as any cold, blonde English girl, and he'll be proud of me, and every man will envy him. I shall wrong him less than I should have wronged John Burke. I should have hated John if I had married him, for he'd expect love, where Strathay will be content to give it. Why, the one honest thing I've done was to break with John.

I wish I could afford to keep on being honest!

5

The Love of Lord Strathay

May 5.

L ord deliver me from the well-meaning!

Because of one pestilential dun, I've done what the weary waiting for money, money, money would never have driven me to do. I've been to Uncle, unknown to his wife, to ask advice. I might have known better.

It was with a wildly beating pulse that I entered the familiar little private office, thinking that Ned might be on the other side of the partition —near enough, perhaps, to hear me; that he might at any moment rap upon the door and enter the room as he used to do, upon such flimsy errands! I wondered how he would look, and what he'd say if he came; but he never did come, though the talk was long enough, mercy knows; long and profitless.

It was hard, with that cold sinking at my heart, to talk to the Judge, as he sat with his keen eyes fixed upon me, leaning back in his chair, at times frowning absent-mindedly.

"I've come to tell you—I've written home for money," I began breathlessly to explain. "But they don't understand, of course—it isn't half what I need, now. I really don't quite know what to do. And so I came to—"

My words died away into unintelligibility.

"Anticipated your allowance a little? Well, well, how much do you need?" he asked indulgently.

"I don't exactly know; not much," I cried eagerly, "I haven't asked Father to send it all at once. Two or three thousand dollars would be a great help—for the present."

"Two or three thousand! Is it little Nelly Winship who is talking about thousands? And what important scheme has she in mind?"

His tone was playful.

"To pay my bills.'"

"Bills aggregating thousands?" He dropped his paper cutter sharply. "Is it possible that in so short a time—if the recital be not too painful, pray explain."

"Oh, it's simple enough; the dressmaker would say: 'Do let me make you this, it's such a pleasure to fit you;' or, 'That would be the rage, if you'd introduce it.' And Mrs. Van Dam begged me to buy a hat from a protegee just starting in business, because it would be a help to have the beautiful Miss Winship for a customer. It did help the milliner, too, for I bought three and they were printed in the papers. But she wants her pay just as if it hadn't been worth the price twice over as an advertisement. And all the things for the flat—"

"Furniture?"

"Why, yes; we've rearranged the place and I've contributed a little. Uncle Timothy, you can see—I need more money than other women. I can't walk without attracting notice, and cab hire or a carriage by the month—and—and I can't shop for myself, you don't know what a difference that makes; and—oh, everything is different! Why, I've just had my portrait painted. But Father isn't a poor man."

"He is poor, measured by New York standards. And he is sending you a great deal of money."

"Yes, but—I must have a *lot* more."

The Judge frowned slowly, considering what he had heard. Finally he said, slowly shaking his head:—

"Doubtless we should have warned you, upon your coming to New York, but I did not anticipate that one of your substantial Western stock would develop habits of extravagance; nor were they apparent while you were with us. I cannot think it was altogether our fault, and certainly it was not your father's. I am not unmindful of the recent unsettling experiences which furnish excuse for confusion of ideas; but, Nelly, I appeal to a head that should be logical, even if—I have never thought it giddy with adulation—to see the facts as they exist. You must yield to your aunt's wish and return to her or to Marcia—"

"Impossible!"

"—you must bring me your bills; doubtless we can give up the furniture—"

"Give it up!"

The coolly spoken words struck to my heart. Why, we had just finished arranging it! But he misunderstood my exclamation, and added:—

"I comprehend your reluctance, and I confess that I should little like to advise returning goods bought in good faith, if there were any chance of payment; but—let me see; are you of age?"

"Why, yes; just twenty-one."

"Is it possible? How time passes, to be sure! Yet—ah, the point is not important; the tradespeople should not have trusted you. Consider that you are unable to pay; the less of two evils is to return the goods as soon as possible, that they may be received undamaged."

"Oh, it's not so bad as that?" I said hastily. "Nearly everybody is willing to wait, and I—you know Aunt Frank doesn't want me, and I should be a —white elephant to Miss Baker. I must live somewhere. It's not my fault if my only friends are rich, and if I—but why can't Father—"

"I do not believe your father can pay your debts," he interrupted, "in addition to the generous sums he has already forwarded, unless—surely you were not suggesting that he should mortgage the farm in order to—pay for paintings?"

"I didn't mean that at all!" I cried; "I never thought of that. But how *do* people—"

"You and I must do what is to be done, if possible without distressing him," he said; "your father is not so young as he once was. If you have bought things for which your allowance will not pay, although"—he hesitated a moment, "—the situation is—ah—trying to Mrs. Whitney. I suppose her half of the common stock is secure?"

"Her half!"

"Has she been leaning upon your slender purse?" he asked not unkindly.

"Why—she saves money by me and I increase her social importance. Of course she had furniture, but it was old and—and—"

I could not find the words to explain to a man my horror of ugliness. He wouldn't have understood.

"Well, well, it makes no difference now. I must arrange matters for you, and I think you will agree, upon reflection, that the first step must be to give up whatever we can."

"But, Uncle," I tried to speak calmly, to show him the situation", "Mrs. Whitney is a Van Dam, and they befriended me when—why, they would never forgive me; it would be ruin. And even from the practical standpoint —you wouldn't like to have your lawbooks sold, would you? Well, people have introduced me—and pretty furniture and pretty clothes and not to have any scandal or any talk—oh, you can see!"

"In the light of reports that reach me," said the Judge, "I might suppose that you"—he hesitated a moment, then continued, in an attempt at a bantering manner, "that you refer to your luxuries as preliminary to— ah—matrimony, which is said to be the only gainful occupation that my sex leaves almost exclusively to yours, and in which fine clothing is undoubtedly an adjuvant. But observation leads me to think that it is a business less profitable than is often imagined. Hm!"

He drummed on the table, and when he continued, he seemed talking to gain time, considering what he wished to say.

"I grant you," he said with his cumbrous playfulness, "that the sensibility of flesh and blood to beauty is as broad a fact as the effect of heat or cold. It is so universally recognised that we take a pretty girl, like original sin or the curse of labour, as a *chose jugeé*. Her sway must have begun with the glacial drifters and the kitchen middeners and the Engis skull man, when they and the rest of the paleoliths were battling with the dodo and the dinornis and the didifornis, and had no time for the cult of beauty except by proxy. Did it ever occur to you that we men drove a hard bargain with your sex when we compelled you to beauty, made you carry the topknots and the tail-feathers? Men propose marriage, women adorn themselves to listen. Let women choose their mates, and they might go as plain as peahens; and men would strut about, displaying wattles, combs and argus-eyed plumes."

"Women would be less beautiful if they proposed?"

"Some could not be, I fear." He pulled down his brows, considering the proposition, then shook his head positively, with a little sigh. "You will remember—was it not Darwin who said that women, in order to attract men, borrow the plumage of male birds, which these have acquired to please the females of their kind? Beauty must be the first law of life to the sex that has not the privilege of choosing. Under the circumstances, it is surprising how much of plainness women have preserved. Possibly because of the extraordinary directions which beauty culture may take. Burton asserts that the Somali choose wives by ranging the women in line for inspection; she wins a husband of note who projects farthest *a tergo*. Yet among famous Greek statues there is also a steatopygous Venus."

The office boy came to the door, and his knock woke Uncle out of his revery. He excused himself to his caller, and, returning to me, went on.

"I have been—ah—I admit, rather evading the personal question. I wish, without seeking embarrassing confidences, to remind you that young people are apt to think bad matters—other than business matters—worse than they are. I am not asking questions, but, when I was younger, cynicism usually hid but ill the scars of heartache. Do not, I pray you, throw yourself away in the gloom of momentary unhappiness."

Did he guess—about Ned? That I was the one most hurt there? He should never know that I winced. I shrugged my shoulders, ignoring his fatherly glance, and faced him with a stare meant to be brazen.

"You do not at the present time believe in sentiment?" he said. "Then I shall adapt my argument to your whim of practicality, and speak of the rumours which connect your name with that of young Lord Strathay."

"Oh; that boy!"

"I presume you are right; he does seem to have fallen deeply in love with you. But—if indeed, you are dazzled by the glamour of a title—do not be too confident of his fealty. I know men better than you know them, my dear. Man loves beauty, but he does not always want to marry it. The rare white swan is admired, but the little brown partridge, clucking as she marshals her covey of chicks, is the type of the marrying woman. Again, no man is master of himself. That Strathay wishes to marry you, I can understand; but, perhaps, when he is not under the spell of your presence, he falls to wondering how you will pronounce the social shibboleths, and may let 'I dare not' wait upon 'I would.' It is idle to deny that, admitting as one must the existence of lines of social cleavage in modern life, it is often a mistake to overstep their boundaries in matrimony; though as to international alliances—"

"Oh," I said, interrupting his prosings with a light laugh, "you mustn't take the matter *au sérieux*."

"I take it so because it is serious." The Judge's eyes and his tone were very grave. "Forgive me if I remind you that these *obiter dicta* have grown out of a discussion of your money affairs, wherein you are bankrupt. If— and I ask your pardon if the supposition does you wrong—if you are relying on a brilliant marriage to help you out of financial difficulties—"

He hesitated a moment, then went on slowly: "Perhaps I ought to warn you that, if at any time this does become a serious matter, you will have powerful opposition. I had not intended to tell you—though now I deem it best—that Mr. Stephen Allardyce Poultney has lately done me the honour to call; and—"

"Lord Strathay's cousin?" I thought he could hear the thrumming of my heart. This was why he had beaten so long about the bush! "Was he—was he speaking about me?"

I felt a sudden chill of apprehension, and almost feared to hear the answer.

"He was; he came to the point with a refreshing directness worthy of a business man, and said that he wanted to know all about you."

"And you—"

"I need not trouble you with our conversation. In view of the attentions which his Lordship has been paying you, his cousin felt it a duty, he intimated, to make inquiries. He did not care a button, I inferred, for your position here, as it could not affect Lord Strathay's in England; but he had read the newspapers with pardonable perplexity, and asked if you were really the only daughter of a bonanza farmer. I did not feel it necessary to enter into particulars, but informed him that your father was rich in honesty and in the possession of a daughter good and beautiful enough for any Lord that lives. He thanked me and said 'quite so,' as Englishmen usually do say when they disagree with one. He added that he would try to get the poor beggar—for so he referred to his kinsman—away fishing.

"You will note that, in the higher social strata, the choice of matrimonial partners has progressed beyond the personal selection so confidently assumed by the scientists, and has become a matter for relatives to—"

"And my only relative in New York," I said slowly, wondering how fatal was this unexpected news, "has made it impossible for me to achieve a success that was almost within my grasp."

I don't see that the remark was so very terrible, but he looked at me with an odd air of astonishment and consternation. Then he seemed to consider it best to treat my natural disappointment as a joke.

"Not very serious is this conversation, as you have reminded me," he said. "You don't wish me to tell that which is not?"

"Why, naturally—no." I was stunned, but I forced a laugh. "But it *is* funny. Why—I was nearer landing the prize than I supposed, wasn't I?—that is, if I had wanted to land it?"

"Um—yes; it was rather close. But in this world you'll find strong men often dissuading weak ones from action briefly meditated."

He gazed at me solemnly, portentously, critically.

"Yes," I said, trying to speak with careless ease; "one Lord gone, but there are others. Don't be too hard upon Strathay, though. He's not so bad. His estates are not heavily encumbered, and he's as likely now to wed a music hall singer as a daughter of the Beerage. Perhaps such a marriage as he might have offered is not the best in life, but it is something that women who love their daughters as well as you love yours are glad to arrange for them. I should have made Strathay a very decent wife—"

But at the word I stopped; something in the sound of it shattered my cool philosophy.

"Of course, of course," Uncle assented. Then after a pause he went on, hesitatingly. "Nelly, these are not matters for a man to discuss with you. Why don't you run in and talk with your aunt?"

I hadn't the least intention of calling, but I answered him according to his folly.

"I must, some time; but I'm so worried—"

"Ah, yes; those debts. Could you not, if you are determined not to come home to us, seek less expensive apartments? You know that for any wants in reason your aunt and I—"

"I—I can't, just yet," I faltered, with a dreary vision before my eyes of such a boarding house as that from which Kitty rescued me.

"Very well, Nelly, but think about it; you will see that to go on as you are doing would be only throwing money into a bottomless pit. But bring me your bills tomorrow; I must have facts and figures, if we are to straighten your affairs. Now—you need money—"

He was fumbling for his check book. Badly as I needed help, instinctively I cried:—

"Oh, no; not that!"

"Quite sure? It is the situation that troubles you and not the butcher, the baker—"

"Quite sure."

"I desist. But sleep on what I have said. Remember that I am in your father's place, that I—your aunt and I—are very anxious about you."

He took my hand, seeming as perplexed as I am myself. He looked affectionate enough, but so futile.

So I came away heartsick. It's useless to argue with Judge Baker. He's a plebeian from his thick shoe soles to his thin hair; but he's honest. And yet —if he had been less ponderously precise—he might have said: "Why, really, I don't exactly know. Mr. Winship is a well-to-do man. It has been years since I knew, but I can ascertain and—"

Or he might just have told the plain truth—that Father has a large Western farm. Englishmen think all Western folks are rich. Why, I believe Meg Van Dam would dower me if I were to marry Strathay. I could make it worth her while. It wouldn't be the first arrangement of that sort in New York, either.

If only Strathay had seen me once more, no power on earth could have prevented an avowal; and marriage with a peer of England would have given me a station befitting my beauty.

But perhaps it's not too late. Strathay may not heed his cousin. If he comes wooing again, I shall not be so silly as I was the last time. Strange that I have not seen him. Can he have gone already?

I might do the London season by borrowing from Meg. It would cost a fortune, and—unless Strathay does propose—perhaps even she wouldn't care to finance me now.

I wish—

Oh, I wish I could get out of my dreams the ghastly form of Darmstetter, as I saw him dead at my feet! He haunts me all day long, and all the night I dream of him!

And I wish I had not broken John Burke's honest heart—how wistful he looked, as he waited for me at the door of the office and helped me to my carriage! Perhaps Ned wasn't in the building; perhaps—he may have avoided me.

I wish I had not brought him sorrow, and I wish—

No, I don't! I just hope Milly is even more wretched than I am!

Father really might mortgage. I could easily pay it back. I wonder I never thought of that. I'll ask him. I will not take my bills to Judge Baker—to be lectured on the dodo and on lines of social cleavage—as if any man could be a match for me.

I'll never go back to Aunt Frank! There is Bellmer, now—and Strathay must soon return to New York, to sail.

6

Little Brown Partridges

May 20.

I wonder if I couldn't *earn* money. For the last week—nothing but trouble. No check from Father. Hugh Bellmer I have not seen. Strathay has really gone, spirited away by that superior cousin.

And Mrs. Whitney has deserted me—oh, if it were not for money troubles, I wouldn't mind that, cruel as was the manner of it!

Of course the newspapers soon learned that Strathay had left town. Trust them for that; and to make sensational use of it! The first I knew of it, indeed, was when one day Cadge came bursting into the room.

"Isn't it a shame?" she began in her piercing voice; as ever at fever heat of unrest, she waved at me a folded newspaper.

"Emphatically; but what is it?"

"That fierce tale of the *Echo*; haven't seen it? We couldn't print a line. Big Tom says the chief has put his foot down; won't have stories about women in private life, you know—without their consent. But why didn't you—why can't you give us a whack at it?"

"Because there isn't a word of truth in the whole disgusting—what does it say?"

I had seized the sheet from her hands and rapidly glanced over the staring headlines. Eagerly she interrupted me:—

"Oh, isn't it the worst ever? But I see how it happened. They must have sent out a leg man to get facts, and when no one would talk, they stirred this up in the office. But—not to print, now—what *are* you going to do with His Lordship? Honest, Princess?"

"Nothing; there's absolutely nothing between us. He's a nice fellow, and I like him, and we're good friends; that's all. I—I knew he was going; fishing."

"Well, I'm glad of that. But so must I be going."

And she whisked out of the room, leaving in my hands this astounding outrage upon truth and decency:

BY EDWARD PEPPER

HELEN WINSHIP is the most extraordinary woman living;

The most beautiful woman in the world;

A scientist of national repute;

She has just passed through a tragedy which has left an impress upon her whole life;

Most wonderful of all, she is the only American girl who has ever refused a titled lover.

This is her life story, told for the first time:—

Chapter I.—Death:
A WOMAN's scream of agony!

A strange scene, like an alchemist's den, the light of falling day reflected from test tubes and crucibles, revealing in dark corners uncouth appliances, queer diagrams, strange odours. Upon the floor the inert figure of the foremost of New York's chemists; above his prostrate form, wild-eyed with horror at seeing his dramatic death, a beautiful woman, the most beautiful in the world.

This was the end of Prof. Carl Darmstetter;

This was how the legacy of science came to Helen Winship.

To carry it out, she has refused a title.

Chapter II.—Love:
BORN UPON a Western farm, Helen Winship's father is a yeoman of the sturdy stock that has laid the world under tribute for its daily bread.

Early she made the choice that devotes her life to science. She was the confidant of the dead chemist, whose torch of knowledge she took up firm-handed, when it fell from his nerveless fingers.

She is vowed as a vestal virgin to science.

Strange whim of destiny! Across this maiden life of devoted study came the shadow of a great name which for two hundred years has been blazoned upon the pages of England's history.

In the loom of fate the modest gray warp of Helen Winship's life crossed the gay woof of a Lord of high degree, and left a strange mark upon the web of time.
Love came to her—many times; but came at last in a guise that seldom woos in vain.

Chapter III.—Sacrifice:
WHO HAS forgotten the memorable scene in the Metropolitan Opera House, when the beautiful Miss Winship took the vast audience by storm, causing almost a panic, which was exclusively reported in these columns?

It was followed by a greater sensation.

Rumour ran through the ranks of the Four Hundred, and the rustle of it was as the wind in a great forest. For one of the proudest titles from beyond the sea, before which the wealth and fashion of the city had marshalled their attractions, had passed them by to kneel at the feet of the lovely scholar.

The Earl of Strathay is the twelfth Earl of his house. He is twenty-one years old. His mother, the Countess Strathay, famous as a beauty, has been prominent in the "Prince's set."

Witley Castle, his seat, is one of the show places of England, though financially embarrassed by the follies of the late Earl.

It was Lord Strathay's intention, upon landing in New York to go West in a week; but he looked upon the fair investigator, and to look is to love.

He laid his title at the feet of the lovely daughter of Democracy, but with that smile whose sweetness is a marvel to all men, she shook her beautiful head.

She was wedded to learning.

Fretted by the pain, he plunged into the wilderness to hide like a wounded deer.

What shall be said of this beautiful woman, for whom men sigh as for the unattainable? That she is lovely as the morning? All New York knows it. That her walk is like a lily's swaying in the wind, her voice is the sweetest music that ever ravished ear, her hair a lure for sunbeams? It is the commonplace of conversation at every smart house.

For this lovely woman of science is no ascetic. She moves by right of beauty and high purpose, in the best society. This farmer's daughter walks among the proudest in the land, and none there is to compare with her.

Like the Admirable Crichton, no art is to her unknown, no accomplishment by her neglected. Her eager soul, not satisfied with dominion over the realm of beauty and of love, would have all knowledge for its sphere.

Amusing, isn't it?—to one who is not the heroine of the tale! The tragedy of Darmstetter revived, my scientific attainments—but oh, the worst—the worst of all—is the wicked lie that I am in the "best society."

Why, the very day before, we had been "at home," Mrs. Whitney and I, and hardly a soul that counts was here. Mrs. Van Dam had a convenient headache; I haven't seen her since Peggy's wedding. If she had not been so very civil—she and Mrs. Henry—I might think that even then she suspected that Strathay—

There were a few correct, vapid young men in gray trousers and long frock coats among our guests that day, but none worth serious attention. And the women!

One creature tucked tracks under the tea cloth, whereat Mrs. Whitney's pinched nose was elevated. Ethel saw the action—in spite of her mother and sister, the poor girl clings to me; I suppose it's natural that *she* should love beauty—and hopping round the table at the first chance, she pulled out one, chuckling mightily.

"'Favour is deceitful and beauty is vain,'" she quoted in undertone; "oh, Nelly, take your share of the unco guid and the riders of hobby horses, and be thankful it's no larger."

Ethel doesn't know how great it is. There was the woman who insists on gloating over me as a proof of the superiority of her sex; the woman who had written a book, the woman who would talk about Karma, and the woman—there was more than one—who would talk about the Earl.

After they had gone, Mrs. Whitney's disgust was as plain as her horror of their appetite for cake and other creature comforts. But the storm broke in earnest a day or two later, after the last reception we shall ever hold together.

I can't describe it. I don't understand it. Women are fast leaving the city; it was too late for an "evening."

But that made no difference; I do not deceive myself. I am pressing with my shoulders against a mountain barrier—the prejudice of women—and it never, never yields. Active opposition I could fight; but the tactics are now to ignore me. In response to cards, I get "regrets," or women simply stay away.

Men—ah, yes, there are always men, and many of them like as well as admire me. But there is a subtle something that affects every man's thought of a woman of whom women disapprove. They don't condemn me—ah, a man can be generous!—they imagine they allow for women's jealousies; but deep in their hearts lies hid the suspicion that only women are qualified judges of women. They respect me, but they reserve judgment; and they do not wholly respect themselves, for in order to see me, they evade their lawful guardians—their wives and mothers.

It may have been the wine—I overheard two young cads making free of my house to discuss my affairs.

"Mrs. Terry really dragged Hughy out of town?" one of them asked, assuming a familiarity with Bellmer that I suspect he cannot claim.

"Guess so; he's playing horse with old Bellmer's money; always wrong side of the betting."

"Needs Keeley cure. Good natured cuss; wonder if the Winship'll get him."

"Lay ye three to one—say twenties—that he gets away, like that Strathay—"

I addressed some smiling speech to the wretches, but through the whole evening my cheeks did not cease to burn.

When the last guest had gone, tired and hysterical as she was, Mrs. Whitney began a long tirade.

"It must be stopped! It must be stopped!" she cried, pacing back and forth.

The blaze of anger improved her. She must have been a handsome woman once—tall and slender, with fine dark eyes that roll about dramatically.

"I don't see what there is to stop," I said, perversity taking possession of me, though at heart I quite agreed with her estimate of the evening. "The object of an entertainment being to entertain, why shouldn't the men I know come to ours? If they stayed away, you'd be disappointed; but when they come, as they did tonight, you're frightened, or pretend to be."

"I'm not frightened; I'm appalled. I don't mean Mr. Burke, though he's a detrimental—and, by the way, he was as much distressed tonight as I was. I mean the men who have families—wives and daughters! Why didn't they bring 'em—or stay away?"

"I'd thank John Burke to mind his own business," I cried hotly. "He doesn't have to come here unless he wants to."

"There is only one way," she went on, as if speaking to herself, pacing the floor and fanning herself violently—for her face, and especially her nose, was as red as a beet; she really laces disgracefully—"there's only one way; I must fall ill at once. I must have nervous prostration, or—it's nearly June. I shall leave town. Heavens! What a night!"

"You're assuming a great deal. Our arrangements were made by two, and are hardly to be broken by one. You can't agree to matronize me—let me buy furniture for you, and then abandon me, cut off my social opportunities—leave me—"

"Social opportunity! Social collapse! Disgrace! Why, your prospects were really extraordinary. But now! Where was Meg tonight? Where was Mrs. Marmaduke? Why did my own sister-in-law stay away?"

"I don't know; do you?"

Her harangue begun, she couldn't stop. "Where's Strathay?" she demanded. "Gone; and no announcement—what was the matter? Needn't tell me you refused him! And why is the letter box always full of duns? Can't you pay your bills? Why didn't you say so earlier? Would have saved us both a deal of trouble!"

"I didn't tell you I had money."

"You played the part, ordering dresses fit for a Duchess, and things for the flat. You spent enough on a wedding gift for Peggy—or was it a promise to spend?—to support a family a month—peace offering because you'd abused her!—Of course if you'd made the great success everybody expected, you'd be on the top wave, and so should I. I don't deny I thought of that. But now—an evening like this—no women worth counting and a horde of men—well, it's bad enough for me, but it's worse for you. No one'll say I brought 'em."

"Oh, no," I assented.

"It comes to this, then," she went on at full heat, flushing and fanning herself still more violently; "either you or I must leave this house, and at once."

"Well, I sha'n't."

And so she did!

Whose fault was it that we were left in such a predicament—that of the inexperienced girl, or the chaperon's? What is a chaperon for? Mrs. Whitney has treated me shamefully, shamefully! Here I am all by myself, and I don't know what to do.

Ah, well, I must play my own hand. She shall regret this night's work, if I marry rank or money.

It is so strange how everyone prospers except poor, baffled, loveless me, who have the greatest gift of all. I wonder if it is really Nature's law that the very beautiful must suffer; if this is her way of equalizing the lot of the poor and plain and lowly; her law of compensation to make the splendid creatures walk lonely and in sorrow all their days while plain ones coo and are happy. Was Uncle Tim right about the little brown partridges?

If I were superstitious or easily disheartened, I should say—but I am neither! I shall succeed. I will take my place by right of beauty or die fighting! If I see Lord Strathay again, he shall marry me within a week. They shall call it "one of those romantic weddings."

I can't live here alone. I have nothing to fall back upon; nothing but a father who doesn't answer my letters, and Judge Baker who lectures me in polysyllables, and John Burke—poor old John; what a good fellow he is!—who simply loves me; and Mrs. Van Dam, who was my friend as long as she hoped to rise by my beauty to higher place, but who has headaches now; and Mrs. Marmaduke—

I don't understand her desertion.

Ah—yes, there is another, my constant companion now.

He is an old man, thin and sallow. He lies prone on the floor, staring at me with dead, sightless eyes. He whispers from muted lips "Delilah!" and the sound of it is in my ears day and night; day and night!

My God! It will drive me mad!

7

Letters and Science

May 29.

I 've revised my opinion of the newspapers. the *Star* has done me a good turn, a great service.

I had tried to borrow money of Cadge, for the third time, and she told me she had none—which was true, or she would have let me have it. Then she said:—

"Why don't you sell a story to some paper—either something very scientific, or else, 'Who's the Handsomest Man in New York?' or—"

"I think I ought to get something from them, after all the stuff they've printed; but how? To whom do I go?"

"Nobody! Heavens!" cried Cadge. "Want to create an earthquake on Park Row? You're a disturber of traffic. Let me manage. I know the ropes and it helps me at the office to bring in hot features. They might give you fifty for it, too."

And I actually did get $50 for digging out of the text books an essay on Rats as Disseminators of Bubonic Plague; they only used a little of it, but the pictures and the signature and the nonsense about me as a scientist were the real thing, Cadge said.

The money, the money, the money was the real thing to me! It has given me a breathing spell—. that and the hundred for signing a patent medicine testimonial; but I had to sacrifice more than half I got from both sources to pacify greedy creditors. And a month between remittances, and so little when they come! Father *can't* refuse to mortgage; why doesn't he write to me?

The day I took the article to Cadge I had a long talk with her and with Pros. Reid, who spends at the eyrie every hour he can spare. One must have some society or go crazy, though perhaps they aren't exactly what I'd choose if my kingdom had opened to me.

Pros. has shrewd eyes that inspire confidence—gray eyes with the tired night work look in them. He talks amazing slang at times, at others not at all; and I wish everyone might be as kind and thoughtful.

I could think of nothing all the evening but my bills, and at last I was moved to ask him abruptly:—

"What can a girl do to get money, Pros.?"

"'Pends on the girl."

"This girl; a somewhat educated person; and grasping. One who wants much money and wants it right now."

"Princesses don't earn money; they have it."

"Suppose the Princess were enchanted—or—or something? Oh, you may not think me serious, but I really don't know what I shall do, if my ship doesn't come in pretty soon."

He looked quizzically at me; he thinks I plead poverty as a joke; Cadge would never tell him how I have tried to borrow.

"'Twould be a hard case, supposing it possible," he said, "because you would want a good deal of money, and because you'd be a bother to have 'round—too beautiful. You couldn't sell many newspaper stories, because you'd soon cease to be a novelty as a special, and would get a press ticket to City Hall Park. Reporting's another coloured horse altogether—poor pay, and takes training to get it. Beauty's a disadvantage even there; too much beauty. Tell you what you could do, though, if ever you *should* want to earn money—go on the stage."

"Girl I knew," said Cadge, "made a pot of money going round to summer resorts, giving women lessons, energizing and decomposing; kind of Delsarte; said it made her 'most die—to see 'em rolling on the floor like elephants, trying to get lean, and eating 'emselves fat four times a day, with caramels between—and not be able to laugh. Might try the Barnard girls. It can't be sure beauty to be up there; I've seen some of 'em. Say now; that's not so bad—'How to be Helen; in Twenty Lessons.' Or say, Princess; answer the great question: 'Does Soap Hurt the Skin?'"

She grinned. Cadge fancies, I suppose, that by any mail I may get a big check from home.

"You display almost human intelligence," said Pros, admiringly; "stage's better, though."

"But, Mr. Reid, that's too public."

"Inherited instinct; no more public than—than being a beauty." He gazed at me with mild audacity,—"Money getting's prosaic, off the stage. Most girls who want cash become tiddlety-wink typewriters at eight per; bargain price; fully worth four. Now that isn't your class; if $8 a week would satisfy you, which it wouldn't, do you suppose there's an office in town that'd have you? Men won't subject their clerks to the white light of beauty; wives won't stand for it, either. There are places where no girl can get work unless she's pulchritudinous. Catch the idea? A pretty London barmaid can't draw more beer than an ugly one, but draws more custom. What's a Princess to do with such jobs? You'd be like the man who wouldn't be fool enough to marry any woman who'd be fool enough to have him—in getting work, I mean. This is the other side of all that rot about Woman's Century and Woman's Widening Sphere. Never go into an office, Miss Winship; my wife won't, when we're married."

"'Cause she'll be in one already," interrupted Cadge; "why, if I had to mope 'round all day in a flat, I'd be driven to drink—club tea. Imagine it; Cadge Bryant a clubwoman!"

"Clubwomaning is exciting enough, election time."

"But men get money," I persisted. "Isn't there anything a girl can do?"

"I've a sister," said Reid, "—other sister out in Cincinnati—who wants a profession; law's the one I'm recommending. It's so harmless. Course she'll never have any practice; she won't get out and hustle with the greasy Yahoudis who run the bar now-a-days. No, so long as my sister has the career fever, I say law, every time. Cadge, why don't you study law?"

"The dear boy does so enjoy talking nonsense," Cadge explained indulgently.

"In ordinary business," Reid went on, "pretty women are only employed as lures for men. Swell milliners have 'em to overawe with their great grieving eyes the Hubbies who're inclined to kick at market rates for bonnets. Now there's dry goods, chief theme of half the race. You'd think there'd be a show there for a pretty girl; well, there ain't. It's retail trade; one girl can sell about as many papers of pins in a day as another."

"Some pretty cloak and suit models get big wages," said Cadge.

"Yes, in the jobbing houses. That's wholesale trade, and every dicker counts. Have to corset themselves to death, though."

"It's a fact," Cadge put in. "Many's the filler I've written about it. Girl has to destroy her beauty to get a living by her beauty."

"Sure! Fashions not made to fit women, but women to fit fashions. Then those girls have an awful time, if they're careful about their associates. Why, it's getting so a model is expected to sell goods herself— held responsible if she doesn't. No sale, no job next week. See the situation," Pros. added, "—on the one hand the buyer, a vain man away from home, with thousands to invest; on the other a girl who must get that money for her firm. Well, of course it's not so bad as that, but—"

"But *I* wouldn't corset myself Redfern shape and go into such horrid places for the world," I cried.

No more than Judge Baker, or Father, or anyone else, could Reid see my situation. What do I care about earning $8 a week—or $80? I must have a great deal of money, at once; to pay my debts and to live upon. Men get money quickly—in Wall Street or by inventions or—

"Course not," said Pros. "You're the Princess; and Princesses may be Honorary Presidents and ask questions and take an interest, but they don't do things."

"Pros. is right about the stage," said Cadge; "that's the best sort of wholesale business. You sell a chance to look at you to fifteen hundred people at once; and folks can't paw you over to see how your clothes fit, either. I'd like it myself, but I'm too—well, after all, I might do; I'm at least picturesquely ugly."

And so the antiphony of discouragement ended in a laugh.

I wonder—women on the stage do get big sums, and they often graduate from it to society. If even a music hall singer can become a duchess—

Bellmer's father made his money in sugar, they say. If I had it, I could storm any position. I suppose Mrs. Terry has shooed him off on that automobile tour I heard about; but he must come back—and so must Strathay.

I can't wait long, I'm not safe an hour from human vultures hungry for money, though I've none to yield them.

I must do something. No sooner had Mrs. Whitney vanished from the flat in a whirlwind of tears and reproaches than in came the furniture man, as if he had been watching the house, to threaten that, unless I pay at once, he will take away everything. He was not rude in words, but oh, so different from the oily people who sold me the things. His ferret eyes searched the apartment; he seemed counting every article.

"The furniture's safe," I said; "it won't walk away."

"Of course it's safe," he answered with a suspicion of a sneer; "but when'll it be paid for?"

"I don't know; go away!" I said. "I've written to my father."

The fellow looked at me with open admiration.

"Better 'tend to this thing; better write again to—your father," he said and walked off, leaving me cold and tremulous with rage.

I must have imagined the pause, the inflection; but he has me under surveillance. Like a thief!

I flew to the dining room and swallowed a glass of sherry, for I was faint and quivering; but before I had turned from the sideboard Cadge bounced into the room, tearing through the flat to find me, and stopped to stare, open-eyed.

"Drop that!" she cried.

"Oh, don't preach! I've just been having such a time!"

"Everybody has 'em; I've had fifty a year for fifty years. And I don't mind your drowning sorrow in the flowing bowl, either. But do it like a man, in company. Honest now, Helen."

She changed the subject abruptly to the errand that had brought her; but, before she went away, she looked curiously at the sideboard and said: —

"Helen, you really don't—"

"Mercy, no! Scarcely at table, even. Why I used to be shocked to see how things to drink are thrust upon women, even in department stores. But they're not all deadly; there's 'creme de menthe' now—the pep'mint extract Ma used to give me for stomachache."

Cadge laughed with me, but she turned quickly grave again.

"Mind what I tell you, Princess," she said, "and never, never drink even 'pep'mint extract' in the house like that, alone; if you do, I see your finish; reporters learn a thing or two."

She's right—for ordinary women. But I told her the truth; I don't care for wine. I've seen girls flushed at dinner, but I know too much of physiology, and I care too much for my beauty.

Still, in emergencies—

Emergencies—oh! I could have named to her the very day I first tasted wine. It was here in the Nicaragua, the day Darmstetter—

Well, well,—I mustn't think about that. I can't understand why I don't hear from Father. Impossible to make him see how different are my present tastes and pressing needs from those I brought from home. I hope he won't delay long about the money.

My position is becoming intolerable. I owe the butcher, grocer, furniture dealer, photographer—and the milliner is the worst of all. The money I got from the *Star* is filched from me by people who need it far less than I. Why, I even owe money to the maids, and I can't discharge either of them, because I'd have to pay her. But they must somehow be sent away.

My position is becoming intolerable.

I wonder if Father couldn't sell the farm. That would bring more than a mortgage; but it might take months, and even then I need in a single year more than all he has in the world.

Will any woman who reads the story of my life—the real story which sometime I shall write, leaving out the paltry details which now harass me —will any woman believe that the most beautiful woman in the world in the wonderful year, of the finding of the Bacillus actually thought of tramping the streets, looking for work, like a story heroine seeking her fortune? I shall have to do something—anything!

But I can't work; I'm not calm enough, and it would ruin my beauty.

The luck must change!

Sometimes I see more clearly than the sordidness of this horrible existence, a big palace with a terraced front and a mile long drive straight to the park gate, past great trees and turf that is always green; and long rows of stately ladies looking down on me from their frames on the lofty wall beside soldiers that have stood silent guard there three hundred years. I can see a beautiful woman courtesying to a Queen and all the world reading it in the morning paper; and a big town house with myriad lights blinking through the fog outside, where shivering wretches watch the carriages drive up to my door. For twenty—no thirty years—I might be the one inimitable and wholly adorable being, clothed with rare garments, blazing with jewels, confidant of statesmen, maker of the men who make history. History! I should *be* history!

I could do it all myself—I have never had a chance, never yet the glimmer of a chance, but I could do anything, conquer anything, achieve anything!

It is so little that I ask—the money to live upon, and a chance, only the chance—it is maddening to be denied that!—and fair play to live my life and carry out my destiny.

There was a time when I wanted less, expected less; like Cadge with queer, devoted Pros. or Kitty Reid, her hair blowing about her face, happy with her daubs, messing about in the studio. Was I happier when I was like that? I would not go back to it! I would not barter my beauty for any other gift on earth. I shall fight and fight to the last ditch. I don't propose to be a pawn on the chess board.

If it comes to that, I shall know what to do!

8

A Chaperon on a Cattle Train

June 4.

This has been one of my worst days, and I have for a long time had no days but bad ones. Three things have happened, either one of which would alone have been a calamity. Together they crush, they frighten, they humiliate me!

This morning came this letter from Father:—

Hannibal, May 31.

DEAR NELLY:—

I take my pen in hand to tell you that we are all well and hope that you are the same. It was a very cold winter and we were so put to it to get water for the stock after the dry fall that I am thinking of putting down a driven well this summer if I can find the money. Ma has a sprained wrist which is painful but not serious. John Burke sent home some little items from the papers. We are glad that you have been having a good time. We were glad that you had gone to Timothy's house, though John Burke said the girl you were with before was very nice. But twas right not to stay long enough to wear out your welcome. I do not see how I can get so much money.

I have sent you all I had by me and we have been pinched a good deal too. I had a chance of a pass on a cattle train and Ma said why don't you go east yourself and see Nelly. But I said no school's most done and she'll be coming home and how can I leave? Shaw said she we can tend to everything all right so maybe I will come. I have written to Timothy and will do as he says. I have a feeling Daughter that you need someone by you in the city. Ma sends her love and asks why you don't write oftener. We wouldn't scarcely know what you was doing at all if it wasn't for John.

Your Loving Father,

EZRA D. WINSHIP.

It seems I'm to have a new chaperon. He's a little stiff in the joints and his face is wrinkled and his talk is not that of society and he's coming out of the West on a cattle train. Good Lord!

Oh, yes, he'll come. Uncle Timothy'll urge him to take me back to the farm.

I won't go back! As soon as I had read this news I started for the Imperial Theatre to see the manager. I walked, for I have no more credit at the livery stable; and I was grimly amused to see in the shop windows the "Winship hats" and graceful "Winship scarves" that are coining money for other people while I have scarcely carfare.

The unusual exercise may have tired me, or perhaps it was some lingering remnant of the old farm superstition against the theatre that made me slacken my steps as I neared the office. I remembered my father's tremulous voice cautioning me against playhouses before I started for the city.

"Now don't ye go near them places," he said, wiping his nose and dodging about the corners of his eyes. "They're bad for young girls."

Why do I think of these things? If he cares so much for me, why doesn't he get me the money I asked for; instead of coming here on a cattle train?

Whatever the reason, Puritanic training or fear of my errand, I walked slowly back and forth in front of the dingy little office of the theatre for some time before I conquered my irresolution and went desperately into the place.

They told me the manager was out, but after a little waiting I began to suspect that this was a dingy white lie, and so it proved; for when I lifted my veil and blushing like a school girl, told the people in the office who I was, at once someone scurried into a little den and presently came out to say that Mr. Blumenthal had "returned."

Oh, the manager's an important person in his way; he has theatres in every part of the country and is a busy man. But he was willing enough to see me when his stupid people had let him know that I was the Miss Winship! Sorry as was my heart, I felt a thrill of triumph at this new proof of my fame and the power beauty gives.

When I entered his office, a bald little man turned from a litter of papers and looked at me with frank, business-like curiosity, as if he had a perfect right to do so—and indeed he had. I was not there to barter talent, but to rent my face. I understood that; but perhaps for this very reason my tongue tripped as it has seldom done of late when I blunderingly explained my errand.

"Guess we can do something for you," he said promptly. "Of course there's a horde of applicants, but you're exceptional; you know that."

He smiled good-naturedly, and I felt at once relieved and indignant that he should treat as an everyday affair the step I had pondered during so many sleepless nights.

"Must remember though," he added, "on the stage a passably pretty woman with a good nose, who has command of her features and can summon expression to them, often appears more beautiful than a goddess-faced stick. However, it's worth trying. I don't believe you're a stick. Ah,—would you walk on?"

"I don't understand."

"Stage slang; would you be willing to go on as a minor character—wear fine clothes and be looked at without saying much—at first, you know? Or—of course your idea's to star—you got a backer?"

"I don't understand that, either."

"Someone to pay the bills while you're being taught. To hire a company and a theatre as a gamble."

"Impossible! I want money at once. I supposed that my—my beauty would command a position on the stage; it's certainly a bar to employment off it."

"Of course it would; yes, yes, but not immediately. Why, even Mrs. Farquhar had to have long and expensive training before she made her debut. And you know what a scandal there had been about her!

"Not that there's been any about you," he added hastily, to my look of amazement. "But you know—ah—public mention of any sort piques curiosity. Er—what's your act?"

"My act?"

"Yes; what can you do?"

"Sing a little; nothing else. I thought of opera."

This proposition didn't seem to strike him favourably.

"I don't know—" he hesitated. "You have a wonderful speaking voice, and you've been advertised to beat the band. Who's your press agent?"

"I don't quite know what a press agent is; but I'm sure I never had any."

"Well, you don't need any. Now that I see you—, but I fancied months ago that you were probably getting ready for this. Suppose you sing a little song for me."

We stumbled through dim passages to the stage, half-lighted by a window or two high overhead. Mr. Blumenthal sat alone in the orchestra, and I summoned all my resolution, and then, frightened and ashamed and desperate, I sang the "Sehnsucht," following it with what Cadge calls a "good yelling song" to show the power of my voice.

Then the rotund little manager rolled silently back to the office, and I knew as I followed him that I had been judged by a different standard from that of an applauding drawing room.

"Well!" said he, when we had regained his room. "You are a marvel! Sing by all means; but, if you must have immediate results, not in opera. Music halls get pretty much the most profitable part of the business since they became so fashionable in London. Tell you what I'll do.—I'll give you a short trial at—say a hundred a week. You've a wonderful voice and no training; but any teacher can soon put you in shape to sing a few showy songs. Give me an option on your services for a longer term at a higher figure, if you take to the business and it takes to you, and you can start in next month at the roof garden."

"The roof garden!" I cried out; but then I saw how foolish it would be to feel affronted at this common man with money who would rank me as an attraction among acrobats and trick dogs.

"I shouldn't like that," I said more calmly; "people are very foolish, of course, but I've been told that—that if I were to sing in public, my appearance would mark a new era in music; now, I wouldn't care to sing in such a place; I had hoped, too, that I could get more—more salary."

"Would seem so, wouldn't it?" said Mr. Blumenthal. "But it's a fair offer. Tell you why.

"You'll take with an audience, for a short run, anyhow, if you've got—er—temperament; but I run the risk that you haven't. I spend considerable money getting you ready to appear, and then you're on the stage only a few minutes. Another thing: Most people nowadays are short sighted; you have to capture 'em in the mass—two Topsies, four Uncle Toms, eight Markses the lawyers, twenty chorus girls kicking at once—big stage picture, you know, not the individual. And the individual must have the large manner. Yes, yes; I use you for bait to draw people, but I need other performers to amuse 'em after they're here. They want to feel that there's 'something doing' all the while, something different. Curiosity wouldn't last long; either you'd turn out an artist and—er—do what a music hall audience wants done, or you'd fail. In the former case you could command more money; never so much as people say, though. There's so many liars."

"I—I'll think over your offer," I said. "I wouldn't have to wear—"

"Costumes of approved brevity? No; at least not to start with."

Mr. Blumenthal also had risen. He looked at me, as if aroused to my ignorance of things theatrical, with a more personal and kindly interest.

"Sorry my offer doesn't strike you favourably," he said. "I'd like mighty well to bring you out; but if you hold off for opera—that isn't my line, though—mind you, I don't say it could be done; but if someone were found to put up the money, would you wait and study? Know what you'd be undertaking, I suppose—hard work, regular hours, open air, steady habits? That's the life of a singer. Your health good? No nerves? We might make a deal, if you mean business. Trouble is, so many beautiful women think beauty as an asset is worth more than it is; it makes 'em careless about studying while they're young, and it can't last—"

I never heard the end of that sentence. I flew home and went straight to my mirror. Sure enough, I fancied I saw a haggard look about the eyes—

My God! This gift of beauty doesn't confer immunity from fatigue, accident, old age. This loveliness must fade and crack and wrinkle, these full organ tones must shrivel to a shrill pipe; and I—I! shall one day be a tottering old woman, bent, gray, hideous!

And all the little disfiguring hurts of life—they frighten me! I never enter a train that I do not think, with a shudder, of derailment and bleeding gashes and white scars; or cross a street without looking about for the waving hoofs of runaway horses that shall beat me down, or for some bicycle rider who might roll me over in a limp heap on the paving stones.

Yesterday I saw a horrid creature; her face blotched with red by acid stain or by a birth mark. Why does she not kill herself? Why didn't she die before I saw her? I shall dream of her for months—of her and Darmstetter, old and wrinkled as I shall be some day, and dead—with that same awful look in my fixed eyes!

Ah, what a Nelly I have come to be! Is it possible that I once rode frisky colts bareback and had no nerves! I mustn't have nerves! They make one old. Mr. Blumenthal said so. But how to avoid them? Oh, I must be careful; so careful! How do women dare to ride bicycles?

And this theatrical Napoleon, part of whose business is the appraisement of beauty—did he suspect that mine was less than perfect? It was perfect a month ago.

He couldn't have meant that, or he was trying to make a better bargain by cheapening the wares I brought—

But I can't go upon the stage. How could I have thought of it? I mustn't subject myself to the late hours, the grease paint, the bad air! Of what use would be a mint of money, if I lost my beauty?

I steadied my nerves with a tiny glass of Curaçoa, and looked again. The face in the mirror was beautiful, beautiful! There is no other like it! And gazing upon radiant Her, I might have recovered myself but for the third untoward event of the day.

It came in the shape of Bellmer.

Perhaps I ought not to have seen him alone, but it is hard for one who has lived in the free atmosphere of the prairie, and has been a bachelor girl in New York with Kitty Reid to think about caution. Besides, it was such a blessed relief to see his full-moon face rise above the darkness of my troubles! I greeted him with my sweetest smile, and did my very best to make myself agreeable.

"You've been out of town, haven't you?" I asked when the talk began to flag, as it soon does with Hughy.

"Aw, yes," he said; "pickin' up a record or two, with my 'mobe;' y' ought to see it; it's a beauty, gasolene, you know. Awful nuisance, punctures, though. Cost me thirteen dollars to repair one; vulcanize the tire, y'see. Tires weigh thirty pounds each; awful lot, ain't it? Stripped one right off, though, trying to turn in the mud; fastened on with half-inch spikes, too. Can't I persuade you to—aw—take a spin some day? Where's Mrs. Whitney?"

"Gone to the country; she—she's ill."

"Awful tabby, wa'n't she?"

"Oh, no; I like her very much, but she was in a hurry to leave town."

"So Aunt Terry said. Awf'ly down on you, Aunt Terry is," he drawled with even more than his usual tactlessness, "but I stand up for you, I assuah you, Miss Winship. I tell her you're awf'ly sensible an' jolly—lettin' a fellow come like this, now, and talk to you's jolly, ain't it? An' you will try my mobe? Awf'ly jolly 'twould be to take a spin."

"Very jolly indeed," I said. I turned my head that I might not see his shining scalp. Thank heaven, I thought, Hughy doesn't know enough to be deterred by two rejections, nor even by the gossip about Strathay. I wished —it was wicked, of course—I wished I were his widow; but I was determined not to repeat such folly as I had shown about the Earl.

"Very jolly," I repeated, "but you don't know what a coward I am; I believe I'd be afraid."

"Aw, no, Miss Winship," he remonstrated; "afraid of the mobe? Aw, no; not with me. I'll teach you how to run it, I do assuah you; awf'ly jolly that would be."

"Why, yes; that would be nice, of course," I said; "but—"

Oh, how shall I tell the rest? I was afraid of the machine; I knew I could never mount it, with his hand on the lever; I was just trying to refuse without offending him.

"—I'm such a coward, really," I went on; I smiled painstakingly into his stupid pink face that seemed suddenly to have grown pinker; and then I felt my smile stiffen upon my lips, for he had whirled around on the piano stool on which he was sitting, and he smiled back at me, but not as he would have done in Mrs. Whitney's presence. He—he leered!

"You wouldn't be afraid, with me, y' know,—" was all he said, but he rose as if to come nearer me.

"Oh, yes, I should—I should—" I stammered; I couldn't move; I couldn't look away from him.

I seemed face to face with some foolish, grinning masque of horror. My heart beat as I think a bird's must when a snake has eyed it; and a cold moisture broke out upon me.

"Oh, yes, I should!" I cried as I broke loose from the spell of terror, and made some halting excuse to get rid of him. I didn't dare even wait to see him leave the room, but fled from it myself, conscious as I went of his open-mouthed stare, and of his detaining: "Aw, now, Miss Winship—"

To get as far away as possible, I retreated to the kitchen, where I surprised Nora and Annie in conclave. They seized the opportunity to "give notice." Nora has a sweetheart and is to be married; Annie has invented the excuse of an ailing mother, because she dares not stay alone with me. They are both afraid, now that Mrs. Whitney—selfish creature! —has gone, and left me helpless against the world.

At any other time the news would have been a fresh calamity—for how can I pay them, or how get rid of them without paying? But with the memory of that awful scene in my head, I could think of nothing else. I don't know what I said in reply.

Bellmer's insult has stayed with me and haunted me. I had bearded a theatrical manager in his den and had been received with kindness and courtesy. He had even assumed that some things in the profession about which I was inquiring might be trying to a tenderly reared girl, and that he ought to give me advice and warnings. But this Thing bearing a gentleman's repute; this bat-brained darling of a society that I'm not thought good enough to enter, had insulted me like a boor under my own roof; and he would probably boast of it like a boor to others as base as himself! The poverty of it, the grossness of it!

I'm not ignorant, now. I know there's a way open to me—God knows I never mean to walk on it—but if ever I do go, open-eyed, into what the world calls wrong to end my worries, it will be at the invitation of one who has at least the manner of a gentleman!

Sometimes I wonder if I did right about Ned. If he had known that I loved him, if I had made it plain, if I were even now to tell him all the truth.—But he said—

I hate him! The whole world's against me, but I won't be beaten! I won't go back to the farm with Father. I will not give up the fight!

What shall I do?

9

A Burst of Sunlight

June 8.

They say the darkest hour comes just before the dawn. It was so with me. My troubles grew too great to bear, then vanished in an hour.

Fate couldn't forever frown. I knew there must be help; some hand outstretched in a pitiless world.

Really I am almost happy, for in the most unexpected and yet the most natural fashion, my perplexities have vanished; and I believe that my life will not be, after all, a failure.

The hour before the dawn was more than dark. It was dreary. In the morning I did not care to go out, and no one came except one strange man who besieged the door—there have been many such here recently, dunning and dunning and dunning, until my patience was worn to shreds. This was a decent-looking fellow with a thin face, a mustache dyed black and a carefully unkeen expression that noticed everything.

"Miss Winship?" he said, and upon my acknowledging the name, he placed a paper in my hands and went away. I was so relieved because he said nothing about wanting "a little money on account;" he wasn't even coarsely insolent, like so many of them. He did look surprised at my appearance; so surprised that his explanation of his errand died away into an unintelligible murmur. But I wasn't curious about it.

I tried to read a newspaper, only to gather from some headlines that Strathay and his cousin were passengers by an outgoing steamship. I wonder if it was all money, money, that kept him from me—or was it more than half the fear of beauty?

I couldn't read anything else, not even a note from Mrs. Marmaduke; it was dated from her country place; she hoped to see me—"in the autumn!" Peggy is in Europe; the General's going if she's not gone already. "May see you at the wedding of that odd Miss Bryant," ran her last brusque message. "I begged an invitation; really I like her. But the chances are against my being here."

All gone, I thought; my last hope, all my friends.

I had then no hope of it, no joy in life, no happiness even in my beauty. Oh, I was wretched!

There was a note from Mrs. Baker; I compelled myself to glance at that, and when I had done so, seized my hat and veil. She would call, it said, that afternoon!

With no thought but of escape, I left the house; I cared not where I went, nor what I did. I knew the Judge had sent Aunt Frank to pry into my troubles; I walked with feverish haste, I would have liked to fly to avoid her. My hands shook.

Oh, I was wretched!

As I passed the Park, I saw that spring had leaped to summer and the trees waved fresh, green branches in the air—just such trees as John and I walked under, less than a year ago, making great plans for a golden future; and a golden future there must be, but I had then no hope of it, no joy in life, no happiness even in my beauty. One only thought spurred me on, to forget past, present and future; to buy forgetfulness by any caprice; to win diversion by any adventure.

After some time I saw that I was in a side street whose number seemed familiar; self-searching at last recalled to me that on this street lived two rival faith healers, about whose lively competition for clients Cadge had once told us girls a funny story.

Could there have come to my thought some hope of finding rest from sorrow in the leading of another mind? Impossible to say. I was near insanity, I think. I chose the nearer practitioner and rang the bell.

I can smile now at memory of the stuffy little parlour into which I was ushered, but I did not smile then at it, nor at the middle-aged woman who received me with a set smile of stereotyped placidity. Her name, I think, was Mallard.

"Have you a conviction of disease, my daughter?" she asked, in a low voice with a caressing overtone gurgling in its cadences. "You look as radiant as the morn. You should not think ill."

"I am not ill," I replied; "but the world is harsh."

"The world is the expression of our sense life to the spirit," she cooed. "We do not live or die, but we pass through the phenomena. Through the purifying of our thoughts we will gradually become more and more ethereal until we are translated."

I felt that momentary shiver that folk tales tells us is caused by someone walking over our graves.

"I'm in no haste to be translated," I said.

"No one need be translated until she is ready—unless she has enemies.

Are you suffering from the errors of others? Has anyone felt fear for you? That would account for what the world calls unhappiness. Is someone trying to influence your subjective state?"

"I am convinced of it," I said with wasted sarcasm. "But you can do nothing for me; you can't—can you work on unbelievers?"

"Most assuredly. We are channels through which truth must flow to our patients. I need not tell you what I myself have done."—Mrs. Mallard modestly cast down her eyes.—"Mrs. Eddy has healed carous bones and cancers. I—some of our healers can dissuade the conviction of decayed teeth. The 'filling,' as the world calls it, is, in such cases, pink and very durable. If these marvels can be wrought upon the body, why may not the mind be led toward healing? Confide; confide."

"Heal the world of its hate of me," I cried out. "What you say is all so vague. Does the mind exist?"

"It Is the only thing that does exist. Without mind man and the universe would collapse; the winds would weary and the world stand still. Sin-tossed humanity, expressed in tempest and flood, the divine mind calms and limits with a word."

I rose hastily to go. Chance alone and weariness of life had led me to enter the woman's parlor, but there was no forgetfulness in it. Impatience spurred me to be moving, and I turned to the door, with the polite fiction that I was leaving town but might soon consult the healer.

"That makes no difference," she persisted, getting between me and the door. "We treat many cases, of belief in unhappiness by the absent method. From 9 to 10 A. M. we go into the Silence for our Eastern patients. Our ten o'clock is nine o'clock for those living in the central time belt. At 11 A. M. it is nine for those in Denver or Rocky Mountain time region. Thus we are in the Silence during the entire forenoon, but it is always nine for the patient. Will you not arrange for treatment; you really look very badly?"

"Not today." I pushed past her.

To my astonishment the woman followed me to the outer door, abruptly changing her tone.

"I know very well why you don't get healed," she said. "You fill your mind with antagonistic thoughts by reading papers that are fighting someone on every page. You want to get into some kind of society where you can pay $15 or $20 a week and get free healing, and you are disap-pointed because I won't give you my time and strength for nothing, so that you can have the money to go somewhere and have a good time. Oh, I know you society people!"

By degrees her voice had lost its cooing tone and had risen to a shriek. I was amazed—until I remembered the rival across the street, who was probably watching me from behind closed blinds.

As I walked away with the woman's angry words ringing after me from the doorstep, I was divided between amusement and despair; I cannot express it by any other phrase. And that cynical mingling of feelings was the nearest approach to contentment that I had known for days.

The feeling died away; reaction came. It was the worst hour of my life. The thought of suicide—the respite I had always held in reserve against a day too evil to be borne—pressed upon my mind.

I wandered to a ferry and crossed the East River to some unfamiliar suburb where saloons were thicker than I had ever before seen them; and all the way over I looked at the turbid water and knew in my heart that I should never have the courage to throw my beautiful body into that foul tide.

From the ferry I presently reached a vast, forbidding cemetery, and as I went among the crowded graves there came floating out from a little chapel the sound of prayers intoned for the dead. I almost envied them; almost wished that I, too, might be laid to rest in the little churchyard at home.

Then I lay down flat upon the turf in a lonely place, and tried to think of myself as dead. Never had the pulse beat stronger in my veins then at that moment. There were little living things all around me, joying in the warm sun; tiny insects that crawled, unrebuked, over my gown, so busy, so happy in their way, with their petty affairs all prospering, that I wondered why I should be so out of tune with the world. And then a rain of tears gushed from my eyes. I do not think that anyone who should have seen me there could have guessed that the prone and weeping woman was the most beautiful of created things; I do not think I have an enemy so bitter that she would not have pitied me.

I tried to think, but I was too tired. I had a vision of myself returning to the narrow round of farm life, to Ma's reproaches, to dreary, grinding toil that I might win back dollar by dollar the money I had squandered— my back bent, my face seamed, my hands marred, like Aunt Emily's; and I shuddered and wept and grovelled before fate.

Then I saw myself remaining in the city, seeking work and finding nothing. Teach I could not; every door was barred except—I saw myself before the footlights, coarsened, swallowing greedily the applause of a music hall audience, taking a husband from that audience perhaps—a brute like Bellmer! Better die!

But as the vision passed, a great desire of life grew upon me. It seemed monstrous, hideous, that I should ever die or be unhappy; the fighting instinct sent the blood galloping. I sat erect.

Then I noticed that the sun was gone, and the evening cool was rapidly falling. The little people of the grass whose affairs I had idly watched I could no longer see—gone to their homes maybe; and I turned to mine, desolate as it was, hungry and chilled and alone.

And that evening John Burke brought the sunshine.

10

Plighted Troth

"**H**elen, you seem tired," John said as I met him at the door—at first I peeped out from behind it, I remember, as if I feared the bogeyman—"Have you been too hard at work?"

"I've been out all the afternoon," I said, "and I suppose I am rather tired, but it was pleasant and warm; and I wore a veil."

There was a little awkward pause after I had ushered him to the reception room, and then, guiding the talk through channels he thought safe, he spoke about his law work, the amusing things that happen at the office, his gratifying progress in his profession.

"Oh," I said, "talking of the law reminds me—some stupid paper was left here today."

I found with some difficulty and handed to him the stiff folded legal cap the man had brought.

He glanced through it with apprehensive surprise, skipping the long sentences to the end.

"Why, this is returnable tomorrow," he said; "Nelly, I had no idea you were in such urgent money troubles; why didn't you send for me at once; this morning?"

"Oh, if that's all—I've had so many duns that I'm tired of them: tired to death of them."

"But this isn't a dun," he began in the unnaturally quiet tone of a man who is trying to keep his temper and isn't going to succeed. "It is a court order; and people don't ignore court orders unless they want to get into trouble. This paper calls you to court tomorrow morning in supplementary proceedings."

"I don't know what they are."

"You don't want to know what they are. You mustn't know. It's an ordeal so terrible that most creditors employ it only as a last resort, especially against a woman. This plaintiff, being herself a woman, is less merciful."

"Why is it so terrible? I have no money; they can't make me pay what I haven't got, can they? Is it the Inquisition?"

"Yes, of a sort; it's an inquiry into your ability to pay, and almost no question that could throw light upon that is barred. You'll be asked about your business in New York, your income and expenses, your family and your father's means. It will be a turning inside out of your most intimate affairs."

"Why, I should expect all that," I said.

"But, Nelly—" he hesitated. "You're alone here?"

He had not before alluded to Mrs. Whitney, though I suppose he understood that she had gone; I appreciated his delicacy.

"I'm afraid you'll be asked about that," he went on; "asked, I mean, how a young woman without money maintains a fine apartment. They'll inquire about your servants, the daily expenses of your table, your wine bills, if you ever have any; then they'll question you about your visitors, their character and number, and try to wring admissions from you, and to give sinister shades to innocent relations. The reporters will all be there, a swarm of them. You're a semi-public character, more's the pity, and some lawyers like to be known for their severity to debtors. What a field day for the press! The beautiful Miss Winship in supplementary proceedings— columns of testimony, pages of pictures—! Ugh! In a word, the experience is so severe that you cannot undergo it."

"I don't see how it's to be helped; is it a crime to live alone?" I said. "I won't ask Uncle Timothy for money—and have Aunt Frank know about it."

Again he hesitated, then he said more slowly, but plumping out the last words in a kind of desperation: "I've heard a woman—once—asked if she had a lover—to pay the money, you know."

I didn't understand at first; then a flush deepened upon my face.

"They wouldn't dare! This woman knows all about me; why, she's Meg Van Dam's dressmaker; Mrs. Whitney's too—" I said.

"I've heard it done," John repeated patiently. "You must pardon me. I didn't want to go into this phase of it, but it may explain what, with your permission, I am about to do. Now, before I go—for I must go at once to find this attorney, at his house, the Democratic Club, anywhere—I must be frank with you."

He was already at the door, where he turned and faced me, looking almost handsome in his sturdy manliness, his colour heightened by excitement.

"I must tell you one thing," he went on very slowly. "I haven't in all the world a fraction of the money called for by this one bill; but in a way I have made some success. I am beginning to be known. If I myself offer terms, so much cash down, so much a month, pledging my word for the payment, the woman's lawyer will agree. She'll be glad to get the money in that way, or in any way. But I must guard your reputation. I shall tell plaintiff's counsel that you are my affianced wife, that I didn't know how badly you were in debt—both statements are true—and that I assume payment. I wish to assure you that, in thus asserting our old relation, I shall not presume upon the liberty I am obliged to take."

I think I have treated John badly; yet he brought me help. And he had no thought of recompense. Since he has seen how useless it was, he has ceased to pester me with love making, but has been simply, kindly helpful. And I have been so lonely, so harassed and tormented.

It was far enough from my thoughts to do such a thing, but as I stood dumbly looking at him, it flashed upon me that here, after all, was the man who had always loved me, always helped me, always respected me. I almost loved him in return. Why not try to reward his devotion, and throw my distracted self upon his protection?

"I would not have you tell a lie for me, John," said I uncertainly, holding out my hands and smiling softly into his eyes.

"I don't understand—" he stood irresolute, yet moved, I could see, by my beauty. "Do you mean—" and he slowly approached, peering from under his contracted brows as if trying to read my eyes.

"I mean that I have treated you very badly; and that I am sorry," I whispered, hiding my head with a little sigh upon his shoulder; and after a time he put his arms about me gently as if half afraid, and was silent. I felt how good he was, how strong and patient, and was at peace. I knew I could trust him.

So we stood for a little while at the dividing line between the future and the past. I do not know what were his thoughts, but I had not been so much at rest for a long, long time—not since I came from home to New York.

Then with a sigh of quiet content, he said in a low and gentle voice, "It's a strange thing to hurry away now, Nelly; but you know I have so much to do before I can rest tonight. I must speak of this: Now—now that we are to belong to each other always—I must know exactly about all your affairs, so that I can arrange them. There are other debts?"

The word grated upon my nerves, I had been so glad to forget.

"Yes, I'm afraid I owe a lot of money, but must we—just tonight?" I asked.

"I'm afraid it's safest. It is not alone that you will be able to forget the matter sooner if you confide in me now, but how can we know that these proceedings will not be repeated if I don't attend promptly to everything? Someone else may bring suit tomorrow, and another the next day, giving you no peace. I'm sorry, but it is the best way. Tell me everything now, and I will arrange with them all, and need never mention the subject again. Then you can be at peace."

"Well, if I must—"

It seemed impossible to go on. Even the thought of how good he was and how he had taken up my burden when it was too heavy for my own strength made it harder to face the horrible business.

"—I owe ten dollars to Kitty Reid, and about twenty-five to Cadge," I admitted. "I didn't mean to borrow of them, but I had to do it, just lately—"

"Poor child!" said John, stroking my hand with his big, warm paw, as he would a baby's. "Poor child!"

"I've bills somewhere for everything else—"

It was like digging among the ruins of my past greatness to pull out the crumpled papers from my writing desk, reminding me of the gay scenes that for me were no more; but John quietly took them from me, and began smoothing them and laying them in methodical piles and making notes of amounts and names.

"I've refused all these to Uncle Timothy; he's been worrying me with questions—" I said desperately.

"Three florists, two confectioners," he enumerated, as if he had not heard me.

"—Women eat sweets by the ton, but lately there have been few of 'em in this house. Then here are the accounts for newspaper clippings, you know; Shanks and Romeike; but they're trifles."

"You must have been a good customer," John said, glancing about the dishevelled flat—I hadn't had the heart to rearrange it since Mrs. Whitney left. "From the look of the place, I believe you would have bought a mummy or a heathen god, if anybody had suggested it to you."

"I have a little heathen god—Gautama; alabaster—and a mummied cat."

"And you're very fond of that? But no matter. Shoemaker and milliner and furniture man; that makes eleven."

He lengthened his list on the margin of a newspaper.

"Well, I never paid Van Nostrand for that painting, and I've even forgotten how much he said it would be. And there's a photograph bill—a perfectly scandalous one—and another dressmaker; Mrs. Edgar; I went back to her after Meg's woman got crusty, but she never'll sue me. And the Japanese furniture shop and—another photographer—and here's the bill for bric-a-brac—that's sixteen. The wine account—there is one, but it ought to be Mrs. Whitney's; for entertaining. I suppose Pa and Ma would say that was a very wicked bill, now wouldn't they, Schoolmaster?"

"They would indeed, Helen 'Lizy; I'm not sure that I don't agree with them. By the way, does your father know about all this?"

"Yes, a little. I've begged him for money, but he won't mortgage the farm. And Judge Baker knows. He wants me to come back to his house, but of course I won't do it. I guess he's sent for Father; Pa's coming East soon, on a cattle train pass."

"A cattle train!"

John stabbed the paper viciously, then he said more gently:—

"A cattle train is cold comfort for a substantial farmer at his time of life; and I don't think we will let him mortgage."

That young man will need discipline; but I imagine he was thinking less about my poor old father than about—well, I needn't have mentioned the Baker house, but what does he really know of how I came to leave it? Perhaps suspicion and bitter memories made my retort more spirited than it need have been.

"We won't discuss that, please," I said with hauteur; "and we won't be too emphatic about what is past. It *is* past. I'll find out what is a proper scale of expenditure for a young lawyer's wife in New York, and I shall not exceed it. I've been living very economically for the sphere that seemed open to me. Perhaps I ought not to have tried it; but I think you should blame those who lured me into extravagance and then deserted me. I've had a terrible, terrible experience! Do you know that? And I was within an ace of becoming an ornament of the British peerage. Did you know that?"

"Yes; I don't blame you for refusing, either; some girls don't seem to have the necessary strength of mind. No; I'm not blaming anybody for anything. Nelly, next week it will be a year since our first betrothal; do you remember? Haven't you, after all, loved me a little, all the time?"

He looked at me wistfully.

"At least," I said, "I didn't love Lord Strathay."

I didn't think it necessary to correct him as to my refusal of the Earl.

"We'll see if Kitty won't take you in again until we can be married," he said, jabbing the paper again and changing the subject almost brusquely. "If you don't want to go back to your aunt, that'll be better than a boarding house, won't it? You pay the girls out of this, and I'll look after the other bills. There's a good fellow. Now, then what's No. 18?"

I fingered with an odd reluctance the little roll of bills he handed me, though it was like a life buoy to a drowning sailor.

"You'd better," he said, with quiet decision, cutting short my hesitation. "The girls won't need to know where it comes from, or that I know anything about it. It's ever so much nicer that way, don't you think?"

I put the money with my pride into my pocket, and continued sorting out bills from the rubbish. In all we scheduled over forty before we gave it up. Besides the Van Nostrand painting and one or two accounts that probably escaped us, I found that I owed between $4,000 and $5,000.

"That is the whole of my dowry, John," I said.

"I would as willingly accept you as a portionless bride," he declaimed in theatrical fashion; and then we both broke into hysterical laughter.

"Never mind," he said, at last, wiping his eyes. "I never dreamed that all this rubbish about you could cost so much; I ought to have had my eyes open. But now we aren't going to worry one little worry, are we? I'll straighten it all out in time. And now I really must go."

And so he went away with a parting kiss, leaving me very happy. I don't know that I love him; or rather I know that I don't—but I shall be good to him and make him so happy that he'll forget all the trouble I have cost him. Dear old unselfish, patient John!

And I am more content and less torn by anxiety than I have been for many a long day. It is such a relief!

And so I'm thinking it over. Even from the selfish standpoint I have not done so badly. John is developing wonderfully. He is not so destitute of social finesse as when he came, his language is better, his bearing more confident. He makes a good figure in evening dress. He will be a famous success in the law, and, with a beautiful wife to help him, he should go far. He may be President some day, or Minister to the Court of St. James, or a Justice of the Supreme Court.

Whatever his career, I shall help him. I have the power to do things in the world as well as he. And once married, I may almost choose my friends and his associates. The women will no longer fear me so much. He shall not regret this night's work.

So that is settled. I am so relieved, and more tired than I have ever guessed a woman could be. Tired, tired, tired!

I'm sure it is the best thing I could do, now; but—Judge Baker is right! What was it he said? "A loveless marriage,"—Oh, well, since I broke Ned Hynes's heart by setting a silly little girl to drive him away, and broke my own by breaking his, I haven't much cared what becomes of me; only to be at peace.

It will be a relief to move out of this accursed flat, where I have spent the gloomiest hours of my life.

Book V:
The End of the Beginning

(From the Shorthand Notes of John Burke.)

1

The Deeds of the Farm

Sunday, June 13.

In three days it will be a year since Helen promised to marry me, and on that anniversary she will be my wife.

It is strange how exactly according to my plan things have come about—and how differently from all that I have dreamed.

She is the most beautiful woman in the world; she is to be my wife sooner than I dared to hope—and—I must be good to her. I must love her.

Did I ever doubt my love until she claimed it five days ago with such confidence in my loyalty? In that moment, as I went to her, as I took her in my arms, as I felt that she needed me and trusted me, with the suddenness of a revelation I knew—

It was hard to meet Ethel—and Milly and Mrs. Baker afterwards.

Today, in preparing to move to our new home, I came across the rough notes I wrote last December, when the marvel of Helen's beauty was fresh to me. As I read the disjointed and half incredulous words I had set to paper, I found myself living over again those days of Faery and enchantment.

Custom has somewhat dulled the shock of her beauty; I have grown quickly used to her as the most radiantly lovely of created beings; my mind has been drawn to dwell upon moral problems and to sorrow at seeing her gradually become the victim of her beauty—her nature, once as fine as the outward form that clothes it, warped by constant adulation, envy and strife; until—

But it is a miracle! As unbelievable, as unthinkable as it was on the very first day when that glowing dream of loveliness made manifest floated toward me in the little room overlooking Union Square, and I was near swooning with pure delight of vision.

Beautiful; wonderful! She didn't love me then and she doesn't now; but the most marvellous woman in the world needs me—and I will not fail her.

I wish I could take her out of the city for a change of mental atmosphere. She shrinks from her father's suggestion of a summer on the farm. But in time her wholesome nature must reassert itself; she must become, if not again the fresh, light-hearted girl I knew a year ago, a sweet and gracious woman whose sufferings will have added pathos to her charm.

And even now she's not to be judged like other women; before the shining of her beauty, reproach falls powerless. It is my sacred task to guard her—to soothe her awakening from all that nightmare of inflated hopes and vain imaginings. Kitty Reid and—yes, and little Ethel—will help me.

Kitty is a good fellow.

"Why, cert.," she said when I begged her last Wednesday to take care of Helen. "Married! Did you say married? Oh, Cadge, quit pegging shoes!"

Jumping up from the drawing table, Kitty left streams of India ink making her beastesses all tigers while she called to Miss Bryant, who was pounding viciously upon a typewriter:—

"Cadge, did you hear? Cadge! The Princess is going to be married. 'Course you remember, Mr. Burke, Cadge is going to be married herself Saturday."

"Don't be too sure of it," returned Miss Bryant, "and do let me finish this sentence. Ten to one Pros. or I'll be grabbed off for an assignment Saturday evening 'fore we can be married. But the Princess is different; she has leisure. Burke, shake!"

She sprang up to take my hand, her eyes shining with excitement.

Kitty hurried with me to the Nicaragua, where she pounced upon Helen, her red curls madly bobbing.

"What a bride you'll make!" she cried fondly. "Going to be married from the den, aren't you? Oh, I'm up to my eyes in weddings; Cadge simply won't attend to anything. But what have you been doing to your-self? Come here, Helen."

She pushed the proud, pale beauty into a chair, smothering her with kisses and the piles of cushions that seem to add bliss to women's joys and soften all their griefs.

"Tired, aren't you?" she purred. "Needed me. Now just you sit and talk with Mr. Burke and I'll pack up your brittle-brac in three no-times. Clesta, —where's that imp?"

She called to the little combination maid and model who had accom-panied us.

"Clesta's afraid of you, Helen. 'Why'd ye fetch me 'long?' she whim-pers. 'Miss Kitty, why'd ye fetch me 'long?' Huh, I 'member how you used to have his picture with yours in a white and gold frame!"

Helen scarcely replied to Kitty's raptures. She laid her head back half-protestingly among her cushions, showing her long, exquisite throat. For an instant she let her shadowy lashes droop over the everchanging lustre of her eyes. I couldn't help thinking of a great, glorious bird of heaven resting with broken wing.

"Poor little Princess!" said Kitty, who hardly comes to Helen's shoulder. Then we all laughed.

Kitty stayed at the Nicaragua that night, and when I came Thursday afternoon she stopped me outside the door, to say:—

"I wouldn't let Helen talk too much; she's nervous."

"Can you tell me what is the matter with her?" I asked. "I don't think she's well."

"Oh, nothing. You know—she's been worrying." Then loyal Kitty spoke purposely of commonplaces. "General must have danced her off her feet. Darmstetter's death upset her terribly, too. She never will speak of it. But she'll be as right as right with me. Bring her 'round as soon as the man comes for the trunks. You've only to head up a barrel of dishes, quick, 'fore Clesta gets in any fine work smashing 'em."

As I passed through the hall, littered with trunks and packing cases, to the dismantled parlour, Helen looked up from a mass of old letters and dance cards.

"I'm sorting my—souvenirs," she said.

The face she lifted was white, only the lips richly red, with a shade of fatigue under the haunting eyes. The graceful figure in its close-fitting dress looked a trifle less round than it had done earlier in the winter, and one fair arm, as it escaped from its flowing sleeve, was almost thin.

"Dear," I said wistfully, for something in her drooping attitude smote me to remorse and inspired me with tenderness; "will you really trust your life to me?"

She leaned towards me, and beauty breathed about her as a spell. I bent till my lips caressed her perfumed hair; and then—I saw among the rubbish on her desk something that made me interrupt the words we might have spoken.

"What's that?" I asked. "Not—pawn tickets?"

"For a necklace," she said; "and this—this must be my diamond—"

"Pawned and not paid for!"

She offered me the tickets, only half understanding, her great eyes as innocent as they were lovely.

"I had forgotten," she said. "I only found them when I came to—"

She brushed the rubbish of her winter's triumphs and disappointments to the floor, and turned from it with a little, disdainful movement.

"I had to pay the maids," she said simply.

"Nelly, why—why didn't you come to me sooner?"

With a bump against the door, Clesta sidled into the room awestruck and smutched, bearing a tray.

"Miss Kitty said," she stammered, "as how I should make tea." And as soon as she had found a resting place for her burden, the frightened girl made a dash for the door.

Before Helen had finished drinking, there was a stir in the hall, and then the sound of a familiar voice startled us.

"Wa-al, Helen 'Lizy," it said. "How ye do, John? Don't git up; I can set till ye're through."

And Mr. Winship himself stood before us, stoop-shouldered, roughly dressed from the cattle cars, his kindly old eyes twinkling, his good face all glorified by the honest love and pride shining through its plainness.

"Why, Father!" cried Helen with a start.

She looked at him with a nervous repugnance to his appearance, which she tried to subdue. He did not seem to notice it.

"Wa'n't lookin' for me yit-a-while, was ye?" he asked. "Kind o' thought I'd s'prise ye. Did s'prise the man down in the hall. Didn't want to let me in till I told him who I was. Little gal in the entry says ye're movin'; ye do look all tore up, for a fac'."

Mr. Winship has grown old within the year. His hair has whitened and his bushy eyebrows; but the grip of his hand, the sound of his homely speech, seemed to wake me from some ugly dream. Here we were together again in the wholesome daylight, Father Winship, little Helen 'Lizy and the Schoolmaster, and all must yet be well.

Mr. Winship sighed with deep content as he sank into a chair, his eyes scarcely leaving Helen. He owned himself beat out and glad of a dish of tea; but when Clesta had served him in her scuttling crab fashion, he would stop in the middle of a sentence, with saucer half lifted, to gaze with perplexed, wistful tenderness at his stately daughter.

She is the child of his old age; I think he must be long past sixty, and fast growing feeble. The instinct of father love has grown in him so refined that he sees the soul and not the envelope. Grand and beautiful as she is to others, to him she is still his little Nelly.

He would not even own that he thought her altered.

"I d'know," he said, a shade of anxiety blending with the old fond pride. "Fust-off, Sis didn't look jes' nat'ral, spite of all the picters she's sent us; but that was her long-tailed dress, mebbe. W'en she's a young one, Ma was all for tyin' back her ears and pinchin' her nose with a clo'espin—to make it straight or so'thin'; but I says to Ma, w'en Helen 'Lizy lef' home, 'don't ye be one mite afeard,' I says, 'but what them bright eyes'll outshine the peaked city gals.' Guess they have, sort o', eh, Sis; f'om what John's been writin'?"

"I don't know, Father."

"Don't ye—don't ye want t' hear 'bout the folks? Brought ye heaps o' messages. Frenchy, now—him that worked for us—druv over f'om the Merriam place to know 'f 'twas true that city folks made a catouse over ye. He'd heard the men readin' 'bout ye in the papers.

"'Wa-al,' I says to Frenchy, 'Helen 'Lizy was al'ays han'some.'

"'D'know 'bout zat,' says Frenchy, only he says it in his lingo, 'but she was one vair cute li'l gal.'

"'Han'some as a picter,' I tol' him; 'an' cutes' little tyke y'ever see.'"

"How is Mother?" asked Helen constrainedly.

"Ma's lottin' on havin' ye home; wants t' hear all 'bout the good times. School done? All packed and ready for a start, ain't ye? But ye don't seem to be feeling any too good. Don't New York agree with ye, Sissy? Been studying too hard?"

"She is a goot organism; New York agrees vit her," I said. "Wasn't that how poor old Darmstetter put it, Nelly? Mr. Winship, Nelly has over-worked, but with your consent, she is about to let a tyrannical husband take care of her."

At my heedless mention of Darmstetter, Helen's white face grew whiter. Her trembling hand strayed, seeking support.

"Al'ays s'posed you'n' Sis'd be marryin' some day," said Mr. Winship, dubiously watching her, while he stroked his beard; "but seems mos's if ye'd better wait a spell, till Ma's chirked her up some. Han'some place here."

His eyes examined the luxurious, disordered room.

"These here things ain't yourn, Sis?"

"Not all of them."

"I ain't refusin' to let Sis marry, if ye're both sot on't," he conceded. Then he caught sight of the Van Nostrand painting, and his slow glance travelled from it to Helen. "That done for you, Sis? I never helt with bare necks. Yes, Sis can marry, if she says so, though Ma wants her home. But she ain't been writin' real cheerful. She—she's asked for money, that's the size on't. An' here ye are up in arms an' she nigh sick. I don't want nothing hid away f'om me; how come ye livin' in a place like this?"

He rose laboriously, surveying through the open doorway the beautiful hall and the dining room; while I interposed some jesting talk on other matters, for I had hoped to get Helen out of the Nicaragua before her father's arrival, and still hoped to spare him knowledge of our worst troubles.

"If Sis has been buyin' all this here, I ain't denying that I'll feel the expense," he said, sticking to the subject; "but I guess we can manage."

Fumbling for his wallet, he drew some papers from it and handed them to Helen, adding:—

"There, Sis; there they are."

"Money, Father?" she asked with indifference. "I don't believe I need any."

"Don't ye? Ye wrote 'bout mortgagin'. I didn't want to do it, 'count o' Ma, partly; but we kep' worryin' an' worryin' 'bout ye. Ma couldn't sleep o' nights or eat her victuals; an fin'lly—'Ezry,' she says, 'we was possessed to let Helen 'Lizy, at her age, an' all the chick or child we got, go off alone to the city. Ezry,' she says, 'you go fetch her home. Like's not Tim can let ye have the money,' she says; 'his wife bein' an own cousin, right in the family, y'know.' So I've brought the deeds, Sis, an'—"

"What!" cried Helen, starting up. "The deeds of the farm? Let me see!"

She reached out a shaking hand for the papers.

"I'll pay you back!" she cried. "Why didn't you come sooner? How much can you get? How much money?"

"Not much more'n three thousan', I'm afeared, on a mortgage; cap'tal's kind o' skeery—but Tim—"

"Three thousand dollars!"

Laughing hysterically, she fell back in her chair.

"I had ought 'a come sooner; an' three thousan' ain't a gre't deal, I don't suppose, here in the city; but it's been spend, spend—not that I grutch it—an' things ain't so flourishin' as they was. I'm gittin' too old to manage, mebbe—"

"Mr. Winship," I said, "Nelly has told you the truth; she doesn't need money; she—"

"Three thousand will save me!" Helen cried. "I can pay a little to everybody. I can hold out, I can—"

"Please, Miss—the furniture—"

Behind Clesta appeared two men who gaped at Helen in momentary forgetfulness of their errand.

Helen's creditors have proved more than reasonable, with the exception of the furniture people; their demands were such that there seemed no alternative but to surrender the goods. As the men who came for them advanced into the room, stammering questions about the articles they were to remove, Helen struggled to her feet and started to meet them, then stopped, clutching at a table for support. Their eyes never left her face.

"Are they takin' your things, Sis?" asked Mr. Winship.

Her feverish glance answered him.

"What's to pay?" he inquired.

"Want to keep the stuff, Boss?" asked the head packer.

"Yes," I said, seeing her distress, and resolving desperately to find the means, somehow.

"It ain't none o' your look-out," interposed Mr. Winship. "Sis ain't a-goin' to be beholden to her husband, not till she's married. Ezry Winship al'ays has done for his own, an' he proposes to do, jes' as fur's he's able. Sis'll tell ye I hain't stented her—What's to pay?"

I couldn't see all his savings go for gauds!

"You may take the goods," I said to the men, with sudden revulsion of feeling. "There's no room for them," I added gruffly to Mr. Winship, "in our—the rooms—where we are to live."

"All right, Boss," said the head packer; "which gent speaks for the lady?"

"Father!" Helen gasped.

"What's to pay?" insisted Mr. Winship.

"Take the goods," I repeated.

"All right, Boss;" and the two men went about their work, still glancing at us with sidelong looks of curiosity.

Helen gazed at me with eyes that stabbed. Then slowly her glance dulled. She dropped on a packing box and sat silent—a bowed figure of despair—forgetting apparently that she was not alone.

Mr. Winship made no further attempt to interfere with events. He stood by Helen's side, puzzled and taciturn.

I, too, was silent, reproaching myself for the brutality of my action, unable to decide what I should have done or ought to do. Helen herself had suggested that we give up the furniture, and I had not mourned the necessity, for I hated the stuff, with its reminders of the General and the Whitney woman and Bellmer and the Earl and all those strange people that I used to see around her. But I might have known that she could not, all at once, wean herself from the trumpery.

A minute later Clesta ushered in the man who was to take the trunks, and when I had given him his directions, I asked, "Shall we go, Nelly?"

"If ye ain't reconciled to movin'—" Mr. Winship began.

But Helen answered neither of us. Her eyes were bent upon the floor, and a look, not now of resentment, but of—was it fear?—had slowly crept upon her face. Her hands were clenched.

Darmstetter! Instinct—or memory of my careless words spoken but a little earlier—told me the truth. The growing pallor of her cheek spoke her thought. How that tragedy haunts her! The face I looked upon was at the last almost ghastly.

"Nelly—" I said, very gently.

She looked around with the slow bewilderment that I once saw on the face of a sleepwalker. Her eyes saw through us, and past us, fixed upon some invisible horror. She was heedless of the familiar scene, the figures grouped about her. Then there came a sudden flush to her face, a quick recoil of terror; she shuddered as if waking from a nightmare.

"Why do we stay here?" she cried starting up with sudden, panic strength. "Let's get out of this horrible place! Let's go! Oh, let's go! Let's go!"

And so it was, in sorrow and with dark forebodings, that we left the gay rooms where Helen had so passionately enjoyed her little flight in the sunshine.

The drive through the streets was at first silent. Shutting her eyes, she leaned back in the carriage. Sometimes she shuddered convulsively.

"Where ye goin'?" Mr. Winship asked at last, peering out at the carriage window. Indeed the trip to Fourteenth Street seemed interminable to me, and I didn't wonder at his impatience.

The simple question broke down Helen's reserve.

"Anywhere!" she sobbed, breaking into violent, hysterical tears. "I didn't want to stay there! I didn't want the furniture! I didn't want it! I don't want money! Father, you needn't mortgage!"

"We'll talk 'bout that some other time," said Mr. Winship soothingly. "Nevermind now, Sissy."

"Ye'll take good care of Helen 'Lizy?" he said to Cadge and Kitty when we had half carried her up the long flights of stairs to the studio. He seemed to take no notice of the strange furnishings of the loft, but his furrowed brow smoothed itself as he looked into the hospitable faces of the two girls.

"Ye'll take good care of her?" he repeated simply. "I'm afeard my daughter ain't very well."

"We will; we will!" they assured him eagerly; and indeed it seemed that Helen had found her needed rest, for she bade us good night almost cheerfully.

2

Cadge's Assignment

"**Y**ou say Winship is around at your place?" asked Judge Baker Friday morning. I had before told him about the approaching marriage. "The dear old boy! I am very glad."

"He wants to talk with you about a mortgage," I said bluntly. "Can you dissuade him? I think the situation in its main features is no secret to you."

The Judge frowned in surprise. "You don't mean that she—"

"Of course Helen has refused her father's offer. We have so arranged everything that no help from him is needed, but he may be rather obstinate, for I'm afraid she wrote to him, suggesting—I mean, she now regrets it," I added.

"Ah, those regrets! Those regrets!" He sat silent for a moment, thinking deeply. "That phase of an otherwise rosy situation is unfortunate. I will do my best with Winship, and you must explain to me your proposed arrangements; for I claim an uncle's privilege to be of use to Nelly, and she, with perhaps natural reticence, has acquainted me only partially with her affairs. I rejoice to hear that she now wishes to spare her father, but—you will pardon me, Burke?—she was hasty; she was hasty. It is easier to set forces of love or hate moving than to check them in motion. Sometimes I think, Burke, that people were in certain ways less reckless in the good old days when they had perpetually before their eyes the vision of a hair-trigger God, always cocked and ready to shoot if they crossed the line of duty. But Nelly is coming bravely through a severe test of character. May I offer you both my heartiest—"

It was just at that happy moment that the office boy announced Mr. Winship to share the Judge's kind wishes; and by good luck in came also Mrs. Baker, but a moment behind him.

"Why, Ezra!" she chirped in a flutter of amazed cordiality at sight of her husband's visitor. "You in New York? Why, for Nelly's wedding, of course! John Burke, why've you kept us in the dark these months and months? I'm—I'm really ashamed of you!"

Her plump gloved hands seized Mr. Winship's, while her small, swift, bird-like eyes looked reproach at me.

"Patience, Mrs. Baker; patience!" rejoined the Judge. "Is not an engaged man entitled to his secrets? Has it escaped your memory how, once upon a time, you and I—."

"There, now, Bake! Stop, can't you?" she interrupted with vehement good nature; and I ceased to intrude upon the three old friends.

That afternoon, when I sought Helen at the studio, I was more surprised than I should have been, and wonderfully relieved to discover the result of their conference.

Ignorant of any quarrel and overflowing with anxiety, Helen's father had unbosomed his anxieties about her health and accomplished what no diplomacy could have done. Mrs. Baker had flown with him to the studio, where, constrained by his presence, Helen had submitted to an incredible truce with her aunt.

"I told Tim'thy an' Frances we'd eat Sunday dinner with 'em," Mr. Winship told me; "an' they say you'n' Sis had ought to be married f'om their house. Good idee, seems to me, though Sis here don't take to it, somehow."

"Oh, I suppose I can endure Aunt Frank," said Helen, making savage dabs at Cadge's typewriter; "if you wish it—you and John."

She was making a great effort for her father's sake, and I could not exclaim against her chilly reception of the olive branch.

"It'll please Ma, w'en she comes to hear 'bout it; she thinks a sight of Frank Baker," urged Mr. Winship.

"'Fraid I'll have to tackle someb'dy else 'bout that money," he went on after a pause; "Tim'thy says he ain't got a cent loose, jest now. I did kind o' want to keep it quiet, keep it to the fambly like, but I can git it; I can git th' money; on'y it'll take time."

"Why, Father, I begged you not to try," said Helen impatiently. "I don't need money; ask John."

"W'at you've spent can't come on John," declared Mr. Winship; "I'll have to be inquirin' 'round. But I'm glad to see ye lookin' brighter'n you did yist'day, Sissy; Tim'thy's wife'll have an eye on ye. She's comin' here agin tomorrer, she says, to a weddin'. You didn't tell me 'bout anyone gittin' married—not in sich a hurry, not tomorrer. W'ich gal is it?"

"Wouldn't think it was Cadge, would you?" laughed Kitty, staggering into the room under the weight of a big palm. "Next chum I have, it'll be in the contract that, in case of emergency, she helps run her own wedding. 'Course Helen's all right with me—or will be, once Caroline Bryant's disposed of."

In spite of the confusion of the wedding preparations, Helen did do credit to Kitty's nursing; and last evening, when there came the climax of all the bustle, she seemed stronger even than on Friday.

It was a night to remember!

The big Indians of the canvasses peeped grimly from ambushes of flowers and tall ferns, as the studio door opened and Kitty came running to meet me, her cheeks flushed and her curls in a hurricane.

"'Most time for the minister," she cried breathlessly, "and not a sign of Cadge! Not a sign! And I want to tell you—Helen's sorry we invited the General, but she won't come, so that's no matter; but the Bakers—do they like him?"

"Like the minister?"

"Like Ned Hynes?" panted Kitty. "When we asked 'em yesterday, I forgot, but he'll be here. Pros. and he belong to a downtown club—'At the Sign of the Skull and Crossbones'—or something—"

"Well?"

"Oh, it's all right, but I thought I'd tell you. If only Cadge'd come! That's what eating me!" Kitty groaned. "But do you see our Princess? All she needed was me to make her comfy. Shall I get you the least little bit of colour, out of a box, Helen? Or—no; you're too lovely. But come, you must have some roses."

As Helen joined us, very pale in her shimmering dress, with her hair like an aureole about her head, she looked a tall, white Grace, a swaying lily shining in the dusky place. Almost with the old reverence I whispered:

—

"You are the most beautiful of woman!"

"Do I please you, Sir?" she said, smiling as she moved away again with Kitty. "Won't you see to Father? He's come without his necktie."

"Sho, Sis!" said Mr. Winship; "don't my beard hide it? Declare I clean forgot."

Soon Helen returned to pin a flower at my buttonhole.

"Where *can* Cadge be?" she cried gaily; but her hands shook and she dropped the rose. "Do you suppose she's interviewing a lunatic asylum?"

What had changed her voice and burned fever spots in her cheeks? I wasn't so indifferent as I had seemed to Kitty's news. Had she told Helen, too, that Ned Hynes—what was he to my betrothed?

"Can't you rest somewhere and just show for the ceremony?" I said, "Nelly, you're not strong."

"There's not a place big enough for a mouse. But did you mean it? Do I really look well tonight? Am I just as beautiful as I was three-four months ago, or have I—"

"Oh, do slip out and 'phone the *Star!* I can feel my hair whitening," whispered Kitty, turning to me hastily, as a couple of women entered. "See, folks are beginning to come."

I went out into the warm and rainy night, but there was no Cadge at the *Star* office. By the time I had returned with this information, the eyry held a considerable gathering. Mrs. Baker had arrived, and her two daughters; but I had no time to wonder at Milly's coming, for behind me entered Mrs. Van Dam and then, among a group of strangers, I noticed Hynes.

Involuntarily, at sight of him, my eyes turned to Helen; but not a muscle of her face betrayed deeper feeling than polite pleasure as she helped Kitty receive the wedding guests, greeting the General cordially, Hynes with graciousness.

Kitty's welcome to Mrs. Van Dam would have been irresistibly funny, if I had had eyes to see the humour.

"Cadge promised to be home early," she sputtered, "but probably she's telling someone this minute: 'Oh, I'll be there in time; I don't need much—not much more than the programme.'

"Can't *you* guess where she is, Pros.?" she implored in an undertone, as her brother approached us. "If the minister gets here before Cadge does, I'll cut her off with a shilling."

"What an interesting place!" exclaimed Mrs. Van Dam, examining her surroundings through her quizzing glasses. "I've heard so much about your paintings, Miss Reid. And what an astonishing girl, this Miss Bryant! Where can she be? Helen, you sly girl, I hear news about you."

"Oh, very likely Miss Bryant is out of town," Reid answered for her with a quiet smile. "She'll show up after the paper goes to press, if not sooner."

"On her wedding day! The girl's a genius! And when may that be? When will the—ah—when will the paper go to press?"

"They take copy up to two o'clock for the second edition. But she maybe here at any moment."

The General stared at him with amazement.

"Oh, you don't know Cadge," sighed Kitty, "if you think she'd be jarred by her own wedding. But we must do something. Everybody's here and waiting. Sing, Helen, won't you? Oh, do sing."

Helen had not joined in the rapid conversation. Now she smiled assent with stately compliance. Undulating across the studio, she returned with a mandolin—not the one I remembered, but a pretty bit of workmanship in inlaid wood. Bending above this, she relieved the wait by merry, lilting tunes like the music of a bobolink, while Kitty fidgetted in and out, the puckers in her forehead every minute growing deeper.

While I listened to the gladsome music, my glance strayed to Milly, but she was almost hidden by the curtains of the tepee; and then to Ned, who sat with his face turned partly away from us. I noticed that he looked gaunt, and I found a bitter satisfaction in the thought that, perhaps, in Helen's "three-four months" he had not seen, until that night, either of the women with whose lives his own had been entangled.

"Just one more," begged Kitty, when Helen stopped. "You're my only hope; do sing, Helen."

Dropping the mandolin, Helen began without accompaniment "The King of Thule:"—

> *"'There stood the old carouser,*
> *And drank the last life glow;*
> *And hurled the hallowed goblet*
> *Into the tide below.*
>
> *"He saw it plunging and filling,*
> *And sinking deep in the sea;*
> *Then fell his eyelids forever,*
> *And never more drank he!'"*

It was the ballad she had sung at Christmas—in what different mood! Then her voice had been as carefree as a bird's carol, but now it lent to the limpid simplicity of the air a sobbing, shuddering sweetness—an almost weird intensity that strangely affected her listeners.

When she had finished, something like a gasp went through the room. With a heartbreaking coldness I felt that I was her only unmoved auditor, or—no; Ned seemed studying with weary disapproval the pattern of his shoes.

"Love and death; and at a wedding!" Mrs. Van Dam shivered. "Something more cheerful, Helen."

"Let's go—let's go and eat up Cadge's spread; that'd be cheerful," sniffed Kitty, her hot, nervous hand patting Helen's shoulder. "The Princess's tired. But we must do something."

"Eat the wedding supper before the wedding. Original, I must say!"

But the General willingly enough helped Kitty to marshal us into the crowded little dining room; where Helen and I found ourselves beside Mr. Winship and Ethel. Her father accepted Helen's music with as little surprise as he had shown at her beauty.

"Comin' home pretty soon, ain't ye," he asked, "to give us some hymn tunes Sunday evenings? W'at'll I git for ye? Must be hungry after so much singing."

"I'm afraid I wasn't in voice tonight," said she rather wearily.

"Not in voice!" protested Ethel with shy enthusiasm; "why, Nelly, I never before heard even you sing like that; it was—it was—oh, it was wonderful!"

I dared not look at her, yet I saw every movement of the slight little figure—saw the blush of eagerness that mounted even to the blonde little curls about her forehead; and, retreating impatiently, I tried to follow Mr. Winship's example, as he waited on the company with a quaintly fine courtesy. Indeed, he made quite a conquest of the General, who presently, after chatting with him for some time with keen interest, asked abruptly:—

"Why haven't we had him here before? So interesting, such an original! Room here for you, Milly. Some salad, please, Mr. Hynes."

Hynes's pinched face took colour. With alacrity he obeyed the General's orders, fetching plates and glasses, and hovering about the group that included Milly and her mother, until Mrs. Baker's face began to wear a disturbed flush, though Milly's small, white features remained impassive.

I watched the little drama with dawning comprehension. Then Ned did not—Helen—it was really Ethel's sister with whom he longed to make peace, while I—Ethel—

Helen's voice roused me.

"Can't we go into the other room?" she asked. "I'm tired; can't we go and sit quietly together?"

With the fading of the glow and colour left by the music, she looked indeed tired, almost haggard. In spite of the regal self possession with which she rose, drawing Ethel with her, I knew in the face of Milly's triumph—yes, I had known before—why her restless spirit had spurred her on to such flights of folly; why she had—she brings no love to me; has she perhaps offered pity?

We turned together to the door, but there was a sound of hurrying feet, and Miss Bryant rushed before us, followed by a big bearded giant of a man.

"Forbear and eat no more till my necessities be served," she declaimed, advancing to the table. "Food has not passed my lips today; or—not much food."

"Cadge!" gasped Helen with a choking laugh, sinking again upon her chair.

Reid calmly extended a plate of salad to his betrothed, while Kitty groaned, scandalized:—

"You mustn't eat now! You mustn't! Where've you been? Look at the state you're in! *Don't* eat, Cadge; you must dress this minute!"

"Bridgeport," returned Miss Bryant, grinning benevolently on the wedding guests, her wet hair clinging about her face, her shirt waist dampened the raindrops that trickled from her hatbrim. "Driving an antelope to a racing sulky. If *I* bear marks, y'ought to see the antelope; *and* the sulky! Seven column picture, Kitty; I've made a layout. You must get right at it—antelope kicking the atmosphere into small pieces—"

"Cadge," suggested Reid, mildly, "our train leaves at midnight."

"We'll make it; but this story must come out whether or not 'Mrs. Prosper K. Reid' does. Won't dress, but—say, just you show my wedding gown, Kitty; not for publication but as an evidence—more salad, Pros."

Kitty ran and brought a billowy mass of fleecy white stuff, and Cadge stood, devouring salad, over the dainty thing, gesticulating at it with her fork and explaining its beauties:—

"You can see for yourselves it's swell. Mrs. Edgar fitted me at the *Star* office, with furious mugmakers pounding on the door."

"With *what*?" gasped the General.

"Mugmakers; alleged artists; after an old photo. Anyhow, it's money in Mrs. Edgar's pocket. One of her biggest customers owes her a lot, she says, and she can't get a cent; needed cash to pay her rent; little boy ill, too. My, but I'm hungry! Can't I eat while I'm being married?"

I felt Helen start; I remembered that I had seen Mrs. Edgar's name among her bills. Poor girl!

And then the wedding; and the practical Cadge surprised us all.

All her soul was shining in her eyes as she said, "I will." She looked upon Pros. with the shy love of a girl who has loved but once. For a brief minute we saw the depth, the earnestness, the affection that in her seek so often the mask of frivolity, and I wouldn't be surprised if more than one tempest-tossed soul envied her peace, her love, her certitude.

The ceremony was short. The giant, who proved to be Big Tom, gave away the bride. As the couple rushed off for a brief honeymoon, the newly made Mrs. Reid—still with the shimmer of tears in her beautiful eyes—tried hard to resume her old manner.

"'Member, Kitty," she called back from the stairway in a voice that trembled, "you can't make that antelope cavort too lively. Brown'll send photographs in the morning."

Soon only Mr. Winship and I were left with Kitty and Helen and the painted Indians.

"What a Cadge!" said Helen languidly, as she walked with us to the door. "But she's the best girl in the world."

I believe she's pretty nearly right. I haven't always done Miss Bryant justice. My mind dwelt upon the lovely picture she had made of trust and happiness; and I wondered whether my own wife would show shining, happy eyes like hers when—In my restless dreams the vision of them lingered, grotesquely alternating with a swaying figure driving a shadowy antelope—a figure that was sometimes Helen's and sometimes little Ethel's—until I waked—

And thus began today—it has been the hardest day in a hard week.

It is three hours now, maybe, since we returned from Mrs. Baker's Sunday dinner. A love feast after a feud is trying, but Helen was brave. Mrs. Baker is too honest for diplomacy, and at first I watched Helen nervously, as she sat in the familiar library, a red spot in each cheek, pitting a quiet hauteur against the embarrassed chirpings of her aunt and Milly's sphynx-like silence.

But little by little the cordiality of the Judge and of his tactful sister, helped by Ethel's radiant delight and Mr. Winship's pleasure in the visit, gave another flavour to the dinner than that of the fatted calf, and warmed the atmosphere out of its chill reminiscence of the encounter with Hynes.

The children, too, were a resource, though for a minute Joy was a terror. Baker, junior, was offering me a Kodak picture, when she came running up to look at it.

"You can have it," said Boy; "it's clearer than the one you liked the other day."

"Thath me!" cried Joy, with a fiendish hop and skip. "Me'n Efel on 'e thidewalk. Mither Burke, you like me'n Efel?"

"I like you very much."

"Efel too, or o'ny me? Mr. Burke, w'y you don't like Efel too?"

Like Ethel—the shy little wild flower! Like Ethel!

"Say, Mr. Burke," said Boy opportunely, "here's an envelope to put it in."

"W'at I like," Mr. Winship said, his frosty blue eyes twinkling with enjoyment, "is to see Sis here gittin' a good dose o' home folks; do her more good'n med'cine."

And almost he seemed right, for, as the minutes wore on, a brighter colour rose to Helen's cheeks, and the marvellous charm she knows so well how to use held us fascinated. She waged a war of jests with the Judge and fell back into her old caressing ways with Miss Baker. Ethel could scarcely contain her happiness, and even Milly showed signs of melting.

I brought Helen away as early as I could—as soon as we had completed plans for a quiet wedding next Wednesday.

"I hope you're proud of her, Ezra," declared Mrs. Baker as we took leave; "she told you she's refused a title? But there! All foreigners break their wives' hearts—Nelly's a sensible girl! You didn't expect, though, to find New York crazy over her?"

"Oh, I don't know; Helen 'Lizy's ma was a hansome girl; Sis here had ought to be satisfied if she wears a half as well."

"Come again thoon to thing to Joy," lisped the baby; "Joy loveth you tho muth."

Helen buried her face in the yellow curls, and when she turned away her eyes were wet.

I stayed at the studio only long enough to beg Kitty to see that her charge rests. Just as we were parting at the door, Helen turned full on me her great, lambent eyes.

"Do you love me?" she asked suddenly.

"Why, I loved you," I replied, "when you were a little freckled Nelly in pigtails."

And that, at least, is true! God help me to be kind to the most beautiful woman in the world!

3

"P.P.C."

June 21, 19—.

Helen and I were to have been married just a year ago. Today I have been going over her own story of her life—of her meeting with Darmstetter, of the blight he cast upon her, of her growth in loveliness, her brief fluttering in the sunshine, her failure, her supping with sorrow, her death.

I must bring to a close the record of this miracle.

This who was the most extraordinary woman that ever lived, was also little Nellie Winship. Again as I remember her as she was—a thing of such vital force that no man could be unmoved in her presence, of such supernal loveliness that words can never tell of it—again I feel that I must be in an ugly dream. But this bit of paper, blotted with tears and stained with wine and ashes, tells me that there was no mistake.

She had seemed in high spirits that Sunday at the Bakers', though she was tired when we returned to the studio. Mr. Winship and I made no stop. Pros. and Cadge were enjoying their brief honeymoon trip and so Kitty and Helen were left together.

Monday morning I went first to the rooms I had taken; Kitty was to be there later, arranging our little furniture. She was to live with us for a time and care for Nelly. But when I reached the office, there lay on my desk a telegram.

"Helen is ill; come," it read.

Helen lay, as if sleeping, upon a couch.

Cadge met me at the studio door, white-faced, strangely, silently gentle. From a tumbled heap among the cushions of the tepee came a voice like Kitty's, moaning. Cadge tried to speak, but could only point to the little bedroom.

There, in the straight white dress she wore at the wedding, Helen lay, as if sleeping, upon a couch. Floods of shining hair fell about her shoulders. In the white dignity of death her face was marvellous. All trace of stress and strain had left it, replaced by an enigmatic calm. She looked not merely beautiful, but Beauty's self vouchsafed to mortal eyes.

I do not know how long I gazed. Vaguely, between Kitty's sobs, I heard the ticking of a watch.

"For another woman of such loveliness," at length said a reverent voice behind me, "we must wait the final evolution of humanity."

Dr. Upton, one of Reid's friends whom I had seen at the wedding, had reached the house before me. He had been examining a glass, a spoon and some other objects so quietly that I had not heard. He said that Helen had been dead some hours.

Mechanically I listened, but it was not until afterward that I understood the full purport of his speech or of Kitty's story of the night and morning. Their words reached me as if spoken from some great distance by the people who live in dreams.

Kitty had come to us; she stood in the doorway, white and shaking.

"Helen—Helen's head ached," she sobbed, "and she begged me to brush her hair, but when I began, she said it hurt, and told me to stop; then she fell to writing. I coaxed her to come to bed, for I thought she was ill; but she called me 'Kathryn' and then I knew I couldn't manage her.

Oh, I was wicked, wicked; but I was afraid of her, always—you know. So I —oh, how could I?—I fixed a screen against the light and lay down, meaning to try again in a few minutes; but the instant my head touched the pillow I must have dropped asleep. The last thing I said was: 'Shall I tell Morphy you're coming?' I was so tired that I don't know whether she answered. And this morning—oh, I can't believe it; Oh, Helen, Helen!"

"And this morning?" prompted Dr. Upton.

"This morning when—when I waked and saw her on the couch, I wondered why she hadn't come to bed; but I dropped a shawl over her and tiptoed out. It wasn't until half-past eight that I tried—oh, I can't! I can't! Don't ask me!"

Kitty's voice was lost in hysterical chokings.

Dr. Upton handed me Helen's visiting card. Below the name was scrawled: "P. P. C."

"It was found pinned to Miss Reid's bedspread," he said; "is that Miss Winship's handwriting?"

"Yes," I answered. The shaky letters were unrecognisable.

"Don't you see! To say farewell," wailed Kitty. "She's done it a hundred times when she started for school before I was up. Barnard is so far. Oh, I can't bear it! How could you, Helen?"

"Don't, Kitty," said Cadge, drawing her from the room.

The doctor motioned me to a table behind the screen of which Kitty had spoken. There Helen had sat, there lay her writing case, the key sealed in an envelope addressed to me. Picking up a slip of paper torn from a letter pad, he asked:—

"Is this also Miss Winship's writing?"

He held it out to me and I read the single line:—

"Don't tell Father."

Dazed, half-comprehending, I repeated: "Yes."

Upton had found nothing else, except Helen's watch, open beside the writing case, and a glass that still held a little sherry. At this he looked with sombre intelligence and set it carefully aside.

Nothing in the room had been disturbed. Helen's chair had the look of having been pushed from the table as she rose but a minute before. Near it on an easel stood the Van Nostrand picture, smiling—smiling, as if it had seen no tragedy. On the floor was a little ash as of charred paper.

In a few minutes Mrs. Reid and Kitty returned with Mr. Winship. Through the fog that enveloped me I saw with dull curiosity that they had told him something that he didn't understand.

He could not believe Helen dead, but knelt by her side and coaxed her to wake, rubbing her fair, slender hands between his leathery palms and calling her by every pet name of her childhood.

"It's on'y your ol' Dad, Sis," he crooned. "Jes' come to fetch ye t' yer Ma; that's all. I know yer tired—plum tired out; but Ma 'n' me'll take care on ye." It was pitiful to hear him.

He desisted at last and looked back at us with a mien of anger.

"Do suthin', some o' ye," he snarled, "'stid o' standin' round like gumps! Speak to me, Poppet; tell yer ol' Pap w'at ails ye. Fetch some hot water, you gals! Ain't ye got no sense? Rub her feet; an' her hands. Speak to me, Sissy —why don't ye?"

As the truth slowly won over him, he straightened himself, one hand still clasping Helen's cold one.

"It's sudden; sudden," he said. "Doctor, w'at ailed my little Nelly?"

Still numbly inquisitive, I waited. The old man couldn't see the truth, the horrible truth. What would the doctor say?

It was Cadge's voice that broke the silence; gentle, assured, yet with a note almost of defiance.

"We think—in fact, Helen overstudied," she said. "We've been much worried about her."

Dr. Upton turned abruptly. Cadge's irregular, mobile face for once was still, its quiet demand bent full upon him. His answering look refused her, but the effort was obvious with which he spoke to the broken man waiting his verdict.

"Miss Winship—your daughter—" he began.

The words died. Cadge's steady black eyes controlled him.

"Wa-al?"

The doctor bowed his head over Helen. I was listening again to her watch that ticked insistently. "Don't tell Father! Don't tell Father!" it said over and over, over and over, louder and louder, until the words echoed from every corner of the room.

They must hear! That was why she had left it!

"I ast ye w'at ailed my little girl."

"Cardiac asthenia—heart failure," said Dr. Upton, abruptly.

Kitty threw herself upon Cadge, kissing her convulsively, while Mr. Winship persisted:—

"Sis was firstrate yist'day; w'at fetched the attack on?"

As gently as Cadge herself, Dr. Upton answered:—

"Mr. Winship, your daughter wasn't so strong as she seemed. There was much in her condition to cause anxiety. I'll be back in an hour," he added, moving hastily, as Reid entered, toward the door.

Could I let him shoulder the responsibility of concealment? And if I refused? Publicity—an inquest? At last I was alive to the situation; in silent gratitude I wrung Upton's hand, but he took no notice of me. As he passed Reid he growled:—

"Your wife's a good woman to tie to, Pros. She's all right. Lucky she was telegraphed for."

Cadge had begun to talk in low tones to Mr. Winship. He did not seem to listen, but the quiet voice soothed him. Gradually his gray, set features relaxed, though he would not submit to be led from the bedside.

"Ma was right," he said at last, broken and querulous. "We'd never ought to have let her come to the city. Ye say she'll be famous? Sissy, my poor little Poppet, w'at good to ye is fame; w'at good is all your studyin'?"

I DID NOT open Helen's writing case for weeks; not until after my return from the dreary journey West with Mr. Winship.

Stunned by the shock of her death, bearing not only my grief but the knowledge that her father and mother must hold me in part responsible for her fatal coming to New York, I could not face the secret of her choice of death rather than marriage with me.

It was a hot July night when I turned the key that guarded the secret.

I found the story of the Bacillus, the curse that killed Darmstetter, that killed Helen. With it was a letter that I have read a thousand times—this letter that I am now reading. The scent of roses still breathes from it. On the last page there are splashes of wine.

This is what it says:—

JOHN: I cannot bear it. Prof. Darmstetter gave me death when he gave me beauty.

I am not a coward; but what is left? I am tired, wretched; there is no place for me.

The Bacillus has defeated every wish it has aroused. It has refused me love, ambition, honest work. From men it has compelled fear; from women hate; it has cut me off from my kind.

You saw Ned smiling into Milly's pale eyes. I should not have cared, I who was to marry you, but—I love him; you know it—you have known it since my heart broke, since I tore it out and swore to reign, to dazzle, to be Queen of the world.

You know what came of my ambitions. The world treated my beauty as a menace; it struck me down. Then I asked to earn my bread; but without you I might have starved. You were my refuge— and you—you love a cripple!

Why didn't I guess? I would have been glad, for Ethel is a dear child, and I had given you sorrow enough. I did not love you; I do not think I have pretended to love you. But can no man help seeming to care for me—help caring while he is with me? Ned told me he did not love; but you, you I trusted; you would have married me, not letting me know—

Ethel limps, she is plain. Plain as I was when you adored my ugly face, my freckles. Does beauty kill love, or do men see beauty only where they love? Little brown partridges, little brown partridges—

The Bacillus is a cheat; every woman to her lover is the most beautiful!

Ethel's good. You would have found me conspicuous, an annoyance among people who shrink from the extraordinary. I have been fond of Ethel.

I was marrying you to get my debts paid—you knew that—but there was more. You must believe—you know there was more. I thought you loved me. Was that strange? How many times have you spoken to me of love? I wanted to show my gratitude, to make you happy, since happiness was not for me. I would have tried; I would have buried my own misery; buried everything but the sense of your goodness. I would have given you the cooperation of a clever woman. I would have given you the affection you know I have always felt. I would have worked, planned, compelled success for you.

But that's over. Ethel is a dear child. I will not stand between you and Ethel.

Don't pity me. I need no pity. I would endure yesterday and today a thousand times for the sake of the first hour of my beauty. Would I change now to be like Ethel, to be white putty like Milly—to have your love, or Ned's? Beauty—I can die with it sooner than drown it in tears.

Don't tell Father. He will suffer; but less than if I went home to eat my heart out in repinings, to grow old and ugly, cursing the world. I have lived too long. I am already less beautiful.

If I could destroy the secret! Death, leaving that behind, is crucifixion. But I was the first, I was the first! That dead face so gray and old—"Delilah!" it mows at me. I keep my promise! I haven't robbed you, you shall have your fame! I, too, I shall never be forgotten!

John, take the secret. Keep my word for me. If you doubt the discovery, try it on an enemy. If you think my sorrow could have been avoided, offer the Bacillus as a wedding gift to—.

Give Milly, who has Ned's love, my beauty? Would it turn him from her? If I thought it—But even for that, there shall be no other! It shall go first. Forever and forever my name, my face,—

"Delilah!" It grins, it gibbers. Wait for no tests. Print quick! Tomorrow, today—it's almost day. Give him what he wants, John —"Delilah!"

Why do you come back, dead face, dead eyes? Haven't I promised? You shall have print, type, a million circulation! Go away, you're dead! What's fame to youth, health, life? It's you who rob and kill. I won't look—I won't! If I wake Kitty, could she help? I won't look, I'm going mad!

Gone! I must hurry. He might come back. Shall I leave the secret? It's life for life, we're even. If beauty were cheap, who'd care for it? It's death to be first, but afterwards—nothing! If I burned it—but no—I promised—.

Why not?

"Delilah!" Your health, dead eyes! I haf put t'e bacillus of perfect vine into t'e new grape juice, and I svear it's—Prosit, dead eyes!— here's a P.P.C.; quickest goodby—Poor Kitty! You'll be sorry for the most beautiful woman in the—

The Bacillus of Beauty has had its victim.

Why do I keep the wine-splashed, rose-breathing letter? Why read over and over the fragments of Helen's journal? Better remember my little schoolmate as she was before the poison stung her. Might she, with time and contact with life, have reacted against the virus, or must such loveliness be fatal to what is best in woman? Who can answer? Helen is dead, Darmstetter is dead, and the Bacillus—

The Bacillus shall have no other victim.

We who were near to Helen have been slow to recover from the shock and the bitterness of her death. Her father and mother have nothing to hold them to life; they are uprooted. Ned has grieved for her with bitter self-reproach, though he is happy with Milly. Ethel and I—

But tonight I can think only of Helen.

The End

A Request

If you liked this book, please take the time to leave a review on the site where you purchased it and/or on one of the social media reading sites like Goodreads. Tell your friends that you enjoyed it. Suggest it as reading for your local book club. Request it at your local library (or more than one local library). This helps others learn more about the book and gets the word out.

Please use the #bacillusofbeauty and #hemeleinpubs tags on social media.

Thank you for your time, and thank you for reading this book!

Find more exciting books to read at hemelein.com.

HEMELEIN PUBLICATIONS

About the Author

HARRIET STARK was born in Payson, Utah Territory, in the United States of America on September 23, 1868, daughter of Daniel Stark and Anna Piscilla Beckenhead. Her father was born in Nova Scotia, Canada, and her mother in Birmingham, England. At some point between her birth and 1870, her family moved to St. Joseph, Rio Virgin County, Utah Territory (somewhere near Amber, Nevada today).

She married Lewis William Barry Wride on May 18, 1897 in Logan, Utah, and—by the time of the 1900 release of *The Bacillus of Beauty*—she, her husband, and their four daughters were living in Payson on a farm. Eventually, they had eleven children, though two died within a year of being born.

They didn't have running water on their farm, so she had to manually pump water from the well and carry it to the house multiple times daily. Harriet made clothing by hand for herself and her children, and she could recreate clothing patterns simply by looking at a picture and then reproducing it on newspaper in the size she needed.

Her husband died on March 7, 1934 in Payson at age 71 after an accidental fall. Harriet lived a decade longer before succumbing to pneumonia —brought on by ten years of pulmonary tuberculosis—on August 23, 1944 in Payson. She was 75 years old.

Her only known published speculative fiction work is *The Bacillus of Beauty*, originally published in 1900 by Frederick A. Stokes Company in New York City.

About the Essayist

LEE ALLRED's fiction has appeared in *Asimov's Science Fiction* and *Pulphouse* magazines, as well as in dozens of science fiction anthologies such as the acclaimed *Fiction River* series and Baen's *Alternate Generals III* and *Drakas!* volumes.

He has scripted fan-favorite stories for Marvel (*Fantastic Four*), DC Comics (*Batman '66, Batman Black and White*), and IDW (*Dick Tracy*). He wrote *Bug! The Adventures of Forager* for Gerard Way's (of *My Chemical Romance / Umbrella Academy* fame) quirky Young Animal comic book imprint line.

His novella, "For the Strength of the Hills", was named a Sidewise Award for Alternate History finalist. A great love of history and historical detail infuses all of his work, whether he's writing steampunk, vampire tales, alternate history, or military SF.

After serving three tours in Iraq for the United States Air Force, Lee retired as a Master Sergeant. You can find out more at leeallred.com.

 x.com/lee_allred

About the Illustrator

JESS SMART SMILEY has written and illustrated over 20 books for young readers (which have been translated into 4 different languages) and loves sharing his passion for storytelling with creators of all ages and skill levels.

A lifelong resident of Utah, Jess has had the pleasure of creating several works for Utah cities, including a library card for the Provo Library, large-scale murals along the Provo River Trail and for the Orem City Center Park, and illustrations for the Oremfest summer festival.

Jess works in a wide range of subject matter, media, and techniques. Though typically recognized for his bright and colorful illustrations for children, Jess welcomed the opportunity to focus on drawing with pen and ink for *The Bacillus of Beauty*.

Jess is the recipient of the 2023 Krider Prize for Creativity, named a "Top 40" by Utah Valley Magazine, nominated for a Ringo Award, has been an invited guest at Salt Lake Fan X since its inception, and was a Guest of Honor at the 2023 Life, the Universe, and Everything symposium on science fiction and fantasy.

His bestselling comics-based activity book *Let's Make Comics* debuted at #1 in 4 categories and has been celebrated by creators of all ages, parents, teachers, librarians, and industry professionals.

Jess has consulted on hundreds of creative projects, and helped thousands of children, teens, and adults around the world to create their first comics. Additionally, Jess has taught writing, drawing, cartooning, and storytelling workshops at the Charles M. Schulz Museum in Santa Rosa, California, as well as at Higher Ground Learning in Salt Lake City and Thanksgiving Point in Lehi, Utah.

Learn more at jess-smiley.com.

facebook.com/jess.smart.smiley.draws

x.com/jess_smiley

instagram.com/jess.smart.smiley

tiktok.com/@jess.smart.smiley

linkedin.com/in/jess-smart-smiley-23255b6

About the Cover Artist

GEORGE FREDERIC WATTS was born in Marylebone, Middlesex, England on February 23, 1817. He was in poor health much of his childhood, and his mother died when he was young, so he was raised and schooled by his father. At the age of ten, he showed artistic aptitude, so he began training with the sculptor William Behnes. When he was 18, he enrolled at the Royal Academy. He closely studied the Elgin Marbles in the British Museum, learning much from them.

After winning an art competition, he studied in Florence, Italy from 1843–1847 before returning to London. After having little success in finding a building where he could create a large fresco, he spent most of the rest of his career working in oils. After helping his friend, Henry Thoby Prinsep, obtain a 21-year lease on Little Holland House in Kensington, Watts lived with them for the length of the lease.

During that time, he married the actress Ellen Terry (the subject of *Choosing*, the cover painting of this collection) a few days shy of her 17th birthday in 1864. Ten months after the marriage, Terry eloped with another man and Watts requested a divorce. The divorce didn't take effect until 1877, however.

In 1871, Watts had a new home built in London, and purchased a home near Freshwater on the Isle of Wight near those of his friends, including Alfred, Lord Tennyson. He also had a home built for the Prinseps family nearby. Watts remarried in 1886 to Mary Fraser Tytler—a Scottish designer and potter—and they build a home named Limnerslease near Compton in Surrey.

While married, they worked on a number of projects together, including the Watts Mortuary Chapel in Compton and the Watts Gallery. The latter was the first gallery in England to be built and devoted to a single artist. Today, it is the only such gallery still operating. Watts painted a version of his painting, *The All-Pervading*, for the chapel, completing it only three months prior to his death.

Queen Victoria twice offered him the title of Baronet, but he refused both times. Watts was made a member of the Royal Academy in 1867, and he was named one of the original recipients of the new Order of Merit. The latter was awarded to him by King Edward VII at a ceremony on August 8, 1902.

Watts died in London on July 1, 1904, at the age of 87.

About the Editor

JOE MONSON worked at many different jobs before trying his hand at writing and editing fiction.

He edits the LTUE Benefit Anthologies series with Jaleta Clegg: *Trace the Stars* (2019), *A Dragon and Her Girl* (2020), *Twilight Tales* (2021), *Parliament of Wizards* (2022), *A Hero of a Different Stripe* (2023), *Troubadours and Space Princesses* (2024), and the forthcoming *Dog Save the King* (2025) and *Honor Among the Stars* (2026).

Joe edited *A Universe of Stories* (2021) and *The Horror at Pooh Corner* (2024), all of the works in the Legacy of the Corridor publication series, and has many other fun projects in the works.

He has written many short stories and is currently working on the first book in a space opera adventure novel series. He collects science fiction and fantasy art, but not as much as Paul (as if that was even possible). He lives in the tops of the mountains with his lovely and talented wife, their three amazing children, and their pet library.

Learn more at joemonson.com.

facebook.com/joe.monson.editor

x.com/JoeMonsonAuthor

Milton Keynes UK
Ingram Content Group UK Ltd.
UKHW011822140624
444031UK00010B/152/J